REDEEMING THE RAKE

AGENTS OF ESPIONAGE
BOOK THREE

LORRI DUDLEY

WILD HEART
BOOKS

Cover design by: Carpe Librum Book Design

ISBN-13:

I have swept away your offenses like a cloud,
your sins like the morning mist.
Return to me,
For I have redeemed you.
~ Isaiah 44:22 (NIV)

CHAPTER 1

London, England, *1818*

"Y ou've gone and gotten yourself into a fine mess this time."

Lord Jacob Langford Warren, third son to the fifth Duke of Warren, inwardly cringed at his brother's cutting words. He swallowed under the tight knot of his cravat.

Robert's face colored red, tinging it purple. "I have never been more disappointed in you."

Jacob itched to take the blasted cravat off. Instead, he relaxed his muscles and inhaled slowly to calm the simmering anger corroding his insides. He ran the back of his hand across his brow to smooth the crease that formed between his eyebrows under duress. It would give his emotions away if not under strict supervision, a most unfortunate trait for card playing and espionage, but he'd learned to control it. This, however, was not a card game. It was a disaster with a small, unexpected opportunity, and if he seized the proper moment, it could drastically change his life.

"Are you aware that when your mouth opens, Father's words come out?" Jacob draped his arm over the back of his chair in his brother's townhome study and flashed a crooked smile. Even though Robert, the Marquis of Sudbury, sounded like Father, he wasn't a brooding tyrant. His eldest brother could still see reason.

Well, maybe not at the moment.

Robert paced behind his large mahogany desk with stiff, jerky movements. The bulging vein in the center of his forehead throbbed the same way their father's did before he exploded into a rage. Robert, however, wouldn't be half in his cups at this early hour.

Even the mere thought of their father filled Jacob's senses with the burning, sweet stench of whiskey breath. Fortunately, unlike their father, Robert's tone was born out of concern.

Robert rambled on, something about position and responsibility. He stopped pacing in front of the paned glass window framed by rich velvet curtains with dangling tassels. Everything about the room exhibited the power and grandeur of their station. Beyond Robert's bent elbows and fisted hands on his hips, movement out the window drew Jacob's attention as a crested coach passed on the street. In less than a month, carriages would jam the road as the Quality returned in their splendor for the frivolity and enjoyment of the Season. If all went well, Jacob would escape the superficial bombast and finish his investigation in the uncomplicated quiet of the Cotswolds.

The pitch and volume of Robert's voice rose. "Someone in this room must act like an adult."

Jacob waited for his brother to continue. When he didn't, Jacob drew his chin back and snorted. "Well, it's certainly not going to be me."

"Do you hold no regard for your own life?"

He shrugged. "I enjoy making my guardian angel perspire a little."

His brother's nostrils flared in a most unbecoming manner. "Your reckless behavior will get you killed, and if it doesn't, Father will kill you himself." Robert ran a hand over the top of his head, causing a section of his hair to stick out like a bird's ruffled feathers. "And think about poor Mother and her heart. Father gives her plenty of anguish, and it's not helping that Alex is chasing some ballerina in Prussia. Do you truly mean to add to it?"

Jacob had no response to that. His reserved brother doing something radical by pursuing a working woman in what was considered a debased art form was upsetting to Mother and poor timing for Jacob's plan. The last person he wanted to harm was their mother, but the truth behind why he acted like a cad in public would send her into an apoplectic fit. Besides, he was forbidden from telling his family the truth. It was rule number one in spying for the Home Office. *Tell no one.*

Robert slammed his palms on the desk and leaned forward. "I do not relish looking our mother in the eye and informing her that her youngest son is dead."

Jacob swallowed, his cravat growing even more constricting. In his life as a spy, he often tread a fine line between living and dying. He preferred to concentrate on the former and not the latter.

"It is only by the grace of God that I'm not standing here right now doing just that." Robert composed his features, and his voice lowered to an eerie calm. "Pack your things. I'm sending you to the country, far away from London, your fast-set friends, and Father's wrath."

Jacob recognized the rigid set of his brother's jaw. He couldn't be persuaded once the muscle in his lower jaw remained taut. Better to work where he still had an advantage and play his cards carefully. He stuffed his hand into his jacket and felt the smooth edge of the latest missive, detailing the intelligence he'd requested. Its mere existence acted as a catalyst of encouragement.

"I'll die of boredom." Jacob sighed, hoping it sounded full of disdain. "Surely, that isn't what you want to become of me? A withered recluse like Aunt Louisa in Sylvanwood?"

Robert's lips curled, but then his eyes lit.

Jacob held his breath. *Take the hint.*

"Sylvanwood." A slow smile spread across Robert's face. "It would be difficult for you to find trouble in the rural village of Sylvanwood. Maybe you should pay our aunt a visit. Brownstone Hall has fallen under my care since our uncle passed without heirs. The arrival of her darling nephew to manage the much-needed repairs to Brownstone Hall could be a blessing to you both."

A surge of excitement raced through Jacob's blood, but he mustn't appear eager.

Be glib but not derisive.

"You want me to play the role of a lady's companion?" Jacob crossed his arms like a rebellious child, but his eyes assessed Robert's every movement, from the cords in his neck to the twitching muscle at his temple.

"More like her steward." Robert's shoulders relaxed, and his facial coloring returned to normal.

Jacob rolled his lips to contain the triumphant smile that trembled the corners of his mouth. Victory was assured. Life may have dealt him a bad hand, but he'd used his wits to turn it into a winning play. He was about to embark on a mission to right his wrongs from six summers ago.

Robert straightened and his jaw set the same way it did when they were kids and about to face a reprimand. Robert would stand tall with his chin high, and Jacob would do his best to emulate him even if his knees were shaking. How many times had Robert placed a hand on Jacob's shoulder as if to infuse him with strength? It was as if, even as a child, he'd known their punishment would hurt but would be for their own good, and they'd come out stronger in the end.

Jacob's sudden desire to reveal all to Robert and plead for forgiveness and understanding almost overran his good sense. Now was not the time.

Robert raised a brow. "Plan to leave before the week's end." He pushed back his jacket and hooked his left thumb into the top of his pantaloons. "Think of it as a fresh start." He walked around his desk and clapped his other hand on Jacob's shoulder. "An opportunity to turn your blackened reputation around in a town where no one knows of your libertine ways."

~

*J*acob pushed back the curtain of his town coach. London proper melted away into lush, rolling hills as he traveled to Sylvanwood. A farmer's wife hung laundry on the line and waved to her husband and son, around five or six years old, walking behind a horse-drawn plow. The father pointed to the field and leaned toward his son as if teaching him how best to get the land to produce.

Jacob twisted his head to follow the father-son pair through the window until they passed out of sight. He'd longed for his father to have such moments with him, and to do the same with his children in the future.

The intricacies of his assignment and all that could go wrong had run through his brain—his approach, misinformation, non-cooperation—and robbed him of much needed sleep the prior evening. His current weariness made reviewing his strategy challenging. He leaned his head against the window and stared at the passing landscape, trying to get some shuteye by counting sheep.

Jacob's eyelids grew heavy as the rhythmic swaying of the

Warren town coach lulled him. "Sixty-three, sixty-four, sixty-five, sixty-six...sixty..."

The carriage door slammed open.

Jacob jerked awake, but the lingering haze of a deep slumber fogged his consciousness. "What in thunder—?"

Two hands grasped his lapels and heaved him off his seat. Jacob's shoulder smacked the door, nearly throwing his arm out of the socket.

A masked face blocked out the bright sun. The man snarled at Jacob before tossing him onto the roadside.

Jacob landed on his hurt shoulder and skidded across the damp ground. The musty scent of earth filled his nostrils. He shook his head to clear away the grogginess of sleep and stared at the grass stains now marring his favorite pair of buckskin breeches.

"You might be a bit too enthusiastic about your work." Jacob felt for the note in his pocket, relieved he hadn't left it in the coach. He pushed off the ground to his knees. His fingers clenched into fists, ready to swing.

The click of a round loading into a gun's chamber froze him.

"Whoa." Jacob raised his hands. Blasted highwaymen. He should have been more cautious, but it was rare indeed for bandits to pillage at such an early hour—in broad daylight. He'd erred in stashing his pistol between the cushions instead of on his person. "Take what you need and be on your way."

A groan sounded to his right. His footman and coachman lay semi-conscious, sprawled in the dirt. The coachman stirred, but a booted assailant kicked him in the gut, and he stilled.

"If it's money you're after, you've looted the wrong carriage. A third son doesn't have a pocket to let."

"It's the pretty price on yer head that will be fillin' our pockets." The masked man's lips curled.

"Truly?" Jacob snorted. "A price on my head? Is that what they told you?"

The man bent and once again grabbed Jacob's lapels. "Ye're worth more dead than alive."

The cold malice in the man's eyes sent pinpricks down Jacob's spine. Men like this fed on fear, so Jacob flashed a smile and chuckled.

"What are you laughin' at?" the man asked, revealing a set of rotting teeth and releasing the stench of his putrid breath.

"I'm merely waiting to see what other hummers you've been told."

The ruffian shoved Jacob back into the dirt and turned to a man Jacob hadn't noticed rounding the back of the carriage. "Ya'd better have me money."

"Enough! You will get yours as soon as the job is finished." A pair of well-polished Hessian boots stepped closer to Jacob. "If a third son is meant for the clergy, then you'll get your money when he meets his maker."

The voice sounded familiar, but the highwayman's back blocked a clear view of the other man's face. "Clever." Jacob used a flippant tone despite his shoulder aching like the devil and twisted to get a look at the ruffian. "I admire a man with a quick retort. It's practically a requirement for those who run with the fast set. Say, have we met?"

His remark earned him a kick to the stomach. He toppled into the dry grass as waves of pain and nausea swept through him.

"Blindfold and tie the coachman and servant to a tree in the woods. Except for this one. Tie and gag him. I want Lord Warren to look upon my face as I put a bullet in his chest."

The rogue's boot heel dug into Jacob's upper back. Rough hands yanked his arms behind him and bound his wrists together. Hemp fibers from the rope bit into his skin.

The hooligan clamped on his upper arm, and he was

hauled to his feet. Jacob clenched his teeth against a dirty rag that a masked man forced against his mouth. Another punch to the gut weakened Jacob, and the bandit shoved the rag deep into Jacob's throat. It tasted of grime and sweat and smelled like horseflesh. He gagged and tried to spit it out, but a rope was tied tight to hold it in place.

His assailant spun him to face the highwayman funding the operation. Except it wasn't a highwayman.

Even though the man wore a mask, Jacob recognized the vile hatred emanating from the depths of Lord Benton's eyes.

A sickening grin twisted the man's lips. "Let's take a walk, shall we?" He waved toward the woods with the point of his gun. "I don't want anyone finding your body until the birds have picked your bones dry. By then, I'll be long gone with a nice alibi."

Jacob's heartbeat stalled, then leapt to a speed close to exploding.

Lord Benton would like nothing more than to gain the satisfaction that he failed to achieve during their duel. The man was supposed to delope. Shooting one's gun in the air was the respectable thing to do in a duel, but Benton wanted Jacob dead. While Jacob stood in the rain-soaked field of Hyde Park, still woozy from the aftereffects of a jolly night of carousing, Benton took a shot that would have put a hole in Jacob's chest. Except, as luck would have it, God intervened.

Due to the deluge of rain that early morn, moisture must have gotten into Benton's flintlock, failing to ignite the main powder charge in the barrel. It was the only explanation short of a miracle when, after a flash in the pan, Benton's gun exploded into a heap of twisted metal.

As the required surgeon on the dueling field worked, Benton cursed words even Jacob hadn't heard. Benton was lucky. Though he'd been badly burned, he walked away with all his fingers.

The point of Benton's gun jabbed Jacob's back. He'd brought this on himself when he'd been discovered in Lady Benton's bedchamber. Just a misunderstanding. He'd sought nothing more than information regarding nighttime raids targeting nobility, but he'd couldn't explain his secretive actions, nor did he have the time before jumping out the second-story window—either that or he'd have been pushed.

Benton laughed. "Where are your brothers, Warren? Unable to come to your aid? Oh, that's right, they're too far away to rescue their worthless scoundrel of a younger brother."

The two other bandits trailing behind them snickered.

Jacob could only offer strangled sounds past the gag. He wanted to tell Benton he wouldn't get away with this. Robert's influence and reach extended farther than Benton realized, but it came out as gibberish against the gag.

"Can't talk your way out of this one." Benton's laughter hissed through his teeth. "That sly tongue and clever wit may work on the dimwitted brains of the weaker sex, but it is useless on me."

The man was deranged.

Funny how, when faced with impending death, the simple things in life stood out in his memory. He remembered racing his brothers through a field similar to this one. He remembered building forts in a grove of trees along the hillside identical to the ones he saw in the distance. He saw Sarah's smiling face before she surprised him with a passionate kiss behind a large oak tree. Later that day, he'd fallen out of that same tree and twisted his ankle. His brothers carried him home to his mother, who held him in her arms and whispered, "Everything will be fine," in her soft, tender voice. She stayed with him until the physician arrived.

Jacob would give anything to hear her whisper those words now.

"Even the weather can't save you today." Benton shoved him forward.

The sky appeared extra blue. Sprigs of new growth deep within the old dried and withered grass reached toward the heavens as if begging for the sun's energy and life. Birds took to flight, and rabbits stilled as Benton prodded Jacob forward. The small creatures were blissfully unaware of the shadow of death that loomed in his wake.

CHAPTER 2

*E*mily Ann Thompson inspected one of her paintbrushes by pushing the bristles against her palm. A swirl of white leaked out between the strands. She dipped the brush back into the mineral spirits and swished it around, working out the remaining paint with her fingers.

Mama shuffled into the kitchen. Her prim collar encircled her neck, and her beautiful chestnut hair, now more gray than brown, was pulled back into a lace cap. She waved her hand in front of her nose. "Emily, I do wish you'd wash those outside. The smell of mineral spirits is souring my stomach for the midday meal."

"I'm almost finished." Emily tested the brush. The fluids came out clear, so she toweled it dry and capped the jar of solvent.

Mrs. Hayes, their elderly maid-of-all-work who'd been with the family since long before Emily was born, leaned into the steam rising from the boiling pot and inhaled the savory aroma of simmering beef. "A bit more sage, I believe, and a pinch of parsley." She cracked open the earthenware jar of spices and sprinkled in the ingredients. "It merely needs to simmer for a wee bit." She removed the spoon and placed a lid on the pot.

Mama peered at Emily with a furrowed brow. One side of her mouth turned up into a dry smile that appeared more like a frown. "I do wish you'd stick to watercolors. It's much more ladylike. Painting with oils is a man's pursuit."

"Commissioned portraits pay the most coin, and they are done in oils."

"If your papa were listening, he'd tell you that God will provide."

Emily stuck a pin to cap her paint and placed it into the airtight earthenware jar. "God has always provided for us, and I know He will continue to do so, but I want to be a good steward of my talents. Some extra funds to help ensure Christian's proper schooling will take some pressure off Papa."

Mama sighed and crossed her arms. "Christian is very fortunate to have siblings who dote on him so. Speaking of your papa, Mrs. Hayes jarred more of her delicious preserves. I was hoping you could take some to him to give out at the church. The rest I'll distribute when I make my rounds to the parishioners." She glanced at the back door. "Oh, and could you take Mr. Mathis his bow and arrows? He popped in yesterday to say hello and left them by the door. I daresay he was disappointed he missed you."

Peter Mathis's hopeful eyes had searched the church sanctuary on Sunday before he spotted her. He was a gentleman farmer and a close friend of her older brother, Samuel. It was well known that he showed a partiality for Emily, and most assumed she would one day become his wife. She should be honored, for he was a good man, but the thought of marrying him left a weary lifelessness hanging on her spirit.

Mama pointed at the quiver, leaning in the corner against the doorframe. "I meant to ask Samuel to return them, but he left for Mr. Mathis's house this morning before I remembered it."

Emily untied her painting apron strings and dipped her head to pull it off. "I would be happy to take it to Mr. Mathis." She folded the smock and placed it on the counter. "Especially now that the painting is finished and I have a bit of time to myself again."

"It's done?" Mama clasped her hands under her chin. "Let me see."

Mama hobbled out of the kitchen and across the hall to where Emily had set up a small studio. Emily and Mrs. Hayes followed in her wake.

The finished portrait of young master Danbury rested on an easel in the conservatory. It had taken longer to paint than she'd hoped because Mr. Danbury, the subject's father, had decided upon a specific outdoor setting as a background. Winter had stayed overly long this year, and her fingers froze each time she'd attempted to sketch out a proper scene to recreate later inside the warm comfort of her home. If he'd only requested an indoor backdrop, such as the bookshelves of a library or, even better, a cheery fireplace, the portrait could have been finished a month ago. She sighed. No matter. It was finally done, and she could collect her commission. And without a moment to spare, for the materials she ordered for her next piece would arrive early next week and she'd need the coin.

"Oh, Emily." Mama stopped a few feet from the portrait and touched Emily's back. "It came out wonderful. It is a perfect rendering of young Danbury. Look at the detail in the folds of his cravat."

"'Tis very well done, miss." Mrs. Hayes patted her shoulder. "He looks much like his father, but ya still captured the wee twinkle in his eye."

Mama chuckled. "I can imagine he was a hard one to keep still."

"Not as challenging as Christian, but Lord Danbury's son is also four years older." She smiled at Mrs. Hayes. "I had to keep bribing him with the promise of a freshly baked tart. Your confectionary skills were a blessing."

"Och, which reminds me, I have biscuits baking." Mrs. Hayes shuffled back into the kitchen.

"And I need to be heading out." Emily kissed her mother's wrinkled cheek.

"Where has Phoebe been this past week? She hasn't come by to visit."

Emily froze. Phoebe's betrayal still stung, but she hadn't explained their falling out to Mama. "She has much to prepare for her season in London, and her mother has been keeping her busy with fittings and such. I ran into her yesterday."

"Well, if you see her again, give my regards to her and Lady Dorsham."

Emily strode back to the kitchen and removed her bonnet from the peg near the back door.

She glanced out the window at the bright sun. Drips of ice ran off the roof into the rain barrel, proving the temperature had warmed. "I think I shall do some sketching while I'm out." She grabbed her pelisse from off the hook and shrugged it on.

Mrs. Hayes passed Emily her satchel with her sketchpad and charcoal.

Emily slung it over her shoulder.

Mrs. Hayes walked into the pantry and returned with two jars of blackberry jam. "Are ye gonna take the road and go through town?" She wrapped the jars in cloth before handing them to Emily, who carefully tucked them in with her art supplies.

"Unchaperoned? Definitely not."

"Ah, I keep forgetting you've come of age. You'll always be a wee thing in my eyes. I'd go with ye, but someone must stay and watch the stew."

"I'll take the path through the woods," Emily said. "That way, no one will know. I shall not tarnish the Thompson name by setting tongues a-wagging."

"You've always conducted yerself as a lady." Mrs. Hayes bent to peek on the biscuits.

Emily's younger brother scurried into the kitchen and slid to a stop, eyeing Emily's coat. "I want to go with you." Christian implored her with tilted brows, a look that only puppies and small children could master.

She resisted the urge to scoop him up and kiss his neck until he belly laughed. "You don't know where I'm going." Emily ruffled his blond locks.

He shrugged. "You're going out."

She chuckled. "Indeed, but to sketch. You'll be bored and listless. I can't get a thing done when you keep running off."

"I won't. I can stay still." He froze, pretending to be a statue. "See."

"Ya can't stay that way fer long," Mrs. Hayes said.

Emily removed her bonnet from the hook. "If ever there was a boy of five who couldn't sit still, 'tis you, Christian."

"Your mama and me wear out trying to keep up with the lad." Their elderly housekeeper moved to the window, the soft light illuminating her face.

Emily instinctively reached for her sketchbook, but it was already tucked away in her satchel. "Besides, you haven't finished your chores yet. Samuel asked you to have the wood stacked before he returned."

Christian released a sigh. "I shall do it later. I promise. The sun is still rising."

"Do not procrastinate." Emily turned and issued him one of Mama's famous looks. "The best way to get something done is to begin."

He tipped his head back and drooped his shoulders in a pout.

"When I return," Emily said as she tied her bonnet strings under her chin, "perhaps we can stroll over to see how the Edinburgs' new colt is faring."

"'Huzzah!" He leapt about the kitchen, imitating a horse's gallop.

Emily smiled as she seized Mr. Mathis's bow and quiver and slid the strap over her shoulder. She exited through the parsonage's back door, hurried past what would become their herb garden, skirted the pond, and moved onto the well-traversed path that led into the woods.

A few hours to herself seemed lovely. Sunlight filtered through the pines, creating a beautiful contrast of lights and darks. She inhaled a deep breath of air, crisp like the bite into a cold apple. The homey scent of burning firewood hung in the breeze.

Turtledoves cooed and skylarks chirped among the tree branches. The damp sod cushioned the soles of Emily's kid boots as the familiar scent of oak and pine embraced her like a hug. A lock of hair escaped her coiffure and dangled between her eyes. She shifted the pack on her shoulder and swiped the errant hair back behind her ear with her index finger. A palette of colors spread out before her. The sky's phthalo blue contrasted against the tree branches' dark umber. Fresh sprouts, a cadmium green, pushed their way through the yellow ochre color of the pine needle mulch. The bright sun cast highlights on the eastern side of the trees. Someday, after Christian was through his schooling, she'd have the luxury of painting for enjoyment instead of for commissions.

The heavy moss that lined the north side of the trees grew thinner as she approached the clearing. She quietly snuck to the tree line and peeked her head around a trunk, hoping to spot a deer drinking from the nearby stream. The higher vantage point on the small wooded hillside afforded her a glorious view of the winding ribbon creek. Perhaps she could bring out her charcoals and get a quick sketch in before she met with Samuel and Mr. Mathis.

A murmur sounded down the steep slope of the one-sided ravine to her left. Two men, less than thirty yards away, tromped through the field toward the creek bank. Two other men hung back near the road. Emily frowned. *Drat.* Their commotion would have scared away the deer.

Sunlight glinted off something metal, and Emily squinted for a better view. What was that? One man wore a mask and pointed a pistol into the other man's back.

She gasped and flung herself out of sight against the rough bark.

Her chest tightened, reducing her breathing to quick abrupt pants. What could she do? Should she scream? If she did, the footpad would know her location. Should she run home to get help? But the victim could be dead by then.

Oh, dear Lord. Do something. A man is about to be killed.

An arrow shifted in the quiver and tapped the side of her head.

The bow and arrows. Emily's heart stilled. *Oh, Jesus, give me the strength.*

She carefully slid an arrow from the quiver and notched it to the bow as Samuel had taught her from a young age. Her toes tingled, and her knees were weak as she forced her foot to step out from behind the tree, careful to keep most of her body protected.

As the men reached the creek's edge, the masked man shoved the other to his knees. "This should be far enough. The wild animals will take care of your body before anyone even knows you're missing."

Emily forced her lungs to breathe. The captive's hands and

mouth were bound, yet he didn't cower. He held himself erect. His snow-white shirt gently ruffled in the light breeze.

It might soon be covered in blood.

A cold sweat chilled her body as she lifted her bow. *Thank You, Lord, for blessing me with a steady hand.*

The masked man paced erratically back and forth behind his captive, yelling until his face turned scarlet as a ripe tomato. Emily couldn't make out a word the man screamed over the rush of her own blood in her ears. Papa had always said anger can run like acid through a man's veins. If this man spit, surely the grass would die.

The cur raised the gun to the back of the bound man's head.

The captive closed his eyes.

Lord, guide me.

Her brother's instructions filled her mind as she exhaled a slow breath, focused on the target, and released the bow's string.

Her arrow sliced through the air, landing a few inches below his shoulder. The man grasped his upper arm where the arrow remained lodged and hollered in pain. His pistol dropped to the ground.

The captive threw his body on top of the weapon, the tall reeds obscuring her view of him except the crown of his head.

Two other men ran over, coming from the direction of the road. They must've seen the arrow stuck in the man's arm because they retreated.

Emily notched another.

Blood dripped off the masked man's elbow. He scanned the forest, and Emily dropped back behind the tree. She could sense the man's outrage, which felt like a tangible blast. He cursed in words that Emily had never heard and she hoped would never hear again.

The captive righted himself onto his knees, the pistol

clutched in his hands. Little good it would do him with his wrists tied behind his back.

The masked man kicked his captive upside his head, knocking him facedown into the creek.

The man didn't move or struggle. *Merciful heavens.* Was he unconscious and drowning in the water?

She let a second arrow fly. It hit its mark as she intended, directly at the man's feet as a warning that he'd better run. The man turned and sprinted toward the road still clutching his arm.

Just in case the man changed his mind, she notched another arrow. Each second seemed drawn into long minutes as she waited for the man to flee far enough for her to come out of hiding, all the while knowing the captive might be dying.

She glanced at his partially submerged body. The slow current dragged him into the water well past his waist. Soon he'd float downstream.

He needed her.

She skidded down the embankment, lifted her skirts, and leapt across a narrow section of the stream—a feat of which her brothers would be proud. When she reached his side, the man's body hung limp. His shirt and hair undulated with flowing water.

Emily grabbed his boot to keep his body from slipping farther into the running stream. With a strength she hadn't known she possessed, she heaved him from the creek and rolled him onto his back. She yanked his gag down around his neck. His face was tinged an eerie pale blue, and the sight ripped a startled yelp from her lips. She dropped to the ground beside him and listened for any sound. Nothing. He wasn't breathing. She pushed on his chest. His shirt clung to his broad shoulders, and the water chilled her hands. Matted dark-blond hair stuck to his forehead.

"Don't die!" *God, please don't let him die!*

She pushed again, applying more pressure. *Come on.* She stilled, listening for breaths. The scent of wet male invaded her senses.

Please, please, please.

Emily leaned farther over him, raising her knee onto his stomach for better leverage. She jammed her hands repeatedly onto his chest, risking cracking his ribs, desperate to get the water out of his lungs.

"In Jesus's name. You will live!"

CHAPTER 3

*J*acob jarred awake for the second time that morning. Creek water projected out of his mouth, along with what might have been a small minnow. He hacked out a cough and drew glorious air into his lungs.

He was alive, blessedly, wondrously, alive, albeit wet and chilled.

He opened his eyes, but Lord Benton wasn't sneering at him. Instead, he peered into the angelic face of a woman. Her finely arched brows knit together as she leaned over him. The bite of the freezing water fell away as Jacob dissolved into a pair of soft amber eyes. She had finely molded cheekbones and a small chin. An unruly lock of thick mahogany hair dangled over her forehead, brushing his. Her rosy lips parted, and she panted as if she'd exerted herself overmuch.

Suddenly, his day seemed vastly improved.

No longer gagged, he instinctively shifted to draw this fetching display of beauty to himself and kiss her soundly. But the rope cutting into his wrists reminded him his hands were still bound. An utter shame, for he hated a missed opportunity.

"Praise God. I thought you were dead." Her features relaxed.

As did I. "Are you my guardian angel?" His voice cracked on the last word.

The furrow in her brow returned. "I beg your pardon?"

He cleared his throat. "A woodland fairy?"

She blinked, her thick lashes sweeping over those enchanting eyes.

"A Valkyrie, maybe?"

"A what?"

"A Valkyrie. A noble maiden carrying a slain warrior to Valhalla."

Her alluring mouth curved into a frown. "The lack of air has addled your wits."

He relished the warmth of her hand seeping through his shirt. "Quite so, or maybe the lack of blood to my brain." He lowered his gaze to where her hands pressed on his chest and her shin rested on his hip. Her knee dug into his stomach.

"Oh!" She scrambled off him backward in a crab-like crawl. She glanced around as if to ensure there were no witnesses before she jumped to stand. "Right. Dreadfully sorry."

A becoming blush tinted her cheeks. The rose color contrasted against the paleness of her skin and drew out the amber in her eyes.

He resolved to make her blush often in the future.

She shook the wrinkles out of her gown, made of a sturdy fabric. He'd like to see her dressed in soft muslin or perhaps silk. Definitely silk.

He shook his head to clear it. Why was he thinking such things about a servant woman? Maybe the water *had* addled his wits.

Addled or not, he continued lying on the ground, gazing at this captivating female.

"Do you think the rogues will return?" She looked over her

shoulder. Her profile displayed the pertness of her nose, petite and fitting for her features.

"Doubtful." Knowing Lord Benton, he'd run straight to the nearest tavern and toss back some spirits before calling for a surgeon. The men would follow Benton's purse looking for the pay due them. "But it's best not to wait around in case they do." Plus, Jacob needed to check on his coachman and servant, but he couldn't rush back in case one of the highwaymen lingered to search his coach. Best to go slowly and not put his rescuer in harm's way. Jacob rolled to his side, putting his weight on his bruised shoulder. He winced and dragged his legs underneath him until he rested on his knees.

"Here, let me help you." She bent and picked at the knots binding his hands until they came undone. "There."

"Much better." Jacob pushed off the ground and rose to his feet. He rubbed his wrists where the restraints had left red marks. "It's amazing how often we take the use of our hands for granted."

Her lips spread into a shy smile. "Especially when you're swimming."

A sense of humor. He returned her smile. "Most definitely." He dipped his head in salute. "I must thank you, miss…"

"Emily Thompson." She bobbed a polite curtsy.

Her neck curved in a graceful ark the likes of which would make swans jealous.

She cleared her throat, and his line of vision settled back on those enthralling amber eyes as he untied the loose hanging gag from around his neck.

A crow cawed.

She jumped at the sound and gazed at the field's perimeter.

"How poorly done of me." He tried to regain her attention. "I've been remiss in all the excitement, but since your excellent marksmanship has my assailants running for the hills." He bowed. "Lord Jacob Warren, at your service." He hit her with a smile that would flutter many a fan in a London ballroom.

"Pleased to meet you, my lord." She glanced over her shoulder, scanning the road as if to reassure herself the bandits weren't returning.

She appeared unaffected by his charms. Not his best day. He would have to try harder.

"The pleasure is all mine." He procured her hand and raised it to his lips. "Especially since you saved my life. I shall forever be in your debt." He lowered his voice to a baritone. "And endeavor to make my gratitude known."

～

*H*is gaze locked on hers, and Emily couldn't look away. The devilish charm in his smile caused her stomach to flop about like a fish on land, and his blue eyes twinkled as if communicating a shared secret. She knew nothing of flirting, but something inside told her this was how it was done, and Lord Jacob Warren was the master.

His lips lingered over her hand a tad too long.

Emily yanked her hand away. "Should we hide or something in case they return?"

Lord Warren beckoned her and silently skirted the wooded edge of the field. She picked up the quiver and followed. He paused and listened, then scanned the road. "It appears their leader's off to lick his wounds, and without him, the rest have scattered. Thanks to you."

There was that lopsided smile again. Heat rushed to her cheeks. This stranger had become too comfortable around her too quickly. Was it due to the harrowing circumstances? Saving someone's life—and having been saved—must bond people quicker than normal. However, it was situations like this she needed to avoid—not saving a man's life but interacting with a man as if a future together were possible.

The twinkle in his smoky-blue eyes goaded her to forget herself and the circumstances of her birth. The jaunty twist to his full lower lip teased as if to provoke her smile, but she mustn't lose her head. She checked the top button of her blouse and clasped her hands in front of her. Since she learned the truth about her actual birth mother, it was imperative that she remain above reproach.

"Miss Thompson, could you perhaps tell me *where* I've had the good fortune of making your acquaintance?"

"Sylvanwood, outside of Gloucester in the Cotswolds."

"Splendid. I was practically at Brownstone Hall before being accosted."

She cleared her throat and worked to keep the shock out of her tone. "You are to reside at Brownstone Hall?"

"You know of the place?"

"Um, well, yes..." An image of the manor with its strange inhabitants, locked shutters, and overgrown vines floated through her mind. Emily knew the manor home well, for a far corner of Brownstone Hall's grounds abutted their field.

"Why does your response give you pause?"

"I didn't know Lady Athol had any relatives. I've never seen a soul visit."

"Which is what I am here to remedy. My brother sent me because we fear the estate has fallen into disrepair, and I'm to attend to it. Among other things."

"I'm certain it will improve under your supervision." She forced a positive tone, but her incredulity caused her words to sound measured.

He ran a hand over the top of his head, and water droplets dripped over his shoulders and back. "Why do I have the impression you're saying that because it couldn't get any worse?"

"It is—ah—merely in need of sprucing."

"Indeed. Your hesitation doesn't give me much encouragement."

"I apologize." What was she apologizing for? Her hesitation? Or for not conveying the full truth of the wretched condition of Brownstone hall, which a person couldn't fathom until seen firsthand. *Lord, forgive me.* Definitely the latter.

"No need. My brother warned me about the sad state of Brownstone Hall from my aunt's missive." His eyes widened, and the muscles around his jaw tightened. He patted the top of his breeches before stuffing a hand into his pocket.

"Is something amiss?"

A whoosh of air slid from his lips, and his mouth relaxed along with his shoulders. "I-I feared the letter with the estate's address might have gotten ruined during my unfortunate swim, but it feels dry."

"No need to fret. Everyone in Sylvanwood knows where Brownstone Hall is. It's on this side of town. One could walk from here."

He shivered, his lips graying from the cold.

"Do you have a coat?" she asked.

"In my carriage."

"Is it safe to head in that direction?"

He took her hand and placed it in the crook of his arm. "In my experience, it doesn't take much to scare off highwaymen."

"You have a history of being accosted by highwaymen?" Emily hesitated at the gentleman's bold maneuver and glanced about. What if someone witnessed her strolling with a stranger?

A snorted chuckle emanated from his nose. "Touché, Miss Thompson. How astute of you. No, I haven't made it a practice to be accosted, but unfortunately, I have several friends who've had—well—similar encounters."

The timbre of his voice vibrated through her, his closeness

setting her nerves on edge. She moved to put some distance between them.

Lord Warren placed a reassuring hand over hers, holding her fast. Their gazes met. A beseeching in the depths of his eyes reminded her of a small boy pleading for attention, much the way Christian often did.

She bit the inside of her cheeks to keep the smile from her lips and fought the giddiness welling within her. *Keep your head.*

He nudged her forward, and they fell into a stroll. "Sylvanwood," he said. "Isn't that a bit redundant for a name? Wooded wood?"

She had always thought it a strange name for a town. The whole set of circumstances seemed ludicrous. She had rescued a man from certain death, they were walking through a field unchaperoned, and now he made small talk as though he courted her. Might as well make light of the situation. "We take our trees very seriously."

He graced her with another one of his captivating smiles. "I admire your quick wit, Miss Thompson. Most charming. I look forward to more verbal swordplay with you."

The sparkle in his eyes sounded an alarm in her head. She must end this acquaintance as quickly as possible. "I have very little free time with all my responsibilities to the parsonage."

"You're married to the vicar?" He scowled. "I did not see a ring."

She glanced at her hands. *Oh, piffle.* She wasn't supposed to come across anyone besides her brother and Mr. Mathis, so she hadn't bothered to wear her gloves. "I'm the vicar's daughter."

A rabbit in the tall grass darted into its burrow.

He murmured, "I enjoy a challenge."

At least that's what she thought she heard, and what was that supposed to mean? Part of her wanted to duck into a hole like the rabbit. Instead, she shrugged the quiver strap closer.

"How did you become such a superb marksman?"

"My older brother."

"We have that in common, except for I have two. The oldest is dreadfully bossy."

"Mine, too, believes he knows best, but he has a good heart and good intentions."

"How charitable of you." He grinned. The sun's position behind him illuminated his blond hair, making it glow like a halo. The strong angles of his face and chin held nice lines.

She should paint him in this light.

Merciful heavens. Where did that thought come from? She wouldn't be painting him in this light or any other light.

"You and your brother must join me for target practice. I'm certain you can find some free time to indulge the man whose life you saved. Being new to town, I'd be delighted to make the acquaintance—"

Twigs snapped to their left.

She gripped his sleeve, imagining that highwayman returning to exact his revenge.

But her brother Samuel and Peter Mathis broke into the clearing.

She jerked her arm from Lord Warren's grasp. Oh, the talking-to she'd receive later if Peter—er—Mr. Mathis noticed. It was challenging to remember that she must now refer to the boy she'd grown up playing with as Mr. Mathis. Had her brother and Mr. Mathis heard the commotion all the way to Mr. Mathis's house?

She swallowed. "I believe you'll be afforded the opportunity now."

Samuel skidded to a halt, shotgun in his hand and breathing hard.

Mr. Mathis stopped close behind. His white-blond hair rose from a deep reddened crease in his forehead. "We heard yelling and came running." He pinned Lord Warren with a protective glare. "Who is this bloke?"

"No one." Emily stepped to the side to increase the distance between them.

Lord Warren lifted an eyebrow.

No one? He was the son of a peer of the realm. "I-I mean..." She was making a mull of things, but being spotted alone with a man in the woods, as innocent as it was, could reflect poorly upon her reputation.

"I spied him through the woods. He was about to be killed by highwaymen. By chance, I had your bow with me, so I shot the man with an arrow, and he ran off."

"You got him?" The quantity of Samuel's freckles appeared to grow with his excitement, giving his bran face a tanned complexion. He glanced about as if to find a pierced dead body among the tall grass.

"I aimed for his shoulder but struck his arm above the elbow."

"Well done, Em." Samuel slapped her on the back, pushing her forward a half step.

Mr. Mathis was not impressed. "What were you thinking, confronting a bandit by yourself?"

Lord Warren stepped forward. "If she hadn't, I'd most certainly be dead. If not shot, then drowned." He glanced back at the creek and rubbed the back of his head. "Probably both." His casual smile returned, and his hand dropped to his side. "Fortunately for me, I have a damsel who rescued me from distress."

All eyes were on her—staring. "I've only just met him." Her words came out rushed. "Nothing untoward happened." She pressed her lips tight and gulped.

Her brother eyed her as if she'd taken leave of her senses, and she fought the urge to hide her face in her hands. She'd said too much and only made this situation worse.

Lord Warren raised his eyebrows at her before clearing his throat and easing the moment's awkwardness. "Do let me introduce myself." He spoke to Samuel. "Lord Jacob Warren, pleased to make your acquaintance." He dipped his head. "I'm in your sister's debt. She is an incredible marksman."

"She learned from my instruction." Samuel's chest puffed. "Name's Samuel Thompson, and this is Peter Mathis. He lives around the bend there." Samuel nodded toward the woods, and Lord Warren glanced that way.

"Mr. Mathis." Emily searched the ground. "One of your arrows should be around here somewhere." A hint of royal blue from the fletching of Mr. Mathis's arrow stuck out among the yellow blades of grass. She yanked the shaft up. "Here it is."

She held it up for everyone to see and strolled back to the group. "I'm afraid the other one is embedded in the bandit's arm." She shrugged off the quiver's shoulder strap and handed it to Mr. Mathis.

He grimaced at her. "What if he'd shot back?"

Emily raised her chin a notch. "I aimed for the hand holding the weapon."

"But you could have missed." His nostrils flared.

Samuel shook his head at his friend. "She's never missed a target."

"This was the first time her target was a man." Mr. Mathis tilted his head heavenward. "God forgive you."

Emily ruffled at Mr. Mathis's accusations. He was acting strangely. Didn't he realize she hadn't had any other choice?

"Knowing how Em can aim"—Samuel whistled—"the rogue should count it as a blessing that she wasn't aiming for his heart."

"I, for one, am grateful. She saved my hide." Lord Warren craned his neck in the direction the masked man had run. "I should see about my coachman and footman. Last I saw, they were lying in the grass, knocked out cold."

Emily gasped. "Good heavens." How could they have stood around chatting while his men were hurt?

Lord Warren lightly gripped her elbow, sending tingles across her skin. "It may not be a scene fit for a lady." A crease formed along the bridge of his nose, his concern as clear as the cerulean blue of his eyes. "Even if the lady is a Valkyrie."

"Perhaps you should see your sister home." Mr. Mathis's hand cut between them and scooted Emily in Samuel's direction. "And I'll see what aid I can give."

Samuel spoke to Lord Warren. "Peter apprentices with our town physician."

Lord Warren bowed. "It has been a pleasure meeting you, Miss Thompson. You have my deepest gratitude for your quick aid and my admiration for your skills."

Emily's stomach flipped and somersaulted. She nodded to Lord Warren before accepting Samuel's arm, keeping herself from looking back as they strode toward home.

Samuel aided her across the embankment.

The corner of her sketchpad peeked from behind the tree—forgotten in all the commotion. Before entering the tree-lined path, she allowed herself one glance back.

At the same moment, Lord Warren peered over his shoulder. Their gazes locked.

He smiled.

Emily scrambled to catch up with her brother and the shelter of the woods. Her mind continued to stray to dangerous places it shouldn't go—to a pair of cerulean-blue eyes, a teasing roguish grin, and a longing to be wooed by Lord Warren.

◌

*U*sually, Jacob was an excellent judge of character, an asset that often benefited him at cards and espionage, but he couldn't quite figure Mr. Mathis out. The exceedingly fair Nordic man appeared upset with Miss Thompson. Jacob had had his fair share of run-ins with jealous men, and he was certain this one intended to leg-shackle himself to Miss Thompson.

Better Mr. Mathis than Jacob. Women were a fun diversion, but nothing more. Anything deeper led to heartache or trouble, perhaps both.

Dead grass rustled beneath their boots.

"How did you come to be wet?" Mathis issued a sideways glance.

"The bandit knocked me unconscious into the water."

"Miss Thompson pulled you out?"

"I believe so." He doubted Lord Benton would have pulled him out.

"She touched you?"

Definitely jealous. He should tread lightly. "From the tenderness in my ribs, more like pummeled my chest until I started breathing."

Mathis's frown deepened. "If you are truly thankful for Miss Thompson saving your life, then I would appreciate you not revealing this detail when you retell today's events. I shall not have her reputation suffering for her good deed."

"Indeed," Jacob said. "You have my word."

Mathis's frown didn't lessen.

Jacob pressed a hand to his chest. His sore muscles and skin protested. "I do believe I'll be sporting a fair number of bruises tomorrow." Between the highwaymen's rough handling and Miss Thompson's revival techniques, his body ached, but he was alive. "I'm appreciative for the chance to be feeling anything. At the moment, a little soreness and a few aches are welcome."

His coach and team had been led into a small clearing of the woods just off the other side of the road. The horses munched on the nearby weeds. According to the tracks in the mud, Lord Benton and his highwaymen had fled in the direction of London. If he ever caught another glimpse of Lord Benton, he'd hate to think what he'd do to the odious man. This was the second time Benton had tried to kill him. Jacob wouldn't allow a third.

A muffled sound came from deeper in the woods.

Mathis notched an arrow to his bow and turned that direction in one swift movement.

Jacob dashed to retrieve his pistol from between the cushions inside the carriage. Clutching it, he nodded to Mathis. They converged into the underbrush toward the sound.

Behind a bush, his coachman and footman lay gagged and tied to an oak tree.

Jacob lowered his weapon, and their eyes lit with relief upon spying their employer.

He and Mathis worked to untie them. As Mathis examined the servants physically, Jacob interrogated them. Besides a few bumps and bruises, the pair were in good health. Mathis and Jacob held the steeds steady as the coachman and footman readied the carriage.

"Where are you headed?" Mathis asked.

"Brownstone Hall."

His pale eyebrows rose. "Truly?"

"The astonished reactions to my residing at Brownstone Hall are beginning to dishearten me. I heard it needs work, but how bad could it be?"

Mathis chuckled.

"I'd hoped Miss Thompson was jesting."

Mathis slipped between the mares and patted one's neck. "What brings you to Sylvanwood?"

"I've come to visit my aunt and oversee the repairs to Brownstone Hall."

"Not to court Miss Dorsham?"

Jacob didn't know this Miss Dorsham, but he laughed. He couldn't help it. The events of this day bordered on the absurd.

Mathis didn't appear amused.

Jacob covered his mouth with his hand until his composure returned and cleared his throat. "No, no. I left London to escape the marriage mart and their ambitious mamas. I'm in the prime of my youth. There'll be no settling down for me in the near future. At some point, I will have to become leg shackled, but that time is far off."

"Well, the ladies here are unlike those who reside in London." Mathis's white face reddened. "You understand?"

All he understood was that this man was possessive and overbearing where the ladies of Sylanwood were concerned. Jacob put a hand to his aching head and leaned his elbow against the coach. Maybe it was because his head hurt, or perhaps it was because he'd had quite enough madness for one day, but he nodded.

A cynical smile passed over Mathis's face. "Well, good. You should report the incident to the magistrate. I can direct your man to his house. It's on the way." Mathis turned and spoke to the coachman, giving him directions.

Jacob thanked Mr. Mathis for his help as the footman opened the carriage door. Jacob climbed in and watched from the window as the odd man disappeared back into the woods.

He collapsed against the seat cushions. Today's brush with death had been a little too close.

He rubbed his face with one hand.

His handler would never believe he'd been saved by a Valkyrie.

CHAPTER 4

The following morning, Emily sketched the neighbor's horses and field before her. She put down her charcoal to blend the dark lines with her index finger, but her hands trembled, making the work difficult. She'd brought her sketchbook to calm her unsettled nerves, but a wry grin and a pair of twinkling eyes kept appearing on the page. She exhaled and smoothed a shadow along the mare's neck. Shading captured the sharp angles of the horse's perked ears and the shimmer of its coat reflecting off its muscular form, especially how it contrasted with the fuzzy newborn hair of its wobbly, knobby-kneed colt.

The foal's birth was a sign that spring was on its way despite the chill in the air. The sun shone off the grassy field with a whitish-yellow glow, melting the fine layer of frost and filling her nostrils with the scent of damp earth.

"May I feed them? Please, pretty please." Christian's bright eyes met hers.

Emily rose from the cut tree trunk which served as her chair and placed her sketchbook and charcoal pencil down. "Only the mother."

"Because the baby drinks milk?"

"That's correct." She tousled his hair. "You're a bright young man."

Emily passed him a carrot from the satchel she'd packed, and Christian eagerly fed it to the chestnut mare.

She flipped the page, her fingers sketching in light, quick strokes to capture the joy and eagerness on Christian's face. His small hands clutched the crossbeam of the fence, likely more to keep himself from jumping than for support. He beamed a big smile at her, displaying the gap where his two front teeth used to be. Emily grinned at his rosy cheeks and blue eyes shining with delight. Nothing pleased Christian more than to be around horses, so she often trekked over to their neighbor's land to see what new mounts had been acquired.

"Emily!"

She stiffened, recognizing the familiar voice of her friend— amend that—her *so-called* friend.

Phoebe Dorsham waved from her phaeton as it drew to a stop. She grabbed her white ermine muff before she hopped down and tied the horses' reins to the gatepost. Her chaperone, Miss Neves, who was notorious for nodding off, slumbered peacefully in the double seat.

Emily wiped a charcoal smudge off her worn pelisse and clasped her blackened fingers behind her back before turning to face the petulant storm dressed in ruffles and lace who had been her childhood companion.

With the beauty and grace of a butterfly, Phoebe daintily picked her way along the knoll's crest in her kid leather boots to where Emily stood. These days, Phoebe was less like a butterfly and more like a bee, soft and fuzzy but with the threat of a sting.

Christian waved at Miss Dorsham before stepping up onto the wooden crossbeam. He turned his attention back to the unsteady colt with its widespread legs grazing next to his mother.

"I've missed you." Phoebe kissed Emily on either side of her cheeks. "It has been an age." Her blond, hot-ironed curls brushed Emily's face before she pulled back. Being several inches taller, Phoebe peered down at her. "I have missed our tea parties and romps through the woods."

Would Phoebe pretend as though nothing happened? The guard on Emily's tongue almost let loose. She wanted to settle this here and now, but Papa's words echoed in her mind—*Remember, you're a child of God and a representative of His kingdom.* Instead of lashing out, she asked, "Why, Phoebe? Why would you gossip to your mother about something I told you should remain private?" Emily crossed her arms as if they could keep her hurt inside. "I confided in you. I trusted you."

Phoebe bit her bottom lip, looking contrite. "I was curious about the man who appeared on your doorstep. How could I not be? His questions about your brother and your births— why, that was the most interesting thing to happen in Slyvanwood in an age."

Emily waved her hand to signal Phoebe to lower her voice so Christian didn't overhear. For the thousandth time, she questioned God as to why Phoebe had been visiting when the stranger came asking about things that were not his concern.

"I truly am sorry." Phoebe's gaze lowered, along with her volume. "But aren't you the least bit curious about how the man discovered the name of your birth mother?"

"Not in the least. He was merely seeking trouble." God forgive the partial lie. The man was a problem, and his visit while Mama and Papa were at the church had raised a thousand questions in her mind. What if her birth mother or one of Christian's birth parents sent the man looking for them?

Emily wanted more answers than she'd gotten from the stranger who'd knocked on the door and offered a cordial bow to her and Phoebe. He said he was trying to locate a relative, and she'd been happy to comply, answering most of his questions about the town they'd lived in prior and confirming the names of Mama's cousins. It was only once he started asking Emily about Christian's birth that her protective side sent the man packing. He'd been taking his leave when he paused and asked if she'd heard of a famous opera singer and informed her of her birth mother's identity. Phoebe's startled gasp still echoed in Emily's mind. She denied the relation, but he passed her a hand-copied page of a church registry where her birth date and birth parents were noted. Phoebe instructed him to get out and slammed the door on his retreating form.

"Not being able to call upon you has been awful for me, too," Phoebe said, "but it shall blow over. I promise. You're my closest friend, and I won't let anything separate us. I'll convince Mama to come around. She's already shown signs of mellowing, especially since she's consumed with preparations for the upcoming season." She twisted her muff and attempted a wobbly smile. "You know how I am. My tongue always gets ahead of me."

Emily used to adore Phoebe's vivacious boldness, but now Emily's reputation might lie shredded in the aftermath of her friend's loose tongue. Years ago, she would have told Phoebe what had transpired by the creek the day before, but Phoebe had proved she couldn't be trusted.

"It will not get out," Phoebe said, "and even if it does, the vicar raised you. Everyone will respect you out of regard for him and his wife."

"My parents." The words burst forth from her lips. "Merely because a woman gave me birth doesn't make her my mama."

"Quite right." Phoebe blanched and backstepped. "I do apologize."

"And what of your mama? You're not allowed to even visit

with me. She would faint if she knew we were speaking right now."

Phoebe removed a hand from her muff and swatted the air. "Miss Neves put the absurd idea that I shouldn't associate with you in Mama's head." With pursed lips, Phoebe inclined her chin toward her napping chaperone wrapped in the warmth of her shawl. She assumed her chaperone's haughty demeanor. "Because it's not proper for a young lady to consort with someone of questionable birth." She planted her hand on her hip. "It's ludicrous. How can it be fine for us to play together our entire lives, but when new information comes to light, it's no longer proper?"

Emily put a finger to her lips before glancing in Christian's direction. She lowered her voice. "Your mama is looking out for your reputation. She has every intention of you making the match of the season."

"If the season is anything like the Copelands' house party, I shall adore it." Her mouth curved into a dreamy smile. "I've returned as a woman ready for society." Phoebe grew solemn and peered down at Emily. "I promise I will fix it. Not another soul will find out, and I'll convince Mama." She flashed another wobbly smile. "You know I can persuade her of anything." She took one of Emily's hands. "Please forgive me. I need you to visit while I'm in London. You always have been my practical side. How will I survive without you?"

"Quite fine, I imagine."

"See, I need your level head so that things don't seem as dramatic. When you come to visit, you must bring some of your paintings. We will show them to the Royal Academy. I'm certain they will admit you on the spot when they see your talent, and then we can enjoy London together."

"You know I can't. Not now that I know the names of my birth parents. If anyone recognized me, I'd be turned away from every social call."

"Surely, they won't make the association."

"She's a famous opera singer. Her portrait hangs in the Royal Academy, and she's seen on the arm of the Duke of Bedford. We have the same coloring, same shaped face, eyes, nose, and cheekbones."

Phoebe's head lowered, and her shoulders drooped as if she grasped the extent of the problem she'd created in gossiping to her mama about Emily's true birth mother.

"Besides"—Emily waved a hand dismissively—"you will be busy attending balls, and I can't leave Christian." She peered at her younger brother, who'd barely seen five winters.

"By the end of the Season, I will certainly be married, but you can come and stay with me to paint my portrait." Phoebe beamed. "Or my portrait with the children I will have in a few years." She sighed. "Mama is beside herself planning for my coming out. I've been to one dress fitting after another. The seamstress forced me to stay still for so long, I almost turned into one of those Grecian statues."

And that was all Emily would get for an apology. Phoebe never stayed on a topic for long, but she was Emily's longest-standing friend. Their nannies napped them in the same crib. They shared the same schoolroom. They practically shared every waking moment until the day when that horrible stranger came with all his questions. Emily's spirit wrestled with forgiving her. Extending grace to someone who had betrayed her trust posed a challenge.

Perhaps Phoebe was right and word wouldn't get out about her illegitimate birth. Besides, only the Dorsham women knew of her secret. Not even her own family had seen the page from the annals noting the mother she'd never met. Her parents had sat with her when she was of an age of understanding and explained how like a limb had been grafted into a tree, so, too, she'd been grafted into their family. She'd been stunned but reassured because of the immense love of her parents. It wasn't until she broached a marriageable age that the social ramifications of being adopted became apparent. Emily inhaled a deep breath. God help her. She would forgive Phoebe—as long as the gossip died.

"Do you like my new bonnet?" Phoebe asked, posing.

Emily admired the robin's-egg-blue hat with matching ribbons trimmed with silk flowers. "It's quite spring-like, and the color makes your eyes appear blue."

"That's the effect I was hoping for. It is my bane to have been born with boring gray eyes. Do you think I should add feathers? They would provide more height."

Emily's gaze traveled Phoebe's tall, curvaceous form. Next to her friend, Emily always felt like a miniature pony standing next to a Shire horse. Her petite frame, thin bones, and dark hair made her appear more like Phoebe's shadow. "I believe you're tall enough. An eligible suitor lacking in stature may feel uncomfortable with the illusion of your added height."

"Oh, Emily, you are quite right. How am I going to have a successful season without you?"

"I'm certain you will make do."

Phoebe grabbed Emily's arm and glanced over her shoulder at Miss Neves, still asleep in the phaeton. "Speaking of eligible suitors, did you read the latest gossip from London?" Phoebe's eyes glittered.

"You know I don't read the gossip columns."

"Yes, yes." She rolled her gaze heavenward. "Complete nonsense, an abominable waste of time. The vicar wouldn't approve. But what would you do if you didn't have me to keep you abreast of all the *ton's* happenings?"

Remain in innocent bliss with a lot less nonsense crowding my head. Emily shrugged and afforded Phoebe a half smile.

"Lord Jacob Warren, the handsome rogue and youngest son to the Duke of Warren, dueled a couple of days ago at dawn over Lady Lucile Benton."

Warren. Emily's breath caught. Lord Jacob Warren. Was that why he'd come to Sylvanwood—to avoid scandal due to his duel?

"Can you imagine someone dueling over your honor? It's so romantic."

Shooting each other is not romantic. "It's illegal."

Phoebe's pink lips curled into a droll frown. "I do wish you were more prone to flights of fancy. The mere thought of someone dueling over me sends me into a swoon." She waved her muff like a fan in front of her face.

Emily's gaze drifted toward Christian as the colt drew close enough for him to pet.

Lord Warren had dueled over a married woman, which meant he was a known libertine. Heat rose into her neck. She'd associated with him and, *merciful heavens*, Samuel and Mr. Mathis had seen her walking with him in the field—alone.

"It was assumed Lord Benton would delope and leave them both with their lives and honor, but he didn't."

Emily's eyes snapped back to Phoebe. "They fired shots? Lord Warren killed a man?"

"He must have missed. The column referenced them both as alive." Phoebe stuffed her hand back into her muff and shrugged a dainty shoulder. "Lord Benton was said to have been in quite a rage afterward." She clasped her hands and muff to her heart. "I do hope I get an introduction to Lord Warren while I'm in London. I'm dying to see if he's as handsome as the gossip columnists say."

"Only trouble arises from associating with a known rake."

Phoebe shrugged.

A loud snore cut off, and Miss Neves stirred in her seat.

"Oh dear, the beast awakens. I better be off before she sees me with you." She leaned forward and kissed the air near Emily's cheek. "It was lovely to see you."

"Indeed." Emily didn't return the kiss because Phoebe turned and flittered back down the small hill.

"Don't worry. I shall fix this with Mama." Pheobe waved over her shoulder before hiking up her skirts and climbing into the luxurious Phaeton. "With all haste."

As she snapped the reins, the horses pranced along the dusty road. The carriage hit a bump, and Miss Neves's head popped up. She glanced about.

Emily turned back to Christian. "Well, young man, I think it's time we head back home."

"Aww." Christian's shoulders slumped. "Five more minutes? Please?"

"I'm sorry, but there are chores to be done, and the day grows long."

Christian jumped down from the fence and drooped his shoulders. "But I don't want to do chores. I hate chores."

"*Hate* is a strong word."

"Fine. I dislike chores immensely."

Emily laughed as she strolled beside him. She held out her hand, and Christian slid his fingers into hers. "I'll tell you what." She peered into his mopey face. "If you return without a fuss, I will help you hoe the garden."

His head perked up. "Really?"

She nodded.

He leapt into the air, raising one fist high and shouting, "Huzzah!"

The quick change in his demeanor lightened her mood. Still holding her hand, he half walked and half skipped down the lane in Phoebe's wake. The woodlarks chirped around them, and robins plucked fat worms from the ground. As a cloud passed over the sun, the chill in the air returned, and Emily clasped her pelisse tighter around her shoulders.

Christian swung his head to shift his blond hair out of his

eyes. "Why does Lady Dorsham no longer allow you and Phoebe to be friends?"

Emily stopped and peered into his innocent eyes. With a deep inhale and exhale, she asked God to give her the right words. "Some people believe that status and birth determine a person's worth. But they do not."

"What's worth?"

"A value, or a price someone would pay."

"Lady Dorsham thinks you're not worth nothing?"

"Anything." The correction sprang from her lips. She dropped to his eye level and took hold of his arms. "We all have worth. Do you know how I know?"

Christian shook his head.

"Because Jesus paid a high price for us."

"On the cross?"

"Indeed." Emily slid her fingers down his arms and squeezed Christian's hands. "You and I are precious to God." The sudden prick of tears burned the back of her lids. She stared down the empty lane for a moment before meeting his gaze. "And you are precious to me. Never forget that, no matter what."

Mama had given birth to Samuel, but she'd never treated Emily and Christian differently than her actual blood. Just because some stranger came around asking questions didn't mean anything would change. Emily had witnessed Mama's cousin, Sarah, give birth to Christian and reject the child she'd borne. Emily promised in that moment that she'd care for Christian, and no one would keep her from that vow.

She waited for Christian to nod and smiled when he did. They continued their stroll back to the parsonage while Christian rambled about the Edinburgs' new colt.

They reached the garden, and the yeasty smell of bread filled her nostrils. Mrs. Hayes must still be baking. Emily had helped her knead the dough earlier.

Christian released her hand and ran into the house, but Emily maintained a slow pace. Their discussion weighed on her heart.

She'd do anything to protect Christian from vicious town gossip—and growing up around dangerous rogues like Lord Warren.

~

*J*acob tipped his head back to survey the vast front facade of Brownstone Hall. The dilapidated structure, dating back to the early 1700s and the reign of King George II, was still standing but in desperate need of repair. Its solid brownstone façade remained in good condition, but the roof, trim, and windows had taken a beating by both Father Time and Mother Nature. Shutters hung crooked on one hinge—at least, the ones that hadn't fallen off into the overgrown foliage below. Vines crept over the entire first floor as though devouring the structure and dragging it to an earthly grave. Several attic windows gaped open, revealing a dark and empty interior. Some slate roof tiles were missing, and the chimneys appeared to have become nesting grounds for hawks or dens for other ghastly critters.

My aunt lives in this state? The hair on his arms bristled. The conditions looked almost as bad as when he'd been forced to live in a tumbledown shack of a barn for a month while he spied on the Luddites, who were rioting and destroying farm equipment.

The magistrate had insisted Jacob stay the night at their abode. Though he'd planned to go on to Brownstone Hall, the hour had grown late after retelling the tale of the attack and revisiting the site to reenact what happened. Now, after laying eyes on Brownstone Hall's condition, he was grateful for one last night of good sleep. He might not get any in this drafty old place.

All the strange looks when he mentioned Brownstone Hall made sense now. The manor was in worse condition than he'd thought. He sighed but set his jaw. Helping his aunt had to come second to his true mission.

With the butt end of his umbrella, he pushed a shutter off the steps and cleared a path to the front door.

"Milord, let me get that for you." His footman rushed over and lifted the object out of the way. A mangy cat hissed from underneath its shelter before darting into the bushes. The startled footman jumped aside and struggled to gain control of his awkward load.

Jacob ducked as the shutter's top corner careened in his direction.

His man redirected it, leaning the shutter against an overgrown bush.

Jacob stepped up to the arched stone entrance and attempted to lift the door knocker, but it didn't budge. The hinges had rusted. He rapped his knuckles on the oak door in desperate need of repainting.

At the sound, doves flew with flapping wings from off the second-floor window ledge. Minutes ticked by without an answer. He knocked a second time, waited, and then thumped a third, this time with the butt of his umbrella.

At the bottom of the stairs, the footman swatted at an insect hovering about his head.

"Go with the coachman." Jacob inclined his head to the servant. "See if there is anyone within the stables and find out what accommodations they have for the horses." He raised a warning brow. "Be sure to watch your step. I don't want anyone injured."

The men hurried to do his bidding.

Again, Jacob pounded on the door with his fist. This time a murmuring came from within.

"...impatient callers...gonna knock the blasted door down."

Jacob barely caught the muttered words before the door cracked open and an elderly manservant poked his head out. He squinted against the sunlight, his hair tousled as if he'd just been awakened from a nap.

"Good day, sir." Jacob flipped his calling card from his breast pocket. Between two gloved fingers, he extended the rectangular parchment inscribed with his full name to the man.

The servant grasped the card in one hand and patted his pocket with the other until he found his spectacles. He slid the wire rim up the bridge of his nose and around his ears, then held the paper out full arm's length.

"Ah, yes," the man yelled.

Jacob cringed at the volume. Was the man deaf?

The butler's face cracked into a smile. With a grand swing of his arm, he stepped back and opened the door wide. "Her ladyship is expecting you."

Jacob strolled into the foyer. The floors and wooden paneling appeared gray under a thick layer of dust. "Obviously." He couldn't withhold the sarcasm from his voice.

"Pardon, milord?" The manservant leaned forward.

Jacob shook his head as his gaze fell on the chair and blanket resting a few feet from the door. It appeared the man had been sleeping near the entrance. Brilliant. A nearly deaf butler.

He assisted Jacob in shrugging out of his coat, and Jacob handed the servant his hat and umbrella.

The musk of damp wood hung in the air. The little light spilling in through the film of dirt covering the windows illuminated the dust particles into a thousand shimmery stars. White sheets covered the furniture like little lingering ghouls and goblins.

The elderly servant's gait was slow and held the shuffled rhythm of a country-dance step as he led the way. The click of Jacob's boots echoed through the empty manor as he followed. Vague childhood memories of Brownstone Hall flashed—him running across well-polished, checkered floors and shouting to hear his echo in the grand foyer. Compared to their London townhome, Brownstone Hall had seemed like a sprawling mansion, but Jacob also had to have been only four or five years of age when he last visited. His brother's country homes were much larger, but this place had stood out to Jacob as fascinating with its high ceilings and gothic architecture. He'd overheard that his aunt had become a recluse and his mama had tried to convince his father to intervene, but it only threw him into a fit of rage and a rehashing of his last interaction with Jacob's uncle.

"I must say, milord, we are delighted at your visit." The servant opened the door to the front salon, which at least appeared to have been cleaned recently.

Jacob entered the room and strode to its center. Dated furniture formed a semicircle around a faded blue threadbare rug, but at least it was tidy.

"Do have a seat while I summon Lady Athol."

The man flashed Jacob with a delirious smile that reminded him of the Luddites' expressions when they conspired for a raid. Warning flags rose in Jacob's head, but he was being ridiculous. He was losing his touch if he felt threatened by a man who could barely walk. Besides, his family employed the servant.

The butler gestured for him to sit in a wingback chair with a well-worn seat that curved like a soup bowl.

"Er—I prefer to stand."

"Very well, then." He shuffled back down the hall.

Jacob paced the worn path on the blue rug. The floorboards squeaked with each step. Minutes ticked by on the round-faced mantel clock. A sturdy stone fireplace held the remnants of charred wood, and above the mantel rested a gilded picture of a Tuscan landscape. A draft blew through the chimney, and the smell of soot wafted under his nose.

Faded drapes framed the muntin window, and the ledge held a green tinge of mildew. His throat tickled from inhaling so much dust, and he wedged open the sash to allow in fresh air. A shutter crashed into the weeds below, joining its mate. Jacob poked his head outside and sucked in a deep breath.

How could his aunt live like this? His uncle had been a wicked and stubborn man, but who allows their home to fall into such squalor? He hadn't lacked for funds, for he was notorious for his traveling and dolling out money to clubs, card games, and women. Wouldn't he have maintained his own house if at the very least for his pride?

Brownstone Hall didn't need *freshening up*. It required an entire remodel. He had extensive work to oversee, and the weighty toil ahead pressed upon his shoulders.

He would be here longer than anticipated.

But would that be so terrible? He'd have more time for reconnaissance work to seek the proof he needed before moving forward into his new role. There was no rush to return to the city. The frivolity of London's capricious fashionable set grated his nerves. They'd often impress and win a man's favor with their lavish parties, but in the next moment, cut him down with their biting remarks to improve their situation. A simple country stay might be just the thing to help clear his head and regain some direction for his life—as long as he wasn't called away on a separate mission for the Home Office.

A pair of delicate lips slightly curved in a witty smile floated through his memory. Miss Emily Thompson's fresh and wholesome beauty drew him in a way the charming women of the ton hadn't done in a long time. At least, not since Sarah.

No. He couldn't allow anything to distract him from his real reason for being here. Definitely not a pretty face. He fingered a chunk of missing plaster under the windowsill. Not even this dilapidated building could distract him from his purpose—locating his son.

The butler's shuffle-step announced his return, along with two voices outside the drawing room door. Jacob glimpsed the hem of a white gown.

"He's your nephew." The butler's whisper was loud enough for the entire town to hear. "You must see him. He rode all this way."

The hem swished and then disappeared.

"You won't come to any harm," the man said. "I'll ensure it."

More murmuring.

The butler's voice rose. "These old bones can still take a man down!"

An elderly woman was pushed into the open doorway. Was this his Aunt Louisa? His memories of her were hazy, but he recalled her laugh filling the room and her moving in graceful sweeping gestures like a dancer across a floor. This woman with whisps of unkempt hair framing her face, draped in three layers of long shawls as if unable to chase away a chill, blinked at him with a panicked expression.

Jacob greeted his aunt with a smile, but she backed up like a skittish deer. She'd have fled entirely, but the butler's hands stilled her retreat.

"Aunt Louisa?"

She rounded to greet Jacob with a stiff smile. Her white hair, dappled with gray, peeked from under a lace cap. Worry wrinkles creased her forehead, but there were hints of her once being a young beauty with a slender nose and high cheekbones.

"W-welcome, my lord."

Jacob widened his grin, hoping to soften his aunt's unease. "Please, we are family. You may call me Jacob."

The butler nudged her with his elbow.

She swatted at his hand, and the end of her shawl jiggled, waving under her arm. A smile wobbled on her lips as she treaded lightly into the room. "Jacob, I'm pleased you've come."

His aunt's strange reception spoke otherwise, but he wouldn't call his aunt out on her hum. Not yet.

She stopped out of arm's reach and readjusted her wrap. "You resemble your mother. You're a handsome fellow, nothing like your father. How is she? Your mama, that is."

Jacob chuckled at her odd speech cadence and slight against his father. "Mother is well and sends her regards."

"How nice. Would you care for some tea?" Without waiting for an answer, she leaned back and hollered, "Maslow, fetch us tea."

"Right away, my lady." Shuffle steps retreated down the hall.

"Please have a seat." She tugged at her shawls and sat in a wooden chair positioned between the door and the hearth. She gestured for him to sit across from her.

Jacob sat on the sofa, or more accurately, sank into the sofa. It swallowed him until his knees were level with his chin. His backside was wedged into a hole. He struggled to pull himself out, to no avail.

His aunt said nothing, merely regarded his reaction, her body positioned on the chair as if prepared to spring away at any moment.

The awkward situation drew his sarcasm. "Do all your sofas consume people, or am I merely extra delicious?"

She pursed her lips, creating small vertical lines like the markings on a ruler.

He wiggled a bit and managed to cross one leg over the other. "Actually, it's quite comfortable once you get the hang of it. It could become the next fashion trend for furniture."

Her cheekbones rose, and the corners of her eyes crinkled, but she continued to pinch her lips together.

What does it take to get a reaction from her?

He laced his fingers behind his head. "So, tell me, dear Aunt Louisa. How fare things at Brownstone Hall?"

A noise sprang from her throat, and her lips parted into a burst of strangulated laughter. She appeared startled and glanced about as though the sound were foreign.

He smiled at her over his kneecaps.

She turned away, and another bout of choked mirth propelled forth despite her attempt to cover it with her hand. As soon as she appeared to gain some semblance of control, she turned in his direction again, and the hilarity began anew.

This was the woman he remembered from his youth. Not the timid, skittish woman who'd introduced herself today. Unable to resist, Jacob joined in the contagious laughter until the two of them had tears rolling down their cheeks. Today held his vote for the oddest day ever.

"I beg you to have mercy." Jacob raised his hands in surrender. "My stomach is already cramping."

She used the edge of one of her shawls to dab tears from the corners of her eyes and raised her voice so the butler could hear. "Maslow! Do hurry and come help us."

An awkward silence fell. Aunt Louisa dispelled the tension with a few sighs and a discussion on the weather while Jacob shifted to find some sort of a comfortable position until the servant could offer his aid. *Please let the elderly man be strong enough to hoist me out.*

The butler shuffled in carrying the tea tray and rested it on a low table next to Aunt Louisa. She managed whatever it was ladies did with the tea leaves, seeping them in the hot water.

Jacob rocked back and forth to see if some momentum could save him from his confines, but to no avail. "If I could have a little help."

Both his aunt and the butler ignored his plea.

His jaw clenched. Were they both hard of hearing? And

why did his aunt call for the butler's help if she was going to pretend everything was dandy?

Aunt Louisa disposed of the tea leaves and poured a cup, handing it to Maslow, who carried it toward Jacob.

He lifted a hand with a slight shake of his head to decline. How could one partake of tea in this odd manner?

The carpet lip tripped the older man's unsteady steps.

The next moment, tepid tea bathed Jacob's face and the front of his cravat.

His situation wasn't improving.

"My apologies, milord. Let me find you a cloth." Maslow searched a side table drawer.

Jacob held back a growl and wiped the tea from his eyes with his fingertips and the drips from his chin with the back of his hand.

All the while, his aunt surveyed him judiciously instead of apologizing or lending aid.

Rage, the side of him he usually kept contained, welled, ready to explode in a Vesuvian eruption. He clenched his jaw to avoid scolding the inept butler and lashing out at his aunt for her horrible attempt at hospitality. Perhaps the woman was trying to run him out? Did she believe he was here to banish her to a dowager house? After this stunt, he might do just that.

He opened his mouth to launch into a tirade that would rival his father's outbursts.

No. I'm not my father.

The blaze of anger fizzled to a dull simmer. Once, when he was ten and two, he'd vented the rage that boiled inside him and directed a fierce tongue-lashing at his mother. The memory of her frightened expression still pricked him with guilt.

Jacob exhaled a deep breath. The herbal aroma of tea lingered over his skin. He cocked a brow at his aunt and resorted to the usual tactic that defused the igniting powder keg inside of him. "I had planned to bathe later, but this is much more efficient. Tell me"—he licked his lips and kept his tone flippant—"was that Hysson or imperial tea?"

Her face fell slack, and she blinked wide-eyed at him. "Hysson."

"Splendid choice. Good for the complexion."

Aunt Louisa shot Maslow a look.

He eyed his mistress with a stern glance. "Come now, my lady. No more of this."

Aunt Louisa tucked her chin to her chest, and a pink glow stained her cheeks.

"Terribly sorry, milord." Giving up looking for a cloth, the butler finally extended a hand to Jacob and pulled him out of the sofa's jaws. He gestured to a different chair. "This one is a bit more...firm."

Jacob snorted. "I don't see how it could be less."

A smile twitched the corners of Aunt Louisa's lips, and her fingers twisted the hem of one shawl. She peered at him through faded blue eyes. "You must think terribly of me, but I needed to know for certain."

"Beg your pardon?" Jacob tested this chair before sitting fully. "I'm not following."

"You passed my test."

"Test?" Jacob glanced at his aunt and then at Maslow, but the butler busied himself re-pouring the tea.

Aunt Louisa folded her hands and leaned forward. "I needed to ascertain whether you inherited the Warren temper. I won't abide a man who cannot control his anger."

Like my father.

"Ah. I see." Jacob relaxed back in the chair and forced a jesting tone. "And what would have happened if I'd exploded into a rage?"

His aunt's face grew serious. "I would run you off."

"Brilliant. Well, I'm glad I passed the test."

Maslow handed her a cup, then turned to him. "Do you care for sugar? One or two?"

"One."

Jacob accepted the tea and sipped. "You do this to all your visitors?"

"We don't have visitors." Aunt Louisa's gaze dropped to her hands.

Jacob snorted before he could think better of it. "I think I understand why."

"Please, do not believe the worst of me, but I will not be sorry for what I put you through. It is a small thing compared to..." She swallowed.

Jacob sipped the minty liquid and rested the cup and saucer in his lap. He studied his aunt. "Was your late husband prone to such bouts of temper?"

Her gaze slid to the floor, and she nodded. Even though she held the appearance of a mature woman, her demeanor was that of a scared child.

"I'm sorry," he whispered.

She slowly raised her head to meet his gaze. Years of hurt and sorrow tightened her features.

"I, too, have been subject to such tirades." The mere memory of his red-faced father's snarling expression sent a jolt though Jacob's body. "I want no part of them either."

"Your father wasn't always so." Aunt Louisa's eyes grew distant. "Your father used to be funny and carefree, much like yourself."

"Truly?" Jacob couldn't imagine this picture of his father.

"He and I are only a year apart and shared the schoolroom. He had your quick wit and was forever sending myself and our governess into fits of laughter."

Really? Jacob leaned in. "What happened to him?"

She waved her hand. "I don't want to hang a cloud over such a lovely day. Another time, perhaps."

Jacob nodded and gulped his tea. His unsatisfied curiosity longed to press her for an answer, but there would be time, and he didn't want to disrupt their tentative relationship.

"How was your journey?"

He choked out a cough but recovered. "Eventful, but that, too, is a story for another time. Let's merely say I arrived safely."

"Ah, good."

Silence filled the room.

"I must apologize," his aunt said. "I haven't entertained visitors in an age. I fear I'm going about it all wrong."

"Not at all. Other than the sofa incident, and my tea bath, you're doing quite well."

A shy smile flashed across her features. "You must be tired from your travel. Would you like to be shown to your room?"

He shook his head. "I would enjoy a tour of the house. My brother has been good enough to offer my services and his coin to restore the hall to its former splendor."

"He mentioned such in his letter. It is very generous of both him and you. I'm afraid Brownstone Hall has fallen into a state of disrepair. I did my best to maintain appearances for a time, but my husband..." Her eyes hardened. "The truth is, he was a gambler and a spendthrift. There were minimal funds left when he passed. I sold everything I could to pay down his debts. Nothing much remains."

Jacob scooted to the edge of his seat and leaned over to squeeze her hand. "That is why I'm here to help. I only wish you had reached out earlier. Family must stick together."

She lowered her gaze and set her teacup aside. "Let me show you around."

As Aunt Louisa led him through the main floor, her spine remained straight and her hands folded. She kept glancing back as if feeling uneasy about being in front. He recognized the same meek mannerisms he'd often seen in his mother, always treading lightly to avoid his father's wrath.

The manor appeared to have good bones. No expense had been spared when his uncle's great-grandfather originally built the hall. Elaborate Corinthian cornice pillars lined the walls, leading to gold-inlaid ceilings. Large three-tiered chandeliers hung in the center of the dining room. Very little furniture remained, giving the hall a vast and desolate air. She passed through a library and into a well-lit conservatory, where mildew choked his lungs.

"Do you mind if I open a window?"

"If you wish." Her gaze swept over him, but she appeared withdrawn as though his true aunt had retired somewhere deep within. "This was a grand hall in its day. The former lord used to host impressive house parties. People would come and stay for months at a time."

"You never hosted any balls or house parties?"

"No." Her expression remained stoic.

Jacob threaded his hand through his hair and blew out a long breath. He opened another window, and something moved on the ceiling.

Egad. Bats. A shiver of disgust ran through him. *Please don't let there be any in the bedchambers.*

"Your uncle didn't care for visitors. He preferred to visit elsewhere."

"But you didn't?"

"I rattled around in this old house." She murmured, "My gilded cage." Pointing to a side table covered with a sheet, she said, "Please retrieve two candles from under there. Matches are in the drawer."

He folded the sheet back, sending a spray of dust into the air. A brass candelabra with half-melted candles stood underneath on a small table. He tugged open a drawer and found matches.

"Better to explore the rest of this decaying old hall and show you to your chamber so you can get settled. Bring those,

57

in case the clouds shadow the sun." She glided up the side stairs like a ghost from the past.

The upstairs wasn't in too bad of condition. At least the roof seemed to have held. Very few water stains were noticeable on the ceiling. Although the room she said would be his bedchamber had little furniture, it had been cleaned and the bedding changed. A large window, with a balcony he wouldn't dare set foot upon, overlooked an overgrown garden and a pea-soup-green pond.

Aunt Louisa completed the tour of upstairs before leading him down a back staircase through the kitchens and back to the dining room. Her face had paled, and her shoulders stooped until the ends of her shawls dragged in the dust as though moving about the house sapped the life from her. Maybe the memories were too much for her troubled mind. She excused herself to nap and freshen up before supper.

He turned to the picture window and looked out over the overgrown garden of weeds. He'd met Uncle Cyrus once when the man visited their London townhome. Uncle had drunk deep into his cups that night. Jacob hadn't understood the details of their exchange, but his father ended up with a black eye and his uncle a broken nose. Jacob would never forget the sight of his uncle's eyes hardened with malice. Blood gushed from his nose as he spewed curses like vomit on his way out the door. Father forbid anyone to speak of Cyrus Athol again. Jacob learned of his uncle's death when the solicitor appeared at their door with papers for his brother Robert to sign.

Jacob sighed and glanced at the tiered chandelier coated with cobwebs and dust. His mind whirled, forming a list of projects and required materials. He needed to devise a plan. His assignment to fix Brownstone Manor seemed less daunting than meeting his son for the first time, his real reason for traveling to Sylvanwood. And convincing the family that raised his child that he would handle it from here. If all went well, his first priority would be much more rewarding. He strode outside and sought his footman.

The barn was sturdy. Besides an old mule, a couple of barn owls, and the stray he'd glimpsed earlier, his steeds were the only inhabitants. His men fed his horses in the far stall.

Jacob addressed his footman. "Ride into town and hire everyone willing to work. Make sure one of them is a cook—and purchases rations."

"Yes, milord." He bowed and saddled a horse.

Jacob surveyed the grounds. Vines climbed over a walled garden. A wild pasture required a horde of sheep or goats to bring it back into submission. The chicken coop still functioned, and from the clucking sounds, held occupants, but it too needed repairs before the roof caved in. He had an enormous task ahead of him, but he must remember his true intention.

He was here to locate Christian and return to London with his son.

CHAPTER 5

*J*acob rolled his shoulders to reduce tension and snapped the reins. The horses responded, and the curricle lurched, rolling along the dirt road toward the vicar's home.

Pleased to meet you, Christian. I'm your father.

Bah.

He'd run a thousand lines over in his head, but nothing conveyed that he'd searched for five years, took a job with the Home Office for their resources, and sent out teams of private investigators to find his son. Jacob slowly exhaled. He'd know the right thing to say when he saw Christian.

Their meeting was long overdue. He'd arrived in Sylvanwood expecting to search for his son immediately, but the renovation project was absorbing more of his time and energy than he liked. A fleet of workers had swarmed Brownstone Hall. Using his best persuasion techniques and negotiation tactics, he'd convinced his aunt the workers weren't there to hurt her but to help her. After a week of setting up the staff and another week for his aunt to relax and feel comfortable leaving her room, Jacob was finally able to leave her in the care of Maslow and Jacob's newly hired steward, Mr. Welsh.

Two weeks later than expected, Jacob resumed the long-awaited search for his son. He mentally willed the horses to drive faster.

Amid the renovation chaos, Jacob had received a missive from Lieutenant Scar, his handler. The letter hinted that Jacob's holiday could end due to a string of highway robberies targeting nobility in the area. If another occurred, he could get pulled into a mission to stop the band of miscreants. Lieutenant Scar reminded Jacob that duty to his country took precedence, and of course, Jacob didn't disagree. But he needed more time to locate his son. Not to mention that he couldn't leave his aunt to oversee the workers. If he were called to go undercover in a nearby town for this assignment, his time could be in short supply.

The horses' hooves clopped along the road. If all went well, the next hour or two would give direction to his life. Would he immediately step into the role of a father as he'd hoped, or would his son take some convincing to acknowledge and accept him? Despite the crisp air, a fine layer of sweat beaded on his forehead.

Jacob slowed the team of high steppers and curricle he'd purchased from a local baron who needed to pay down some debts. He'd inquired about the name his investigator had uncovered, Rebecca Nichols.

"There's no one in Sylvanwood by that name." The baron must have noticed Jacob's disappointment, for he added, "Unless you mean the vicar's wife, Rebecca? I don't recall her maiden name, but they moved here from Lincolnshire. She has two sons. One who's old enough to take over the parish and another who's about yea high." He'd held a hand to measure waist high.

Someone who'd seen five years would have been around

that tall. Plus, the magistrate, also had vaguely remembered the vicar's wife's prior name having been Nichols. Two hazy recollections and the investigator's partial inquiry was a more solid lead than some of Jacob's past hunches.

"They live in the stone cottage set back toward the woods. Ride past the town center and follow the church road to the end."

The local vicar.

Had Aunt Louisa mentioned him? He didn't think so, yet a memory niggled.

It didn't matter. He'd meet the man and his wife soon enough.

Jacob passed the stone church with its looming tower, pulled up a narrow drive, and parked the team in front of the cottage. He patted the missive inside his coat pocket for reassurance. How many times in the past few weeks had he read it, in anguish, wondering whether his son would be happy to meet his father? Could he right his past wrongs? Was it too late? That was what he was here to discover.

For five years, he'd searched for clues and spent a small fortune to locate his child. It irked him that, after all this time, all he'd known was the child's age until recently. But he was about to find out more—and bring him home. Nothing was going to stop him.

He scanned the grounds. The early yellow blooms of winter aconite were interspersed with purple crocuses along the walk. A few sheep wandered in the far pasture, nibbling on the dead grass.

However, there was no child to be seen. Maybe his investigator had been wrong.

He recalled the letter's words.

I have discovered new information regarding your case. It has been confirmed that the mother, Sarah Nichols, now the Duchess of

*Winsted, did indeed have a cousin, Rebecca Nichols, residing in
Lincolnshire. Her former coachman recalls driving Lady Charlton
to the Nichols' residence, a home of reasonable means, five years
prior. Unfortunately, Mr. Nichols died from illness prior to the birth
of a child and Lady Charlton's departure. The vicar neglected to
record the child's birth in the local parish's annals. According to
neighbors, the widow Nichols relocated to Sylanwood, where she
remarried. I traveled to Sylvanwood to confirm the marriage in the
parish registry and perform interviews but was summoned to
investigate a matter for the crown shortly thereafter. My search
will resume once my duty to his majesty is fulfilled. I do believe we
are on the cusp of finding your son.*

On the cusp. Close enough to raise his hopes, yet far enough
from his reach for frustration to be his constant companion.
This letter combined with what he'd learned from the local
baron assured him he was on the right path. He lowered
himself from his perch and passed the reins off to a groomsman
who stepped out of the stable.

Jacob lifted the gate latch into the walled garden that led to
the front entry. His boots clicked against the slate walkway.
Neatly trimmed boxwood bushes lined the front of the house.
Hung upon the front door, a dried sage and lavender wreath
perfumed the air. Ivy climbed the stone exterior, and flower
buds peeked over the window boxes. Rows of tiny sprouts
labeled with wooden signs boasted of soon-to-be heads of
cabbage, peas, carrots, and the like. Past the sheep grazing in
the far meadow stood an orchard with trees perfect for climbing. The whole scene reminded him of an illustration in the
Mother Goose book his mother read to him as a child.

This was a quaint house for his child to reside—if indeed
he did.

Jacob removed his handkerchief from his pocket and wiped
the perspiration from his brow and hands. Tucking the cloth

away, he sucked in a deep breath and released it before knocking on the oak-paneled door.

The door opened. A round woman with sagging jowls peeked at him from under a ruffled cap.

"Good day. Is the lady of the house at home?" He handed her his card, which she took and examined both sides.

"Do come in, milord. I must check if she's returned, but I know Miss Thompson is about somewhere. You may wait in the drawing room while I find them." She gestured to a door on the right, curtsied, then wobbled down the hall in search of Mrs. Rebecca Nichols or whatever her new married name might be.

Jacob strode into the room and froze. A beautiful woman reclined on the sofa. Bathed in a sunbeam streaming from the picture window, her white gown glowed and her fingers hovered above a sketching pad.

She blinked at him.

Emily?

Er—Miss Thompson, though in his thoughts, calling her by her given name felt right. Well, they *had* shared an intimate near-death experience. It bonded them together in a way. Surely, formalities could be overlooked.

Emily's golden eyes widened. She jolted into a standing position.

"My lord!" Her sketchbook landed with a thud and slid halfway across the hardwood floor.

He bent and lifted it, glancing at the image. A charcoal rendering of his own likeness stared back at him. Though they'd only met one time, she'd drawn him with incredible accuracy. Either she was amazingly talented, or he'd made an impression. Perhaps both.

She swiped at the sketchbook, but he shifted, shielding his gain with his body. A combination of curiosity and prideful satisfaction swelled inside him. Had he invaded her thoughts as much as she had his? He wanted to linger over the drawing and question her about it, but he wouldn't further her embarrassment. Instead, he stifled a smile, his finger catching a previous page and easing it over before turning toward her.

Miss Thompson stared wide-eyed at him. A pinched expression blanched her face as if she waited for the horror of her humiliation to vanquish her.

He dragged his gaze from her doe-like eyes to the sketch of a horse drawn in fine detail from several angles.

"The likeness is incredible."

Miss Thompson stiffened.

He held the pad for her to see. "I can almost hear it munching the grass."

Her shoulders drooped, and a whoosh of breath expelled through her pink lips.

"You're quite good." He started to turn the page, but she snatched the pad from his hands.

"I enjoy drawing." She grasped the book to her chest, and a deep crimson blush stained her cheeks.

Witty, gifted, and lovely.

"I don't mean to pry." He pointed at the book. "It reminds me of George Stubbs. Have you seen any of his paintings?"

She shook her head. "Not unless he's traveled through Sylvanwood."

"Unlikely. I believe Stubbs passed away a couple of years ago, but he was part of the Royal Academy, and a few of his paintings were on display there."

Her brows lifted into a wishful arch at the mention of the academy.

"The second Marquis of Rockingham commissioned him to paint a horse. The piece is titled *Whistlejacket*. It appears so lifelike, you expect it to gallop off."

He stared at her sketchpad, and her arms drew the pad tighter to her chest.

"Yours holds the same feel."

～

$\mathcal{T}$he sound of horses' hooves cantering across sod had pounded in Emily's ears. Her gaze had flicked to the window, but there had been no carriage approaching. It was the thundering of her own heart.

Lord Warren's soft lips contrasted nicely with the chiseled angles of his chin. She'd lost herself while idly sketching those lips and had only heard murmurs in the foyer. She'd assumed the knock was a parishioner looking for her papa and Mrs. Hayes would send them to the church where Papa was working. She hadn't anticipated seeing Lord Warren in their drawing room, his teasing mouth spreading into a dazzling smile and turning her knees to water.

"You could be the next Stubbs." He tapped on her sketch-book, right over her heart. The vibration reverberated to her toes.

Emily shouldn't let a man affect her so.

The doorway still stood empty. *What's taking Mrs. Hayes so long to find Mama?*

"Or DaVinci, another realist artist. You've probably heard of him, Leonardo DaVinci?"

"Indeed. We have several books on him in our library."

Dancing eyes laughed at her. "A bluestocking, then?"

She raised her chin a notch. "There are worse pursuits than knowledge."

"Most certainly." His disarming smile widened to reveal two rows of even white teeth. "I've always enjoyed a woman with a mind."

"Well, you won't find that here—" Emily broke off. "I mean, enjoyment. Of course, I have a mind. It's merely that we are very serious here. My father is the vicar, and my brother Samuel will eventually take over the role."

Good heavens, stop rambling.

His eyes held hers, and friction grew between, as warm and tangible as the updrafts that allow hawks to soar.

"To what do I owe the surprise of your presence?" She tried to match his mocking tone. "Is there another bandit? Shall I get my bow?"

He chuckled, a rich sound emanating from deep inside his chest. "No, I prefer my drama in small doses."

Emily waited for him to explain the reason for his visit.

His gaze drifted to the window, and his smile wobbled. Silence filled the room, only disturbed by the mantel clock ticking.

Did he forget the reason for his visit?

"I..." He peered around. The direct sunlight changed his eye color to a brighter, iridescent blue. "I-I wanted to invite you... and your family, of course, to a dinner party in your honor."

Emily leaned away to the brink of toppling backward. "In my honor?"

"Rightly so, for saving my life."

She shook her head. "I appreciate your thoughtfulness, but there is no need. Do not burden yourself." Heavens above, she could imagine herself near the head of the table with Lady Dorsham frowning at her, ill at ease with someone of questionable birth sitting among them.

"It would be my pleasure." He pushed back the bottom of his tailored jacket, resting his hand on the top of his fawn-colored breeches, and hit her with a lopsided smile. "I won't take no for an answer." One of his eyebrows lifted as if daring her to try.

His aplomb was maddening.

Emily peeled a hand off her pad and shook her palm to decline. "I couldn't—"

"You wouldn't want to disappoint my poor aunt. When she heard the story of your selflessness, she insisted. It may also be an excuse for her to show off the progress of the renovations to Brownstone Hall."

Lady Athol? The woman hadn't shown her face in the village in years. Emily had only glimpsed the woman through the window when she and Mama left jams and other goods on her doorstep as a gesture of goodwill.

Where were her manners? She should have inquired after his aunt earlier. "How fares Lady Athol?"

"Much improved now that she has my company."

Such an arrogant remark.

Her qualm must have shown on her face, for he said, "It's true. I fear she was rather lonely until I arrived. I'm a step up from talking to the wallpaper—" He broke off as if he'd lost concentration and stared over her head. His forehead tightened, creating a crease above the bridge of his nose.

The urge to turn and view what had captured his attention outside clawed at her, but she didn't give in.

The front door opened. Mama entered the hallway and untied her bonnet strings. Mama had taken Christian to visit Mrs. Dyer. Emily had forgotten. Why did Lord Warren addle her wits?

Once again, the man had landed her in an awkward situation. Ladies did not chat in a room with a man unchaperoned. Why hadn't she immediately excused herself? Perhaps she should do so now.

"There ye are." Mrs. Hayes's voice resounded in the hallway. "Ya have a visitor, Mrs. Thompson, waiting for ye in the drawing room."

"A visitor?" Mama turned their direction. Her face radiated sheer joy when she spied Lord Jacob Warren standing near the fireplace.

Emily inwardly groaned. The years as a vicar's wife had

trained her mother to exude a countenance of serene peace no matter what dilemma came her way—except for matchmaking opportunities. Even though Mama approved of Mr. Mathis as a suitable husband for Emily, she bristled when others spoke of their engagement as a forgone conclusion. Mama would pick a thread off Emily's coat or scratch a paint splatter off her cheek and say, *Don't settle for what the world wants. Always be sure the suitor is God's best for you.*

Lord Warren bowed. "I do hope I'm not intruding."

Mama swept into the room. "I daresay, you must be the gentleman Emily encountered by the stream. My son Samuel relayed the entire story. How dreadful for you to have been attacked by a bandit." She put a gloved hand to her chest. "I assure you such things are unheard of in Sylvanwood."

Emily cleared her throat. "Mama, may I introduce Lord Jacob Warren. Lord Jacob, please meet my mother, Mrs. Rebecca Thompson."

He dipped his head in a polite bow and hit her with one of his dashing smiles. "A pleasure to meet you."

Mama was not immune. "The pleasure is all mine." She dipped into a low curtsy.

"I was just informing Miss Thompson how I'd like to invite you and your family to a dinner party as a token of my sincerest gratitude toward your daughter for saving my life."

Mama clasped her hands to her breast. "How lovely. Did you hear that, Emily?"

"Indeed." Emily forced a smile. "But we might be otherwise engaged."

Mama placed a hand on Emily's arm. "We would certainly clear our calendar for such an honor."

"Wonderful. I was thinking three weeks hence." Lord Warren turned his attention to Emily, raising his eyebrows, adding smugness to his I've-got-you grin. "That gives me time to make the arrangements and finish preparing the house."

"And how do things fare at Brownstone Hall?" Mama asked.

An excellent question. Surely, Lord Warren couldn't host a dinner party with the house in its current condition. Emily hoped he wouldn't discern any challenge in her voice. "The inside must have been in good condition if you're able to hold a party."

He rubbed a finger along his bottom lip. "Well, there is that, but I believe I can get everything in working order, not perfect, mind you, but working. We shall only dine, so that narrows the scope a bit."

Had his bottom lip been that full when she'd pulled him from the creek? It held a pleasingly plump quality with the tiniest crease in the center. Her fingers itched to flip open her sketchpad.

The corners of his eyes crinkled as if they shared a secret. Had he caught her staring at his mouth? Emily's ears burned.

Why is he looking at me like that?

A blur outside the window caught her attention—Christian chasing the chickens back toward their coop.

"Emily?" Mama asked. "Have you rung for tea?"

"There hasn't been time. Mrs. Hayes was still searching for you." Emily scooted around their guest to the bellpull and tugged on the rope. "His lordship arrived mere minutes before you entered."

"I do hope you'll stay." Mama issued him one of her I-don't-take-no-for-an-answer looks. "Mrs. Hayes has a fresh batch of scones about to come out of the oven."

"We shouldn't detain his lordship." Emily folded her skirt and resumed her seat. "He's probably busy with meetings and such."

Lord Warren's gaze held hers a moment longer than necessary before he addressed her mother. "I make a point never to turn down a freshly baked scone."

Mama gestured for Lord Warren to be seated. "Our parsonage, I'm certain, is humble compared to your lodgings, but it is quite cozy for our needs." She lowered onto the sofa.

Lord Warren tested the seat cushion with his hand before reclining in the low-backed chair nearest Emily. The man must be particular about the cushiness underneath his backside.

His gaze locked on hers, and one side of his mouth curved. Merriment danced in his eyes as though he laughed at himself, but for the life of her, she couldn't discern why. Very odd.

"So tell me." Mama folded her hands in her lap and leaned forward as she did whenever she visited with parishioners. "How is Lady Athol handling the renovations to Brownstone Hall?"

His fingers tucked around the V of his jacket, and his elbows rested on the chair's arms. "Initially, all the commotion intimidated her, but she's getting along quite well now."

"Oh, I'm so pleased. The manor home was once such a grand estate. It was terrible to watch it fall into a state of disrepair. You do your family and our town a great honor in reviving the lovely home back to its former glory."

Mama's gaze honed in on him as if the rest of the room had vanished. "I'm delighted Lady Athol is allowing visitors. Emily and I have called upon her every week since we moved to Sylvanwood. Each time, we're turned away, but occasionally, she has spoken to me through the open window. God has put a great burden on my heart for that woman. Your visit is a blessing, indeed. And"—her gaze fell upon Emily—"to hold a party in Emily's honor. I cannot think of anything more splendid."

Mucking stables came to mind. As much as Emily would love to assuage her curiosity regarding the inside of Brownstone Manor and the secretive Lady Athol, she couldn't afford to be associated with a known libertine, especially now that she knew her birth mother's identity.

Lord Warren crossed one leg over the other, the epitome of casual elegance. His high-polished boots reflected the sun from the window. He hooked an arm over the backrest as though he reclined among male friends at White's club. Although Emily had never been to London or seen the club on St. James Street, from the gossip column descriptions Phoebe insisted on reading, Emily suspected that was exactly how men would lounge.

"Brilliant. It's settled, then." He eyed Emily in a way that made her stomach feel as though she'd swallowed a goldfish. "I shall send a formal invitation immediately. The hall will still be in a transitional state, but perhaps it will afford me—or rather, my aunt—an excuse for a party in a sennight so everyone can appreciate the changes. A before-and-after celebration."

"How lovely."

Emily didn't agree with her mother but maintained what she hoped was a demure smile.

The front door thrust open and banged against the wall. Christian dashed down the hallway, his hair flopping.

"Stop right there, young man!"

Christian returned to the doorway and peeked inside.

Mama's tone shifted to that of a commander in his majesty's navy. "There shall be no running, and you left the door wide open. After you're done closing it, please remember your manners and greet our guest."

Emily glanced at Lord Warren, certain she'd witness amusement in his expression. Even when he was being naughty, Christian was a delightful boy. But Lord Warren's confident smile faded, and the blood seemed to drain from his face, leaving him as pale as the white lilies that bloomed in the spring garden. He stood and faced the doorway. His hand grasped the chair's backrest, leaving an indentation when he let go.

Christian stepped out of the open doorway. A moment later, the front door closed, and then he trudged into the salon. His little form straightened, and he shoved a lock of blond hair out of his eyes.

Emily and her mother rose. Emily said, "Lord Jacob Warren, may I present my younger brother, Christian Thompson."

"Pleased to meet you." Christian's arm folded across his middle, and he bowed low.

Lord Warren returned the bow with equal emphasis. "The pleasure is all mine, Master Christian."

Christian giggled, his blue eyes dancing and his shoulders shaking. "Call me Christian if you like. Everybody does." He clasped his hands behind his back and shuffled his foot as if dragging something back and forth with his toe. "What I mean by everybody is mainly Mama, Papa, Samuel, and Emily."

"It would please me very much." Lord Warren stared at Christian as if he'd never seen a child before. "How many years are you, Christian?"

"I'm five." His face beamed. "I can read some and count to one hundred, and Samuel's going to show me how to use a bow."

"Not your sister? She's a good shot." Lord Warren sank onto his haunches to be eye level with Christian.

She'd never seen a man take such an interest in a child. Mr. Mathis acknowledged her brother, though it was clear he had no true interest in him. He usually sent him on his way after a few cursory words.

Christian's face wrinkled. "Em teach me? Nah, she's a girl."

"I noticed that."

"I don't like girls. Do you?"

Lord Warren harrumphed. "I daresay, I appreciate the fairer gender."

Christian pursed his lips and shifted them to one side before he shrugged. "I guess you're right. Some are fine." He glanced at Mama and Emily as if accepting them into his inner circle. "But girls are icky." He pushed the hair out of his eyes again. "Say, are you the fellow who was held at gunpoint the other day?"

Mama crossed her arms. "How did you hear about that, young man?"

Christian's eyes widened. "I wasn't eavesdropping."

"Lying is a sin." Mama's tone held an edge.

"I'm not lying. I promise." Christian drew an *X* over his heart with his index finger. "Samuel spoke so loudly my ears couldn't help but hear."

A broad grin broke over Lord Warren's face.

Mama's face remained stern. "You are not to go repeating the story. Do you understand me? That's how gossip spreads."

"Yes, Mama." Christian turned his attention back to Lord Warren. "Were you scared?"

"I have to admit, I was a bit frightened. My future looked bleak at that moment. Fortunately, your sister came along, or I wouldn't be standing here today."

"It's good for the highwaymen that I wasn't there. I would have given them a thrashing." Christian side-stepped with his hip thrust forward and mimed punching an invisible foe.

Lord Warren chuckled. "That rogue was fortunate, indeed."

Mrs. Hayes carried in the tea service and a plate of scones, and Christian, still demonstrating his fighting prowess, backed into her legs. The teapot teetered.

"Christian!" Emily reached for him, but Lord Warren caught the pot with his gloved hands, righting it.

"Thank you." Mama put a hand over her heart. "You averted disaster. Praise God."

Christian stilled, his chin drooping into his chest and his gaze on Mama, knowing he was in trouble.

But Mama just gestured toward the open door. "Run along and see to your chores."

"Yes, Mama." He turned toward the door but paused and peered over his shoulder. "I hope to see you again."

Lord Warren bowed his head. "I shall make certain of it."

A small smile quirked the corners of Christian's lips, and he dashed down the hall.

Lord Warren stared at the empty doorway long after Christian departed.

After Mrs. Hayes placed the tea service on the table, Emily poured three cups. "Would you care for one or two lumps of sugar in your tea?"

Lord Warren slid back into his chair, but his gaze grew distant.

She awaited his response.

He blinked. "I beg your pardon?"

"Would you like one lump or two?"

"One, please."

The man's unabashed self-confidence appeared to have dried like the morning mist. He seemed bewildered, as if lost in a vivid dream. Most curious.

He accepted the cup and saucer she passed to him.

Emily handed Mama her tea.

"I haven't been inside Brownstone Hall in an age," Mama said. "I'm certain there must be much work to do."

"Quite." He slid his cup onto the table. "Indeed, there is so much work that I'm afraid I must be going."

"But you haven't finished your tea." Emily wanted him to leave, or so she told herself. But her heart sank at the prospect.

"I beg your forgiveness, but I must join you at a later date." He rose and bowed. "Lovely meeting you, Mrs. Thompson." He inclined his head to Emily. "Splendid to see you again, Miss Thompson."

He stopped in the doorway, resting a hand on the frame. "Mrs. Thompson, I'm looking to employ more workers and servants for Brownstone Hall. I would ask that you send anyone seeking employment my way. I would be much obliged."

"Most certainly. I can already think of several. I shall notify them immediately."

He patted the frame and nodded before seeing himself out.

The door had barely shut before Mama stood and rang for Mrs. Hayes. The housekeeper poked her head around the doorway. "We've been invited to attend a dinner party at Brownstone Hall. Have a footman fetch the proper trunks from the attic. We'll want to wear our best attire. They must be aired out and altered immediately."

Emily forced her heartbeat to remain steady and picked up her sketchpad but didn't open it. She tried to resist but couldn't help stealing a glance out the window.

Lord Warren stood in the drive, staring off into the sky and idly slapping his leather gloves against his leg while the groomsman pulled his curricle around. He handed over the reins, and Lord Warren climbed into the driver's seat. He glanced back at the house. Her gaze locked with his through the window and held for a long moment before he tipped his hat with his finger.

Her pulse quickened.

He snapped the reins, and his carriage retreated down the lane.

Truly, what is that man about?

CHAPTER 6

"*A* party? Here?" His aunt stared at him wide-eyed. Although she was seated, she pinched the table's edge as if to keep herself from falling.

One side of the sheet covering the enormous banquet table had been pulled back to allow room for him and Aunt Louisa to eat dinner. Brownstone Hall's kitchens were deep amid renovations. Fortunately, a woman from town had been hired to make their meals in her home and have them delivered.

Jacob chewed a savory piece of meat. He'd hoped to dine alone to allow time to recover from the shock of meeting his son, but Aunt Louisa had held supper for him.

Jacob speared a slice of tenderloin and dredged it through a flavorful gravy. He'd given up on any semblance of peace. The constant hammering, sawing, and shouting of workers were bad enough, but the clamoring of questions in his mind regarding Christian made tranquility impossible. Since he'd already relayed his harrowing escape from death, he'd decided to break the rest of the news to his aunt.

Maybe that should've waited until morning.

He pasted on his most charming smile. "I told them we'd

host a party in Miss Thompson's honor, since she saved my life." Jacob rolled a detestable Brussels spout away from the rest of his food with his fork.

Aunt Louisa paled and drew back in her seat.

"It will be good for the town to see the progress on Brownstone Hall and for you to make an appearance again in society after all these years. Consider it your second coming out."

She blanched until she tinged a bit blue.

Wrong thing to say, apparently. "There is nothing to worry about. I will take care of all the details. All you need to do that evening is to sit and eat dinner. I'll draw the conversation my way."

Her mouth opened and closed, clearly wanting to speak but unable to make her voice work.

Under normal circumstances, he'd throw out some lighthearted quip, but his heart felt too heavy. Part of him wanted to open the windows and shout for joy. He was a father who'd found his son—a healthy, happy young man. The other part was burdened with indecision. Now what? He'd planned to bring his son back to London, but now he hesitated to reveal himself. If he did, how would he answer his son's questions about his mother or where Jacob had been all this time? And the Thompson family seemed like lovely people. Could he pull Christian away from the only family he's ever known? He also couldn't bear not being part of his son's life. He must seek to know the Thompsons better for Christian's sake, then he could decide the best course of action.

With all that to consider, Jacob found himself fussing over something as trivial as a party. A celebration had been an impulsive suggestion to explain his presence in the Thompsons' drawing room other than being there to claim his son.

Aunt Louisa's gaze flicked to his and then away. Obviously, she had more to discuss. When she still stayed silent, he raised a brow.

The spark in her eyes dulled as though she was withdrawing to some place deep inside herself.

Jacob felt like a cad. A party was an immense task for someone who hadn't had company in over thirty years.

"Aunt Louisa, I must apologize. Today was a trying day, and I fear I'm terrible company. Please forgive me. Is there something more about the party you'd like to discuss?"

"I don't mean to be a veritable goose. The Thompsons are dears. Miss Thompson and her mother bring jams and fresh bread to Brownstone Hall weekly." She frowned. "I don't come to the door, but one day, Miss Thompson caught me spying from the window, and she waved." A brief smile flickered on her lips. "I waved back, and now we communicate in a way. She waves. I wave. When the weather is pleasant, Mrs. Thompson and I will speak through the open window."

The full impact of the lonely life his aunt had led hit him like a musket ball to the chest. It was time for her to make friends again.

"I know we've only been reacquainted for a little over a fortnight," she said, "but since you returned from town, you've seemed rather irritable. Is everything all right?"

He leaned back in his chair. "Am I that obvious?"

Her gaze dropped back to her plate, and she raised her shoulders in the slightest shrug.

Jacob chuckled. "You know, I can't remember the last time someone asked me how I fared." He patted his fingertips on the table. "In London, most people are only concerned for themselves. It's rare for anyone to think of someone else, unless it's to wonder what the other person thinks of them."

Aunt Louisa smiled. "I gather things have changed little since I last visited London."

"And when was that?"

"For my coming out." A tiny grin erupted as if a fond memory wavered her lips. "Seventeen eighty-one. I was still a green girl back then, awestruck by the excitement and glamour of the ton and parties." The tiny lines around her eyes and mouth softened, giving her a youthful appearance.

"You must have been a prime article, taking beaus by storm." He sobered his expression. "You still hold a classic beauty."

Two red splotches on his aunt's cheeks warmed her pale coloring.

"You are too kind." She shook her head. "I recall how mercenary the ladies of the ton could behave. I probably acted in a similar manner. I believed it was my one chance to change the direction of my life." The creases around her mouth returned. "Ultimately, my father had the final say in my future."

"He chose my uncle for your husband?"

"I'd hoped to finish the season, but your uncle was in a hurry to marry. Bans were posted, and I was whisked away to Sylvanwood within a month." Her countenance fell as if a heavy weight rested on her shoulders. "I haven't left since."

"Not even to see relatives?"

"Your mother brought you here to visit once."

He nodded. "I remember it vaguely. I liked to yell and hear my echo through the hall."

A broad smile swept across her features. "You hooted and hollered for hours." She swallowed and fiddled with her napkin. "Athol preferred me to be here in case he decided to return home unexpectedly. He'd fly into a rage even if I had merely gone to the market. Servants ventured into town, not the mistress of the house. I was to stay here and do his bidding."

Jacob's jaw tensed. His uncle made Jacob's father seem like an angel. His temper was fierce and scathing, but as far as Jacob knew, he'd never laid a finger on Mother.

His aunt tucked a gray lock under her cap. He would like to have seen her in her prime before his uncle altered her into a wounded animal. Uncle Cyrus was a coward. How could a man abuse a woman?

A string of beautiful faces floated through his memory, women with whom Jacob had an encounter. They had been starved for attention. He gave it freely, collecting their affection as a man would collect snuff boxes.

The tenderloin turned to sawdust in his mouth.

A second musket ball of guilt tore through his chest, leaving a hole where his heart used to beat. He'd been so focused on proving to Sarah that he could replace her as easily as she had him that he'd forgotten that each woman was someone's daughter, someone's sister, or someone's niece.

Aunt Louisa laughed nervously. "And here I am, blithering on about me when I meant to ask about you."

Before he could respond, Maslow appeared at her elbow and removed their plates.

She straightened the dessert silverware in front of her. "Did your conversation with the Thompsons go well?"

Jacob inhaled. He could steer the conversation in two different directions—keep it light and circumspect, or be truthful and sobering. He'd grown tired of the former. Significant risk and judgement could come with the latter, but his aunt had been open with him. If anyone could be forgiving, it might be her.

"I met their youngest son."

"Oh? I haven't seen him yet, but Mrs. Thompson mentioned she had a young son. She'd moved here from up north." She tapped her chin. "How many years ago was that?"

"Five," Jacob said. "It was five years ago."

"What is his name?"

"Christian."

"Yes, that's right." Aunt Louisa nodded. "Christ follower."

Christian. He liked his son's name, but Jacob's actions may have turned God away. He hadn't been in a church since his brother's marriage and even longer before then. Knowing his sinful nature, Jacob was surprised lightning hadn't struck when he entered the building. Maybe there was hope for his son. Perhaps Christian could be redeemed, but Jacob's sins were far too great.

"I'm his father."

Aunt Louisa's lips parted.

Blast. Why had he blurted it out? Couldn't he have found a tactful way to soften the information for his aunt? He'd already hit her with the blow of a party and now followed by planting a facer that he had a child out of wedlock.

To her credit, she subdued her shock quickly. "I see. I wondered if there might be another reason you came to see an old aunt you'd only met once. Checking on your son makes much more sense."

"You probably think the worst of me, and you'd be correct." Jacob massaged the tight muscles in the back of his neck.

"The fact that you're here to find him tells me you feel remorse."

"I wanted to marry her—Christian's birth mother."

"Why don't you tell me the story?"

Surprisingly, her eyes held no condemnation. In their faded blue depths, he only saw concern and sympathy.

"I was home on holiday from university." He gathered his strength for the spectrum of emotions he knew was coming. "I encountered Sarah at a country dance. Her family didn't live far from mine, but I hadn't seen her since she was a child. While I was at Cambridge, she'd blossomed into a woman. Her marriage had been pre-arranged by her father, who was of the same ilk as mine." He lifted his eyebrows at Aunt Louisa. "The same ilk as his brother."

Aunt Louisa nodded her understanding.

"She was rebelling against his overbearing behavior. Who could blame her for wanting to choose her own life? Certainly not me. When she flirted with me and encouraged my advances, I was smitten. Not only was she beautiful, but she knew her own mind."

His chest tingled at the memory of young love—the palpitations of excitement, the carefree spirit of innocence, the belief that he'd always feel what he felt at that time, as if nothing could bruise such pure emotions.

How naïve he'd been.

"She arranged for clandestine visits," he explained. "I fancied myself in love. I believed with my whole heart that the feelings were mutual. She never gave me a reason to think otherwise."

Aunt Louisa remained silent as if she knew how painful this was to reveal. Her gaze never left him, though she occasionally nodded to show she listened.

"One night, Sarah summoned me to our secret spot." Jacob swallowed against the wave of pain constricting his chest. "She was crying and admitted she was with child. I should have been ashamed by our actions, but at the idea that we'd created a life together—a part of her and a part of me—I was elated. I proposed to her immediately, excited for a life together, a child, and our prospects, but when I fell to one knee, she sobbed even harder. I thought she was concerned about any rumors and explained an early firstborn child was common. No one needed to know. I never thought... All our time together, as much as we cared for each other, it never occurred to me that she would marry the man her father had chosen. But that man was the Duke of Charlton. I'm merely a third son."

Aunt Louisa's gaze dropped to his hands, and he followed her gaze to find he'd curled them into fists. He slid them under the table, not wanting her to be alarmed by his anger.

"She wrote me a letter stating her plans to disappear until their child was born—and then marry the duke. In the end, she wanted to be a duchess more than she wanted to be a mother. More than she wanted me."

Even after all those years, he couldn't erase the bitterness in his voice.

"I'm sorry." The compassion in Aunt Louisa's eyes brought a lump to his throat.

"Eventually, I realized my love had been nothing more than mere infatuation, but I never forgot she'd borne a child, my child."

"Of course, you didn't. How could a caring father forget his own son?"

Jacob struggled to find his voice to continue. "Sarah had mentioned, after refusing my proposal plans, that she would visit a distant cousin, but she never said who kept our child or where I could find him. I was in shock over her denial, not thinking she'd never let me see the baby. I hired a private investigator to research her family. I even called upon Sarah after she married. She received me into her personal drawing room and voiced her desire to continue our past relationship, but I pushed her away. She had a husband." His voice dripped with disdain. "We stood in his house."

Jacob shook his head. "I'll never forget the way her nostrils flared and the ugly set of her jaw when she discovered I was there to gather information regarding our child." A harsh laugh erupted from his throat. "The only instruction I received was from her butler as he tossed me out on my ear. 'Don't come back.'"

"And you're certain that Christian is your son?"

He nodded. "Christian has my coloring." He could also claim the child's eyes, smile, and stature. "Seeing him today was like looking at myself when I was a boy."

While his heart leapt with joy, trepidation raised the hairs on the back of his neck.

I have a son.

He exhaled a deep breath and rubbed his hands down his face.

"What do you plan to do now that you've met him?" Aunt Louisa asked in a soft tone, the same question that had filled Jacob's mind since he'd laid eyes on Christian.

"I came here intending to bring him back with me and set things right, but now I'm not so sure." He met his aunt's gaze, hoping she'd have the answers. "Am I fit to be a father? My reputation is black—dark gray at best."

One of his talents, other than the art of disguise that the Home Office often asked of him, was to charm the wives, sisters, or daughters of various persons of interest to extract information. He flattered, flirted, and enticed them through seduction—but never bedded them. He'd learned his lesson. One son to locate was enough.

How could he be a father while leading a libertine's life surrounded by debauchery? He was the furthest thing from a role model for a young boy.

Aunt Louisa reached out and squeezed his hand. "It doesn't matter how you got that reputation. What matters is that you don't have to keep it."

He couldn't move beyond his doubts. "I'm also my father's son, and you know how he is, filled with rage and dipping deep in his cups. What if I turn out the same way?"

"You've chosen to keep your anger at bay." She harrumphed. "If holding you captive in a chair and flinging tea in your face didn't fly you into the boughs, then you've a good grasp on your emotions."

Aunt Louisa was right. He didn't have to continue this destructive path. He could change direction, maybe even stay here and not return to London. He could start a new life.

His eldest brother had changed. Perhaps he could too. Robert had chosen a wife and settled down. He'd been fortunate in discovering Nora. A good-natured, respectable woman was rare among London's *ton,* especially the fast set in which circles Jacob ran. He could never abide living a life with the women of his acquaintance—a fickle lot, the entire bunch, seeking to marry the fortune, not the man, so they could be lavished in jewels and furs.

The meager holdings of a third-born son weren't enough to turn the heads of the elite.

His charm worked to his advantage. Married women, widows with their own means, and genteel ladies wishing to improve their rank sought him out with a fervor that—frankly—scared him. His reputation as a rake horrified chaperones but seemed to increase the young ladies' ardor. Not one of the numerous women who sought his affections took the time to know him. None of them knew he awoke each morning and watched the sunrise alone, that he enjoyed fixing things, or that he hated the taste of Brussels sprouts. From what he'd experienced from his interactions with Sarah and other women, he'd decided women were a capricious gender who sought to benefit themselves. So he played their games but only to his advantage.

But now he'd met his son. Christian was real, not merely a thought that occupied the back of his mind every minute of every day.

He put his napkin on the table and leaned back in his chair. "I don't know how a bachelor's life could compare with the good upbringing Christian is receiving at the Thompsons' household."

Aunt Louisa remained silent, nodding for him to continue.

"But now that I've seen him, how can I stand by and watch the boy grow from a distance?" He stood and paced the length of the table. "Then there's the issue of his illegitimacy. If I stay with the Thompsons, people might speculate about me and my past. Some will assume Christian was baseborn even though the Thompsons did a bang-up job, making Christian appear to society that he's their legitimate son." He turned and faced Aunt Louisa. "But if I bring Christian into my home without a wife, there will be no question about the child's bi-blow status."

"These are all good questions to bring before God," Aunt Louisa said.

Jacob snorted. "God doesn't want to hear from the likes of me."

She frowned. "When Jesus was alive, with whom did He spend most of His time?"

How did they get on this subject? "I guess His disciples."

"Who else?"

Jacob should've paid more attention during church. "There was that Samaritan woman."

His aunt nodded, encouraging him to go on.

"And that tax collector chap, Zack something..."

"Zacchaeus."

"Yes, the tax collector that everyone despised." Jacob snapped his fingers. "And then there were those people from whom he cast out demons. And the woman caught in adultery."

He was on a roll.

"They were all sinners." Aunt Louisa nodded as if she'd made some important point. "If there is one thing I've learned, it's that God cares for all His children, especially the broken-hearted. He came to redeem us through His blood and offer forgiveness for our sins. Jesus came to give people like you and me a new life." She leaned in closer, the intensity in her faded blue eyes reaching into the darkness of his soul. "You are exactly who He wants to hear from."

CHAPTER 7

*T*he following morning, Emily sat on the wooden bridge overlooking the rushing stream, swinging her crossed legs and sketching the scenery. Upstream, Christian sailed the toy boat Samuel had made for him. The small craft bobbed and dipped as it rode the rapids.

Christian shouted commands at the pretend crew to hoist the beams and lower the stern. If he accidentally released the string, she sat stationed with a branch ready to prevent the boat from sailing into the reeds and becoming entangled.

While Christian amused himself, Emily shaded in her rendering of Christian playing at the riverbank and mulled over the odd encounter with Jacob—er, Lord Warren.

"Good day, Miss Thompson, Master Christian." Lord Warren's voice rang out as if she'd conjured him from her thoughts.

She snapped her head up to find him approaching up the narrow path atop a black stallion. He appeared one with the horse, matching the fluid movements of its sinewy torso and flank. He reined the horse to a neat stop, his muscular legs straining against the buckskin fabric of his breeches.

Christian waved in greeting, his enthusiasm shaking his entire body. "Good day, Lord Warren."

Swinging a leg over, the gentleman slid off the horse's back. He led his mount to a grassy section next to the bridge and tied the reins to the railing before tipping his hat at Emily.

She bobbed her head, hoping he couldn't sense her nervousness. Would being seen with a rogue like Lord Jacob Warren hurt her reputation, even though they were out in the open and Christian was with her? She made sure her skirts covered her ankles.

But Lord Warren barely gave her a nod before he turned to Christian. "And what have you got there?"

"It's my sailboat." He held up the string, and the boat jerked through the water.

"What have you christened it?"

Christian's head cocked to the side. "What's Chriseneenid?"

One side of Lord Warren's mouth pulled into a playful smile. "Christened. I was asking what you've named your boat."

"Oh, I haven't a name for it yet."

"A boat must be christened before it sets sail. Reel it back in."

Christian did as instructed, and Lord Warren squatted next to him to inspect the boat. "What would be a good name?"

The sight of the man and the boy... Emily's hand moved across the pad, sketching Lord Warren's form.

Christian shrugged.

"Well, my brother named his boat *Nora's Pin Money*, but that wouldn't work for you. Nora is his wife. A lot of men name their boats after their wives, mothers, or sisters. You could name it *The Emily*."

Christian dug the toe of his boot into the dirt. "Well, *The Emily* sounds nice and all, but it's rather girlie."

Lord Warren glanced in Emily's direction with an I-tried sort of shrug.

"What else?" Christian asked.

"If you like puns, you could call it *Seize the Day*, but spell seize, *s-e-a-s*."

"How else would you spell *seas*?" Christian wrinkled his nose.

"With an *i* and a *z*." Lord Warren waved his hand. "Never mind. How about something that sounds tougher, like Pirate Catcher or Shark Hunter?"

"Pirate Catcher." Christian galloped a couple of steps out and a couple steps back. "I like that one." He extended his arm as if holding a sword. "Fire in the hole!" He shouted. "Ye better stand down and stop yer pillaging, or we'll fill you full of lead."

Lord Warren met her gaze with a conspiring wink, and Emily laughed.

At least he's fond of children.

He joined in playing pirates with Christian, and she sketched the outline of his hair as the sun illuminated it.

Funny. In the sun, Christian's and Lord Warren's hair was the same hue. She leaned against the bridge's railing post and swung her legs as she captured the innocent scene.

The man making cannon noises with her younger brother seemed so contrary to the one depicted in the gossip columns that she found it hard to believe they were one and the same. Lord Warren's rakish reputation had spread like household gossip upon his arrival. Yet, due to his title, the townsfolk seemed willing to overlook such accusations.

If word got out about her birth, would the town make allowances because they knew who she truly was?

Christian handed Lord Warren the string to sail the boat. It was his turn to be at the helm. Lord Warren propped a booted foot on a log and molded his hands as if peering through a telescope in a fair imitation of a Royal Navy captain.

Emily added some finishing touches to her sketch. She flipped the pages back to the drawing she rendered from memory, adding details she hadn't remembered, such as the tiny scar near his hairline and how one eyebrow held more of a mocking tilt than the other.

When Christian tired of playing with his boat, he tied the string to a low branch and dragged Lord Warren to his horse for an introduction. The man hefted Christian onto the saddle and had him hold the reins while he paraded his horse in a circle.

"Look, Em. I'm riding a horse." Christian's face could barely contain his excitement.

"And doing a bang-up job of it." Lord Warren winked at Christian. "I might add."

Emily squared off Lord Warren's chin a tad more and added a few tendrils of hair that curled under his collar.

He wiped the road dust off his hands and aided Christian's dismount, and Christian ran back to battle the imaginary pirates as Lord Warren sauntered in her direction. Emily flipped her sketchbook closed and laid it on the wood.

He settled beside her on the bridge but didn't look in her direction. "He has quite an imagination."

"Indeed."

Christian tossed a rock like a cannonball into the water, careful not to hit his wooden ship.

"My lord, I must thank you—"

"Please, call me Warren or Jacob," he said in a matter-of-fact tone. He still didn't glance in her direction. "We are neighbors and all."

"I couldn't be so forward—"

He cut her off with an intimate sideways glance. "You pushed water out of my lungs to save my life. First names should be acceptable, at least when we're alone."

"We're not alone," she said, her voice barely a squeak.

He challenged her with a raised brow. "I hardly think Christian shall mind you calling me Jacob."

"But there are rules."

"Indeed, but why stick with decorum when so many other options exist?"

She fought back a smile but failed. "I wanted to thank you for hosting a party in my honor. I appreciate the gesture, but truly, it is unnecessary. I would have done the same for any man needing rescuing."

His hand thumped against his chest as if he clutched his heart. "And I thought my dashing good looks brought a damsel to my rescue."

Emily felt tempted to push him into the water. "Truly. There is no need."

"Ah, but I have an ulterior motive. You see, hosting is putting your guests first. Entertaining is showing off. I intend to do the latter under the guise of the former."

At his sly expression, Emily burst into laughter, her shoulders shaking with mirth.

~

*J*acob savored the musical quality of her laugh. Emily Thompson did not hold a title, wealth, or a lush, voluptuous body, but she plagued his thoughts. Her unique beauty might not be of the fashionable blond-haired, blue-eyed sort, but she was striking, nonetheless. Her elegance seemed to radiate from within.

They sat quietly. He liked that she didn't ramble on as though silence were a form of torture.

A content smile settled on her soft features as she studied the toy ship, clinging to the string as the current churned against it. Even her ear was lovely—small, delicate, and pinned nicely against the side of her head.

Something stirred inside him.

Emily Thompson was an unknown. Since she'd speared his

assailant with her arrow, Cupid also seemed to have pierced Jacob's heart with one. She found her way into his thoughts daily, if not hourly. When she saved him, she somehow restarted his heart, made him feel again. Helped him view individuals as people instead of a means to an end. But his rusty heart groaned in disapproval, fearing it couldn't survive another betrayal like Sarah's.

Emily was nothing like Sarah. She was an open book. All her emotions registered on her face for all to see, and watching the display teetered him on a precipice. If his heart toppled over the edge, would he be left battered and bruised, or would he soar like an eagle?

Life was about taking risks, but since Sarah, he'd been careful not to risk his heart.

He knew better.

The corner of Emily's sketchpad caught his eye. He grasped it and flipped it open to the middle.

Emily gasped. "Wait."

She tried to snatch it, but he turned his back toward her. "I'm merely checking your skill to confirm the missive I sent to Lady Kauffman about your talent doesn't need to be rescinded."

"You sent Lady Kauffman a missive? About me?"

The shock in her voice proved she knew exactly who Kauffman was—the woman sat on the Royal Academy board. But more than that, Emily's surprise caused his lips to twitch with laughter. He stared at a cozy picture of her mother sitting in a rocking chair, sewing. It appeared so lifelike, he almost expected the image to blink.

Jacob flipped the page to find Samuel positioned in a tree stand as a deer emerged from the woods. She'd even captured the tautness of his trigger finger, poised and ready.

"These are quite good."

"Please, give it back." She leaned around him and grappled for the pad.

He stood and shrugged her off. "Sorry, I don't take orders."

She scrambled to her feet and came around the other side.

He turned the other direction. "In truth, I barely take suggestions."

"Lord Warren."

He glared at her over his shoulder and flipped to the next page.

"Jacob!"

"Much better." He smiled before his gaze fell on the image of his face staring back at him. His breath caught.

She'd drawn him precisely, from the sweep of hair across his brow to the slight cleft in his chin. It was remarkable. His lips were turned up at the corners in a self-confident smile. She'd even drawn the crease in his bottom lip. *Extraordinary.*

There was an intimacy in knowing every crevice of his face, and she had captured him perfectly.

He turned to her, but humility rendered him speechless.

Emily's cheeks blazed bright pink. "I-I do these sorts of studies whenever I'm commissioned. I—it's necessary to practice."

He flipped the page to find an image of his profile. Even his hair curled in the right direction. "I no longer doubt your capabilities."

He flipped again to find the exact rendering of their surroundings, with Christian sailing his boat and the creek swelling around it. Jacob was kneeling beside him. "You did this just now?"

She moistened her lips.

"You drew this entire scene that quickly." He pointed at his image. "You even drew the tassels on my boots."

"I have an eye for detail."

"Incredible." He flipped back to the beginning and paged through the sketchbook slowly, studying. There were drawings of Christian galloping on a stick horse, a man he assumed was the vicar practicing a sermon behind the podium, her other brother, Samuel, carrying Christian on his shoulders. "Amazing. I can tell they are teasing each other by the glint of mischief you captured in their eyes."

Emily sighed. "They are forever jesting with one another."

"It's what brothers do."

"You are fond of your brother?" She was watching him closely.

"*Brothers*." He snorted. "I have two. Alex is between Robert and me. As a second son, he's often overshadowed by our brother, the marquis, but he's managed to stay out of the gossip columns. Sadly, I learned that trick too late."

"You don't care for your reputation?"

"I'm not particularly fond of black. I prefer color, a shade of blue or perhaps violet."

Her lips curled into a smile, and his chest swelled with pleasure. She grasped his humor. Not all women did.

"I appreciate color."

Jacob read into her words. He lowered to sit on the bridge and aided her to rest beside him.

"What is your family like?" she asked.

He pictured his father's sneer, his mother's fabricated smile, Robert's controlling reach, and Alex's quiet removal. And then, there was him—a constant source of disappointment.

"It's much like any other family of the *ton*." He flipped to a picture of Emily's family dining together and laughing. "It's not like yours, but I wish it could be."

"Is your family not close?"

"We are, in a way. Robert and I are the most similar, so I frustrate him immensely. He believes he can tell me what I should and shouldn't do, but he also takes the brunt of my father's wrath. For that, I hold him in high regard and try to appease him, but I usually fail miserably."

"What about your other brother?"

"Alex is withdrawn. We get along well, but he's a serious fellow and doesn't appreciate my witty banter."

"Does your witty banter typically get you into trouble?"

"Perhaps...well, yes."

"It sounds as though your middle brother avoids conflict."

"Quite right." Alex often retreated from a room when tempers ran hot.

"And your parents?"

"Mother is full of life, but she, too, doesn't like strife. She's forever covering up for us so as not to stir my father's anger." He smiled. "One time, when I was about Christian's age, I caught a frog and brought it into the house. Mother saw my new pet and pointed toward the door. Unfortunately, at that moment, my father entered the room behind us. She snatched the frog from my dirty hands and stuffed it down the front of her gown. When my father addressed me, I was in a state of shock and couldn't respond. He rounded on my mother, demanding she explain my insolence. She opened her mouth to speak, but that happy little frog nestled in such a warm, cozy spot chose that moment to chirp its glee. Mother jerked in surprise, and it appeared as though she had hiccupped. I couldn't help but snicker, which made Father even more livid. He forbade Mother from consuming spirits during the day before giving me a good thrashing and sending me to bed without supper." Jacob flipped the page back to where he'd begun and passed the sketchpad to Emily. "Mother served me cold porridge for an entire week."

"Your poor mother." Emily bit her lower lip to contain her smile, but her brows tilted in a display of sympathy.

"Catch it! Catch it quick!" Christian shouted and ran after the loose ship careening toward them.

Emily grabbed the emergency retrieval branch next to her and redirected the boat toward them. Jacob gripped the rail and reached for the ship, but it veered closer to Emily. She leaned down and snagged the toy before it sailed past into the reeds. Her balance slipped, and she tipped toward the swirling water.

Jacob wrapped his arm around her waist and jerked her against himself. She crashed into his side and jabbed him in the arm with the dripping toy boat.

Emily gasped. Her lips parted scarcely an inch from his. Her chest rose and fell in rhythm with the beating of his heart. He peered into the depths of her amber eyes.

The toy boat tilted, and a trickle of water seeped through the material of his breeches, cooling the heat that flared under his skin.

She lowered her gaze and squirmed against his hold.

He released her. "If you'd planned to bathe, you should have brought a towel."

She shook her head. "It was certainly not my intention. Thank you."

"It seems I've saved *you* this time." He was sure to put much mirth into his tone. "We're even."

Christian ran across the bridge. His boots clopped against the wooden planks. "Hurrah! You saved the *Pirate Chaser.*"

"It has survived for another day of pirate hunting." Jacob plucked the ship from his lap and handed it to Christian.

The boy darted off to sail again.

He turned to face Emily, and her delicate eyebrows arched.

Why in heaven would she look at him as though he'd gone mad? Didn't he just rescue her? "Did I miss something?"

She lowered her chin, which emphasized her furrowed brow. "You believe saving me from a swim is the same as shooting your attacker, dragging you half dead out of a creek, and pounding on your chest until life returned to your blue face?"

He held his hands up. "I'm not here to split hairs."

She arched an eyebrow.

"I will submit to the lady's good judgement."

"Then I shall add wise to your list of attributes."

The pert smile she issued him unfurled a desire for closeness he'd long since tucked away. The forgotten sensation disentangled itself from the dirt and decay and lifted its head like a new leaf to the sun.

Was five years long enough for the fallow ground of his heart to heal? Or would the new sprout be killed by an unexpected frost?

~

*J*acob slid into a wooden bench seat across from Lieutenant Scar at a table in the New Inn of Little Barrington. Smoke from the fire blended with the smell of fresh-cut wood stacked to the right of the hearth. Few patrons frequented the pub at such an early hour—only the innkeeper, who dried glasses, and a man deep in his cups on the other end of the bar.

"Lieutenant?" Jacob acknowledged his handler. "I hear congratulations are in order."

Scar snorted. "Don't make much of it just because I sit behind a desk more than venture into the field."

"Lieutenant Spark's shoes are a hard pair to fill." Jacob accepted the mug of ale from the barmaid. "But there's not a better man for the job."

"I appreciate the sentiments. How is the search for your son?" Scar blew the foam from his mug and sipped.

"I've located him and even spent time with him." He smiled, thinking of Christian sailing his boat. "He looks like me and has many of my tendencies, but..." Jacob puffed his cheeks and exhaled. "You're a papa, and you know me as well as my family. Do you think I'd make a good father?"

"I'm new to parenting, so I may not be the best source." Scar peered at the flames dancing in the hearth. "But we've worked a lot of assignments together, and I've witnessed you risk your life for your country. You stared down the barrel of a crazed traitor's gun bent on vengeance and didn't flinch. You've talked sense into irate men and de-escalated tense situations so that good men on both sides could live another day. The crown asked you to flatter, court, and seduce noblewomen to gather crucial information, but you do everything in your power to keep the women's innocence and hearts intact. Not all agents are as kind. You have honor, good character, and you put others above yourself. Those are commendable traits for a father to pass down to a child." Scar's gaze honed on Jacob. "Not to mention, you've turned over heaven and earth to locate the boy. You've the makings of a splendid father."

Unused to compliments, especially from his hardened handler, heat rose into Jacob's cheeks. He ran a hand over the lower half of his face to hide it. "My plan is to get to know the Thompson family better—get their approval to make Christian's transition easier."

The barmaid smiled at Jacob as she leaned over to wipe off a table. He looked away. His tastes now inclined toward artists with expressive eyes and pert little noses.

Scar waited for the barmaid to return to the kitchen and leaned forward. "Lord Benton's back on the move."

"With the wound in his shoulder, he'll have to leave the pillaging to his cronies."

His handler frowned. "You've had an encounter?"

"Lord Benton accosted me in my coach and meant to kill me. He's still bitter about my last assignment."

"Your intelligence gathered during that party set him in our sights."

Jacob shrugged. "He didn't enjoy discovering me in his wife's bedchamber."

"You think his attack was a revenge plot? Shouldn't he have received his satisfaction on the dueling field?"

"He won't be satisfied until I'm pushing up flowers."

"Let's not allow that to happen, but we must take this highway robbing ring down from the top. Threats to nobles and aristocrats, especially when their wives are with them, puts pressure on the crown." Scar leaned his forearms on the table and whispered, "There've been nighttime carriage raids on the post road near here. Lord and Lady Memphis were leaving Lady Crawford's private house party."

"You think Benton is behind this?"

"That's what I want you to find out"—a determined glint sparked in Scar's gaze—"by going undercover as Lord and Lady Dorsham's driver."

CHAPTER 8

*O*n the way to Brownstone Hall, Emily shifted to better view the passing scenery through the coach window and take her mind off the looming social engagement. The old rusty springs of their conveyance groaned, and she tugged on the bodice of her gown to keep her corset from pinching her side.

The night she'd dreaded had arrived too quickly. She'd be expected to mingle with Sylvanwood's elites, who'd give her the cut direct if they knew the truth of her birth. After hours of preparing, primping, and having her breathing constrained by a corset, she was stuffed into a gown that almost weighed as much as she, with superfluous layers of embroidered lace. Mama flashed her a disapproving glare and pursed her lips because Emily had refused the elaborate feathers she'd wanted to add to her coiffure.

"Stop fidgeting." Mama sighed. "You look lovely."

"I'm not used to this cut." She adjusted the fabric of her bodice.

"It's fine." Mama's eyes dropped to Emily's chest. "The square cut is in fashion."

Samuel glanced her way and shrugged. "Phoebe will probably wear a dress cut much lower—"

Papa shook his head, and Samuel quieted.

Phoebe probably would choose a lower-cut bodice, but that didn't make Emily feel better. A reputation defined a woman and determined her opportunities. If one were extraordinarily rich, then society might make an exception to their risqué dress or behavior. The Thompson family did not struggle for funds, but they were not swimming-in-lard wealthy.

Tonight would be Emily's first time sitting in the same room with Lady Dorsham since Phoebe had informed her mama that Emily was adopted. Had Phoebe convinced her mama to hold Emily's secret, or would the gossip be too juicy to Lady Dorsham to hold inside? Would the dinner guests outright shun the honoree, or would they merely speak about her behind her back? If it was the latter, she'd be the last to know. Rumors were never shared with the object of said gossip.

Mama picked a loose thread from Papa's jacket.

"Stop fussing, dear." But Papa grinned, obviously not minding her attention.

They'd sacrificed so much to improve their children's lot in life. To take in someone else's unwanted babies, Mama had uprooted from friends and family so that no one would know Emily and Christian were illegitimate. Papa had married her, knowing full well that Emily and Christian weren't hers from her first marriage.

Emily remembered the snide remarks of her old neighbors as a young child. The pain of being snubbed by the other children, and the wide berth people gave her family as they passed, as though being baseborn were contagious.

If Phoebe didn't keep her word, if the knowledge of Emily's birth leaked out, it wouldn't only be Emily who suffered the consequences. Papa could lose the parsonage for not being forthright with his congregation. Samuel could lose his apprenticeship, and Christian could learn he was adopted and suffer the consequences the same as Emily herself would.

She must keep the truth from getting out.

The air inside the carriage had warmed. Mama fanned herself. "I do hope it's a lovely evening. I found Lord Warren to be a delightful fellow."

In Mama's opinion, Lord Warren, with his title and connections, would make Emily an excellent match, but Emily could never set foot in London. It would be best for her to settle in the country—and for Mr. Mathis. Why couldn't her heart skip in Mr. Mathis's company the way it did around Jacob?

Funny how quickly she'd shifted from thinking of her childhood friend by his first name.

And how, just as quickly, Lord Warren had become *Jacob* in her thoughts.

The gates at Brownstone Hall were swung wide, so different from the way they usually appeared, with the intimidating wrought-iron spikes locked tightly. Mama and she often hitched the horses to the gate and trekked the long drive to leave a food basket.

Mama patted Samuel on the knee. "Look at how much his lordship has already improved the property."

Samuel pulled back the curtain with his index finger. "Indeed. It shall bring more enthusiasm to Sylvanwood. Lord Warren's arrival is a blessing to our town."

Truly? A blessing? Why, then, did she feel the need to pray for protection?

The tall grass and overgrown weeds had been replaced by a manicured lawn, the broken shutters removed. The ivy vines that had overrun the house had been trimmed back, and the dilapidated columns flanking the front steps repainted.

The Dorshams' town coach moved from the door toward the stable, which meant Phoebe was in attendance, and the Geyers' and Hamsteads' gigs were already parked. Even the magistrate, Mr. Fiske, and his wife would dine with them in her honor.

Would Lady Dorsham give her the cut direct? No, of course not. Emily waved the thought away. Lady Dorsham would never blatantly disrespect the vicar. She'd merely nod and say, *Good evening, Miss Thompson*, and walk past.

Their coachman drew the horses to a stop in front of the entrance. A footman in brown-toned livery, which complemented the stonework and hall's name, opened the carriage door. The scent of lilacs laced the evening air and filled Emily's lungs as she alighted. She shook out her hands to combat the nervous tingling in her limbs and focused on the front steps instead of the imposing home.

A fresh coat of varnish glossed the main entrance, and the elderly butler, Mr. Maslow, who bellowed the hymns at church, pushed open the doors as they ascended the front steps. Like the footman, he was dressed in brown livery. If Phoebe were beside her, she would comment on how Lord Petersham, the famous dandy from the gossip papers, had made brown all the rage in London.

Mama handed the butler their card, and Maslow belted out their names so loudly that she imagined St. Peter wincing at the pearly gates.

So much for a discreet entrance.

Emily slid in behind Samuel, but Mama looped her arm through Emily's and drew her forward in line with the rest of the family.

The white marble floors with black diamond accents gleamed. The ornate Corinthian columns were freshly whitewashed, the faint odor of oil solvent lingering. Inlaid, gold-leafed trim shone, competing with the sparkling triple-tiered chandeliers.

Guests clustered in groups in the large open parlor as footmen carried hors d'oeuvres on silver platters. Sylvanwood's most prestigious residents were in attendance at the dinner party—the Dorshams, the magistrate and his family, and Sir Hamilton, a local knighted for his service for the king—but their provincial ways probably seemed lacking compared to the elite members of the ton among which Jacob would normally mingle. Twenty or so townspeople engaged in conversation, but a couple glanced her way, one being Mr. Mathis, who nodded to the magistrate and headed in their direction.

Mama and Papa exchanged comments about the change to the manor, but Emily issued Samuel a sidelong glance to state, *stick together.* He nodded and Emily relaxed.

"Good evening, Miss Thompson." Mr. Mathis touched her elbow.

Had he been waiting for her to arrive?

His gaze flicked to her gown and then to her father. "I'm surprised by your choice of gown."

Emily restrained her hands from pulling up the tulle tucker hiding her bosom. "We were just commenting on the changes to Brownstone Hall."

"Indeed." Mr. Mathis pivoted to examine the room. "I was here as a child when the hall was in its splendor. My father was Lord Athol's estate manager until my uncle passed and my family inherited his lands." One side of his mouth lifted in a smirk. "Much has changed since then."

A boisterous laugh erupted across the foyer. Jacob's infectious warmth singled him out of the crowd.

Emily's heart hitched, spreading nervous tingles through her system. She and her family crossed the foyer and descended the few steps into the parlor.

While conversing with Phoebe and Lady Dorsham, Jacob glanced in her direction and flashed a confident smile. He wore an elegant evening jacket of dark-blue kerseymere with a brilliant white waistcoat and dark trousers, every bit the high-born society leader and son of a duke. He excused himself and strode in her direction, maneuvering around guests with a panther-like stride.

He bowed and introduced himself to Papa. "Pleased to finally meet you, Reverend. Mrs. Thompson, delighted to see you again." He nodded to Samuel. "Same to you, Mr. Thompson, Mr. Mathis." Jacob looked at Emily, and his grin broadened. "And our guest of honor." He scooped Emily's gloved hand and bowed over it, keeping hold a tad longer than customary and drawing heat to her cheeks. "Welcome, Miss Thompson. You look radiant this evening."

His gaze locked on hers, and Emily, unaccustomed to such attention, murmured her thanks and curtsied.

He turned his full attention to Mama, bowing over her hand. "Mrs. Thompson, may I say how charming you look in that color of green?"

Mama blushed and fluttered her fan.

His brows drew together. "I know the color has a specific name, but it's eluding me."

Her family shifted to regard Emily.

She shrank under the scrutiny but mumbled, "That shade of green is called celadon."

"Quite right, I was going to say sea-green, but celadon sounds better." Jacob's eyes glinted with sarcasm.

The man enjoyed teasing her.

Samuel beamed, his easygoing smile expanding his freckles. "Emily is a brilliant artist."

"Indeed," Mama said. "You must come again to visit, and she shall show you her work. It is exceedingly good. She has plans to send a portfolio to the Royal Academy."

Emily inwardly sighed. Those had been her plans until she learned her birth mother's identity.

"Really." Jacob's gaze settled upon her. "A marksman and an artist." Funny how he pretended this was new information. "What other impressive skills do you hold, Miss Thompson?"

Why did her stomach somersault whenever he peered at her like that? "I believe everything has been brought to light, my lord."

Samuel wouldn't let the comment stand. "But you forgot to mention how you seat a horse well and have a proclivity with children, especially our youngest brother."

Something flashed in Jacob's eyes, but it was too fleeting to register. He lifted a brow, and the timber of his voice vibrated the fine hairs on her skin. "A talented woman, indeed."

"Her true gift to her future husband will be in how well she manages a household." Mr. Mathis stepped closer to her side. His words seemed like a compliment, but his reproving tone hinted that it was a slight against her.

Papa gazed about the room. "Brownstone Hall looks splendid. It's astounding what you've done with the place in such a short time."

"The work has progressed quite well, indeed." Jacob leaned into the family's circle and whispered, "As long as you stay within these three rooms." He drew a triangle in the air with his finger, implying the foyer, parlor, and what she assumed must be the dining room, but she couldn't be certain for the doors were closed. "I fear what people may say if they stray beyond this general area."

"Do not fret. We won't be fixing our eyes on what is seen, but instead on what is unseen." Papa inclined his head in Lady Athol's direction, who was speaking to Lady Dorsham near the entrance of the dining room, and a spark of approval lit his eyes. "It's the heart changes for which we extend our gratitude."

"I admit..." Jacob glanced at his aunt. "I've stretched her beyond what she finds comfortable, but Aunt Louisa has handled the renovations and party planning well."

"I hope you were able to gather the help you needed?"

Jacob dipped his head. "Indeed. Thanks to Mrs. Thompson's recommendations, workers lined up outside my door. I am grateful for your assistance."

"You're very welcome." Mama's gaze shifted over Jacob's shoulder where Lady Athol disengaged from the Dorshams to speak with the butler. "Ah, here comes Lady Dorsham and Phoebe, how lovely." Mama smiled to greet them.

Emily stiffened.

Mr. Mathis straightened and smoothed his jacket.

While the others were distracted by Lady Dorsham's approach, Jacob whispered in Emily's ear, "Valkyries also seat a horse well."

A slight gasp escaped her lips, setting his eyes twinkling.

And... *Was that a wink?* Did the man have the audacity to wink at her in public?

He spun and greeted Phoebe and her mother. "I believe you all are acquainted with each other?"

Lady Dorsham curtsied to the Thompsons and Jacob. "Indeed, my daughter and Miss Thompson shared the same schoolroom. Allowing Miss Thompson access to Phoebe's governess was the least I could do for the good vicar's family for overseeing our small parish."

The ostrich feathers in Phoebe's coiffure shook as she flashed Emily an isn't-he-handsome look before practically swooning.

Beside her, Mr. Mathis tensed.

If Mr. Mathis's inclination toward modesty was making him uncomfortable around Phoebe's daring fashion, he showed no disapproval and greeted her with an eager smile. "Phoebe...er, Miss Dorsham." His voice cracked. "Your hair looks...rather nice this evening."

"Quite." Jacob arched a brow. "I haven't seen the like of such a hairstyle in London. At least, not yet."

Was that another trace of sarcasm in his voice? He showed no sign of mockery on his face.

Her friend giggled and fluttered her fan with delight.

"Phoebe is making her debut this season, my lord," Lady Dorsham told Jacob. "I do hope you'll be returning to London before the end the Season."

"It depends upon the renovations." Jacob graced Phoebe with one of his captivating smiles. "I'm certain Miss Dorsham will be the season's catch."

Phoebe's fanning doubled its rhythm.

A servant signaled to Jacob.

"The meal is ready. It is time for us to be seated." He nodded to the footmen standing in front of the dining room, and they swung the doors open in a grand gesture. A long mahogany banquet table that could easily seat twenty people filled the spacious area. Large fruit-and-flower arrangements in silver bowls graced the center, alternating with six-piece candelabras.

Jacob maneuvered through the crowd and offered Lady Athol a hold on his arm.

When Lady Athol's gaze fell upon Emily, Emily waved as she did whenever she left treats at the door.

A small smile curved Lady Athol's lips. Even though she clenched Jacob's arm with her gloved hands, she exuded elegance and grace, returning the wave with a slight raising of her hand.

Jacob escorted Lady Athol into the dining room, and the rest of the guests followed.

Samuel held his arm out for Phoebe, but she hesitated, likely hoping to acquire a higher-ranking escort. When no others rushed forward, she permitted Samuel to lead her.

Mr. Mathis took Emily's hand and placed it in the crook of his arm as she'd expected.

The guests seated themselves in typical fashion, according to rank and alternating male and female. Lady Dorsham and Phoebe settled near Jacob at the head of the table. The

Thompson family shuffled to the lower-ranking middle, except Papa, who had been asked to take the gentleman's place of honor next to Lady Athol. Emily could only reason it was due to her father's age or being the town's reverend, for there were higher-ranking men in the room.

After everyone was seated, Jacob held up his glass.

The room's noise dwindled, and she shifted to better view their host.

Before he spoke, his gaze settled on Emily. He frowned. "This will not do."

A footman pulled out his chair, and their host strode the length of the table.

To Emily's horror, he stopped behind her. "My guest of honor must be seated in a *place* of honor."

"It's quite all right..."

But a footman pulled out her chair, and Jacob tugged on her hand.

Mortified into compliance, she allowed him to guide her. Her dread doubled when she realized there wasn't an open seat. Where would Jacob settle her? Would a footman bring another chair?

Jacob waved his hand. "Please, everyone on the right side of the table, shift over one seat so we can make room for Miss Thompson. Her quick thinking saved me from certain death at the hands of highwaymen."

Lady Dorsham stammered, "But she's...she's..."

Emily inched closer to the butler pouring wine into glasses. One bump of her hip would create enough of a distraction to drown out Lady Dorsham's next words. But she dared not.

Lady Dorsham's voice trailed off, but Emily knew the direction of her thoughts. *She's of questionable birth, base-born, a bi-blow.*

*J*acob's glare cut off Lady Dorsham mid-sentence. He had no idea what she'd meant to say, but her flared nostrils and pinched expression announced it would not have been complimentary to Miss Thompson.

Silence as thick as London's fog hung over the room.

"The vicar's daughter." Lady Dorsham shifted one chair.

The gall of this social-climbing mother astounded him. That she'd attempt to humiliate Miss Thompson, who once shared her daughter's schoolroom, to obtain a better seat for herself.

He drew Emily closer to his side, away from the woman's vile tongue, hoping to infuse her with some of his strength. She appeared so delicate—a beautiful flower among a roomful of weeds. But he'd witnessed her strength by the creek.

Jacob pulled out Emily's chair himself. "Please be seated."

She sat but kept her eyes on the empty plate before her.

He raised his glass again. "A toast to the lovely woman beside me, Miss Thompson. I owe her my life and a debt of gratitude. May your aim always be sure and your arrows quick, and may I never find myself unfortunate enough to become your target."

Guests chuckled at his quip and clinked their glasses.

Peter Mathis remained straight-faced. *Perhaps the man needs to think he had a little competition so he'd not presume Emily was his.*

Emily flushed a becoming shade of pink.

Jacob resumed his seat at the head of the table as footmen carried in large trays and placed them on the sideboard.

At a nod from Jacob, the vicar rose and blessed the food. Turtle soup and an assortment of breads and cheeses were served.

His aunt's nerves seemed to settle as the magistrate and his wife engaged her in conversation. She was handling herself famously. The cornered animal look in her eyes lifted, probably due to the patient and good-natured vicar nearby. His presence kept wagging tongues in check, and Mr. Thompson's lively chatter must have helped.

Jacob raised his glass and saluted his aunt's efforts.

Beside him, Emily remained quiet, leaving him no choice but to endure Miss Dorsham on his left as she raved over the soup, dominating his attention. She leaned toward him until the bodice of her gown brushed his sleeve.

He tucked his hand in his lap, imagining the poor chaperone, who would be busy with her flirtatious charge during the young lady's coming out this spring.

Miss Dorsham was a pretty chit with soft blond curls and a ripe figure, much like the women who fought for Jacob's attention in London. But he'd witnessed the conniving, deceptive tactics they used and to what ends they would go to climb the social ladder. She would be an easy conquest if he were a cad who took advantage of innocents. Disrupting her advances might be amusing.

When her satin slipper brushed his leg, he turned to Emily. "Miss Thompson."

She froze and lowered her spoon to her soup, her gaze sliding his direction.

"What types of paintings do you typically create?"

"Portraits, mostly." One shoulder issued a dainty shrug. "Some landscapes for my own enjoyment." She turned back to her soup as if to end the conversation, but he would have none of it.

"Ah, if the landscapes are for your pleasure, then the portraits must be for commissions?"

Her jaw tensed. "Indeed."

"To save for membership dues to The Royal Academy?"

Miss Dorsham shifted in her seat and cleared her throat as if to interject.

Jacob ignored her. Painting his portrait would be the perfect excuse to get to know Christian's family and to see his son. "I would love to commission you for a painting. I was thinking of a full-length portrait of myself to hang in the hall and remind my older brother of his love for his youngest sibling." He glanced from Miss Dorsham to Miss Thompson and added in a conspiring tone, "Or at the very least, irritate him every time he walks in the front door."

"Oh, Emily." Miss Dorsham leaned across the table and tapped it above Emily's place setting. A bobbing ostrich feather in her coiffure brushed his temple as he looked away from the scandalous view of skin. "An opportunity to paint his lordship, and a full-length portrait. How generous." Sitting back, Miss Dorsham touched her throat and peered at him over her shoulder. "You are too kind, my lord."

Jacob cringed at Miss Dorsham's tone, insinuating that Emily needed the money.

"Emily is splendid with a paint brush. You'll be amazed." Miss Dorsham pouted. "I insist on tagging along and entertaining both of you while you work. It shall be splendid. I can read or sing, or we could merely chat." Her focus shifted to him. "I've been dying to know more about London and hoped you'd share all the ins and outs."

"I'm afraid I'm already scheduled to paint the magistrate's son." Emily shook her head.

"Pish posh. I will speak with them. They should wait until fall, anyway." Miss Dorsham faced him and lowered her voice. "Young Fredrick had an awkward growth spurt. The poor chap wouldn't want his gangly body commemorated for all time."

Emily's eyebrows drew together, watching Miss Dorsham.

Jacob hid his smile behind his glass and sipped. "Then Miss Thompson is willing?"

"Of course, Emily agrees." Miss Dorsham's enthusiasm oozed thicker than the dinner's sauces. "We're inseparable"—

her face reddened suddenly—"at least until recently, with all the preparations for my season, but I have missed her company."

Emily leveled Miss Dorsham with a glare before shaking her head at him. "I do not have a proper studio in which to paint a full-length portrait."

"Oh, but certainly, his lordship wants his portrait done here." Miss Dorsham glanced at him for affirmation.

The Thompsons' home would be best, but it would be rude to insist upon her painting him at the parsonage, so he shrugged.

Emily rested her fork at the top of her plate and said in a prim voice, "I do not have a chaperone, for Mrs. Hayes is needed at home."

Jacob smothered his grin at the female battle of wills— Phoebe who seemed determined to win his affections and Emily...why would Emily not want to paint his portrait? His smile withered. It didn't bode well for him if it was due to his reputation. All the more reason to be in her company, so he could win over her approval and learn more about the family that raised Christian.

"Another reason for me to accompany you. Miss Neves can serve as a chaperone for both of us. Besides, Lady Athol shall be here. Won't she?"

Seeing Aunt Louisa conversing with Mrs. Thompson swelled Jacob's heart with pride. The night was faring remarkably well. "Indeed. I believe some female company might be just the thing."

Emily's face paled. She whispered in a tight voice, "Phoebe, your mother shall not approve."

"Mama," Miss Dorsham called across the table.

Jacob stiffened at the woman's bold disregard of etiquette.

Her mother did the same. "Darling, lower your voice. It is not polite to beckon across the table."

"His lordship has asked Emily to paint his portrait, and you know how tedious those sittings can be. I offered my services to entertain them. We are merely looking for your consent."

Her mother glanced around at the luxury surrounding her, the centerpieces and the team of footmen. Her regard seemed to settle on the elegant cut of Jacob's coat and the sapphire winking at her in his neckcloth. He could almost hear the marriage banns being announced in her head. "Well, of course, my dear, as long as you bring Mrs. Neves, I think it's a lovely idea."

"Splendid." Miss Dorsham beamed.

"Splendid," Jacob echoed and turned to Emily.

Emily glared at what Jacob deemed her fickle friend, and her head gave the tiniest shake.

"What do you say, Miss Thompson?" Jacob asked. Candlelight shimmered in the reflection of her amber eyes, causing them to glow. Drawn into their depths, he wouldn't accept her refusal. "Shall I add the price to my brother's bill?"

Miss Worsham honed her gaze on Emily. "Your commission could go toward Christian's first semester at Eton."

She visibly wavered.

It was the perfect way for him to indirectly pay for Christian's schooling and learn more about him and his family. He must convince her. "It will provide me with a reason to brag about your work to Lady Kauffman at the Royal Academy."

Emily lowered her voice to a whisper. "You've barely seen my work, only what I can sketch with charcoals."

"Ah, but Miss Worsham claims you are best with a brush, and I'm confident in your skills because of the people who vouch for your talents."

Miss Dorsham nodded. "Emily is very talented. She painted both Mama's and my portraits. They turned out lovely."

"Lady Kauffman would welcome my recommendation. What do you say, Miss Thompson?"

He could see her mind weighing the pros and cons and willed her to say yes.

"Very well." Her desire for the academy must have won out over her wariness.

"Excellent."

Miss Dorsham clapped. "When shall we start? Tomorrow?"

"Tomorrow is the Lord's Day." Emily leaned back as a footman served the main course of prime rib roast with Yorkshire pudding and a side of Brussels sprouts in mustard sauce.

"Monday, then," Miss Dorsham said.

"I must order a canvas made." Emily seemed relieved at the possibility of a reprieve. "Those things can take time."

"I shall provide the canvas." Jacob inhaled the prime rib's savory aroma and raised his fork. "There's one already stretched in the attic."

Another resigned sigh crossed Miss Thompson's lips. "Monday it is."

The guests delved into the tender meat dripping with delectable sauce.

While Sir Hamilton asked Miss Dorsham about fashion, finally dragging her attention away, Jacob's focus drifted to Emily.

Her long lashes dipped and rose as she regarded the other guests, though she never peered in his direction. A tiny dimple flashed with amusement. She must've overheard something, though he paid no attention to the conversation. She sliced off a piece of meat, placed it in her mouth, and delicately chewed. He watched the slender muscles of her neck move as she swallowed.

"Are you enjoying the meal?" He couldn't keep himself from trying to draw her out. She had an odd effect on him.

She dabbed at her mouth with her napkin. "The prime rib is delicious." She nudged a Brussels sprout with her fork. "I've never had a Brussels sprout, and seeing as they don't appeal to you, it has given me pause."

Jacob blinked and leaned in towards her. "I beg your pardon?"

Her eyes widened. "My apologies. I spoke out of turn."

"No, I'm curious whether I heard you correctly." He leaned to one side to study her response. "What did you say gives you pause?"

She swallowed. "It's obvious you don't particularly care for Brussels sprouts." Her gaze drifted to his plate. "You've eaten around them and hidden some under your bread."

Indeed. Most observant.

She tapped the mushy green ball with her fork. "My father doesn't care for them, either, so I've never had them."

"Really?" Jacob's respect grew for the small-town vicar.

"Why do you try to hide your Brussels sprouts?"

"Out of habit." He snorted and rested his fork on the side of his plate. "Our nanny used to force me to eat them." He imitated her stern voice. "'Sprouts are good for a growing man's constitution.' Now that I have a choice, I don't consume them out of sheer rebellion."

Her lips spread into a captivating grin, curving around straight white teeth.

"You know"—she arched a sculpted brow—"a benefit of being the master of the house is that you get to say what can be served, or in this case, *not* served."

"Quite right. Would it offend the cook if I mentioned it immediately?"

"No doubt." She paused and tapped her index finger to her lips. "I believe you'll have to slip your preferences into normal conversation."

"Something like 'the garden is spouting well. Speaking of spouts, I detest the kind from Brussels'?"

"I was thinking more along the lines of"—she mirrored his

lean to one side—"while I was in Brussels, I dearly loved their chocolate, but their sprouts left much to be desired."

He burst out laughing, drawing the attention of those around him.

Emily hid her mirth behind her napkin.

"Along with Brussels sprouts, I shall add cold porridge to the items never to be served."

"Indeed, the devil's food, both of them." She grinned.

Her teasing roused his courage to ask what he'd been dying to know. "How fares Master Christian?"

Her expression brightened. "He's quite well but driving Mama and Papa to perdition. They're getting up in years, and it's a challenge for them to have such an energetic child. I help, but while I was out, Christian chased the chickens about the yard, scaring them so badly they refused to lay eggs for two weeks."

He smothered a chuckle.

"And then, he found Mrs. Hayes's hair powder, patted it all over his body, and pretended to be a ghost. The poor woman almost fainted."

His mouth split into a wide grin. "I did something similar to my mother as a boy." He sobered. "Would the two of you like to join me riding sometime?"

Her lips parted and air whooshed through. "Oh. Christian doesn't have a horse suitable to ride."

Blast. Jacob had forgotten there wasn't a pony in his aunt's stables. He'd have one ordered immediately.

Miss Dorsham cleared her throat. "Mama plans on hosting a party before we travel to London for the season. I do hope you will attend, my lord."

"I'd be careful announcing such." Sir Hamilton perked up. "You'll attract those highwaymen who raid coaches. They particularly like coming out in the evening when the gentry are on their way to a soirée, lightening them of their jewels.

Lord Warren, you were an oddity getting robbed during the day."

Jacob waved in a dismissive gesture. "There's no need to speak of it, thanks to Miss Thompson. Word has it that more raids have taken place on London Road." Most likely, Benton was behind those robberies, too, but to be certain, he must identify the lackies and trace them back to their ringleader. "Have any of the local townsfolk gotten a glimpse of the brigand?"

Sir Hamilton rubbed his chin. "I heard there were two of them."

Technically, there were three. Lord Benton had two lackeys, but as the mastermind, Benton wouldn't need to participate in the robberies. He might have made a special appearance because of his vendetta against Jacob.

"Nimble and short of stature." Sir Hamilton pulled back his large shoulders and patted his round stomach. "Rules me out."

Lord Benton also, but the hearsay must be wrong. According to Lieutenant Scar, the other coach robberies took place after dark and Benton would keep his distance. If rumors were correct, he didn't like getting his hands dirty. Or it could be a separate ring altogether and Benton's daytime attack was merely a strike of vengeance.

"They keep their faces covered," Sir Hamilton said, "but I heard one has light eyes."

Jacob frowned. "They could determine eye color in the moonlight?"

Sir Hamilton shrugged and squirmed in his seat. The man didn't appear to like Jacob questioning his knowledge even if it was hearsay.

"I heard Lady Templeton was accosted on her way to the Partridges' house party." Miss Dorsham seemed eager to share the gossip she'd heard, retelling what she knew of the robbery, then effectively using the Partridges' party to switch the topic back to her gathering. Jacob asked questions about the highwaymen, but it became apparent the other guests knew little.

Even as Miss Dorsham droned on, he found his attention on Emily. A wisp of hair escaped her chignon and dangled alongside her cheek, and the tiniest bit of dried blue paint tipped the loose strands as she studied each guest as though memorizing the scene to recreate later. Was she as keenly aware of his every move as he was of hers? She'd noticed his aversion to Brussels sprouts, so perhaps. She'd also proved to have a quick mind and pleasant sense of humor.

He found himself wanting to gain her approval and show his admiration for her. But why did he admire her so? Because she'd noticed he disliked Brussels sprouts?

A future with a vicar's daughter wasn't likely with his reputation, and he certainly wasn't seeking a wife. But she sparked an appreciation inside him, and a small part of the bitter acid that had corroded his heart washed away.

CHAPTER 9

The following morning, with Emily's becoming blush and musical laughter lingering in his mind, Jacob did the unthinkable. He stepped through the doors of Sylvanwood's church. He pulled the wrought-iron handle, swung the door wide, and glanced at the ceiling's beams, waiting for the lightning strike that would end his sorry life. When no flash occurred, he removed his hat, and the sexton ushered him to an empty box, opening the small door for him to be seated on the pew.

Jacob shifted on the hard bench, trying to find a comfortable position. By Jove, it was warm in the nave, yet no one else seemed to be sweating. Jacob unfolded his handkerchief and mopped the perspiration from his brow. Reverend Thompson stood behind a tall podium and announced the blessed arrival of baby Jonah, the firstborn child of the town's blacksmith.

Several rows up and across the aisle, Miss Dorsham peered over her shoulder and issued Jacob a coquettish smile.

He nodded and scanned the crowd. A row in front of him, the magistrate's balding head gleamed a high-polished shine that any boot-back would strive to achieve, and the man's wife stared straight ahead. Behind the Dorshams, the store clerk who'd assisted Jacob in ordering materials sat beside what he presumed from their similar profiles were the clerk's elderly father and mother.

Soft blond curls tinged a blue hue from the sunlight cascading through the stained-glass window caught Jacob's eye. Christian sat in the front row with Samuel on his right and Emily on his left. The boy wiggled, and Emily glanced down at him with love. A second later, she did so again, but this time with a look of silent reprimand.

Jacob, too, had struggled to remain still in church when he was a child. He angled for a better view.

Emily whispered something to Christian, and Jacob admired the fine line of her profile until Miss Dorsham leaned forward, blocking his view. She must have thought he was looking at her, for she lowered her lashes and fanned herself.

Lady Dorsham glanced over her shoulder, a satisfied grin curling her lips.

Marriage-mart mamas. He wasn't certain who was more troublesome, young women or their mothers.

He raised his gaze to the picturesque windows so they'd believe he was merely admiring the stained glass depiction of scales falling from the Apostle Paul's eyes. At least he thought it to be the Apostle Paul. Mother would be horrified at how little he remembered of Bible stories.

The rustic stone walls of this quaint church sanctuary wasn't as elaborate as the church his mother had dragged him to as a boy in London. Back then he'd felt like a tiny ant in the three-story nave beneath buttressed ceilings and hardly understood a word spoken.

He rose with the congregation and sang a few hymns. Lady Dorsham's bellowing voice sounded like a crow cawing. At the conclusion of the last song, Mr. Thompson dove into his speech, and Jacob listened, forgetting about the other congregants. Even though Mr. Thompson spoke to the crowd, his words hit Jacob's heart as if they'd been written for him.

"God has a plan for your life." He paused and surveyed the congregation. "It's written in 2 Corinthians 3:5. We cannot claim competence of ourselves, for our competence comes from God." The vicar bent over the podium until his chest touched the open Bible. "He will use your past hurts and failures to develop your character, and if you humbly rely upon Him, God will raise you up, so that"—the reverend gestured as if pulling someone up onto the platform—"you can reach back down and pull others out of the pit. For God wants all His children to be redeemed."

The proverbial lightning bolt Jacob expected upon entering the church now struck his chest. Heat collected under his collar, and he ran his index finger along the edge of his cravat to cool his neck. Could God have a plan for a worthless third son who could only boast of being a dandy spy—lucky with cards and able to draw a woman's fancy?

The vicar closed his Bible, prayed, and blessed his congregants before dismissing them. The congregants rose and filed out of the church, but Jacob remained seated to wait for the crowd to clear. His heart brimmed with questions regarding the message he hoped to ask the vicar.

"My lord." Miss Dorsham stood over him and smiled prettily. "How lovely for you to attend our humble place of worship. I'm certain it's nothing like London's beautiful, spired cathedrals."

Out of politeness, he rose. "Sylvanwood's church holds a certain beauty, as does its parishioners."

Miss Dorsham's eyes sparkled at the compliment.

The platitude rolled off his tongue, too late for him to rescind. The last thing he needed was to encourage the chit.

"I'm so looking forward to our meeting tomorrow." Her eyes shimmered with a mischievous glint.

When had he set a meeting with Miss Dorsham? "My apologies, but to what meeting are you referring?"

"Why, our engagement for your portrait. The one Miss Thompson will be painting."

"How could I forget? Please forgive me."

"Of course." She lowered her lashes. "I daresay all the renovations at Brownstone Hall must be occupying your thoughts."

"Rightly so. I look forward to breaking the monotony with the delightful company of such lovely ladies." There he went again with the accolades. Had he no reign over his tongue?

She met his eyes with a bold gaze. "Would you be so kind as to walk me to my carriage?"

God help the poor bloke in London for whom Miss Dorsham set her cap. "You'll have to excuse me. I'd like to have a word with the vicar."

Her lower lip extended in a dainty little pout, but she stepped aside to let him pass.

Jacob strode to the front of the church, where Mr. Thompson smiled a greeting. "Lord Warren. Glad to see you in church on the Lord's Day."

"You have a fine congregation I enjoyed your...ah..." *Sermon? Homily? Liturgy?* "Talk. I wondered about God wanting everyone to be redeemed." Even sinners like himself? "How does one determine if we hold God's favor and what His plan is for our lives?"

"God reveals His will in various ways, but it may differ from person to person." The vicar folded his hands across his stomach. "Have you asked God to show you?"

Jacob lowered his voice. "And how might I do that?"

Mr. Thompson's eyes twinkled. "You pray."

"Ah. I see." But he didn't. He hadn't prayed since he was in leading strings, and even then, he never recalled hearing God answer.

Another parishioner approached the vicar, and Jacob

excused himself. When he turned, he almost stepped on Christian.

"Good day, milord." The boy stood tall in his Sunday best.

Jacob squatted on his haunches. "And good day to you, fine sir."

The tow-headed, cherub-faced boy's blue eyes filled with intent. "Are those your blood cattle out front? The ones attached to the landau?"

Jacob's heart warmed. His son was interested in horses—something else they shared in common. "If it's the matching pair of black thoroughbreds, then yes. Would you like a closer inspection?"

"Most definitely."

"Then, off we go."

"Huzzah!" Christian hopped-stepped toward a side door. "This way. I know a shortcut."

Christian's enthusiasm warmed Jacob's chest as he followed him outside into the tepid sunshine. He ran to Jacob's horses and petted the neck of the one named Goliath.

"Are they from Arabia? The land where the men have the crescent swords?" He slashed the air with his hand, and Goliath drew back.

"Easy now." Jacob calmed the horse with a caress to its nose. "Indeed. How do you know of Arabia?"

"We have a book on horses in our library." Christian had mentioned he could read, but Jacob figured he'd meant basic words like *hat* and *cat*, not a complete book.

"And you've read it? At your age?"

"Emily helps me." Christian's head rolled back, and his shoulders drooped, leaving his dangling arms in a sway. "She turns it into a learning lesson."

"I know how that can be." Another hidden talent of Emily's. "What is your favorite horse?"

"Lipizzaner stallions. They can do all sorts of tricks."

"You're right. Very impressive. You know your horseflesh. My brother owns one. He's a beauty."

Christian's eyes flashed. "I wish I could see it. Em painted me a picture of one. It hangs over my bed."

Em. The simple nickname suited her. "Do you paint?"

"No, painting is boring." His eyebrows rose. "Unless you're painting horses, but they're hard. I tried to paint one, but it looked like a dog."

"It's probably better than what I could do. I'm afraid I can only draw stick figures, and even those aren't very good."

"That's okay. Not everyone can do art. Papa told me to keep trying different things until God shows me what talents He's given me."

"Your papa told me to pray."

Christian petted Goliath's nose. "Yeah, that would work too."

"Have you ever done that? Pray, I mean."

"All the time."

The other horse, Comet, nuzzled Christian's sleeve, and Christian shifted his attention to it.

"How do you go about it?" Jacob asked. "The praying."

Christian peered at Jacob as if he'd never heard such a silly question.

Folks lingered outside the church, but no one appeared to notice him asking a five-year-old for advice. "I mean...people have different styles. Do you have a specific phrase or method for...say, praying to God to show you your purpose?"

"Naw, I talk like we're talking now."

"And God speaks back to you?"

Christian giggled. "No, silly. Not out loud." His blond brows wrinkled together as he mulled it over. "Well, He did speak to Moses through a bush, so He *can* speak out loud. Papa said He speaks into your heart, real quiet, so you have to listen closely."

"Christian! There you are." Emily strode toward them, her eyes honed on her brother.

"Em—" Jacob pressed his lips together. After her courageous rescue and their conversation during dinner, he'd thought of her as Emily. Her name reminded him of a summer's day or a fluffy cloud floating in a blue sky. He'd dreamt about her last night. Nothing remarkable. He'd merely felt her presence and been comforted by it. His Valkyrie.

"Papa told me to keep an eye on you, and I didn't know where you'd run off." She placed a protective hand on Christian's shoulder.

"Miss Thompson." Jacob stepped away from Goliath's side into her line of vision.

"Good day, milord." Her brow furrowed. "I didn't realize you attended church."

Jacob flashed her a saucy grin. "I've heard it's good for the soul."

Her bonnet framed the delicate features in her face, and the breeze tugged at her pale green gown, hugging it to her slight figure.

"It's a lovely day." He glanced up at the clear sky. "Would you and Christian care to join me for a ride through town? My team could use some exercise."

Christian jumped about and tugged on her skirt. "Could we? Could we, please?"

"No, we couldn't." She leveled her gaze on Jacob. "It wouldn't be proper."

He pushed back his jacket and rested his hand on his hip. "It's an open carriage. There could be no impropriety, especially with Master Christian riding along."

"Please, Em." Christian hit her with his big blue-eyed stare, which compelled a person to want to lay the world at the child's feet.

Jacob fought back a smile. Another trait he'd inherited from his father. "I shall promise to keep to the main road."

"Well..."

Jacob raised slanted brows in his best pleading look.

Christian spoke for him. "Pretty please..."

She sighed. "Mama and Samuel will be preoccupied at the church for some time." She rolled her lips, a seemingly unconscious gesture that heightened the rosy color of her sensual mouth. "I will concede if you promise to make it a fast trip."

Jacob drew an X over his heart with his index finger.

She left to inform Samuel—who spoke to congregants near the church entrance—of their short jaunt and returned with a nod that they could leave.

"Hurrah!" Christian scrambled into the curricle.

Jacob offered his hand to assist Miss Thompson and glimpsed her slender ankles as she boarded. He climbed aboard on the other side so that Christian rode between them. With a flick of his wrists, he snapped the reins, and the team trotted toward town.

"Did you enjoy dining last evening?" Jacob asked.

"Surprisingly, I did. It was kind of you to invite us."

His head swung in her direction. "Surprising?" He tried not to sound as affronted as he felt. "That you enjoyed yourself at a party hosted by me?"

She flushed and stared down at her hands. "That was poorly done of me and not what I meant."

"What did you mean?"

In the silence, the clopping of horses' hooves grew louder.

Christian leaned forward so far to see the horses that he practically stood. Emily tugged him back into a seated position.

"It's not that you didn't throw a lovely party," she said. "The evening was splendid, and what you've done to Brownstone Hall in such a short time is commendable. Even the scrolling on the cornices has been restored."

His chest swelled, knowing she'd noticed the places he'd enjoyed refurbishing most. "A little paint hides a multitude of sins."

She intrigued and captivated him—made him feel fresh and new. Still, a voice in his head, remarkably similar to his father's, told him he was a sluggard and an irredeemable rogue who'd never aspire to anything. The day after he'd overheard his father say that last bit, he strode into the War Department's Home Office and offered his services.

"Good day, milord. Miss Thompson," Mrs. Brunson, the barrister's wife, called as they passed.

Jacob tipped his hat. "You were saying?"

Emily wouldn't look at him, merely stared straight ahead with her lips drawn into a tight line.

It didn't seem she meant to continue. He repeated her sentence to jog her memory, "I throw a lovely party, but...?"

"Look at the set of grays!" Christian pointed at the magistrate's team.

Jacob smiled and dipped his hat at the man as the horses pranced past pulling his carriage.

Emily shrank back in her seat each time they spotted another person, or more likely, each time someone spotted them. Was she ashamed to be seen with him? As the son of a duke, he wasn't accustomed to women not wanting to be seen with him.

Emily was different. She didn't flirt or vie for his attention. Of course, the daughter of the town vicar wouldn't behave in such a manner, but to cringe and try to hide? Had his reputation preceded him to this small town?

She glanced back over her shoulder. "I believe it's best if we head back to the church."

"Aww," Christian whined.

Emily ran her fingernails lightly across Christian's back in a motherly gesture. Jacob found a spot in the road to swing the team wide and bring them back around.

Why did he care what she thought of him? Was it because she was Christian's sister or something more? He needed to stay focused on the objective. He swiveled in Christian's direction. "How would you like to help me drive the team for a bit?"

"Really? You'd let me?" Christian rounded on Emily. "Can I?"

She raised a brow at Jacob. "You believe he can manage?"

He handed the reins to Christian but looped an arm over the boy and grasped his hands. He held them tight, showing him how to keep the team steady. Christian smiled so big his mouth hung open.

"Loosen up a little and give them some freedom to go."

Teaching Christian how to drive a team was the perfect excuse to keep the pace a little slower and extend their visit. Christian's eagerness to learn caused Jacob's heart to swell, and he was surprised by the sense of fulfillment at the chance to pass his knowledge down to his son. He wanted to hold on to this feeling, what it was like to act as a father would.

Emily watched them with a mild smile. She shifted a bit in her seat to face him. "Did you enjoy today's message?"

"I found it interesting. Do you believe God wants to save all people, not just good people?"

"The Bible states in 2 Peter that God is patient with us, not wanting anyone to perish but all to come to repentance. So yes, that includes the good and bad."

"But I thought God hated sinners."

"God hates sin, not sinners. All of us have sinned and fallen short of the glory of God. That's why it was necessary to send His son Jesus to die. He took the weight of our sins and nailed them to the cross."

"So we can be washed clean." He'd heard that message

before, but this time, it held more clarity—struck him differently.

Emily brushed her fingers through the back of Christian's hair. "God dearly loves all of us. We are His children."

"Sometimes, it's hard to remember that."

"Why?"

He studied Christian's small hands enfolded in his. "It's difficult to think of God as a loving father when your own father only sees you as a disappointment." Jacob would never do the same to his son.

He tried to remember a time when his father hadn't glared at him in shame or remorse. "To my father, I'm more of a backup to the backup plan. He's invested most of his time in my eldest brother, Robert, and then Alex. I was always more of an afterthought, so I never saw him much." Jacob frowned. "I still don't, but when I do, he makes it abundantly clear that he isn't impressed with my life choices."

"What would he have you do?"

"Purchase a commission in the military or his majesty's navy like a typical third son."

"And why haven't you?"

Funny. He couldn't recall anyone besides Robert asking him why he hadn't enlisted. "It's a bit embarrassing, actually."

Her long lashes swept up as she met his gaze. She was so open and curious. He hadn't seen the like in ages, definitely not among the jaded set in which he ran. The sudden compulsion to spill all his faults overruled logic.

"It's a wretched problem."

"You don't have to explain if you don't want—"

"I cannot abide the sight of blood."

Her eyes widened the tiniest bit.

"I swoon like a woman at the first drop of red." Which was why he'd become a spy and used his charm as a weapon to obtain information. Less chance of witnessing a bloody battle.

However, there was that one time at Willowstone Farm when things went awry, and a horse thief was shot. Jacob had fallen to his knees and blacked out. Fortunately, he'd come to quickly, and in the chaos, his associates hadn't noticed.

Emily's brows raised. "Truly?"

"Can you imagine me in the middle of the battlefield?"

She fought a smile but failed. "But when my arrow hit the bandit, there was blood."

"Probably the reason I ended face down in the creek. I froze at the sight instead of ducking before his boot met with the side of my head."

Emily's face contorted, and an odd noise escaped her nose.

"Don't you dare laugh." He feigned offense. "I told you in great confidence. Do not have me regret it."

"How dreadful." She pinched her lips together and struggled to appear sympathetic, but the corners of her lips twitched.

Christian sat on the edge of the bench seat and concentrated on the team with an expression of sheer joy.

"It's a blasted curse. Quite humiliating. It also ruined my career as a pugilist."

Emily covered her mouth with her hand to smother her giggles.

"It is why you will never find me at the Fives Court betting on a prize match either." He tilted his eyebrows like his father's hounds did when they were being denied a treat.

"Well, I should hope not. The law forbids boxing matches."

"That, too, put a damper on my pugilist aspirations."

Emily lost the battle against her laughter, and Jacob reveled in the sound of it. A dancing tendril teased her graceful neck, writhing a seductive dance in the breeze, ignorant of her prim pose with her hands folded in her lap.

Too soon, they reached the bend and turned onto the church drive.

"Gently pull back on the reins to slow the horses. Like this." Jacob lightly tugged on Christian's hands.

He pulled the reins to his chin.

"Bang-up-to-the-mark job at steering the horses. I do believe you're a natural." Jacob jumped down and lifted Christian out.

The boy beamed as if it were Christmas morning.

Jacob strode to the other side, aiding Emily in alighting from his curricle.

"It has been a lovely afternoon. I daresay it was due to the excellent company." Funny, how the slight touch of her made him feel as though he could conquer the world. When their hands slid apart, he felt a sense of loss.

"Christian, what do you say to his lordship?"

He wrapped his little arms around Jacob's thighs and squeezed, almost tripping him. "Thank you for the lovely time and for letting me drive." His blond head tipped back, and he smiled up at Jacob. "I've got to tell Mama." And with that, he turned and dashed toward the church.

Jacob's chest tightened. A lump rose in his throat, and he cleared it. He clasped his hands behind his back and strolled alongside Emily in Christian's wake. "I look forward to resuming our talk tomorrow."

She faltered a step. "Tomorrow?"

Jacob pinned a smile on his face to not let her witness his disappointment. Was that how Miss Dorsham felt when he didn't recall? "For my portrait."

"Oh, quite right. Tomorrow with Phoebe and her companion."

He stopped outside the large oak door and turned to face her.

Her cheeks reddened under his intense gaze, and she lowered her lashes.

He took her hand. "I shall count the minutes."

The hint of a smile formed before she turned. Jacob pushed open the door, holding it for her. The vicar stood inside alongside Peter Mathis while Christian danced about, explaining how he drove the team.

Jacob inclined his head. "Good day."

Mr. Thompson returned the nod, but his focus drifted to Emily.

Christian rushed over to help hold the door. "And don't worry, Lord Warren. I can keep a secret about the blood thing too."

Emily's laughter burst forth as Christian closed the door, but not before Jacob caught the shaken expression on Mr. Mathis's face. The poor bloke probably didn't know what to think about that statement, and it didn't bode well for Jacob, but a smile marked his lips as he strode back to his conveyance. Tomorrow was looking bright, indeed.

It might remain so, but only until he informed Emily and her parents that he was Christian's father.

Jacob swallowed. The more he learned about Emily and the Thompson family, the more he desired to earn their respect, but wouldn't they despise him once learning the truth? Or would they live out the words the vicar read that God desires everyone to come to redemption? Could they accept him as a new person—a reformed rake?

The right time would present itself.

He hoped.

CHAPTER 10

*E*mily hefted her satchel loaded with art supplies and with her pallet under her arm as she strolled the drive toward Brownstone Hall. Samuel had given her a ride to the bend in the road, but she insisted upon walking the rest of the way so he would not be late for a meeting.

The intimidating wrought-iron gate loomed before her, but few townsfolk drew close enough to admire the intricate beauty of its ebony swirls and scrolling patterns. Her palette board slid into an awkward position. She tucked it back under her arm and pushed the metal gate. It swung open, its old hinges groaning in protest.

The extra money will help Christian be able to attend Eton. She repeated the phrase as a mantra to motivate her not to turn around and go home. *You've painted portraits before.* There was no need to be nervous, but she'd still tossed in bed all last night, ruminating on the teasing smile that set her on edge, wishing for an impossible future.

The pounding of hammers and the grating peel of a saw grew loud as she approached the manor. A gaggle of workers hefted boards and tossed debris out of windows. Upon spying her, the workers paused, the swinging of hammers ceased, and the saw blades stilled.

With all those eyes upon her, Emily faltered, then sped her pace. She should have asked Samuel to escort her to the door. Coming to Brownstone Manor was a terrible mistake. She never should have agreed to paint Lord Warren's portrait. It didn't help that she dreamt about crafting the angle of his chin, the plane of his aristocratic nose, and the curve of his lips. She shouldn't have allowed herself to be swayed.

A stone stabbed her foot's arch through her slipper, and she stumbled, barely regaining her balance.

"Miss Thompson." Jacob called from the side yard, and Emily glanced that way. He shook hands with a bulky worker, perhaps the foreman, for his clothes were tidy and kempt.

Jacob jogged toward her, a broad smile spreading across his features.

"Here, let me carry that for you." He tugged on the shoulder strap of her satchel and grasped her pallet. The sun caught his hair, casting a halo. A light breeze ruffled the wavy tresses, reminding her of how Christian's hair fluttered when he ran around the yard.

Jacob glanced over his shoulder, and the workers resumed their noisy tasks. He offered his arm for her to hold, and they strolled toward the entranceway.

"You are early." One side of his mouth lifted into a crooked smile, emphasizing the crease in the center of his bottom lip and the full softness of it. Her fingertips tingled at the prospect of capturing his provocative mouth and the teasing spark in his eyes.

"Only by a few minutes. Samuel had an early-morning meeting." The spicy citrus scent of lemongrass encircled her like a tender breeze, along with his distinct male smell. Instead of the stuffy formal attire she'd seen him in previously, today he appeared casual in a flowy white linen shirt with the collar undone. A pair of buckskin breeches formed to his legs and led to a couple of tasseled Hessian boots. "How are the repairs going? The place certainly appears to be buzzing with activity."

"Rather well." He paused with one foot on the bottom step leading up to the entrance and placed his hand on an artichoke-shaped stone capping the newel post. "Funny thing, but I'm finding overseeing the daunting project quite agreeable." He scanned the façade. "It's hard to explain, but there's something satisfying about restoring and creating beauty."

The artist in her understood perfectly.

"I know it's not done, and if found out, the upper classes would shun me, but I've enjoyed toiling alongside the workers, getting my hands dirty, working up a sweat." He examined one hand and said with a hint of sarcasm, "Who knew these things could be useful?"

She laughed at his expression of amazement as he studied his palm.

"No doubt"—he shrugged—"I'm shunned by the ton already."

The rumble of a carriage sounded from behind. Emily turned to see Phoebe's phaeton bouncing down the drive.

Phoebe waved, earning a reproachful glare from her chaperone. Her horse drew to a stop in front of the stairs. Dust kicked up about their feet, matting the polish on Jacob's boots.

He lowered Emily's satchel and rested it against the newel post to aid Phoebe and the elderly Miss Neves from their perch. Several groomsmen rushed to care for the horse and conveyance.

Phoebe's fashionable day dress, a white-on-white muslin weave, clung to her figure and scooped low into a square neckline. Her hair had been swept into an elaborate coiffure, and her usually straight locks framed her face with ringlets made from curling papers. She floated to Jacob's side, leaving Emily feeling gauche and dowdy in her sturdy walking dress. A silly thought. There was no point in dressing in something she could ruin with paint.

"My lord, how lovely to see you." Phoebe's lyrical voice sang the words.

"Miss Dorsham." Jacob took her gloved hand and bowed. "You look charming."

Her fingers splayed across her bosom, and she giggled. "Three days in a row of being graced by your presence. I daresay I shall never grow tired of your company." She laced her arm through Jacob's and turned to stroll into Brownstone Hall.

Mrs. Neves shot Emily a downcast glare before falling into step behind them.

Although she didn't blame Phoebe for her mother's decree that Emily was no longer acceptable company, it stung to be treated shabbily.

Jacob halted after a step and pivoted to Emily as he extended his hand. "Shall we?"

"Come along, Emily, it's time to paint," Phoebe said over her shoulder without glancing back.

Emily reached for her supplies.

"Don't worry about your things." He beckoned her forward with an open palm. "A footman shall see to them."

His gaze held hers, pleading. She appreciated that he hadn't treated her like a paid employee, but she had the oddest impression the opportunity he was offering was more than to paint his portrait. She'd had a lovely time during their carriage ride with Christian—too lovely. Could she keep her heart and reputation intact around a notorious rogue, or was she in over her head?

His smile was kind, almost playful. And why shouldn't she be allowed an afternoon doing what she loved and delighting in the company of someone she found enjoyable?

She slid her fingers into his hand. His grip enfolded hers, and his smile skittered her pulse.

The door swung open, and the butler, Mr. Maslow, bowed at his lordship. Jacob nodded in the direction of her satchel, and Mr. Maslow shouted, "I shall see to it immediately."

Phoebe ignored the man as she glided into the great hall.

Emily paused. "Good day to you, Mr. Maslow."

"And good day to you, Miss Thompson."

Jacob strode down the few steps and into the parlor. The clap of his boots against the marble floors echoed in the large room. "I defer to the artist's better judgment. Where is the best location to paint?"

Emily glanced at the windows. "The room with the best natural light would be preferred."

"Ah." He gestured toward the left down the hall. "This way, then."

He stepped aside to let her pass and motioned for Phoebe to do likewise, but Phoebe clung to his arm, leaning so their shoulders touched.

"I haven't seen this wing. I'm certain it's as richly done as the rest."

"It is still a work in progress." Jacob scanned the hall, his gaze lingering on a brown stain on the ceiling alongside a missing piece of crown molding.

Phoebe frowned. "Oh, I was hoping the renovations were finished, for the noise becomes tiresome to my delicate ears."

"I'm afraid I shall have to disappoint you. The hammering has been a constant and shall remain so for another month at the very least. If you must take a break, I can show you to a quieter part of the house."

"How kind." She leaned against his arm with a coy smile. "I'm certain I will grow accustomed to it."

"Here." Jacob nodded toward a door that led to a garden-like conservatory with one wall of windows and stepped aside to allow them to enter before him.

Emily strolled into the morning sunlight spilling in and basked in the warmth. The view showed a stone patio with potted topiaries, withered after years of neglect, and a long man-made pond, its water green with algae and laced with lily pads. At the end of the pond, a solid oak tree stretched out its branches.

She smiled at the beauty waiting to be unleashed. Jacob had confessed earlier his love for restoration. If only she could witness the pride in his eyes when this garden bloomed into a spectacular view. After a little love and care, the landscape could be brought back to life.

"Will it do?" he asked.

"Brilliantly." Emily turned and met his broad smile. Their gazes held. The remembrance of his vulnerability yesterday in sharing his reaction to seeing blood and his ability to laugh at himself created a longing for more of those moments.

"Splendid."

A shiver passed through Emily, yet she was not cold.

"The footman will bring the canvas shortly."

"Is there a piano nearby?" Phoebe placed a possessive hand on his arm. "I was thinking I could play. I also brought the works of Lord Bryon, for I didn't know what books your library might hold."

"How thoughtful of you." He graced Phoebe with a charming smile, and she basked in his attention.

A sour taste filled Emily's mouth.

Jacob and Phoebe were ideal for each other. They came from the same social class. They would make a perfect match. She should be pleased that Jacob was showing her friend interest.

Lady Athol appeared in the hall outside the open door.

"Good morning, dear aunt. I'm glad you could join us." Jacob waved her inside.

The woman stepped into the room like a deer entering a clearing, the fringe on her shawl dangling to the floor.

"You've met Miss Dorsham and Miss Thompson."

The ladies curtsied, and the tension in Lady Athol's frame relaxed.

"And this is Miss Neves, Miss Dorsham's chaperone."

The elderly chaperone curtsied so low she would have toppled if Jacob hadn't caught her elbow.

Lady Athol swallowed and cleared her throat. "It is wonderful to see you, and I cannot wait to watch you paint my nephew, Miss Thompson. I've heard you have an abundance of talent."

Warmth filled Emily at the compliment. "Thank you."

"Please excuse me, for I have a few things to attend to first."

Jacob's brows lowered, and his voice rang in a warning tone. "Aunt Louisa."

"I shall return for tea and biscuits at eleven." She backed from the room and disappeared down the hall like a phantom vision.

A footman carried Emily's satchel inside. Another hefted a large floor easel, and a third lugged in the blank canvas almost as tall as Jacob himself. At least she wouldn't have to shrink his proportions to fit.

The footman glanced at her for placement. She stepped closer to the wall adjacent to the windows. "Right here shall do nicely."

The servants set everything into place as Emily opened her satchel and pulled out her brushes and paints. She donned her full-length apron and tied it about the waist.

Phoebe settled onto the settee and Miss Neves into a low back chair in a shaded area and pulled out her embroidery.

"Where would you like me to stand?" Jacob asked.

Emily peered about the space, tapping her index finger to her lips. "I believe over in the corner." She nodded toward a sunny spot next to the windows.

Jacob shifted nearer the corner.

"You don't have to pose yet. I must first prime the canvas. You may relax." She removed a large brush and earthenware jar from her bag and lifted the lid, dipping her brush into the paint jar. With large strokes, she swept her brush up and down over the canvas.

"Do you plan to change into something more formal?" Phoebe asked. "Perhaps the nice superfine jacket you wore to dinner the other evening?"

"I plan to stay as I am. Robert always dresses bang-up-to-the-knocker. Seeing me painted without a cravat and jacket shall send him into a dudgeon."

Emily crouched to cover the lower sections of canvas. "You seem intent on vexing him."

Jacob grinned. "Do not fear. It is how we express our love for each other."

"Then you must love him dearly." Emily glanced his way before finishing priming the bottom corner.

His grin widened with a mischievous glint. "I do, indeed."

"Tell us about the marquis," Phoebe said. "What is he like?"

Admiration laced Jacob's tone while he spoke of his elder brother's accomplishments, and his voice struck a note of awe when he mentioned the duke and duchess's love for one another.

Emily finished priming. She set her brush down and stepped back. "The canvas is suited better for a standing position, but that can grow tiresome." Emily's gaze settled on a nearby chair. "Would you prefer to sit?"

His shoulders straightened. "Most definitely not." He stood near the window and posed.

Emily examined the lighting, lines, and angles, moving

toward him. His nearness warmed her skin. She cleared her throat and willed the heat from her cheeks before she placed her hands on his shoulders and positioned him to illuminate the right side of his face. When she had him situated just right, she stepped back. Yes, that was it, the halo effect she'd witnessed at the creek and during their carriage ride.

She refused to meet his gaze which lazily roved over her. "Find a relaxed stance you can remain comfortable in for at least an hour."

He shifted his weight and settled upon a pose with one arm resting on the back of a chair, the other hand in his pocket. That suited Emily fine because an hour could be spent painting the hands alone. Only painting one would save her time. The faster she finished, the sooner she'd be paid and away from his unnerving presence. How could she be drawn to a man yet fear those same feelings? Mr. Mathis never made her pulse flutter but nor did he set her on edge.

Phoebe fanned her face. "I daresay. Never has a man looked so virile."

Emily grabbed a piece of charcoal and knelt at his feet. Phoebe had always been outspoken, but her flirtatious comments caused Emily to cringe. Need she be so forward? Emily marked a light outline of his boots and assumed a professional tone. "Please tell the servants not to scrub away the markings, or we shall not remember the exact positioning."

"I haven't posed for a painting in an age," he said.

Emily returned to her canvas, picked a thinner brush, dipped it in a light sienna, and faintly outlined his figure.

"I believe the last time was when I was ten." Jacob grunted. "My father commissioned an artist to paint all four of us together, himself and his three heirs. Never did the time go so slowly or the fine weather call so relentlessly."

"Which is why I offered to come and entertain you." Phoebe picked a bit of lint from her gown and folded her skirts about her. "Mama commissioned Emily to paint my portrait on four occasions. I had to sit still as Emily painted for hours several days on end, so I understand how tedious the time can be."

Emily's jaw tightened. She'd enjoyed her sessions with Phoebe, and if Phoebe had found them tedious, then she certainly hadn't acted it. Phoebe had laughed so hard, her mama scolded her on how proper ladies did not display such emotional abandon.

Emily opened her paints and squeezed good-sized quantities onto her pallet.

"A generous offer." Unable to move, Jacob shifted his eyes to peer at Phoebe. "Thank you."

Emily bent to shape the form of his legs, refusing to admire the snug fit of his buckskin breeches, and lowered to the positioning of his boots from toe to heel.

"Before I begin to read..." Phoebe laid the works of Lord Byron on the settee next to her. "I was hoping you could tell me about London. What shall I expect?"

"Certainly."

Emily could feel the warmth of his stare as she sketched his outline.

"London is a jolly good place to enjoy one's self. There is plenty of entertainment. No one suffers from boredom in the city. The circles in which we run teem with drama." He sniffed, and a faint smile drifted the corners of his lips upward. "Truthfully, I'm growing quite fond of Sylvanwood. The people are friendly, and life seems...simple." He frowned. "Please, do not take offense. I mean that in a good way."

"No, you are correct," Phoebe said. "We are a tolerably dull town, but we are delighted to have your lordship in residence. You have already brought us much excitement, saving us from boredom, which makes you a hero of sorts." Her voice lowered to a purr. "At least to me."

Emily glanced at her friend.

Phoebe's expression seemed to say, *There is nothing wrong with innocent flirtation.*

"You have it reversed. The good people of Sylvanwood tolerate me." A wry smile curved his lips. "*They* are the true heroes."

"Enough about Sylvanwood. I want to hear about London."

"There is much ado about London. Where would you have me focus?"

"On the parties and balls, of course. Whom should I meet? Where should I go?"

Emily grabbed a flat brush and developed the skin tones. Thank heaven she'd bought extra paint. She rarely worked on such a large piece.

"You should start with Almacks, assuming your mother has already secured a voucher."

"Mama has written Lady Jersey," Phoebe said. "We expect it to arrive any day now."

Emily lost herself in the swish of her brush as their banter about Londoners' exploits continued. She could picture Phoebe and Jacob strolling through Hyde Park and dancing together at Almacks. They would make a beautiful couple and have perfect little towheaded children. She should be happy for them.

Lord, why then does my heart ache?

She laid a base coat of skin color before starting on the contours of Jacob's face. His hairline emerged as she dragged the brush over the swell of his cheekbone. It curved like a lover's caress over his jawline and strong chin. When she'd pulled him from the stream and he coughed out the creek water, she'd never seen such a beautiful sight as breath heaving through those firmly molded lips. So much so that tears had stung her eyes, but then he'd asked, "Are you my guardian angel?" At that moment, she'd wanted to be.

Now she knew his reputation. So why did she still long to fill that role? To mean something to him?

She dabbed the bristles in more paint and blended in white highlights. His aristocratic nose took shape. She played with the lowlights of his face but wouldn't be able to create his eyes or lips until the next session, after the base coat dried.

Phoebe rambled on about parties as Emily switched brushes to create the billowing white of his shirt, followed by the tan of his breeches.

She frowned when he shifted his weight. "Do you need a break?"

"Certainly not. I'm enjoying the tingling numbness of my limbs." He flashed her a crooked smile.

"Oh my." Phoebe gestured to the clock in the hall. "It's half past the hour. You've been painting for two hours and must let us stretch our legs." She rose from lounging on the settee and addressed Jacob. "Would you be so good as to give me a tour of the rest of Brownstone Hall?"

"I would be delighted." Jacob smiled. "Miss Thompson?"

Emily waved her hand for them to go on. "I must continue working before the paint dries. Please, do not dally, for the lighting will change."

"We'll be back in a pinch." Jacob raised his elbow, and Phoebe snaked her hand around the crook of his arm. He paused before the doorway. "Should we wake Mrs. Neves?" His head inclined toward Phoebe's chaperone, who'd nodded off in the corner.

"The poor dear needs her rest. Leave her be."

Phoebe sashayed as they exited and laughed at something he said before disappearing around a corner.

Why hadn't Emily joined them? Her heart clenched. She couldn't compete with Phoebe's looks, wealth, and status. Besides, Jacob had a life in London—a place she could never set foot. Her feelings for Jacob were counterproductive. A relationship with him could never be. She must set her unexplainable feelings aside, paint his portrait, and put the money toward Christian's education.

Her brush swept over the canvas, her mind locked in a spectrum of color until she no longer heard Phoebe's chaperone snoring in the corner.

~

"Y ou've seen the foyer and the dining room." Jacob paused in the hallway, unable to resist the opportunity to show off the renovations and his plans. "The library remained in decent condition, just needing a good dusting and wood polish. On the left, we have a drawing room." He pushed the door open wider and leaned against the doorframe for Miss Dorsham to peek inside. "The walls need to be re-papered, and we're having the furniture reupholstered in cream."

Instead of looking, Miss Dorsham squeezed through the doorway. Hooking his arm, she pulled him into the room and rounded on him with puckered lips and closed eyes.

He bit back a chuckle, disentangled his arm from hers, and walked around her to peek out the window, checking on the workmen's progress.

Hinges creaked. He glanced back to find the door closed behind them. Had she nudged it shut with her slippered foot?

"Perhaps we can sit for a moment." She flashed a come-hither smile and sashayed to the sofa. "You must be tired after overseeing all this work and standing for your portrait."

Miss Worsham's minor flirtations seemed comical, but he didn't want to hurt her feelings. She lacked Lady Benton's finesse, but he'd rather not have a repeat of *that* incident. One duel was enough.

"For propriety's sake, let's leave the door open." He stepped toward the exit.

Miss Dorsham ran gloved fingers along the sofa's backrest before she positioned herself between him and the door. "You have such splendid plans and fabulous taste." She toyed with her right glove, exposing her thumb. "I cannot wait to see the manor finished."

Jacob had never been one for the game of cat and mouse, especially when he played the part of the mouse. These games held dire consequences, and he'd had enough. He desired a simpler life.

An image of Emily beside the creek hovered in his mind. Her shy smile as she tucked her hair behind her ear after one of his witty quips.

Once again, Jacob stepped around Miss Worsham. "There are other rooms to see, and Miss Thompson awaits." He reached for the doorknob, but she yanked on his arm. If he hadn't been off kilter, he could have held his balance. Instead, he stumbled onto a nearby settee. Or had he been pushed?

"Oh, Jacob, I have been longing to do this since we first laid eyes on each other." She sprung on him like a cat. Her hands pressed his shoulders, pinning him to the armrest. Her lips crushed his in a demanding kiss.

He gripped her upper arms, pushing her away.

Miss Worsham's bottom lip pouted before her face crumpled and tears fell. Her voice raised a couple octaves into a whine. "You don't think I'm pretty."

Heaven help him. He'd never made a lady burst into tears. How did one handle this sort of situation? "You are a lovely woman."

"I am?" She peered at him with teary eyes and sniffed. "You think so?"

"Remarkably so."

She hugged him, pressing her face into his neck.

"There, there." He awkwardly patted her head, wishing he'd had a sister and not just brothers to have better prepared him on how to react. Women had caused him nothing but problems. Chasing pleasure left him empty. He wanted to settle down and be a father to his son, not a libertine. But if he was caught alone with Miss Worsham, the vicar would never consider him a suitable father for Christian. "Miss Thompson is waiting for us. She will notice our prolonged absence."

Miss Worsham nuzzled his neck.

He jerked away.

Miss Dorsham's hands worked the knot of his cravat. "Emily becomes engrossed in her artwork. I daresay she'll hardly realize we're gone."

He grasped her fingers to still their movement. "I'm sorry if I've given you the wrong impression."

One thing grew abundantly clear. Miss Dorsham was not an innocent. Her experience was evident in her forwardness and her calculations to get him to this point. Jacob pushed her aside and rolled from under her grasp.

A man passed outside the window. Mr. Welsh. Thank God!

"My steward is searching for me." He pointed at the window. "I must see what he needs." Jacob bounded for the door and fled the room.

~

*E*mily finished cleaning her brush and was about to change colors when Phoebe entered the salon, cheeks flushed and mouth curled into a secretive smile. She strolled the perimeter, humming a tune. When she drew closer, Emily noticed her swollen lips and mused hair.

Phoebe caught her staring, and her hands moved to her coiffure. "Goodness. Is it out of place?"

Emily dropped her gaze to her palette. It appeared as if

their tour of the house had turned into something else. How could Jacob who'd been so considerate to her and Christian toy with Phoebe? Her flirtatious friend was acting like a harlot, but didn't a gent know better than to play with an innocent?

Phoebe scooped Emily's hand up and held it between hers. She bit back a smile, but it erupted past her teeth. "Emily. I must tell you the loveliest secret." Phoebe glanced at the sleeping form of Miss Neves and whispered, "His lordship stole a kiss while we were in the drawing room." She sighed heavily. "He is so romantic and charming."

And a rogue.

Emily rounded on her friend. "If your mother found out, banns would be announced tomorrow. Think of the scandal."

"It was a mere kiss, and I don't care a wit if Mama knows." She shrugged. "I know he has a reputation as a rake. It's part of his allure, but you should have seen how he admired me as though I were the only woman in the world."

Emily remembered how his eyes held hers by the creek and on Sunday's carriage ride. She, too, had felt special, but the man was a cad, and Emily was the worst kind of fool. She turned back to her work, picking up a clean brush and adding black to her pallet, deepening the manganese blue color.

"A kiss encourages a man and leads to other things."

"Indeed, marriage. I believed he would have professed his affection for me, but his steward required his presence." Phoebe flounced onto the settee. "Imagine me...part of the *ton*. Lady Phoebe Warren."

Emily lowered her voice in case servants lingered within hearing distance. "My birth mother learned a different result."

"Em. Please trust me." Phoebe's eyes softened with a pleading look. "I understand you're looking out for me, but Lord Warren's lived in a different world than our small town of Sylvanwood. I have my reasons for being so bold."

Phoebe treaded a dangerous path, but Emily knew when

her friend would no longer listen. She dipped the end of her brush in the blue and painted the sky on the canvas. Her hand shook, but thankfully, this required broad strokes. The sweeping motion looked like a strong wind on the canvas, and she added a touch of gray. A storm formed in the far background, barreling in on the unsuspecting outline of Lord Jacob Warren.

A man's throat cleared from behind. She turned to see the libertine in the doorway, tugging the cuffs of his sleeves.

"Ladies, I beg your pardon. There has been an unexpected complication, and duty calls. Today's session must come to an end. We will have to enjoy our tea and sandwiches another time." He glanced at Emily but couldn't quite meet her eyes. "I do hope I haven't inconvenienced you, Miss Thompson."

"It's quite—"

"How dreadful." Phoebe rose from her seat with a pout. "I had hoped we could continue our earlier conversation."

"I'm afraid not."

"Perhaps another time, then." Phoebe flashed him a coy smile.

Emily's stomach twisted.

Jacob shifted his feet. "Miss Thompson, if you need more time to—"

"I am quite finished." She capped the paint tube with a nail and dropped it into her earthenware container.

"It only takes a few days for the paint to dry." Phoebe's eyes locked on her. "Shall we plan to return Thursday at the same hour? You know"—she grinned at Jacob—"because of the similar lighting." She tilted her chin in Emily's direction. "Right, Emily?"

"If his lordship wills it."

He rubbed his forehead.

Emily pinched her lips and glared at him, but he stared at the unshapen form of himself on the canvas.

"So be it."

~

$\mathcal{W}$hile Jacob escorted Phoebe and the sleepy Miss Neves to their phaeton, Emily hurriedly washed her brushes out back with mineral spirits. She allowed the footman to clean her pallet but was particular about her brushes, not wanting them ruined. In her hurried state, she hoped she wouldn't damage her supplies. They would need to be cleaned again at home, but the sooner she left Brownstone Hall, the better.

Emily collected her things and slung her satchel over her shoulder. She strode into the house and rounded the back hall corner, slamming into Jacob's chest. He caught her shoulders, but Emily jumped back, dropping her satchel.

"My apologies." He reached for her bag. "Here, let me help with that."

She clutched the strap. "I've got it."

"I see." He straightened, surprised concern lining his brow. "I'll see you out."

"It is unnecessary. I know the way." She slipped by him, but he stayed at her side.

He cupped her elbow. "I believe it is quite necessary."

"Unhand me."

He pivoted to block her path before letting go. "I fear Miss Dorsham has maligned my character."

"There was no need for her to do so. Your reputation precedes you, and I'm not blind to the misdeeds done today."

His eyes flashed. "You do not know the truth of it."

"I know all that I need to know." She tried to step around him, but he moved with her.

"She kissed me. It was not my intent. I had to fabricate an excuse to escape her advances."

"You expect me to believe that?"

"You're the vicar's daughter." His brows drew together. "Doesn't the Bible say things about grace, forgiveness, and not being quick to judge?"

The cerulean blue of his eyes cut into her like the cold steel of a blade. What she knew and what she felt warred within her.

"I will not be gulled by flummery nor lured by flattery and a handsome face. Phoebe is a naïve, trusting soul, and you are a rake of the worst kind."

His nostrils flared. "So only a woman can be the victim? Is that it?"

"Ha!" Her chest heaved as her breathing swelled. "Are you saying Phoebe—Miss Dorsham—overpowered you and took advantage?"

"Yes!" He shook his head. "No...well, somewhat."

She brushed past him and strode the hall with as brisk of a pace as her skirts would allow.

"Emily, wait." He matched her long strides.

She whirled around. "I don't recall giving you permission to use my given name."

The soles of his shoes slid on the polished floor, and he nearly collided with her. "I merely..." He ran a hand over the back of his head and blew air through his cheeks. "I thought we might be friends."

Had similar words lulled her mother into a man's bed? Emily steeled her resolve against those haunting eyes and tempting lips. "I have my brothers and my family. I don't need friends."

A pained expression flashed in his eyes, and he recoiled as if bitten. A shuttered expression followed, cool and removed. "Very well." He bowed his head. "My butler will have my curricle brought around. I shall see you home."

"It's unnecessary."

"Nevertheless, I will not allow you to walk when I can offer you a ride for, despite your disbelief, *I am* a gentleman."

Emily survived the return trip to the parsonage in stony silence. Despite the buffer of her satchel between them, she could feel the tension in his frame like a winch cranked too far. He pulled in front of the house, jumping down before the horses slowed to a stop. He walked around and reached up to assist her from the carriage. She hesitated, wishing he had let her walk.

"We made it this far." He spit his words like venom. "Do you truly believe I'd maul you on your doorstep?"

Emily accepted his hand and aid. But when he echoed her aloof, "Good day," tears welled in her eyes. She couldn't escape his presence fast enough. She scurried through the front door and up the stairs to her room, where she crumpled onto her bed.

"Are you crying?" Christian's voice sounded from the open doorway.

Emily's head jerked up. She turned and scooted into a seated position, wiping the evidence of her tears away with the back of her hands. "It's nothing."

"Was he mean to you?"

"No, it's not like that. I'm merely...disappointed."

"If he comes here again, I'll pull out my saber and challenge him." He lunged an attack on his pretend foe. "*En garde.*"

Christian's loyalty drew a weak grin, but she would have much to explain if Christian confronted his lordship. She frowned as Jacob's words echoed. *Don't you believe in grace, forgiveness, and not judging?* She stilled Christian's fencing moves with a hand, remembering Jacob's hurt expression. Phoebe had been flirting with him the entire morning. She had always been the one who went after what she wanted, and she'd seemed pleased about having been kissed. Had Emily been too hasty in blaming Jacob? A gentleman should know better, but Jacob's reputation preceded him, and Phoebe still chose to tempt him with all the wiles in her arsenal. "I'm afraid I've handled myself rather poorly. Papa would be disappointed in my unchristian-like behavior."

"Whaddya mean?" Christian blinked at her.

"It's nothing. You are a wonderful protector, and I know I can count on you." She rose and ruffled his blond curls. "But truly, I'm fine. Nothing God can't fix right here." She tapped her index finger to her heart.

Christian shrugged. "Jolly good. I like Lord Warren. I'd hate to have to run him through." He saluted with his invisible sword. "But I will keep my eye on him."

Emily smiled and shook her head at his retreating form. He certainly hadn't learned such bravado from her. She sighed. *Men.*

CHAPTER 11

*W*omen.

Jacob was done with the whole lot of them. Ladies appeared sweet and delectable with soft curves and feminine features, much like a tame house cat. But beware of the slash of their claws and the sinking of their teeth. If only he could ask Lieutenant Scar or Robert for advice. Instead he spent the evening undercover, dressed as the Dorshams' coachman with hopes to put a stop to the highwaymen's robberies.

A cold breeze whipped his face, and he yanked up the woolen scarf he'd wrapped around his neck to hide his identity from the Dorshams.

He'd thought Miss Emily Thompson of a different breed. Once again, he'd thought wrong. The more time he spent with women, the less he understood them.

Jacob steered Goliath up the lane to Brownstone Hall after driving the Dorshams back to Hinwick Manor in the weary pre-dawn hours. He attempted to buoy his spirits by focusing on Christian. He'd located his son—a wondrous feat—and shouldn't let his indecision on how to proceed nor his argument with Emily affect his mood.

Sunday's sermon still pricked at him. He could ask God for wisdom on how to proceed.

But right now? On his horse? In the middle of the night? Wasn't that sacrilegious?

Christian's voice rang in his head. *I just talk to Him.*

Jacob cleared his throat and glanced up at the starry sky. "Good evening, ah...Lord. I was wondering if You could help me know what to do. For Christian's sake, I want to be a better person —a good father. I've made mistakes"—he snorted—"plenty, as I'm sure You're aware, but I want to change, have a fresh start, a new life. Tell me what to do, and I'll do it. Have Your way with me."

The clopping of the horse's hooves was the only audible sound, but a quiet thought echoed in his head. *I love you, My son.*

Jacob's throat constricted.

Foolish. Surely, God hadn't actually spoken to him. Why would He?

How many years growing up had Jacob strived to hear those words from his father—to no avail?

But to believe God would say that? To him?

Lack of sleep was making him delusional.

With a shake of his head, he focused on his assignment. Being the wealthiest family in Sylvanwood, the Dorshams were the most likely targets for the highway robbers. Thankfully, for a few coins and unbeknownst to the Dorshams, one of their drivers had been happy to take the night off. Posing as their coachman had allowed him to surveil the roads while driving Lady and Miss Dorsham to the nearby town of Swindon for a ball. He'd also had the opportunity to listen to the other drivers' comments after he mentioned the highwaymen.

"They rode good horseflesh with admirable skill," the

Flushings' driver said. "Accosted us on a turn. I couldn't outrun them without risking flipping the coach. Well armed, too, both of 'em." The man warmed up to his topic. "The thin one aimed a blunderbuss at me chest and another at Johnny, the footman, while the other bandit lightened Lady Flushing of her jewels."

"The post road ain't safe, but we risk crackin' an axle on some of them backroads," said the Bushnell driver.

As dawn crested, Jacob lumbered up the wide stone steps into Brownstone Hall. The workers were already getting started on their tasks.

The door swung wide for him to enter. "Good morning, milord," his aunt's half-deaf butler said in a booming voice that set Jacob's head throbbing.

"Good morning, Maslow."

Maslow beamed as if thrilled his master referred to him directly. "Mr. Welsh is ready for your meeting. A few letters arrived yesterday. I took it upon myself to put them in your office."

"Splendid."

Jacob greeted his steward outside the study and waved him in before plunking into the chair behind his desk. "You can tell me good news, or you can hand me a drink. Either would do."

His steward scratched his forehead where a scar split the eyebrow into equal halves. "Shall I ring for coffee or tea, milord?"

Jacob shook his head. The poor bloke didn't always understand his sarcasm. Dark circles, probably matching Jacob's own, outlined the man's eyes. Had he spent all night reviewing Aunt Louisa's finances? Jacob liked his attention to detail and ability to do sums in his head. Jacob had taken a risk in hiring him without a local reference, but it had paid off so far. Mr. Welsh had already suggested several efficient changes.

Mr. Welsh flipped through his notes. "The re-shingling of

the roof is coming along favorably, but..." He glanced toward the crystal decanter.

Jacob couldn't help but smile. "I was only jesting about the drink."

The steward relaxed. "The slate above the west wing is in worse shape than we realized. More shingles will need to be ordered."

"How many?"

"Six bundles."

"Place the order. How is the re-glazing of the windows?"

"Slow and tedious, but they are making progress."

"Excellent. We can address the rest tomorrow. What about my correspondence?"

Welsh reached for the opened mail in the silver tray and flipped through the letters. "Lord and Lady Keating heard you were in the area and have invited you to a soiree at their house in Bourton-on-the-Water, and Mr. Beau Brummell has asked you to join him in attendance at the Royal Pavilion in Brighton. Baron Alvanley sent an invitation to his country house for sport hunting with the hounds. Several letters from—ah"—he cleared his throat—"ladies, begging for your return to London." He held out a paper with elegant script. The man's face reddened like an apple, and his eyes did not meet Jacob's. "This one seemed quite urgent."

Jacob accepted the letter and reclined in his chair to read it.

My Dearest Warren,

Oh, how it flatters my heart to hear you dueled my foolish husband for my honor. It makes my sentiments easier to declare. I am in acute torment and candidly confess my motives are far from pure, but my passion takes the place of reason. Since you have proven you share my ardor by your care for me in my wretched state, I beg you to come to London posthaste. How impatiently I await you. While you are off amusing yourself in the countryside, my heart suffers.

> *Truly Yours,*
> *Lucile*

"Lady Benton." Jacob spit the words like a curse. "My good deed has not gone without punishment." He released a bitter laugh. "I help a lady in distress and end up at the end of her husband's pistol. And now, the woman has completely misinterpreted my intentions. Mr. Welsh"—he pointed at the young man—"if you learn one thing from my example, learn this. If a woman starts spewing sentiments of love—*run!* Women are trouble. You're best to leave them well enough alone."

His steward dropped his gaze.

Jacob hadn't inquired about Mr. Welsh's marital status, but by the red tint creeping above his steward's cravat, Jacob would place a high-stakes bet that a thief of the feminine variety had stolen the man's heart.

He tossed the letter onto the desktop. "Please decline her gently but firmly." The night he'd carried Lady Benton to her chamber to sleep off the effects of her heavy imbibing, he'd overheard her seedier guests whispering about Benton organizing the highway heists. He excused himself to use the retiring room and searched Benton's office and later his bedchamber. He had toasted his hostess with the intention of getting her foxed so her tongue would loosen, but she kept the wine and spirits flowing long past his initial salute. His intentions weren't to get her into bed, only to obtain information on behalf of the Home Office.

He swiped a hand through the air. "In fact, respond in the negative to them all. My attention is needed here at Brownstone Hall. One more thing."

"Yes, milord."

"Write my"—how should he address Agent Scar to his

estate manager?—"private investigator. Have him report again on Lord Benton. I want to know the man's exact location." He didn't need the devil to put a bullet in his back the moment he let his guard down. He rose. "That will be all."

Mr. Welsh collected the letters and left the room.

Jacob rested his elbows on the desk and rubbed his eyes. In their secluded meeting places, Sarah had professed similar dribble to him. He'd grown to understand that such words from women like Sarah and Lady Benton weren't professions of love for him. They'd been words of worship to a god of pleasure. He'd merely been one of their sacrificial goats.

It never ended well for the goat.

~

"Oh, Emily, how could you?"

Emily cringed at Phoebe's whine and stepped outside the church, closing the doors behind her. She'd promised Mama she'd gather flowers from the church yard to take to Widow Taylor.

Several weeks had passed since Lord Warren and his jaunty attitude had invaded her world and a few days since she'd begun painting his portrait. Her life had somewhat returned to normal, and she did not need Phoebe upending it again.

Emily placed the cutting shears into the basket and slid it into the crook of her arm. She inhaled deeply before she turned. So much for her private retreat. There would be no peace now that Phoebe had found her.

Phoebe trotted up the walkway, a fierce scowl darkening her complexion. The ruffles on her parasol flopped in tune with her steps.

"Why would you do this to me?" Her chest heaved as if she might burst into tears. "I thought you were my friend."

"Whatever are you talking about?"

She stopped so abruptly that her skirts swayed forward. "You know what I mean. You're ruining everything."

"Truly, I do not." Emily fought the urge to snort and turn away from her friend's drama.

Angry red splotches formed on Phoebe's cheeks. "You told Lord Warren you will no longer be painting his portrait." She put a fisted hand on her hip. "Don't deny it. He told me so when I encountered him at the mercantile."

Emily prayed for patience. She'd sent Jacob a letter yesterday recommending he commission another artist. "If you walk with me to the field to cut flowers, I can explain."

Phoebe glanced at the tips of her fawn-colored kid boots. "We must stay on the stone path."

Emily agreed, and Phoebe fell into step alongside her.

Birds swooped around them, chirping out love songs to potential mates. The warm weather coaxed spring into a premature bloom. Her mother also suggested she clip some daffodils to decorate the church before the next warm day withered them.

"Well?" Phoebe prodded.

How could she explain to her bold-spirited friend that Emily was merely looking out for her reputation without having Phoebe take offense? "It is true. I told Lord Warren I would not continue to be commissioned for his painting." She'd mourned over the loss of funds. She'd need to paint five times the number of portraits to make up for the one lost commission, which could have paid for a semester for Christian at Eton.

Phoebe turned toward her. "Why? You must know my interest in Lord Warren. Do you have no regard for my feelings?"

Emily exhaled slowly to keep from snapping at Phoebe. Her father always said that even if you are right, you can be wrong if you raise your voice. Rarely did anyone in her household scream or yell.

You yelled at Jacob. Emily pushed the belligerent thought aside.

"I do care for you, Phoebe. So much so that I couldn't turn a blind eye to the temptations the both of you face in each other's presence."

Her friend's face brightened. "You believe he is fond of me?"

"I believe the man has earned his blackened reputation, the one you read about in the gossip columns. Stealing a kiss is proof his intentions are less than honorable. I cannot stand by and be party to him assassinating your character."

Phoebe touched Emily's arm, searching her eyes for answers. "But you think he has intentions toward me?"

Emily smothered her groan. Did Phoebe not hear the rest of what she said? She clutched her friend's upper arms to emphasize her point. "Not *good* intentions. I beg you not to play his games. Stay away lest you fall into his trap and end up like my mother did."

Phoebe's gaze dropped, and she swallowed. "Do you think ill of your mother?"

Emily had never discussed her birth mother with anyone. Exhaling a whoosh of air, she let go of Phoebe's arms. "I want to believe the best of her." Emily closed her eyes. "Really, I do, but the truth of it is"—she opened her eyes to face her friend—"I do not know. I shall never know if she made an unwise decision of her own free will or was forced or coerced. All I know is that she had me and left. She did not leave a note and never tried to contact me. How could she do that to a daughter she loved?

Phoebe burst into tears.

Emily put a hand on her weeping friend's shoulder. Whatever was amiss? She didn't have a handkerchief to lend her because hers was in her reticule inside the church. She pulled Phoebe to the low stone wall separating the graveyard from the churchyard, where they sat. Phoebe's parasol fell from her loose fingers as another sob tore from her throat.

"What is the matter?" Emily squeezed Phoebe's hand.

Phoebe inhaled a staccato breath and murmured incoherently before releasing an even louder wail.

Emily leaned in. "Pardon?"

"I need to m-marry."

"Of course. It is the reason your mama is bringing you to London for the season." Emily tried to coax Phoebe to smile or at least stop the flow of tears. "If you are worried you won't find a match, well, that would be ridiculous. The dandies of London will look at your beauty and beg for your hand."

"You think so?" She pulled a handkerchief out of her sleeve and blotted under her eyes.

"I'm most certain of it."

"Oh, Emily, I've missed your encouragement."

"Have no fear. I'm certain that by this time next year, you shall be confessing your vows, perhaps in this very church with me in attendance."

Phoebe's face scrunched again. "I don't have until next year." Her voice raised to a higher pitch. "I need to marry straightaway."

An icy chill washed over Emily. "Why?"

Phoebe put her hands to her face and sobbed.

Emily shifted off the wall to sit on her haunches in front of Phoebe. She pried her friend's hands away from her face. "Tell me the truth of it. What's happened?" She waited as Phoebe got a hold of herself.

"I enjoyed his attention, but then one thing turned into another, and it became more than just a kiss." Phoebe bit her bottom lip and lowered her gaze. "Much more."

Emily gasped. "He tupped with you?"

"I'm in a terrible mess. I don't know who else to turn to."

She bit her quivering bottom lip. "Please, Emily, you must help me gain Lord Warren's affection. What if I'm with child?"

White-hot heat burning in her belly flared into an inferno. "You shall go to him and demand he marry you."

"I can't." She shook her head in such a fervent manner that several golden curls escaped her coiffeur. "Think of the scandal. My reputation."

"If you don't and you are carrying his child, you'll be ruined and so will your family."

Phoebe sniffed. "I'd like a chance to convince him myself. I shall sway him to surrender his bachelor status and make an offer for my hand in short order. But I need your help." She wrapped her arms around her stomach and rocked back and forth. "I can only manage if you aid me in persuading him."

"What do you mean?"

"Sing my praises." She scooted forward to teeter on the edge of the rock wall. "Afford me any opportunity to be alone with him."

Emily hesitated, despising the idea of facing Lord Warren ever again—the despicable blackguard. "I don't—"

"Please, Emily, I don't know what else to do. Help me as my longest, dearest friend."

Emily ached to comfort her, embrace her in a fierce hug, and weep over her ruination. But she hesitated, unsure if that was what Phoebe wanted. Her friend had always been strong-willed and high-spirited. As a child, she'd tested boundaries and dared to question everything. Why hadn't she realized the consequences?

Phoebe would be shunned, an outcast in her own town.

Emily closed her eyes. At least it wasn't her.

Bile soured her stomach. How could she think such thoughts when her friend was in such pain? *God forgive me.*

Silence fell between them except for the twittering of birds in the nearby briar bushes. Even though the sun still shone, what had seemed like a beautiful day had darkened.

Phoebe's eyes filled with a calm as if she had a spot-on plan that would save them. Her calculated look raised the hairs on Emily's arms.

"I have three weeks before we leave for the season. My best recourse is to have Lord Warren fall hopelessly in love with me as quickly as possible so the dates won't appear too amiss if a babe arrives early." Her gaze drifted to the church exterior. "Thankfully, the House of Lords reconvenes later than usual, and I'll arrive in London at the start of the Season." Phoebe clasped Emily's hands. "Lord Warren is a wonderful catch. This might not be the way God intended for us to marry, but I believe He sent Jacob to me. Think of it. The Dorsham name aligned with the son of a duke."

Emily swallowed her shock. Did Phoebe understand what she was saying? Of course, God could forgive her, but she would still have to face the consequences of her actions. Fortunately, she could lean into His strength. "God doesn't condone sin. But, if you ask for God's forgiveness, He will—"

"If I am with child and can't convince Lord Warren"—her tears began in earnest again—"I will have to disappear until my time is over. My child will be left with strangers, much as you were. How could I do that when the child is part of me? What if the people are cruel or the baby is left at a workhouse or grows up as a street urchin? We can't let that happen."

We? Emily would do what she could to help her friend, but saving Phoebe from ruin wasn't Emily's responsibility.

"If I remain here unwed with a babe, we'll be worse than lechers." Phoebe covered her face with her hands. "Without my family to support me, I would have to become a man's mistress and live a life of sin to keep a roof over my child's head." A desperate sob tore from her throat. "You have your painting to sustain you. I have nothing."

Was this how Emily's mother had felt when faced with the same dilemma?

The full weight of Phoebe's situation strangled the air from Emily's lungs. There was no simple solution. Her friend's future appeared bleak—hopeless. Emily put her hands to her cheeks. Had her birth mother's options seemed as abysmal? Had she known another family would provide a better life for her baby than she could? Emily needed time to digest the situation. Most of all, she needed time to pray for God's guidance.

"There is a chance you aren't...that there won't be a child."

"I can't take that gamble." Phoebe clutched Emily's arm. "Please say you'll help me, Em. You, Peter, and Samuel have always saved me from my past scrapes. You are the only one to whom I can turn now. Your goodness and grace have sustained me. I don't know how I will survive if you say no. I need you."

Emily wavered. The best option for Phoebe and the baby was to marry, but life felt out of order. Phoebe being in a motherly way wasn't what Emily had envisioned when she and Phoebe pretend played finding a husband as children.

Jacob's playful smile and teasing blue eyes flashed in her memory. The rake had flirted with her more than once. What kind of a father would he possibly be?

She mustn't think the worst. Perhaps he would fall in love with Phoebe. Perhaps he'd love their child. Wouldn't that be best? Why, then, did unease gnaw at her?

Panic flared Phoebe's nostrils. "Please. At least say you'll continue the painting sessions."

Her nails scraped against the stone wall at the thought of having that rogue in her vicinity. Emily exhaled a long breath. "Fine, but the next session shall be at the parsonage under the careful watch of Mama and Mrs. Hayes. I don't want him doing anything else untoward." The canvas should be dry enough to move, and she'd need to figure out which room had similar lighting.

"I will need opportunities to convince him."

"Then convince him in other ways. No dalliances, especially not under the vicar's roof."

Phoebe nodded. She released Emily and pressed the palms of her hands against the stone. "Do you remember how we used to play in this very field? We'd pluck daisies for our hair."

Emily missed those simpler times. "We also made them into flower bouquets and pretended to be reciting our wedding vows. We were so young. Not a care in the world."

"Promise this will be our secret." Desperation edged Phoebe's words.

Phoebe hadn't kept hers.

"I'm sorry about telling Mama about your birth—truly, I am. I didn't think through the repercussions. Please forgive me. Say you'll hold my confidence."

Phoebe's pleading look always wedged open Emily's compassion, sometimes despite her better judgement. But Emily had no plans to ruin her friend's life by spreading gossip. She nodded.

"I could always count on you." The rigidness left Phoebe's frame.

Birds darted past, calling to their mates, and soon the air filled with the birds' songs.

"I intend to fulfill my childhood dream." Phoebe tilted her face toward the warm sun. "Soon, I'll be married and, within the year, holding a child in my arms. I have become a woman. I shall leave Sylvanwood to begin a life of my own."

Emily mentally steeled herself for the challenge ahead. At least, if she finished the portrait, Christian's schooling would be paid. She would settle for Mr. Mathis, a God-fearing man and gentleman of moderate means.

CHAPTER 12

"Take me to River's Bend Bridge."

Jacob startled awake in the driver's seat and checked to ensure his scarf was pulled up. A drizzling night rain dripped water off the rim of his hat and beaded on his driving coat. He'd sunk into its warmth, catching a quick nap and waiting to see if the Dorshams would attend another soirée. He preferred to spy undercover as a groomsman, coach-man, or the occasional footman over wealthier positions, because the upper classes rarely looked at their servants—at least not fully. The Quality acted as if their hearths miracu-lously lit themselves, or ghosts delivered their food and chauf-feured them around town.

A footman aided Miss Dorsham into the coach. Where was her family or Miss Neves, her chaperone?

"Make haste," she said before the door closed.

Jacob snapped the reins, and the team of horses cantered down the lane. The rain slowed to a drizzle. He checked his pocket watch and tilted it toward the hanging lantern. Who was Miss Dorsham meeting close to midnight? In under ten minutes, they arrived at River's Bend Bridge, where another coach was parked. It had an emblem he didn't recognize. The other driver tipped his hat, and Jacob returned the gesture.

Miss Dorsham flung open the door and jumped down before he could assist her. She dashed to the other coach.

Its door opened, and a man emerged.

She threw herself into his arms, wrapping him in a lover's embrace. At first, the man conceded, his hands roving over her back, but then he pulled back, shaking his head and ushering her into his carriage.

His guess had been correct. Miss Dorsham wasn't an innocent.

Several minutes passed before a muffled argument grew louder inside the closed coach.

"It was a mistake." The man's shout quieted the regular nighttime chirping of crickets and frogs. "I was hurt and lonely."

"You ruined me." Miss Dorsham's shrill voice jerked the other driver upright.

"What would you have me do?" Exasperation weighed the man's words.

The door flung open, and a slippered foot dangled. "This can't be undone."

"Let me help. If you need funds—"

Miss Dorsham fled, her hands covering her face.

Jacob jumped down, ready with the lowered steps, and opened the door to the carriage. Miss Dorsham sobbed into her hands as he aided her inside, got her settled, and returned to his seat.

The rain did little to cool the shame burning under his collar. Sarah had fled with a similar look after he'd proposed. *What would you have me do? Give up my dreams over a child?*

His world had crumbled that night. He'd spent several weeks attempting to change her mind and all the years since searching for his child.

His heart ached for Miss Dorsham. Although her circumstances were different, it seemed she had been rejected by the one who should face it with her.

Her life would never be the same.

He flicked the reins, and the hoofbeats on the dirt-packed road drowned out her sobs.

~

*E*mily spent the next two days mulling over Phoebe's situation. She'd prayed hard, but instead of peace, she felt conflicted and unsettled, tossing and turning these past couple of nights since Phoebe confided her secret.

Morning light streamed through the window as she paced back and forth in the salon-turned-studio. The canvas form of Jacob, which the footman from Brownstone had delivered with the easel, seemed to question her even in its most basic form of mere skin tones.

Can only a woman be a victim?

Phoebe could be very aggressive. When she set her mind to something, she'd stop at nothing to get it, as she had with the Phaeton. She'd pestered her parents until they finally relented and purchased her the four-wheeled open carriage, allowing her to drive despite proper etiquette.

The outline of Jacob's eyes peered back at her from the canvas. *Do you really believe the worst of me?*

Emily swallowed past the lump in her throat and laid out her art supplies.

The light filtered in nicely through the north-facing window of the makeshift studio. An old bed cloth had been laid out beneath the easel to protect the floors. It reminded Emily of the sail on Christian's boat and how Jacob had helped name it the *Pirate Catcher*. He was terrific with children, more patient than Samuel with Christian's active imagination. She smiled at the memory of Jacob and Christian playing pirates. Her traitorous mind switched to the feeling of his arms about her waist as he pulled her to his side to keep her from plunging into the icy river. She'd shivered in the security of his arms—and not from fear or cold.

She was weak. As weak as her birth mother must have been being unmarried and with child. Jacob was a known libertine. He'd been a gentleman in her presence, but to accept the advances of an innocent like Phoebe was not the act of a nobleman. It was even low for a rogue, who'd usually steer clear of innocents, if only out of fear of being forced to the altar.

Oh, why had Emily allowed Phoebe to persuade her to continue the painting sessions? How would she be able to look at him?

Horses' hooves clopped in the distance, drawing nearer. Her fingers tightened on one of the paintbrushes she laid out. Phoebe was bound to come parading down the lane in her phaeton or Jacob in his landau any moment now. Emily's stomach churned, and her palms perspired. All morning, the unsettling feeling of being a participant in something God would frown upon slithered through her conscience.

Lord, forgive me.

She opened her airtight earthenware and spread out her paints by color. The bladder of cadmium yellow was getting low. She must ask the apothecary to send for more. She no longer dared go to London to replenish her supply from the colorman's shop. In the meantime, she'd have to use the color sparingly or mix the pigment with walnut oil herself, which was toilsome, messy work.

Mrs. Hayes knocked on the door and popped her head in. "Lord Jacob Warren has arrived, miss."

Emily wiped her palms down her durable nankeen dress and followed Mrs. Hayes to the front entry.

God, give me strength.

Lord Warren reclined in a low-back chair in the drawing room and held a carved wooden horse in his hands. He rose as she entered.

She stared at the knot in his cravat. "Good morning, my lord."

"Miss Thompson, you look lovely this morning."

Emily's jaw clenched. Did he think his flattery would work on her? Heaven forbid. She fanned out her sturdy painting frock. "I daresay you should have your eyes checked."

"Your dress is merely an adornment." He widened his stance, and a determined smile quirked one side of his mouth. The man seemed to enjoy a challenge. "I was speaking of the glow about you. The freshness of your face."

"You are overly kind. I'm certain London's ladies do so enjoy your flattering tongue."

"Might you have problems accepting a compliment?"

Emily changed the subject. "That's a finely carved steed."

He eyed the wooden piece. "I'm afraid this one is for Christian, but if I'd had known you'd admire it, I'd have purchased two."

Her breath stopped at the boldness of his statement. He, too, appeared surprised by his words, for his gaze dropped, and he ran a hand across the back of his neck.

"Are you aware of the flummery that spills from your lips?"

He shrugged. "Sometimes my mouth gets ahead of me." He shifted the horse in his hands. "Is Master Christian around?"

"Indeed, but not for long. Papa plans to bring him on his rounds today. The elderly of our parish enjoy Christian's lively spirit."

"He is energetic." Jacob broke into a wide grin, his affection for the boy evident. "I found this in a store window." He handed the toy to Emily. "I thought he'd enjoy it."

"How thoughtful of you. Christian will be delighted." The last thing she wanted was for her impressionable younger brother to idolize the likes of Lord Warren. She set the wooden horse aside.

He strolled to the doorway, leaned into the foyer, and called up the stairs in a teasing, boisterous voice. "And where is Master Christian?"

As if waiting for a cue, Christian flung open the other entrance to the parlor, beyond the sight of Lord Warren in the hall, and sped across the room. He swung around Emily and hid behind her skirts.

Jacob used exaggerated footfalls to stomp through the hall as if going in the other direction toward Papa's study. He held a finger to his lips and tiptoed back toward Emily, then snatched the giggling boy from behind her.

Christian reached for her. "Help! Lord Jacob's turned into a green ogre."

"Green. I never said I was green." He ticked Christian's stomach. "I'm a blue ogre."

"Help!" Christian giggled. "They're the worst kind."

Absolutely the worst kind.

Mama opened the door and poked her head inside. "What in heaven's name is going on? Oh." She clasped her hands. "Good afternoon, my lord. Here for a painting session?"

He set Christian down and bowed to Mama. "We have an early sitting to catch the light."

"I'm delighted you're here." She turned her attention to Emily. "Emily, can you watch Christian until your father leaves? He'll wear Papa out before his day begins. This little ruffian has been driving Mrs. Hayes to distraction, and we're in the middle of canning preserves."

Jacob slung Christian over his shoulder like a bundle of sticks. "I might be of assistance."

"Do be careful." Emily held her hands out to catch him if Jacob's grip slipped. "He's only five."

"This shall only take a moment." Jacob wiggled his brows before opening the front door and carrying Christian outside.

Emily froze at the door, which closed in front of her. From inside the house, she followed them from window to window until she reached the salon.

Jacob chased Christian around the grounds, matching smiles gracing their faces. She had to admit, for a rogue, he was great with children.

She finished arranging her paints, only stopping to peer outside when she heard Christian's peals of laughter.

Papa strode down the back stairs and straightened his cravat. "Christian, time to go!"

Emily and Mama met him in the hall to bid him farewell.

Papa kissed each of their cheeks before opening the front door.

Christian hung like a monkey off Lord Warren's back in the front yard.

"Good morning, Lord Warren," Papa said. "I didn't realize you were here."

"Morning, Mr. Thompson." He slid Christian to the ground. "I had hoped to expel some of Christian's energy, but he has unfathomable reserves."

"That is the truth." Papa chuckled. "Have a blessed day. Come along, son."

Jacob reentered the house, a healthy glow added to his face from the exertion. He sat on the tufted sofa in the drawing room.

She stood in the doorway to the foyer and lowered her gaze. "We can begin even though Phoebe hasn't arrived yet."

"One moment, please." He gestured for her to sit in a nearby chair. "I'm glad you allowed the sessions to continue. I promise you, I did nothing untoward with Miss Dorsham. I hope you believe me."

A dalliance with an innocent wasn't untoward? The man

certainly held a deranged sense of morals. Emily gritted her teeth and stared at the hem of her dress.

"I commend you for defending Miss Dorsham the way you did. You are a true friend."

Her stomach twisted.

"Emily." He whispered her name in much the same way a gentle spring breeze ruffled her bonnet strings.

His gaze locked on hers, and she instantly regretted looking up. Jacob searched her eyes as if seeking truth. He was the same man who played pirate with Christian, who'd allowed Christian to steer his team of horses, who'd shared with Emily about his family.

How could this man have had a tryst with her friend?

She hoped he couldn't read the cluster of emotions warring inside.

He slid to the end of the sofa closest to her chair, and his scent of citrus and spice encircled her, enticing her to fill her lungs.

"Devotion and loyalty are admirable qualities." He leaned closer and his shirt tightened.

His nearness and sheer maleness left her dizzy, until the icy fingers of self-loathing penetrated her brain, chasing away such thoughts. How could she feel anything for an unspeakable cad?

"I've had time to realize my part in what transpired with Miss Dorsham. I shall be more careful not to mislead her in the future."

"You do not have any sentiments toward Miss Dorsham?" Her voice sounded tight, stretched taut like her canvases.

"She is a lovely woman, but..." He shook his head. "To be honest, in the past, I might have flirted, exchanging witty banter out of sport." Regret hung heavy in his voice. "I used to be reckless—the third son who could push the boundaries. It became a game in which I held all the cards. I knew when to bluff, when to throw more into the pot, and when to fold." He sighed. "But now, I no longer enjoy the game. I'm ashamed I ever wanted to play. And in Miss Dorsham's case, it's time to fold before the hand is even dealt, because she isn't the right person for me."

The hand hadn't been dealt? What did he mean?

His gaze held hers steady. "I've set my sights on another."

Another? His intense stare heated her cheeks. *Her?* Where was Phoebe?

Phoebe was the one who was supposed to be appealing to Jacob, not her.

Emily folded her hands as she'd seen Mama often do to maintain her calm demeanor, hoping to quell the panic shaking inside her.

"If she'll have me."

The intensity in Jacob's gaze sent Emily's pulse at a frenzied pace. "Perhaps you do not know the goodness of Phoebe's heart."

"I know enough to sit out this game."

"But—" *But what?*

A knock sounded at the front door, and Mrs. Hayes opened it.

A moment later, Phoebe swept into the foyer, her blond curls piled on the crown of her head.

Praise God. Emily jumped up to greet her friend, leaving Jacob in the drawing room.

Far too much creamy white skin showed above Phoebe's low-cut bodice, and her skirts, dampened in the modish style, clung to her curvaceous figure. Miss Neves shadowed her, and Phoebe handed her chaperone her bonnet and shrugged out of her pelisse.

"Good morning. I was determined to be early, yet Lord Warren has beaten me here."

Emily whispered, "How are you feeling this morning?"

"Quite lovely." Phoebe blinked. "Why are you whispering?"

Emily kept her voice low and glanced in Miss Neves's direction, but the chaperone progressed down the hall, passing Mrs. Hayes Pheobe's hat and pelisse. "Because of...you know..."

Phoebe's face remained blank.

"You still feel the same?" She continued to whisper. "Nothing different? No queasiness?" How could Phoebe not understand what she was talking about? Phoebe's condition had been all Emily could think about since their conversation a week ago.

When Phoebe spied Jacob standing in the drawing room, her hand flew to her breast, reminding Emily of the paintings she'd seen of the goddess Aphrodite. "Good morning, my lord."

Jacob's demeanor turned formal, and he nodded his greeting and joined them in the foyer. "Shall we get started?"

Emily led them down the hall to the salon.

Mama met them near the kitchen. "Phoebe, please come with me for a moment. I have a poultice for your mother. I'd like to explain how it should be applied for the aches in her joints."

Phoebe's gaze flittered to Jacob, but she replied through tight lips, "Of course." She followed Mama toward the kitchen and peered back over her shoulder at Lord Warren with a longing look.

In the salon, Emily pointed to where he should stand and prepared her palette while Jacob resumed a similar position to before. She stared at the array of colors, and a rush of excitement tingled her fingers. It might be odd that she always held this same thrill, but the awe of creative potential and the joy of making an image out of blobs of color never diminished. God must have felt the same when he created the earth and heavens.

"You're smiling." Jacob quirked a brow at her, looking exactly like the sketched lines of his portrait, with that mischievous glint and the confident turn of his lips.

"Am I?"

"Indeed."

"I enjoy painting, creating something out of nothing. Twist your torso a bit to the left." Emily held her hands up as if positioning him even though he stood across the room. "And turn your right toe out just a tad."

Jacob adjusted accordingly.

"Perfect. Don't move."

"Have I told you I've been visiting the tenants to introduce myself?"

"And how is that progressing?"

"Quite well, I must say." The corner of his mouth turned up, and his eyes took on a faraway look.

Emily focused on painting his mouth first and then his nose and eyes. She drew a line for the divide of his lips. One end curved up a tad more than the other.

"I never thought engaging and assisting with their needs could be so fulfilling." He raised his brows.

"Don't move." She pointed the paintbrush at him.

"Terribly sorry." He lowered his brows. "I know it would horrify Miss Dorsham, but so far, I've helped build a chicken coop, thatch a roof, and mend a fence." He smiled with his eyes. "The first went smoother than the last."

Emily added the small crease that divided his bottom lip left from right. Why did that little line intrigue her so much?

"I've been warned about the perils of manual labor. Maybe Father's right. Maybe those of the upper crust know better. A gentleman doesn't use his hands, but they have to serve more purpose than guiding a dance partner or holding a hand of cards. I'm expected to lead a frivolous life. I do not have the weight and responsibilities of my older brother, yet I am a man of means. In London, I felt restless, but here, I feel... I don't know. Settled?"

"Useful?"

"Indeed." He grunted. "As though I'm contributing to something greater. Helping things improve."

"Did you dislike your life in London?"

"No, but I grew up faster than most, being a younger brother. I was allowed into White's gentleman's club at a young age because I followed my brothers, and they didn't want to walk me back. I got away with getting in underage because I was tall and no one bothered to complain. Plus, the club's chairman, a friend of my father, had witnessed his temper when Father dipped too deep in his cups. The man pitied me. He'd taught me to gamble, drink, shoot pistols, and woo a lady by the age four and ten."

Emily's jaw clenched, and her gaze flicked from the canvas, but Jacob's eyes held a distant look. How could he speak so liberally? Was he proud of his past? Didn't he fear judgment?

"Eventually, it grew tiresome, but I still sought the same rush of excitement." He cleared his throat and peered at her. "I shouldn't be telling you any of this."

"You do so because you know I can sympathize with not belong—" She coughed. He knew nothing of her illegitimacy. "Because of our not being from Sylvanwood originally, of course."

His eyes tinged with compassion. "I do not know how you understand me so well, but it's true."

Heat rose into her cheeks. "It's normal to idolize your older brothers, but eventually, you have to find your own way. Is that what happened?"

He shrugged. "My brothers were more cautious. I dove in with the fast set. At first, it was thrilling. Their soirées were wilder, more outlandish—even outright salacious. I went along with their antics, but I never felt I belonged. Something didn't sit right with me. I felt like an unwilling participant in a den of fools. Yet I continued to attend their parties because I didn't quite fit in elsewhere."

He shrugged. "The fact that my behavior irritated Robert kept me accepting their invites longer than necessary. Otherwise, I'd probably have sought other pursuits sooner, such as world travel, but even my desire for that has changed."

"Do you and your brother not get along?" Emily added a finishing highlight to his bottom lip before moving to his nose.

"Because we try to irritate each other?" He chuckled. "It's the way we show our love for each other." His gaze grew distant. "I cannot stay in Sylvanwood for forever. Brownstone Hall is my brother's holding." He released a sigh. "But I don't yet desire to return to the city. Here I feel...fresh. New...and needed."

"Because of your accomplishments."

His eyes danced with excitement. "Precisely. Maybe God is revealing His plan for me."

"I must warn you." She peered at the paint swirled on her pallet. "Once you've tasted purpose, you won't be satisfied with merely living."

A grin passed over his features. "I believe you're right. In London, I was existing. Following orders. Doing what I was told. Here, I have a mission to restore Brownstone Hall and its surrounding land, which includes helping its tenants."

"You don't mind that it's not your holding?"

His gaze shifted upward while he considered his answer. "Not entirely. It's something I can do, and do well, to honor my brother for bailing me out of scrapes and to aid Aunt Louisa, who's undergone grave misfortune."

He'd had a lot of past vices, but it seemed he desired to change. She admired his loyalty to his brother and his candor. If she hadn't known what he'd done to Phoebe, she'd believe he was a man of good character.

"I brought the perfect book." Phoebe swept into the room, holding the volume high.

Jacob's smile faded.

She floated over to the settee, sat, and flipped open the

cover. "*Childe Harold's Pilgrimage* by Lord Byron. I heard his prose is sensational, and I've desired to learn why." She looked up. "Have you read it, Lord Warren?"

"I have not." His tone turned formal. "Although, I've heard rumors it resembles his biography, depicting a lamenting libertine."

Emily coughed. How ironic.

Phoebe spread her skirts about her. "Have you met Lord Byron?"

"We run in the same circles." Jacob's brows flicked into a fleeting arch. He glanced at Emily as if awaiting reprimand for moving, but she'd switched to painting his hairline. "We've amused each other with battles of wit, but Byron's remarks slice a bit too deep. It's hard to listen to him reduce grown men to tears."

"Oh." A confused expression passed over Phoebe's face, but she blinked and moved to another topic. "I heard women swoon in his presence."

"Everyone but Lady Annabelle Milbanke, with whom he fancies himself in love, but only because he believes she can redeem his blackened soul."

"I've also heard he's killed a man," Phoebe whispered.

"You keep company with a womanizing murderer?" Emily blurted the words, unable to keep the shock from her voice.

"One reason I have escaped to Sylvanwood, in hopes of lightening my darkened reputation."

Was that why he was here, for a second chance? Did he regret his decisions? Did he lament his liaison with Phoebe? Was that why he was acting stiffly toward her friend? "Papa always quotes First Corinthians. 'Bad company corrupts good character.'"

Phoebe harrumphed. "Let's not get into that. It's time to read." She reclined on the settee and read with a dramatic flair as though performing for a crowd.

Peace settled over Emily as she thinned her paint to shape Jacob's eyes. His spiky lashes broke the line and added to the spark of mischief. She mixed blues to add depth to the celadon shade she'd painted earlier and create that glint she'd often witnessed in his eyes. Should she make them the same blue as the clear afternoon sky, as they'd appeared when she pulled him from the creek bed? Or should she paint his eyes with a tinge of aqua blue, like the color of a Robin Redbreast's eggs that his eyes turned whenever he teased her?

The latter. She added the dark depths of his pupils with the end of her brush and then dabbed the white of the reflected light with the tip. A small dot of pink for the inside corner of each eye, and she added a shadow to the very outside corners as if he held back a smile.

Emily had painted many portraits for elite families in Sylvanwood and surrounding towns. Usually, the subjects focused on an object or out a window. Jacob, however, regarded her as she studied him. Every time her gaze lifted from the canvas, his was on her. She tried to focus on the shape of his eyes and lips, but her stomach fluttered, and her cheeks warmed as their gazes locked.

The slight curve of his mouth lifted higher on one side, and he glanced at Phoebe before his lips parted to reveal a row of straight white teeth.

Emily peeked over her shoulder at Phoebe, who now lay on her side across the settee, a rolling landscape of feminine curves. Her elbow propped her head as her other hand turned the pages. Gone was the dramatic flair. Now she seemed fully absorbed in the heady words of Byron.

"The parted bosom clings to wonted home,
If aught that kindred cheer and welcome hearth;
He that is lonely hither let him roam,
And gaze complacent on congenial earth."

Heavens! What was Phoebe thinking, choosing that book?

She was playing a dangerous game. Emily had heard Lord Byron's writing was exotic, but she'd never imagined a debauched, sullen protagonist. Occasionally, Phoebe paused and lifted her thick lashes, likely to ensure she'd captured Jacob's attention. Didn't she know this was how she wound up in her dilemma?

Emily knew little about wooing a man, but if her friend wanted to lure him into marriage, this was not the way.

Jacob smiled with an amused twist of the lips like one would use to avoid disappointing a child. He met Emily's gaze, and something flashed in their depths. Laughter? Oh, goodness. She wanted to shake Phoebe and tell her she was going about this all wrong. And she would as soon as she had a moment alone with her.

She focused on the canvas. Blue eyes stared back at her. His likeness was taking shape. She feathered his brows with tiny brushstrokes, making sure to turn the ends down, and then checked the real Jacob's eyebrows to ensure her accuracy.

The way he looked at her transported her back to the wooden bridge, where he'd held her in his strong arms to keep her from falling into the river. How was it that the cool blue of his eyes always appeared so warm?

It felt as though he saw past her defenses to her real self, not the cast-off daughter of some noble, or the vicar's adopted daughter, or a woman with secrets. He saw her hidden wit and understood her passion for creating. They had led different lives, but he understood how it felt to not truly fit in.

He certainly was handsome. No wonder women fawned over him and the society papers gossiped about his every attendance, especially with that boyish grin. And that enticing crease in his bottom lip. How would it feel pressed against hers?

God forgive me. What was she thinking? She closed her eyes and gave herself a mental shake. The man was off-limits. Not only because her dearest friend had set her cap for him but also because he was worldly, and she was not.

She kept her eyes closed until her heart settled back into a slow and steady rhythm. Focus on the task at hand.

Otherwise her vulnerable heart would be broken.

Phoebe sat up and placed the book face down on the settee beside her. She fanned herself with her hand. "The room has become a tad warm. Shall I ring for refreshments?"

At least Emily wasn't the only one who felt warm. "Don't get up. I've got it." She ensured her fingers were free of paint before tugging the bellpull. "I could stand a bit of refreshment, and I'm certain Lord Warren could stretch his legs."

Jacob stepped toward her. "I'd like to see the progress."

"It's not finished yet." Emily waved him off, but he walked around her and faced the canvas.

His brows rose. "It is coming along nicely. You've truly captured my face. It's as if I'm looking in a mirror. There's even an essence there."

Emily caught a whiff of lemongrass and inhaled his spicy citrus aroma. The scent suited him. Exotic yet familiar with the promise of excitement.

The crease between his brows deepened. "I appear as if I'm about to smile. Look how my mouth turns up on one side."

Phoebe squeezed in between Emily and Jacob. "You are."

Emily stepped aside so the paint on her hands wouldn't get on Phoebe's muslin day dress.

Phoebe lifted gloved fingers to her lips. "That's unheard of. Maybe for a woman, but men do not smile. At least not in portraits."

"I can fix it." Emily reached for her brush. "I merely paint what I see. You are rarely serious."

He touched her shoulder, and she stilled. The heat of his light grip burned through her sturdy apron and gown. She willed Mrs. Hayes to hurry with the refreshments before she caught fire.

A smile, like the one in the painting, blossomed on his lips and spread into a full-blown grin. "It's perfect. It shall incite my brother all the more, being taunted by my provoking smile." He turned his head to face Emily. "Outstanding."

She dropped her gaze to the floor, hoping he didn't notice the heat in her cheeks. She'd heard plenty of criticism and praise in the past. Why did this man's words affect her so?

"Phoebe." Time to change the subject to Phoebe's attributes. "I've been dying to hear about your party and gowns for London's season." Emily couldn't quite make herself meet Jacob's eyes, so she stared at his chin. "She has a magnificent flair for fashion."

Phoebe flounced back to the settee and patted the cushion beside her. "Please, Lord Warren, have a seat. Your legs must be tired from standing so long."

His gaze lingered on the painting a tad longer before he moved to sit.

"Necklines have lowered substantially." Phoebe fanned her gloved fingers across her chest, highlighting the cleft barely hidden behind the folds of white muslin. "Almost to the point of immodesty."

Emily paused in blending her next color, and her gaze flickered to Miss Neves. The woman merely pulled loop after loop through her embroidery. What sort of chaperone was she?

"Waistlines have also lowered a few inches for a more fitted look." Phoebe's hands slid from under her bosom down her sides and rested at her waist.

Jacob's Adam's apple bobbed, and he shifted in his seat. She tried to warn Phoebe with a quick head shake, but her friend ignored her.

"Men's fashion has also taken a turn." Jacob cleared his

throat. "I have it on Beau Brummel's word that we will see more trousers worn with Hessians or half boots."

Emily relaxed, grateful he'd taken control of the conversation.

"Brims are becoming thinner," he said, "and Brummel wears a beaver hat with the top slightly curved."

"You don't say." Phoebe pulled her fan out of her reticule and toyed with it in front of Jacob, slowly opening then folding it shut.

Emily may not have been to court or had much knowledge of flirting, but Phoebe had read her enough gossip columns to understand the meaning behind the gesture.

Kiss me.

Phoebe issued Emily a hard stare that clearly said, *leave us.*

Emily hesitated.

"I wonder what's taking the tea so long?" Phoebe snapped her fan shut. "Might you run and check, Em?"

As much as Phoebe wanted her to leave, Jacob gave Emily a don't-do-it glare.

"Oh, and look." Phoebe pointed at the brushes. "Your black brush has touched the blue. Perhaps you should wash one."

Emily didn't see a spot of black but took the brush and excused herself. She hurried to the kitchen to ease the tension building in her shoulders. How did Phoebe expect her to sing her friend's praises when she acted like a brazen light-skirt?

Why did her heart have to race every time her gaze locked with Jacob's?

Lord, what am I to do about these feelings?

Mrs. Hayes looked up from readying the tea tray. The lines in her forehead deepened. "What's a matter, luv?"

She held up the brush. "I need to clean a brush."

Mrs. Hayes took the brush from her fingers. "I'll see to that, and tea will be ready in a wee bit. Don't you fret." She rested her other hand on her hip. "His lordship is a polite young man, and kind too. Look at the way he is with Christian." She lowered her voice. "He deserves better than Miss Dorsham."

It wasn't like the housekeeper to be so outspoken. "They are of a similar class, whereas I'm—"

"You're a child of God. He created ye special, and God doesn't make mistakes."

Emily had said those exact words to Christian. She believed them for Christian. Why didn't she believe them for herself?

"It's time for Miss Dorsham to step aside. She's off to London in a few weeks." She pointed at Emily with the dirty brush. "Get back in there and rescue that poor man. The Good Lord knows he needs it." Mrs. Hayes scooted Emily from the kitchen and back into the salon.

When she arrived, Jacob was standing on the opposite side of the room, wielding the book of poetry like a shield. He gave Emily a wide-eyed, what-took-you-so-long stare while Phoebe hit her with a why-did-you-rush-back glare.

Emily could not win in this situation, so she sought refuge in front of her canvas to think.

Mrs. Hayes believed Emily should set her cap for Jacob? It was out of the question. If he'd ruined Phoebe, she wanted nothing to do with the rake. He should do the right thing and marry her whether or not he enjoyed her company.

But Jacob had been acting more like a gentleman than a rogue. It was Phoebe who acted like a wanton woman.

Emily's thoughts whirled. She needed to stall to sort things out. "Have you told Phoebe of your latest progress at Brownstone Hall? She has an eye for fabrics."

CHAPTER 13

*M*iss Dorsham's gloved fingers hooked onto Jacob's upper arm with a tight squeeze. "When I first entered the hall, I noticed the draperies were a bit outdated. Switching to a gold damask print would revive the room, bring out the gilded trim, and give the impression of wealth."

"Because nothing says riches like gold curtains." Jacob waited for her to laugh or smile.

Nothing.

She didn't understand his humor.

Unlike Emily, who smiled as she soaked her brushes in mineral spirits.

Miss Dorsham gasped as if inspiration struck. "And in the dining room, a blue brocade or velvet would look lovely."

Jacob tried to fashion his attention on Miss Dorsham, but she rambled on about fabrics and trims until his eyes started to cross.

The housekeeper bearing a tea tray rescued him.

Miss Dorsham steeped the tea in Emily's stead, pouring a cup for him, Emily, and herself. "How do you like it?"

"Black."

A sultry smile returned to her lips, followed by a giggle. "Of course."

He hadn't meant to infer his reputation nor to be funny. He just wanted his tea black.

Miss Dorsham passed a cup to Emily. Jacob hoped she would join them, but she remained in front of the canvas and painted the background.

Miss Dorsham sat beside him so close that their arms touched.

He scooted away.

When she inched closer, he stood and selected a low-backed chair.

Miss Dorsham blinked, apparently shocked her machinations weren't working on him. But she recovered quickly. "Are you enjoying my reading?"

"You have a flare for the dramatic." He thought he heard Emily snort, but he couldn't be certain.

"I do hope I've helped to take your mind off the weariness of posing."

"The time has flown."

Miss Dorsham sipped her tea, peering at him over the rim. "Are you enjoying Lord Byron's prose?" She shifted to the edge of her seat until their knees brushed. "The man has a beautiful way of expressing the longings of the human heart."

And other areas. "Lord Byron appreciates the human condition and all of its follies." Jacob lifted his glass and gulped the liquid, burning his mouth and leaving a warm path to his stomach.

Miss Dorsham fluffed her skirt, brushing his breeches with her pinkie.

He shifted and crossed one leg over the other, out of her reach. His patience with her unsubtle tactics long since had waned. He had half a mind to give her chaperone a lecture on her responsibilities, but the dozing woman released a snore.

"His prose seems to churn up something from deep within. Don't you think?" She leaned forward, and Jacob averted his gaze. "Especially in 'She Walks with Beauty,' he describes the woman in such an alluring and mysterious way."

"I'm not sure *alluring* is the right adjective. Byron uses the words *calm* and *grace* to describe her." He pressed against the chair's backrest, resisting the urge to rub his temples from a tension ache. "And I know I heard 'innocent' and 'serenely sweet.'"

"But a woman can be both serenely sweet and mysteriously alluring." She stood, running her fingers up his arm, and hovered her lips to his ear. "I can be both," she whispered.

Emily glanced in their direction. If she thought it odd that he was tilting the chair onto two legs to lean back from Miss Dorsham, she didn't comment.

"Ahem." Jacob pressed Miss Dorsham's shoulder away and stood. The chair landed in place. "Are you ready to begin again?"

"If you are," Emily said.

He resumed his position, Miss Dorsham her reading, and Emily her painting.

She studied him, but no matter how hard he tried to catch her eye, she only seemed to peer through him.

Miss Dorsham droned on, and Jacob shifted his weight shaking, the stiffness out of his leg.

"Do you need another break?" Emily asked.

He shook his head. Why did she entice him so? Was it because she posed a challenge? Compared to Miss Dorsham, who placed her cards all on the table, Emily was more like the woman Lord Bryon described. Emily walked in beauty. She epitomized innocent grace, calm eloquence, and sweet serenity.

And yes, that led to mysterious allure. Yet the woman Byron described walked in the darkness of night. Emily did not appear to be deceptive, but Jacob had been lured by such beauty before—and had his heart ripped out.

Women were a distraction, and these two ladies were doing a bang-up job keeping him from his goal. He was here for Christian. He was here to get to know his son and be part of his life. But would learning of his father be beneficial for Christian? Or was the life of a vicar's youngest son better than the life as the son of a reformed libertine?

He needed more intelligence for an informed decision. Perhaps he could secretly interview the family, determine the available future opportunities for Christian, and sort out the facts. He'd start with Emily.

"Tell me, Miss Thompson..."

Miss Dorsham stopped reading with a huff.

Let her be annoyed. He was done with her antics. Jacob directed his question at Emily. "If your eldest brother is to take over the vicarage, what is in store for young Christian? Will he begin apprenticing soon?"

Emily snorted. "I think not. He's five."

"But in a few years, will he?"

"It depends."

"On what?"

She put down her brush. "Maybe we should end our session for the day. The light has shifted."

"Agreed." Miss Dorsham tossed the book on the chair and roused her sleepy chaperone. "Lord Warren, would you be so kind as to see me out?"

Jacob eyed Emily. He wanted to finish the conversation, yet it would be rude to ignore Miss Dorsham. "Of course." He raised his elbow for her to hold but addressed Emily. "The painting's progress is coming along nicely. How many more sittings are necessary?"

"Two, perhaps three."

Miss Dorsham gasped. "That is all?"

"My brother built a tailor's dummy as a model for the clothing. I only needed Lord Warren for his facial features."

"And here I thought I was more than a pretty face."

Emily pressed the back of her hand to her mouth to smother a chuckle.

"But, of course, the real model is preferred?" Miss Dorsham's fingers tightened on his arm.

"Yes, but I must honor Lord Warren's time. I'm certain he has much to do with restoring Brownstone Hall."

Miss Dorsham's lips thinned, and she glared at her friend.

"I appreciate your thoughtfulness." Jacob bowed his head. "Good day, Miss Thompson."

"Good day, Lord Warren, Phoebe."

Miss Dorsham issued her the barest of nods before turning toward the door. Jacob led her from the room, mindful of his jacket, neatly folded over the arm of a chair.

~

*E*mily washed her brushes and put away her paints. The house seemed quiet now. Mrs. Hayes added fuel to the hearth in the kitchen, and Mama sat at the table with paper and quill in hand.

Returning to the salon for one last assessment of the painting, Emily spied Jacob's jacket draped over the settee arm. She grabbed it and dashed to the front door. "Lord Warren?"

The drive was empty, with no sign of either Phoebe or Jacob. His curricle was parked near the barn. He couldn't have left with Phoebe. Her phaeton only seated two.

She strode back into the house, searching the main rooms for any sign of his lordship.

Mama and Mrs. Hayes sat in the kitchen going over the week's meal plan.

"It's the strangest thing." Emily patted the jacket draped over her arm. "Lord Warren's carriage is here, but he is not."

"I saw him walking with Samuel to the east pasture."

Emily trooped out the back door. Rounding the corner, she spied two men struggling to insert a fence crossbeam into a post and recognized Jacob's profile. The white shirt she'd painted moments before was matted with sweat and clung to his broad shoulders.

A lord of the Quality would never be caught toiling in manual labor, yet he guided the post while Samuel lifted the back.

They were both concentrating and didn't see her approach.

"I've got it. Now lift." Jacob clenched his teeth as they strained to direct the stubborn beam.

"Very well, now, push." Jacob glanced up and smiled when he saw her.

Samuel pushed, but Jacob didn't extract his hand in time.

"Blast." He yanked it away and clasped his fingers in his other hand.

Emily rushed forward. "Lord Warren."

His face blanched.

Samuel dropped the cross beam. "Are you all right?"

Emily hopped over the unfinished fence and hurried to Jacob. She reached for his hands. "Is it broken?"

He offered the barest shake of his head.

Emily nodded at the fencepost. "Is there a nail in the beam?"

Samuel examined it. "Indeed, it's rusty and sticking out a bit."

"Is it bleeding?"

His pale face conveyed the answer.

"Let me take a look." She gently pulled his hands toward her. "I suggest you look away."

He did, and she pried his other hand off, leaning closer to inspect. A gash tracked along the outside of his pinky finger. Blood oozed, running down his hand and dripping off before it reached his wrist.

Jacob stiffened. His gaze snapped back to her with a glazed-over, frantic expression, his face tinging so pale he almost appeared green.

"Lord Warren? Are you all right?" Samuel asked.

His eyes rolled back in his head, and he toppled backward into the grass like fallen timber.

Emily dropped to his side. She patted his cheeks. "Jacob, wake up." She shook his shoulders.

When he didn't rouse, she twisted around to peer at Samuel. "Get Mama. Tell her to bring smelling salts and a bandage."

"What happened? I've never seen a man felled by a cut to the hand."

"He can't stomach the sight of blood."

"How do you know—?" Samuel cut off his words.

It *was* a rather intimate thing to know of someone. Would Samuel draw conclusions if she didn't clarify? "He told me it's why he didn't join his majesty's army." Why must she always explain herself? "Now go. Hurry."

He dashed off toward the house.

She placed her hand on Jacob's chest. It rose and fell in rhythm.

Praise God.

The countryside grew silent except for the sheep bleating in the distant field. Once again, she leaned over his sprawled body.

"Why do you continue to put me in these situations?" She pulled a handkerchief out of his coat pocket, still draped over her arm, and tied it over his oozing hand. "I have fought to maintain a spotless reputation to repair the damage my mother caused, but since you arrived, everything has gone awry."

A breeze waved the grass, and a lock of hair fell across his forehead. In rest, he looked boyish, reminding her of Christian. She had the urge to ruffle his hair as she would that of her younger brother. Instead, she brushed the fallen lock aside with her fingertips and traced his contoured hairline over his cheekbone, around the curve of his jaw, and to the square of his chin.

"And why do you make my heart feel like the arrival of spring?" she whispered.

A door slammed, and Mama and Samuel ran toward her.

Emily rose.

"My word." Mama's eyes widened as she saw him. Her gaze raked over Jacob, her face a mask of concern. "I brought the box. Here."

Emily uncapped the bottle of hartshorn and waved it below his nose.

Jacob gasped, and his eyes sprung open. "Egad! What's that awful smell?"

Emily rested back on her haunches.

Mama and Samuel kneeled on his other side, peering down at his lordship.

"What is going on here?" Jacob struggled to sit up.

Samuel put a hand under Jacob's arm and pulled him to a seated position.

Jacob saw the handkerchief tied around his hand and glanced away.

"You fainted," Emily said.

"I did nothing of the sort." Jacob's chin jerked back. "Only women swoon."

Men. Emily snorted. "I beg your pardon." She exaggerated

her tone. "Rather, when you saw the blood on your hand, your body decided it was time for an expedient nap."

His mouth broke into a mischievous smile. "I bring out your satirical side."

She stuffed the cap back on the bottle.

"My lord." Mama dusted a blade of grass off his shoulder and rose. "Let's get you back to the house so we can tend to your injury."

"You may lean on me." Samuel aided Jacob to stand and kept a firm grip on his arm.

"Truly, I'm fine." Jacob waved him off.

Samuel helped Mama rise instead.

Jacob held up his elbow. "Here, Miss Thompson, allow me to escort you."

She tucked her hand in the crook of his arm, and they strolled toward the house. After a few steps, his weight shifted, and he leaned heavily on her instead of vice versa. Emily worked to brace his weight. No one seemed to notice his woozy behavior, and they plodded through the walled-in rose garden and stone patio. Mrs. Hayes opened the paned glass door into the back parlor.

"I'll have the physician summoned right away," Mrs. Hayes said as they passed, then scurried to fluff the pillows on the settee.

"No need to fuss." Jacob sat on the chair and gestured Emily to the settee. "I'm confident that Miss Thompson has sufficiently seen to my wound."

"My apologies for interrupting your task," Jacob said to Samuel.

"Think nothing of it." Samuel stepped forward, his hat between his hands. "The groom will help me when he returns from town."

"Make sure you warn him about the nail."

"I'm going to wheedle it out right now." He bowed and left.

Emily pulled Jacob's hand onto her knee and lifted the edge of the cloth. "The cut needs a good cleaning and to be re-bandaged."

"You're quite knowledgeable about these things. It must be from living with two brothers. I'm in good hands."

Mama passed her the box of bandages. "Let me grab the spirits." She left the room.

Jacob's brows rose. "Are you in need of courage?"

"Heavens, no. I do not partake. Mama swears that a little poured on the wound aids in preventing infection. She says it's the only thing spirits are good for."

"Well, there are others, but it usually ends with a pounding headache."

Mama returned with a bottle of gin.

Mama slid a footstool in front of Jacob and sat. "Under the circumstances, would you care for a glass?"

Jacob peered at the bottle for a long moment but shook his head. "It's a minor cut. Nothing to be worried about."

"You never know about these things. One can't be too careful." Mama patted his good hand. "And do not feel bad. I'm also squeamish. The sight of blood makes me lightheaded."

Emily picked at the handkerchief's knot and murmured under her breath. "Yet only one of you faints."

Jacob shot her a warning glare before addressing her mama. "I don't want you swooning on my account, but your kindness does me good."

Emily pulled out a clean bandage.

"Your daughter was quick to come to my aid. You've done a fine job raising a family."

Mama blushed. *Blushed!*

He wiggled his eyebrows at Emily. "Since it's on the under-side of my hand, let me turn the chair." He scooted the seat to face Mama, his back to Emily. "Now, I can divert your attention away from the fiendish blood." He held his wounded hand back for Emily to bandage.

"You are too kind." Mama's voice flowed like sweet syrup.

His maneuver was genius. It offered Emily a better angle, prevented Jacob from seeing the wound, and made him appear like a gentleman, as if he'd done it on account of Mama. Intelligence, charm, and wit—a lethal combination for innocent women. Yet humbly felled by the sight of blood.

God had a grand sense of humor.

Emily twisted the lid off the gin. The wound was long but not too deep. She held the old dressing under his hand to catch runaway drops.

"This may sting a bit." She fought to keep the smile out of her tone. It would burn something fierce. She poured the liquor into the cut.

He winced and sucked in a breath, jerking his hand.

Emily held it firmly. Men were babies about such things. Her brothers also yelped at the sting, yet Mama said women were hushed for screaming during childbirth.

"Oh, Lord Warren, you are very brave," Mama said. "I assure you, Emily is wise in these ministrations. You must return in a couple of days for her to look at it. She'll want to ensure it's healing properly."

Emily knotted the bandage and set aside the one stained with his blood to be laundered. "All finished."

Jacob turned around.

"Emily," Mama said, rising, "would you be so kind as to see Lord Warren to the door?"

"Certainly."

Mama's gaze bounced between them before she smiled and left the room.

Was she still playing matchmaker? Had she not heard the rumors of his reputation in London? Or was she practicing *do not judge lest ye be judged*?

"After you." Jacob gestured with his hand. As she passed, he said, "Thank you for your assistance back there. Brilliant timing for your arrival since no one else was aware of my... ur...condition."

"You gave Mama quite a start." She strolled down the hall with Jacob behind her. "She doesn't fuss over her sons as much as she did you."

"She cares for each of you dearly. It shows every time she looks at you."

"We are very fortunate to have her love." She opened the door.

Papa's carriage rumbled up the drive.

"Oh, splendid." Emily waved to her papa and brother. "Christian is home. You forgot to present him with your gift."

"Indeed, I'd completely forgotten."

"I believe Mrs. Hayes put it in his chamber. I'll run and fetch it."

Emily dashed upstairs and found the horse where she'd expected. She snatched it and returned to the front door.

Jacob stood at the top of the drive as Christian leapt from the carriage. "Lord Warren, what are you doing here?" He ran to him and danced about in a semi-circle. "Are you here to take the *Pirate Catcher* out sailing again?"

Emily hid the toy behind her back and passed it to Jacob.

"Master Christian, I spotted something in the mercantile window that I knew belonged to you."

"What is it? What is it?" Christian jumped in place.

"Ta-dah." Jacob held the wooden horse.

Christian's eyes widened, and his little hands reached for it with reverence. "It's for me?"

"Indeed."

With a grin almost as wide as his face, Christian took the horse and inspected it.

Emily leaned in and whispered to Jacob. "I don't know where his exuberant personality came from."

"From his father." Jacob didn't take his gaze off Christian. "He gets it from his papa."

Emily glanced at their father, addressing the nearby groom. His eyes sparkled when he delivered his message on Sunday mornings, but otherwise, he was generally calm and steadfast.

The pride lacing Jacob's words seemed odd.

"Do you know what breed it is?" Jacob asked Christian.

"It's a Morgan."

Jacob crouched to Christian's level. "How can you tell?"

"Because of its long neck and legs, and because its body is lean." He gazed at Jacob with a serious expression. "It's a high-stepper. No doubt."

Jacob laughed.

"That's a fine present." Papa stood behind them, his Bible tucked under his arm. "What do you say to Lord Warren for his kindness?"

Christian threw himself at Jacob, wrapping his arms around him and squeezing tight. "Thank you."

Their fair hair melded into one. His words echoed in her ears.

He gets it from his papa.

Christian pulled away, and she looked between them, the man and the boy.

Their likeness seemed uncanny. He'd taken such an interest in Christian, even brought him toys. It couldn't be. Could it? Why hadn't she considered...?

Was Jacob Christian's father?

Papa addressed Jacob. "I met a lady in town who's visiting from London. She claims she knows you." Papa squeezed his eyes shut. "Lady Lu... Lady Lucile. Yes, Lady Lucile Benton, I believe."

Lady Benton. Wasn't that the woman Phoebe read about in

the gossip column? The one whose husband had dueled with Jacob?

"You don't say." Jacob stood, and Christian ran to play with the new toy. "She is a distant acquaintance of mine. A friend of a friend of a friend, that sort of thing."

"She sends her regards." Papa gestured toward the house. "Care to join us for the noontime meal? We sup early in the country."

"Unfortunately, I have another engagement, but I appreciate your hospitality."

"Another time, then." Papa bowed.

Jacob returned the nod. "I would be delighted."

Papa called to Christian. "Make sure you wash up before coming to the table, young man."

"Yes, Papa."

Papa headed into the house.

Jacob watched Christian prance about, holding his new toy high and neighing like a horse. He turned to Emily with a smile as wide as Christian's, but it faded.

"Is something amiss?" He gripped her elbow. "You look pale."

Emily opened her mouth to speak, to accuse, to question, but nothing came out. Her gaze jumped between Christian and Jacob.

He glanced over one shoulder, then the other. "Is there a ghost lingering about?"

Emily's mouth finally loosened. "You're—are you... You and Christian? Are you his...?"

Jacob's eyes widened. He grabbed her hand and yanked her to a stone bench in the rose garden. When he'd settled her, he crouched on his haunches in front of her. His hands cupped her upper arms, and he peered over his shoulder to ensure Christian couldn't overhear. "What are you asking?"

Emily swallowed. "Are you Christian's father? His real father?"

He froze like a cornered animal, braced for an all-out run. But he didn't run.

"Blast." He ran a hand across the back of his head.

"Do not pitch me any gammon. I can see the resemblance."

"You do?" His reaction gave him away. "I'm..." He licked his lips, glanced behind him again, as if she'd allow Christian to creep close and overhear. "I am Christian's father. He's the reason I came to Sylvanwood."

"So you can ease your guilt by buying him a toy and then merrily going on your way?"

"No." His harsh tone split the air, and his grip tightened on her arms. But he immediately relaxed his hold and leaned away. "It's not like that." His tone was pleading. "Let me explain."

"No need. You got a woman with child, and then you did the dishonorable thing and left. You left your child, your blood." Her words punched the air. "You left Christian." Much like Emily's mother had abandoned her. She tried to shift on the stone bench to turn her back or pull away, but he held her firm. "Christian doesn't need another father. He already has one—a good one."

He winced as though she'd slapped him. "I never wanted to leave my son. I'd offered her marriage, but she refused and disappeared for eight months. When she returned, she wouldn't tell me where she went or where he was. I've spent five years searching for him."

"You're going to marry Phoebe, then?"

"What?" His eyes widened, and he shook his head. "Why would you think that?"

"What about her? What if she's with child? Will you leave them to their own devices too?"

He reared back. "What has she told you?" Rage flashed in his eyes. "I haven't been intimate with Miss Dorsham."

Jacob had withheld the truth about being Christian's father. He could be lying now, but it would be hard to feign his reaction.

"She's been having clandestine meetings with someone else." He spoke past a stiff jaw. "Ask her carriage driver or footman. They'll tell you the truth."

This weekend I blossomed into a woman. I met someone, but Mama would disapprove. Phoebe had started to tell her a story the last time she'd come to Emily's house before Jacob came to town. But her words had been interrupted by the knock on the door. The investigator had plagued Emily with questions about Christian, informed her about her true birth parents, and passed her the copied registry page as confirmation.

"Lord Warren," Christian called. "Do you want to play?"

Jacob peered over his shoulder at Christian, and Emily took advantage of his distraction. She yanked free of his grip and darted toward the house.

"Emily, wait!"

She barreled inside and rammed into Peter Mathis, who must have walked over.

He caught her in his arms. "What's wrong?"

Samuel stood beside Mr. Mathis with his brows drawn together, peering at her with concern.

Emily blinked back hot tears burning behind her lids. Her emotions somersaulted. She needed to process this information. "Nothing." She peeked out the window, where Christian and Jacob were talking, probably about horses.

Jacob glanced toward the house, his face tense and drawn.

"What did he do?" Mr. Mathis gave her a tiny shake.

Emily shook her head. "Nothing. I need to freshen up for the noon meal."

Mr. Mathis stared at her. He didn't believe her—she saw it

in his eyes—but he let her go. "I wanted you to know that I must leave for London but shall be back in a fortnight."

She worked to focus on his words and not the tight pain in her chest, choking out her ability to breathe.

He backed up a step and stuffed his hands in his pockets, a muscle twitching in his jaw. "Don't do anything drastic until I return. We can speak more then."

Drastic? She didn't know what he was talking about. What radical thing did he believe her capable of?

"I shall be as rational as ever. Excuse me." She climbed the stairs. As soon as she was out of sight, she fled to her room.

She'd been lied to and deceived. But by whom? A devious rake pretending he'd reformed, or her closest friend?

Emily paced. The woven circular rug was well worn, and she could have walked a hole through it after the number of times she passed over it in the next half hour. What was going to happen to Christian? Could Jacob take him away? Her parents wouldn't allow it. Or would they? If so, would Jacob take Christian to live with him in London? Society would shun Christian for being his bi-blow. Didn't Jacob understand he'd ruin Christian's life? He could pretend Christian was his ward to avoid being ostracized, but even then, tongues would wag.

How would she keep her promise to protect Christian if he lived elsewhere?

Emily flopped onto her bed. Drawings she'd done as a child hung on the walls. She'd been so proud of her artwork back then, but now the drawings appeared infantile compared to her recent work.

Things change. People change.

She was no longer the naïve little girl who drew rainbows and sunshine. The world was full of selfish, dishonorable rogues who romped through life, not caring who they hurt.

"Why, God? How could our birth parents be so cruel? We were their children. Why did they discard us like trash?" A picture of Christian's mother's face floated through her memory—an unhappy young lady who complained of the stuffiness of their small rectory and roamed the fields and moors until her condition became obvious and her lying-in period began. Emily pulled an old sketchbook off her book-shelf and flipped through it. She'd displayed artistic talent even at the age of four and ten. She stopped at a picture of a sad young woman peering out their front window.

Christian's mother, Sarah, had been beautiful. Emily understood how Jacob had been attracted to her.

Memories soured her stomach.

Get it out, Sarah had yelled during her labor. Emily had assisted the midwife until the wail of a baby's cry filled the room. The midwife wrapped Christian in a blanket, and Emily had risen on her toes to peek at her new brother before the woman tried to hand him to his birth mother.

I don't want it. Sarah had pushed the baby away. *Why should I let that thing ruin my life?*

Mama had claimed Sarah's outburst were the pains of labor speaking, but Emily had wondered whether she'd been rejected by her mother in a similar, hurtful way. The thought sparked a protectiveness for her younger brother.

Emily flipped the page to Sarah sitting on the bridge, at their old house in Lincolnshire, her feet dangling in the water. A young man sat beside her, leaning in as though hanging on her every word. The face wasn't Jacob's, but he held a familiarity that Emily couldn't place.

As Sarah met with the young man, she hadn't spotted Emily sketching in the tall grass along the shore. Sarah had never given Emily much notice, anyway.

Christian was now five, and Jacob around three and twenty. When Christian was born, he would have been ten and eight or ten and nine. If Emily's memory served, Sarah had been ten and nine and engaged to a duke. Jacob must have been very convincing to seduce a beautiful woman into risking an advantageous marriage.

Emily would need to be even more on her guard. To think she'd found him amusing, even charming. Thank heavens she discovered the truth before her heart formed an attachment.

No, she needed to be honest with herself. She admitted that she'd begun to have feelings for him.

She squeezed her eyes shut. Jacob was perfect for Phoebe. She, too, was dishonest. Jacob had pawned off his bi-blows, and if he'd spoken the truth, then Phoebe was trying to pawn someone else's child on Jacob.

The two of them would make quite a pair.

CHAPTER 14

From the top of the stone staircase leading to Brownstone Hall's entrance, Maslow greeted Jacob with a smile. "Good afternoon, milord."

He nodded at his butler. This morning, Jacob's steps had been light as he commented on the beautiful weather and how spring seemed right around the corner. Now, he felt as though he dragged leaden soles in his Hessian boots.

He entered the hall and trudged down the polished marble floor. As a child, he would have made a game of the foyer's large checkered flooring, stepping on the white squares and not the black. If only avoiding pitfalls in life were that easy. The mistakes now swirled black, white, and gray in various shapes, sizes, and surprises.

He would never regret having a child, even though he regretted the pain his sin caused and continued to cause others, especially his son.

He'd been foolish to think no one would recognize the resemblance. Part of him was flattered, but the other knew it meant facing facts. Would Emily tell her family? Would they bar him from seeing his son? He rubbed his hands over his face, almost missing Mr. Welsh sitting in a chair outside the study. "Mr. Welsh, good afternoon."

His steward stood, stuffing a ring he'd been examining into his pocket, and bowed. "I'm here for our regular meeting."

"If you're considering proposing to your lady love, I recommend against it. Women only cause problems. The whole lot of them." He entered the study, pulled out his pocket watch, and sank into the leather chair behind the desk. Five past the hour. He'd forgotten the meeting. "I'm a bit distracted. Shall we postpone until tomorrow, or is anything pressing?"

"Nothing that can't wait until tomorrow." Mr. Welch strode to the door but paused and turned. "Actually, there was a caller who was quite determined. Lady Benton. Maslow left her calling card in the silver tray. She is staying at the Rose and Thistle Inn and is"—the young man cleared his throat—"awaiting your visit."

"When did you mail out the response to her last letter?"

"I posted it right away. It should have arrived a week ago."

"Is Lord Benton with her?"

"Not that I know of. Maslow may have gotten a better look within the carriage."

"I'll check with him. That will be all." Jacob waved him away, then rested his elbows on the desk and rubbed his eyes with the palms of his hands.

Why had Lady Benton come to Sylvanwood? The last thing he needed was her creating more scandal. Next time the woman became spoony drunk, he'd let the guests laugh at her passed out on the floor.

What was he thinking? There wouldn't be a next time. He had no desire to return to that crowd. Best for him to resolve any misconceptions or delusions Lady Benton might hold and find out if her husband had been in the area—specifically the night of the Crawford party when highwaymen robbed Lord and Lady Memphis.

Jacob heaved out of the chair and sighed. He needed to keep his reputation clean to make a good impression on the Thompsons, especially now that the truth was out. The public tap room of the inn would create less local gossip and attention since meetings were often held there—both business and private in nature. If only he knew he wasn't walking into Benton's trap.

~

*a*s far as inns went, at least the Rose and Thistle was respectable, with whitewashed walls and dried lavender bouquets that scented the air, blending with the heavy smell of spirits.

A few patrons filled the stools at the bar with mugs set before them. The owner was a friendly chap with a red nose and a boisterous voice with a Scottish lilt. He immediately recognized Jacob even though they'd never met. Word spread quickly when the upper ranks came to small towns.

"I heard a friend is in town and thought I'd pay him a visit." Jacob extended his card to the owner. In his last interaction with Lady Benton, he'd been targeting her to gain intelligence regarding her husband's suspicious affiliations. Information was still his objective, but he was no longer willing to use his old tactics, which made their pending encounter tricky.

"His lordship didn't check in, milord, just her ladyship and" —the owner flashed him a sly look—"I don't think she's expectin' him."

Jacob relaxed, his fingers no longer twitching to grasp the pistol hidden in his coat pocket.

"She's playing cards with friends in our back room." He beckoned him to follow. "Right this way." The man directed him past the stairs leading to the guest rooms to a wooden-paneled rear room.

Laughter sounded, but a curtain over the door blocked his view. Jacob walked slowly, allowing his eyes to adjust to the dim light, and slid his hand into his coat pocket, gripping his pistol just in case. He approached at a narrow angle, staying tight to the wall, and glanced back, orienting where he could be vulnerable to attack. The oblivious owner held the drapery aside and gestured for him to enter. Jacob scanned the room, making out shapes—a cluster of tables and chairs and a group of gents and ladies gathered at the far corner table.

Several barmaids passed out rounds of drinks, but he didn't identify any threats.

"She'd be somewhere in the mix." The owner tipped his head toward the guests, then left.

"There you are, darling." Lady Benton rose from her seat at the card table. A large plume of feathers adorned her hat. "I just knew you'd come."

The male guests at her table politely rose. At a separate table, the dealer paused, and the players swiveled their heads and gaped at Jacob with dazed smiles and half-open eyelids.

Lady Benton sauntered in his direction, but her hat tilted to the right, guiding her body that direction. With a hand on the fireplace mantel, she righted her angle and tried again, stumbling slightly and tumbling into his arms. Jacob yanked his hand out of his pocket in time to catch her.

"I appear to be a touch jug-bitten. I told Lady Anne we'd only have one drink, but these gentlemen bought us more." She shifted in his arms, leaning on his left side. Her face was flushed, and the smell of gin wafted under his nose as she spoke. "Shame on you, Mr. Klay. You've gone and gotten me foxed."

Jacob grasped her upper arms and leaned her against the wall.

She pouted. "I waited for you, darling, but you never came." She reached out a gloved hand as if to caress his face but instead dragged her finger down over his nose and lips. "I'm fed up with wanting. No, I'm fed up with waiting. Did I say waiting or wanting?" She shrugged a sensuous shoulder. "No matter, I'm done with both."

"Lady Benton, I'm not—"

"Shhhh." She held a finger to her lips. "We can talk in the other room." She grabbed his arm, and he allowed her to lead him out into the hall so that they'd have less of an audience. She shielded her eyes with her other hand from the front foyer window's bright light. "I'm here for the Rogers party on Wednesday night and the Simmons party on Friday, but in the meantime, I'm happy to entertain."

Jacob stopped. Lady Rogers and Lady Simmons threw lavish parties at their country estates in surrounding towns that drew the height of the *le bon ton*. Bandits would be drooling to accost the nobility traveling the roads this week.

"The parties will still take place despite the recent robberies?"

"Are you worried for my well-being?" Her gaze rested on his mouth, and she swayed forward, but he shifted, and she fell against his side, laying her head upon his shoulder. She sighed. "The season must go on, and it can't without the pre-season parties. Besides, I heard shots were fired. Maybe they got the fiends?" Lady Benton half sauntered, half stumbled toward the stairs, until it registered that he wouldn't follow.

"Silly, aren't you coming?"

"Where's Lord Benton?" Jacob leveled her with a stern glare.

Her bottom lip protruded into a pout before she broke into giggles. "My husband is traveling. He reinjured his shoulder and has ridden to Bath to heal in the pump house spring waters." Her mouth twisted into a cynical smile. "Or to find solace in that wretched light-skirt love of his." She waved a hand. "No matter. He is not due to return for a fortnight, and I told everyone I was visiting my sickly cousin in Sylvanwood. Only Lady Anne knows the truth, and she'll hold my secrets because I hold hers."

A wicked smile blossomed upon her rouged lips. Lady Benton was known for her beauty. Her red lips and pale skin complemented her silky blond hair, but Jacob saw the bitterness masked by her feminine wiles in that smile. He glimpsed her future self, rotted from the inside out unless she changed.

Sympathy for this broken woman washed over him.

"Lady Benton."

She stepped closer, too close, and her head tipped back. "Darling, call me Lucile." She placed her gloved hand upon his chest.

"I'm not your darling." Jacob seized her wrist and pulled her over to a pair of wingback chairs under the stairs, separated by a small table. He lowered her into one and sat in the other. "When was the last time you saw your husband?"

She closed her eyes and pressed gloved fingers to her temples. "Several Saturdays ago." She peered at him and dropped her hands. "Indeed, we'd argued because he was supposed to escort me to the Crawford party, but he refused because his shoulder was injured. He left for Bath instead."

"Your husband received his shoulder injury when he accosted me on the road in Sylvanwood."

She smothered an eruption of giggles. "Surely, you're mistaken. Benton isn't capable of such a feat."

"His henchmen are, and he had no problem holding a gun to my back."

"Oh, my." Her eyes widened, but she waved her hand dismissively. "We'll need to be more discreet. I'm tired of him ruining my fun."

"There has been a misunderstanding. I am not interested in pursuing a relationship with a married woman—nor any woman, for that matter—until I decide to settle down." An image of Emily's smile as she sat beside him on the bridge flashed before his eyes. But she'd never have him, especially now that she knew he was Christian's father.

"But your letter?" Her brow furrowed. "It practically begged for a much-needed diversion from all the work of restoring the hall. I came as soon as I read it."

He recalled his words to his steward. *Mention that there is much that needs my attention here at Brownstone Hall, and I cannot be otherwise engaged.* "I believe you read too much into what was written."

"But you took me to bed."

Jacob ran a hand across the back of his head. "I aided an inebriated woman in retiring after casting up her accounts in front of her guests, but that was the extent of it."

She blinked and shook her head. "I don't understand."

"That night, you'd dipped too deep in your cups. You wanted to show me your husband's wine collection, but when you stood, you grew dizzy and retched on the floor." He could still hear the laughter of her so-called friends as they cackled over her drunkenness. "I couldn't leave you like that, so I scooped you up. Your footmen were busy cleaning the mess, so your butler, who claimed to have a bad back, directed me to your chamber. I placed you neatly in bed and intended to leave." Or search her husband's chamber for clues of a connection between him and a ring of jewel thieves, but she needn't know that part. "Your husband picked that inopportune time to arrive home. I stole through the second-story window and lowered myself to the first-floor patio."

She frowned.

"Nothing. Happened. Between. Us." Jacob enunciated each word.

"But you dueled?" She leaned forward, resting her arms on the table.

Jacob kept his gaze on her face and not the flesh she

flaunted. "Your husband demanded satisfaction. My honor was at stake. I tried to get him to see reason, but he'd suspected you and didn't believe a word I said."

"He suspects something?" Lady Benton gasped. "Did he say who?"

Jacob snorted. "He was a tad busy aiming his pistol at me."

"Think back." She sobered a little too quickly. "You don't recall him murmuring a name?"

"I'm afraid my attention was elsewhere. Mostly on the barrel of his gun."

She shrugged. "Well, it all worked out, didn't it?"

"If you consider almost dying twice 'working out,'" Jacob murmured.

She frowned. "Are you talking to yourself?"

"Sometimes I need expert advice." Sarcasm laced his tone.

She melted into a seductive pose. "Shall we retire upstairs, then?"

Clearly, she had no other useful information for him. It could have been Benton's plan to rob the Memphis coach on route to Bath.

"I'm rather sleepy." She rose, sauntered to the back stairs, and posed against the railing with the seductive curve of her hip pushed out, as if to entice a fool to follow. She faked a yawn.

"Why don't you go on and clean yourself up a bit?"

Her hand moved to her hair, and she frowned. She climbed the stairs, keeping one hand on the wall for balance. "I'll be waiting. Don't tarry."

He watched her stagger up. Once he heard the door of her room open and close, he placed his hat atop his head and strode out the front exit, wishing the owner a good day.

~

*E*mily lay snug under the covers of her bed, yet she wafted in and out of sleep with images of Jacob haunting her rest. In her dream, Christian played behind her with his carved horse, neighing and prancing it about. Mama, Papa, and Samuel worked the far field in the distance. Jacob stood a few feet away on her other side. He offered one of his lazy smiles that flipped her stomach and sucked the air from her lungs. He extended his open hand, a tempting invitation. She stared at his palm, so strong, so secure, so masculine. She longed to slip her hand into his to feel the warmth of his fingers in hers, but she hesitated.

Could she allow herself to love? Could she draw him into her inner circle? She met those blue eyes so sure, so confident. *Yes.* Her hand reached out as if with a will of its own. Their fingers brushed, and a rush of excitement coursed through her body.

Jacob's hand passed hers, and she frowned as she clasped air. Instead, he reached behind her, grabbing Christian and pulling him away. Christian's small hand waved goodbye, and Jacob led him to his carriage. Emily tried to run after them, but her feet were rooted to the spot. She cried for help, but the words stuck in her throat.

A thud woke her. The Bible she'd fallen asleep reading fell to the floor when she'd rolled. Her heart pounded and her breath came in quick pants. She was in her room. Safe in her bed.

She felt the floor for her Bible. Her fingers found a corner of the leather cover. She set the book on her bedside table and stared at the ceiling.

Lord, You wouldn't allow Jacob to take Christian from us, right? I know You want what's best for Your children, and wouldn't a loving home be better for Christian than the home of a rake? Please don't let this libertine upend our lives.

216

CHAPTER 15

*W*ednesday evening, two days later, Jacob ran into his steward in the stables on his way to go undercover as the Dorshams' driver. He glanced at the repaired thatched roof and noted the renovations. "The barn is coming along." He clapped Mr. Welsh on the shoulder.

His steward winced.

"You all right?" Knotted thread of hastily sewn fabric trailed an inch long down Mr. Welsh's coat sleeve. "What happened to your coat?"

"A loose nail jabbed me in the stables." Mr. Welch raised his elbow and eyed the material before pointing to the spot where the assault took place. "Poked straight through my jacket."

Jacob had had his own run-in with a nail. Lord help him if word got back to Lieutenant Scar that he'd fainted. "We'll need to have the nail dealt with so it doesn't happen again."

"I had it removed. It won't bother anyone else, milord."

He eyed the steward, whose appearance had grown even more haggard in the past few weeks. "Perhaps I should send for the town physician to look at your shoulder. Make sure it's not infected."

"Don't bother." He raised his palm. "It's already healing."

"Very good. Why don't you get some rest, then?" Jacob mounted his horse. "You've been working too hard with the renovations."

Mr. Welsh bowed. "Thank you, milord."

As twilight loomed, Jacob trotted down the lane. A chill left over from winter hung in the air. At the Dorsham estate, he settled his horse inside the farthest stable, paid their coachman to enjoy a night off again, and climbed into the perch of the coach. Only a few minutes passed before the Dorsham family called for their carriage to be brought around. He lowered his beaver hat and tugged his collar points higher to hide his face. Snapping the reins, he urged the team to the main entrance.

The family moved from the house, and the conveyance tilted as Lord Dorsham entered the carriage, followed by his wife and daughter.

As the sinking sun lay shadows across their path, Jacob drove the team along the darkening turnpike toward the Rodgers' party. He scanned for movement—any approaching men on horseback—his weapon ready at his hip.

All remained quiet until he pulled into the Rodgers' drive. Lines of coaches dropped off guests who filed out and entered the Georgian-style home. The windows glowed with the occasional guest passing in front and dimming the chandeliers' blaze.

Lady Dorsham and Miss Dorsham were assisted from the carriage by a footman. They ascended the stairs, Lord Dorsham behind, and handed their card to the butler, who swung the doors wide and announced their arrival.

Jacob pulled the conveyance around to wait and turned his ear to the other coachmen's gossip while watching guests enter the party.

Lady Benton arrived with Lady Ann Fenster.

Several hours passed while Jacob listened to the coachman

mostly complain about their employers and the toll workers who tried to charge double. The number of guests arriving dwindled.

A coach pulled in front of the residence. The emblem and driver's livery looked familiar, but both were hard to determine in the moonlight.

A short man dressed in finery exited the coach. He extended his hand for another passenger, flashing the red silk lining of his cape. Jacob straightened and strained for a better view.

A blond woman emerged, her head lifted high with a sparkling tiara restraining pinned curls.

He held his breath. When she turned toward him, there could be no doubt.

Sarah.

The Duke of Charlton had a holding in the upper Cotswolds, not far from here.

The old, familiar pain struck him in the chest. The hurt remained, but the desire he'd held for so many years had dissipated. She was still beautiful...but not what he wanted. She'd withheld his son from him, and for that reason, any beauty she'd once possessed no longer appealed to him.

Besides, he'd developed an affinity for petite brunettes, vicar's daughters with small pert noses and artistic talent.

"There's the duke and duchess." Burton's driver slapped the shoulder of the coachman parked parallel to him. "I bet you a shilling we'll see the duchess depart in under ten minutes."

The man snorted as his and her grace entered the party. "I'll take that bet."

Another coach reined to a halt in front of the grand manor, and a man exited.

Jacob squinted. He'd seen that tall silhouette before, but where?

A woman descended and tucked her hand into the man's arm.

Lady Copeland?

Hound's teeth.

The tall man... Wasn't he the one who'd had the clandestine meeting with Miss Dorsham? What was Miss Dorsham thinking, dallying with a married man? There was no good ending to that situation. Heaven help her if she wound up carrying his child. She couldn't force a man to the altar if he was already married.

Someone needed to talk sense into Miss Phoebe Dorsham before it was too late, but it couldn't be him. It needed to be a woman.

Emily?

She was Miss Dorsham's closest friend.

A side door opened, and Sarah strode onto the Rodgers' veranda.

A man stepped from the shadows. Jacob was too far away to get a good look at their faces, but the mysterious man appeared hesitant.

Sarah glanced around before approaching the poor lad. She slid her white gloves up his arms and toyed with his hair. She whispered something in the man's ear, and the bloke responded by wrapping her in an embrace and kissing her with the fiery passion of a starved man being offered a delicious treat. The kiss deepened with hands and arms roving over backs and hips.

With a snort, Jacob was ready to look elsewhere. But Sarah broke the kiss and walked away.

The poor fool followed, his palms up as if pleading with her.

Instead of retreating to the garden or greenhouse, where guests met for trysts, she led the man into an unmarked carriage. They climbed inside, the driver cracked his whip, and the coach sped down the lane.

It must be a new trend of the fashionable set to hold their clandestine assignations inside coaches.

"Where do you think those two are off to?" Jacob addressed a nearby coachman, nodding at the retreating coach turning onto the road.

The round-faced man pushed down on the top of his driving hat with the palm of his hand. "I shouldn't be sayin', but she and that young fellow often leave parties together. It's not a secret that the duke and duchess don't hold any love for one another."

Was Sarah's hard heart even capable of love? "Where do they go?"

The man shrugged. "I figure the nearest inn."

"The closest inn is an hour's ride there and back." Jacob checked his watch. It was already past midnight. They wouldn't be returning until three in the morning. "Wouldn't the guests be leaving by then? The duke?"

"Bah." The driver peered toward the door. "The duke dips deep in his cups. I've never seen him leave before my charges, and they often leave with the rising sun."

Jacob had heard rumors of the duke being a gambler but tried not to pay the gossip any heed lest he celebrate the man's shortfalls. Just because wagging tongues said he, too, initially had been beguiled by Sarah didn't make the duke a bad person. Lord knew Jacob was working on his faults.

One of the coachmen he'd spoken to earlier excused himself. He snapped the reins and picked up his charges. The other drivers pulled their coats tight and settled in for a long wait.

Jacob yawned. His eyelids grew heavy as the sound of carriage wheels crunching down the lane grew distant. These late nights were taking their toll. He leaned back in his seat and drifted off for a quick nap.

He jolted awake to the sound of an approaching carriage.

The unmarked conveyance had returned, but only Sarah exited. She checked the positioning of her tiara and, with a defiant air, strode up the stairs, not seeming to care if anyone noticed her return.

Jacob leaned toward the lantern and flicked open his pocket watch. Two in the morning. She certainly hadn't made it to the inn. He snorted. Although, back when she owned his heart, they hadn't needed an inn to escape their fathers' verbal attacks and find comfort in each other's arms. A hayloft had sufficed, but she'd left him for finer things.

He'd have thought she'd hold higher expectations now.

Lady and Miss Dorsham exited the building, and Jacob lowered the brim of his hat and snapped the reins to drive up in front of his charges.

"What a waste of an evening," Miss Dorsham said to her mother as the footman aided Lady Dorsham into the carriage. "I thought for certain Lord Warren would be in attendance." She accepted the footman's help up the mounting block. "Pity because I'd hoped to dance with him without Emily around as a distraction."

Lady Dorsham harrumphed. "She's setting her sights too high with Lord Warren."

Set her sights for him? He wished. Jacob strained to hear more.

"Everyone knows she'll marry Peter Mathis." Miss Dorsham's tone spoke of whining. "Why make things harder for me? Mr. Mathis confided that he left for London to purchase a ring and should be returning—"

The door closed, cutting off the rest of her sentence.

Mathis.

That sour-faced cuffin would snuff the joy out of Emily. An image of her entered his mind. She was dressed in a drab, high-collared gown scrambling to pull over a footstool and hand Mathis his pipe. Mathis would read the paper while she stood dutifully by, ready to wait upon him.

Blast. Jacob snapped the reins a little too hard, and the horses burst forward. Emily believed the worst of him after discovering he was Christian's father. He'd need to find a way to redeem himself in her eyes, and quickly, before Mathis returned.

~

Two days after she'd last seen Jacob, Emily stared at his painted face, so much like the image that had preoccupied her thoughts as of late. She returned her attention to the background and painted the silhouette of a tree against a red sunset. The cool air chilled her nose and cheeks, but her hands remained warm from furiously working to finish the commission and be done with him.

It wasn't her typical choice of backdrop. She preferred blue puffy-cloud skies, but the colors reflected her mood. How could she have been so foolish to think Lord Warren might be a man of character? What did he plan to do next? Would he take Christian from them?

Her tight grip on the brush hindered her from working. She forced her hand to relax.

"Emily, dear," Mama called from the open doorway. "Do come inside. It's almost time for the evening meal, and we're having company. I'll send Samuel to help move the canvas."

She finished the small tree she'd been adding as Samuel arrived to aid her.

"Please tell me our company isn't the chatty Mrs. Evans

with the odd giggle or dreary Mr. French whose only delight in life is to complain."

"Thank heaven, no." Samuel carried the canvas into the salon. "It's—"

"Set it right over there near the window." Emily pointed to the spot, and Samuel grunted when the canvas's edge hit the oil lamp wall fixture. Emily righted it before any oil spilled. Thanking her brother, she said, "You go on and tell Mama I must clean up first. It will only take a minute."

Emily put away her paints and cleaned her brushes. She entered through the kitchen and scampered up the stairs. The clock in the hallway chimed the six o'clock hour. *Drat!* She hadn't even changed.

In her chamber, she quickly stripped out of her sturdy nankeen dress and rang for Mrs. Hayes, who helped her to fasten the buttons on the back of her muslin day gown. She hustled downstairs to the dining room, where she could hear Papa's laughter and forks clanking against china.

"My apologies for being late." She strode into the room and froze.

Jacob was seated beside Papa at the family table. Her mother and Samuel were there as well.

Emily's jaw clenched, and a white-hot flame lit inside her belly.

The gentlemen rose.

"Emily, please have a seat." Mama gestured to the only empty pacesetting at the table, which was, of course, next to Jacob. "Samuel ran into Lord Warren in town, and he was nice enough to agree to join us for supper." She turned her attention back to him. "He was just telling us that his brother, the marquis, is arriving next week to see Brownstone Hall's progress."

Jacob pulled out her chair, and Emily sat.

The men resumed their seats as well.

She said a quick prayer and dug into her food, preferring to focus on eating instead of the infuriating man next to her.

"Nora, my sister-in-law, will be visiting as well. She wants to see the progress and layout before ordering fabrics and whatnot from London." Jacob sipped from his cup.

Emily could feel Samuel's eyes on her, no doubt wondering about her cool behavior.

"Tell us about the marchioness?" Mama cut a piece of ham but didn't remove her gaze from Jacob. "I do hope I get a chance to meet her. We are so blessed to have the privilege of the aristocracy in our town."

"She is a splendid woman filled with grace and a charming personality. She's patient with my dictatorial brother. Also perceptive and merciful, much like your daughter."

Emily felt his regard, but she kept her gaze locked on her mother, who practically glowed from the compliment.

"But is she as talented as our Emily?" Mama said.

"With a brush, no, but she can play the pianoforte like Mozart."

"Truly?"

"I've seen her play his piano concerto number twenty-one blindfolded."

"Remarkable." Papa grunted his approval. "She is talented, indeed. They should be pleased with all your work at Brownstone Hall. I passed by the other day. The home has regained its former splendor."

"It is coming along nicely. Thanks to the help the Sylvanwood community has provided, for finding craftsmen and hiring a small army of workers is a tremendous feat. Once again, I thank you for your assistance."

Samuel swallowed a bite of bread. "When will it be complete?"

"The roof is finished," Jacob said, "and the rotted boards replaced. The west wing still needs a fresh coat of paint, and a few windows need re-glazing, but for the most part, the rest of the work is cosmetic. Hence, why I've asked the marchioness to pay a visit." Emily felt his gaze on her but only allowed herself to look at his right hand holding his fork with a dripping piece of roast speared on the end. "I was hoping Miss Thompson could aid Nora in determining colors. I'm also looking forward to my brother and his wife seeing Miss Thompson's painting. Although, it may not be completed."

"It will be finished." Emily stabbed at a cooked carrot.

"That soon?" Mama drew back.

"I'll make certain of it." The sooner, the better.

Jacob ate a bite of roast and swallowed. "The food is delicious. Thank you for inviting me to dine."

"It's our pleasure," Mama said.

With her fork, Emily pushed the carrot from one side of her plate to the other. "If only Mrs. Hayes had served Brussels sprouts."

Jacob hid a snorted laugh by coughing and sipping from his glass.

"What did you say about Brussels sprouts?" Papa leaned closer.

"They're his lordship's favorite." Emily dared to look at Jacob and wanted to blot out the playful spark in his blue eyes with her paintbrush.

"Had I known, I would have had Mrs. Hayes prepare some." Mama sighed. "I shall note that for next time you dine with us."

Emily muttered, "With any luck, there won't be a next time."

"Did you say something?" Papa stared at her.

"Next time, of course," she said.

"Speak up, my dear. We didn't raise you to mumble." Papa turned his attention to her brother, giving her a moment's reprieve. "So Samuel, how was your visit with the Pearsons today?"

As Samuel recounted his day, and while her parents listened to him, Jacob leaned toward her and whispered, "We need to talk."

She pretended to wipe her mouth. "I don't believe that's necessary."

"I insist."

"Lord Warren"—Papa cut a piece of his roast—"have you taken the time to pray about God's purpose for you?"

Emily focused on her food, trying to appear uninterested.

"I have, and I believe God is answering, but how do I know if I'm hearing God's will or my own?"

Papa sat back in his chair and smiled. "Brilliant question."

"I'd hoped asking God to help me with my situation wasn't being disrespectful."

"Not at all. David brought his questions to God." Papa tapped his fingertips together. "The answer isn't simple. God reveals Himself in different ways to different people. When He called me into ministry, I resisted. I didn't know how to shepherd people. I wasn't an expert on the Bible. I was a sinner. God, however, continued to put the call on my heart. I even tried to go another route—used my savings to buy some land with a plan to become a gentleman farmer, but the restlessness I felt wouldn't go away. The further I drifted from His purpose, the worse it became until I wasn't even sleeping at night. I finally handed my fears over to God and worked to become a vicar. I was installed into a living in Sylvanwood and have found peace and joy in doing God's work." He patted the table. "That's not to say it was an easy road once I submitted to God. I had a fair share of problems, including our first vicarage burning to the ground, but I knew God was for me." He eyed his children. "And 'if God is for me...'"

Emily and Samuel chorused their response. "'Then who can be against me?'"

Papa's proud smile showed his love not only for his children but also for God. He turned to Jacob. "Does that help?"

"Quite." He stared at the basket of rolls in the center of the table. "I have been restless, as though I need to fill a void and haven't been able to. It sounds petty, but I tried to fill the emptiness with parties and outrageous people, but the hole only seemed to grow bigger."

"And you said God is showing you some of your giftings?" Papa sipped his drink.

"Since I've come to Sylvanwood, I've found satisfaction in restoring the Hall—breathing new life into something. I'm meeting the tenants, seeing their needs, and helping however I can. There's a lot of fulfillment in it. The odd thing is that it's not about me. I struggled for so long, stuffing everything into my void, but it never filled. Then I assisted others with their needs and found that my restlessness disappeared. Who would have thought aiding others would help me?"

Papa saluted with his glass. "Welcome to the upside-down world of Jesus, where the meek inherit the earth and the poor in spirit are the greatest in the Kingdom of Heaven. Where we forgive those who have wronged us, and where whatever you do for the least of these you do for God."

"I feel as though I'm moving in the right direction."

Emily sent up a silent prayer of forgiveness for her earlier childish behavior. God was doing a great work in Jacob, and her attitude was a poor example of Christlikeness. *But God, even if Jacob is changing his ways, please don't let him take Christian from us.*

Papa asked Mama to pass him the Bible on the sideboard. When she did, he handed it to Jacob and tapped the cover. "Read this book. I believe you'll find Ecclesiastes and the book of Matthew helpful to answer your questions further."

"Thank you." He flipped it open and stared at the fine print on the pages. "I shall return it to you—"

"Keep it. I have access to more. All the answers can be found within those pages."

"I'm sorry to hear that your first parsonage burned. I hope no one was hurt."

"Praise God everyone got out all right." Mama glanced at the ceiling, sending her thanks to heaven.

"We were newly married, and Christian was just a baby." Papa patted Mama's hand. "A log had rolled out of the hearth. Mrs. Thompson and I were out back planting a garden. Mrs. Hayes was in her pantry packing food baskets to take to the sick. Samuel was in the field."

Emily twisted the napkin in her lap. The memory still raised the fine hair on the back of her neck and brought back the image of flames licking the curtains and her desperation to get to Christian.

Mama put down her fork. "Emily saw the flames first and hollered. I don't know why we hadn't smelled the smoke. It could have been the breeze was blowing the opposite way. Christian was napping in the nursery. I screamed, running toward the house, but Emily burst through the door carrying Christian. We didn't even know she'd gone inside." She splayed a hand over her chest and exhaled as if reliving the moment. "Angels watched over us that day." She issued Emily a motherly smile. "Emily's been protective of Christian ever since."

Emily swallowed the sip of soda water and set her glass down. Her defense of her younger brother started before then. She'd bonded with Christian the day he was born, when she vowed to keep him safe, even from his birth mother, who'd discarded him like an outdated gown. She wanted to glare at Jacob, question him with her eyes if he'd be willing to risk his life for Christian as she had. Mama and Papa would be astounded by her lack of manners, so she kept her gaze on the plate in front of her.

Papa cleared his throat. "Mrs. Hayes ran out, hearing

Mama's scream. She had no idea the house was on fire. The house went up like dry kindling. We lost all our material possessions, but they were only things." He smiled at his family. "Our small community came together, and God raised us from the ashes."

"And you are a tight-knit family because of it," Jacob said.

Papa nodded. "Indeed, we are blessed."

"Where is young Christian?" Jacob asked. "Does he take his meals in the nursery still?"

Emily eyed Jacob, her heart pounding. What was he after?

Mrs. Hayes collected the dishes, and Mama rose. "He's sharing a tutor with our neighbor's son. They are of a similar age. The tutor took them on an outing, but Christian should be along in an hour or so."

The rest of the family and Jacob rose, but Jacob waylaid Papa. "Might I have a moment alone with you?"

"Certainly. Come and join me in my study."

Emily stared at Jacob's retreating form. He didn't walk with his usual swagger. Instead, he respectfully bowed to Papa and trailed him. She itched to follow, to press her ear to the door as she and Samuel used to when Mama and Papa had private discussions. She glanced down at her hands. Her napkin lay twisted into a tight coil between her fingers. She tossed it onto the table and followed her mother into the sitting room.

What was Jacob telling Papa?

Mama picked up her embroidery, and Emily grabbed her sketchbook. After scribbling a mess of lines that didn't take any shape, she put the drawing down and stared at the open door to the hall. She wanted to scream and pound on Papa's study.

She wanted to yell at the man, *You can't take Christian from us!*

~

*J*acob tried to calm his breathing and focus on the spot above the vicar's eyes in between his brows. He found no deep creases there as his father had, the result of holding a constant scowl. But Jacob wasn't facing his father's vicious temper.

He sat opposite the vicar and watched the man over a well-used mahogany desk. Even so, his nerves were screaming and his stomach twisting. Because whether or not they approved, he was already entwined with their family. He wanted to earn their respect, and that started with honesty.

Jacob never had far to fall from his father's already low opinion of him, but the vicar was different. The plummet was a steep drop. This man had welcomed him into his home, to his table. He'd conversed with Jacob as if what Jacob said meant something, as though his opinion held merit. When the truth came out, all of that would change.

"So, Lord Warren..." Mr. Thompson leaned back and laced his fingers across his stomach, reminding Jacob of his older brother, Robert. "You had something you wanted to discuss?"

Jacob scooted forward in his chair and wiped his palms down the top of his breeches. "Since you are a man of the church, I'm going to confess my sins, of which I have many, and ask for your grace, mercy, and forgiveness."

The corner of the vicar's brow twitched, but he held back any display of emotion. It must have taken years of training for such a feat.

Jacob rolled his lips. "As you already may know, I do not hold a good reputation in London, and my ill repute is deserved." He inhaled a breath to steady his nerves. "The summer I graduated from university, I fell in love with a woman of the quality. At least, I thought it was love. She was beautiful, and I was besotted. I planned to marry her, but we did things out of order, and she became with child."

Jacob paused, waiting for a tongue-lashing or, at the very least, a lecture, but none came. He dared not meet the vicar's gaze for fear of seeing the breadth of his disappointment.

"I proposed, but she refused my offer because she endeavored to marry a wealthy, titled aristocrat." He relayed the entire tale with his head hanging, staring at his quivering hands. When he was finished, he glanced up, expecting to see a scowl of loathing, disappointment, or anger.

He didn't expect to find sympathy reflected in the man's eyes.

Jacob exhaled and forced out the words that would surely send the man into a tirade. "Christian is my son."

Mr. Thompson's brows lifted, and his eyes widened, but his surprise lasted only a moment. His face softened. "I see." He closed his eyes, breathing slowly. Was he praying? When he opened his eyes, he didn't smile, but neither did he shout or scowl. "God has been preparing my heart for this. I've had the impression that this day would come since Christian was born. Christian is a joy that God has loaned to us, but I won't place my son into unworthy hands."

Jacob's chest tightened. He wanted to rile at the reverend. Christian was his blood, and he'd altered his entire life in search of him. Who was he to stop him? But looking into the reverend's face, an awareness settled that this man, this family, had also sacrificed much for Christian and loved him dearly.

"God has placed you and Christian in the forefront of my mind lately. You—Christian's father—have been at the top of my prayer list." Mr. Thompson inhaled as if to steady his emotions. "We have always known that you or his mother could appear on our doorstep. We've never regretted adopting. We understood there'd be unanswered questions and stigmas associated with it. At least Christian has the opportunity for some answers." He tilted his head. "I can see the resemblance."

"So did Miss Thompson."

"Emily is more observant than most."

"Indeed. She confronted me a few days ago, and I admitted the truth to her. When you invited me to dinner tonight, it seemed clear she hadn't told you. While I appreciate her silence, it seemed wrong to deceive you and Mrs. Thompson any longer."

"We care for Christian very much."

"I know. It's evident in the boy's actions and confidence. He is well loved here."

"What are your plans?"

Jacob massaged the back of his head. "Truthfully, I don't know. I've been searching for my son for five years. I arrived intending to bring him back with me to London."

"And now?" The vicar's voice sounded tight.

"I want to be part of his life, but I also want what's best for him."

"As do we." Mr. Thompson shifted in his seat. "Besides Emily, is anyone else aware?"

"My aunt, but she keeps to herself and isn't prone to gossip."

Mr. Thompson grunted. "I'd say that's an understatement. Before your arrival, Lady Athol hadn't spoken to anyone except a few words to my wife as long as I'd been in Sylvanwood."

"Lord Athol was an unkind man."

"Your arrival has been good for her." He inhaled a deep breath. "And I believe it will be good for Christian, but informing him must be done properly and with God's guidance."

Jacob leaned forward. "What would you have me do?"

"Pray about it, and so shall I."

Jacob straightened. "That's it?"

He nodded. "There isn't a better source of wisdom than the Almighty. We are not to trust in human wisdom but instead seek God's power. The book of James states that if you seek God's wisdom, He will give it generously without finding fault."

Without finding fault? Jacob blinked. Could God and Mr. Thompson see him for the man he wanted to be and not just the man he used to be?

Mr. Thompson stood, and Jacob followed suit.

They walked toward the door, but Jacob stopped and shook his head. "Why would God bother with me? I have so many shortcomings."

"We all have sinned and fall short of God's glory." Mr. Thompson clasped a hand on Jacob's shoulder. "Sin separates us from God, but Jesus offers us a clean slate. Like the spotless lambs our forefathers sacrificed so the people could be purified before God, Jesus died, offering his blood to cleanse us from our sins." He pulled a well-worn Bible off the bookshelf and read from Psalms. "'As far as the east is from the west, so far hath He removed our transgressions from us.'"

Jacob rubbed his chin. "You can't sail that in a day."

"No, you cannot." Mr. Thompson chuckled and reached for the doorknob. "While you're praying for God's insight with Christian, why don't you ask for God's wisdom with Emily as well?"

"You're right. I owe her an apology, even though she doesn't seem eager to be in my presence right now."

Mr. Thompson clasped Jacob's shoulder. "That's not what I mean, son. I've seen how you look at her, and she holds you in regard also." He snorted. "Maybe not at the moment, but give her time."

Jacob stiffened, and his knees turned as brittle as dried kindling. "You'd consider me for your daughter? What about Mathis? I thought everything was predetermined."

"I will obey whatever God's plans are for my children, for His ways are higher than ours, and we want God's best for all. Whatever He determines that to be." Mr. Thompson swung the door wide.

Jacob's mind whirled, and somehow, his legs held as he

walked through the door. He peered over his shoulder needing one last confirmation that he'd heard correctly. "I have a lot of praying to do, then."

Mr. Thompson's warm gaze held a peace Jacob couldn't fathom. "'Ask and it shall be given to you. Seek and ye shall find. Knock, and it shall be opened unto you.'"

Jacob patted the Bible given to him. "I have some reading to do also."

CHAPTER 16

"Good day, Miss Thompson."

Emily jumped at the voice that had haunted her thoughts and dreams for several days, ever since their shared meal. Why couldn't Jacob just disappear and let things return to how they were? She scooped her package of art supplies off the counter of the mercantile shop and slid it into her satchel.

He lay a toy sailboat on the countertop and pressed a few coins into the clerk's palm.

A snappy comment about his childishness popped into her mind, but she bit her tongue. The last thing she needed was to engage the rogue in conversation.

"Good day, my lord." She strode for the exit.

"Miss Thompson, wait."

She pretended not to hear and kept going until she was halfway through the door. The boat was for Christian. She was sure of it. What were his plans? Her stomach twisted into a hard knot. Did he plan to take Christian from them? Gritting her teeth, she marched back to confront him.

Jacob rushed through a farewell with the store clerk and turned, spotting her. The tension seemed to melt from his frame as he tucked the boat under his arm. The barest hint of a smile curved one side of his mouth, but it disappeared when she grabbed his elbow and pushed him behind a tall display of bolts of material.

"For such a petite frame, you're strong."

She released his arm and leveled him with a glare, jabbing a finger at the toy boat. "That's for Christian, isn't it?"

"It's for me, actually."

She narrowed her eyes. *Do not lie to me.*

He raised his hands in a mock surrender. "I thought Christian and I might race. See whose is the fastest."

"You may buy him toys and the like, but you can't buy his love." She lowered her voice and stepped closer. "You may be his father, but we're the ones who've raised him and shown him love all these years. I will not let you take him away." She rose onto her toes. "That is what you plan to do, isn't it?"

"I don't know what I plan to do." He grasped her elbows. "Your father told me to pray about it."

"Unhand me." She yanked her arms away. "Papa said that?"

The store clerk leaned around a shelf filled with spools of yarn into her line of vision.

Emily smiled and nodded at him. "Lovely weather we're having today, Mr. Marcum."

He frowned. "It's a bit chilly for my taste, and a tad overcast."

A rumble of nervous laughter passed through her lips. "At least spring is on its way."

"So it is." The clerk continued to eye them suspiciously.

Jacob guided her toward the door. "Perhaps we should take in the air."

She grumbled but allowed him to lead her outside.

Rows of quaint shops lined the cobbled road. Colorful sign boards hung above display windows.

He gripped her elbow and led her around the few people peeking in the paned glass or inspecting the displays of fruit and vegetable baskets outside the grocer. Mrs. Hayes, who'd stopped to purchase some items for this week's suppers, put down an onion and shifted into a chaperone role, following a few steps behind.

Emily was aware of every eye that fell upon them. Tongues would wag. Determined to gain an answer, she whispered, "What did God tell you when you prayed?"

Jacob tipped his hat to the fruit vendor. "I believe He suggested I get to know Christian better and allow him to get to know me better. Hence, the toy boat."

"Oh." Emily fumed. How was she supposed to dispute that?

He paused at a small alcove next to the porch of the local inn. "Look, Emily—"

"Miss Thompson." She raised her chin.

"I beg your pardon." His nostrils flared. "Miss Thompson, I have much to discuss with you. I merely need to explain."

"Fine." She crossed her arms. "Explain."

"It may take more than a few minutes." He glanced over his shoulder, and his eyes widened. He turned back and locked eyes with her, pleading for understanding.

The inn's front door opened, and out strolled a woman dressed in an elegant peach-colored cambric robe with an arched collar trimmed with lace. Her bonnet, the same color as her pelisse, sported a curled ostrich feather. She caught sight of him. "Lord Warren?"

He stiffened.

"How wonderful to see you. I was so disappointed when you didn't call yesterday."

"Lady Benton." He flashed a half smile, a weak version of

his natural charm. "How good that we've crossed paths once again."

She stepped out of the inn and onto the porch, her half boots of peach-colored velvet peeking from beneath her full skirt. In her light-blue kid gloves, she dragged two of her long fingers along the railing. Her gaze roved over Emily, her lip curling. "I see you're getting a taste of country life."

The crease between Jacob's brow deepened. "Lady Benton, allow me to introduce Miss Thompson."

Lady Benton's forehead furrowed. "Truly? The vicar's daughter?" She harrumphed. "Miss Dorsham has been keeping me abreast of the goings on in this small town." She turned to Emily. "Or are you the vicar's sister?" She patted the underside of her hair.

"It's both." Emily curtsied but searched for any justification to excuse herself. *A taste of the country life.* Her cheeks burned. "My father is the vicar, and my eldest brother shall someday take over the parsonage."

"Small towns are such a bore." Lady Benton sighed.

Two other women exited the inn, fluttering their fans. Their chatter quieted.

Phoebe, dressed in a pale pink muslin walking gown with long sleeves and antique cuffs, stood partially behind Lady Benton. She adjusted the French tippet of a leopard silk shag hanging about her shoulders.

"If I recall correctly"—Lady Benton stepped aside—"you're both acquainted with Miss Dorsham."

Phoebe glanced up at her name, her eyes widened at Jacob. She smiled at him, then shot Emily a look that conveyed, *What are you doing with the man I've set my cap for?* "Emily, were you looking for me?"

"I was at Mr. Marcum's store purchasing supplies when I ran into Lord Warren." Emily pressed her mouth closed. She'd done nothing wrong and shouldn't feel the need to explain herself.

Lady Benton's other acquaintance stepped around Phoebe, her pale silk gown swishing over lace-trimmed petticoats. *Sarah.* The Duchess of Charlton. Christian's birth mother.

Emily's mouth dropped open, but she quickly snapped it shut.

The duchess placed her gloved hand on the rail and eyed Jacob.

Speaking to Jacob, Lady Benton gestured to Lady Charlton. "You remember my dear friend, her grace, Lady Sarah Winsted, Duchess of Charlton?"

"Indeed." Jacob bowed, color leaching from his face. "Good to see you again, *your grace.*"

Did she hear a twinge of sarcasm lacing his address?

A twitch at the corners of her lips was the only acknowledgment he received.

Emily was outright ignored.

Lady Benton's eyes sparkled as though stimulated by the exchange. "Would you care to join us for a morning cup of chocolate at the bakery on the corner?"

"Seeing as it's two in the afternoon"—his tone was dry—"I must pass on your offer."

Lady Benton shrugged one shoulder, giving him a seductive smile that soured Emily's stomach. "I'd planned to return to London after the Simmons soirée tomorrow evening to prepare for the season, but I may change my mind." She turned her attention to Emily. "Be a dear and pray for safe travel. Nowadays, the country roads are as dangerous as London's rookeries."

Jacob perked up. "Another robbery?"

"Indeed." Lady Benton fanned her face as though she might swoon. "Two highwaymen accosted Lord and Lady Copeland.

Lightened him of his purse and her of a fabulous emerald set I adored."

Jacob gripped the lapels of his jacket. "You note what jewelry everyone wears?"

"Of course. Every woman does." Lady Benton tapped her index finger to her lip. "I didn't see you at the party."

"I was there."

Phoebe's shoulders straightened as she eyed Jacob as if he'd personally insulted her.

"I lingered with the gents," he said, "smoking cheroots and talking politics."

Phoebe pursed her lips, obviously disappointed, while Lady Charlton tugged at the end of her lace cuff as if bored.

Lady Benton rested a gloved hand on his upper arm. "I do hope you visit before I go. I've informed the staff to put their best bottle of brandy aside for me."

"I'm afraid I have plans, but I'm certain others will partake of the spirit with you."

The woman's mouth thinned into a white line. "I see." Her assessing gaze landed on Emily. "Well, when you grow tired of the country, and I daresay you soon shall, you may always visit my London townhome."

"The country air suits me." Jacob stood taller.

Phoebe's eyes sparked.

"So be it." Lady Benton turned, and the three ladies strolled toward the bakery.

Phoebe glanced at them over her shoulder twice before entering the establishment.

Emily narrowed her eyes on Jacob. "An invitation to her townhome?"

～

"*I* can explain." Jacob reached to cup Emily's elbow, but she stepped back.

"I may be green, but I'm not an imbecile." Emily planted her fists on her hips. "She's the one you dueled over."

Behind her, Mrs. Hayes gasped.

Jacob cringed. He'd forgotten about her housekeeper-turned-chaperone. How much had she overheard? "Due to a misunderstanding."

Emily spun to leave, but he grabbed her arm.

"Please." When he was a child, he used to hope, pray, sometimes even beg for his mother to take his side. That small boy did the same with Emily now.

Like Mother, Emily turned away.

"Let me explain."

"I must get back." She peered at him with renewed resolve. "Mrs. Hayes has supper to prepare, and I'm to help."

Jacob turned his pleading gaze on her part-time chaperone.

Mrs. Hayes twisted the fold of her skirt around her finger as if weighing the proper thing with her hope for young love. "There is plenty of time. Supper is an easy fix tonight."

Emily exhaled an exasperated breath and leveled Jacob with a glare. "Fine, but you will be hard pressed to change my mind."

"Challenge accepted." He couldn't fight back a triumphant grin. "We can talk as I escort you home."

He guided her down the main road, maneuvering around shoppers. His pace increased, and he searched for a secluded spot. He needed to speak to her alone—just for a few minutes—to get her to understand. He had wanted to amend his wrongs with Sarah back then, and now he was determined to set things right with Christian. Emily glanced back, and he did the same.

Mrs. Hayes was struggling to keep up.

Emily squeezed his arm. "Please slow down."

"I need to speak with you in private. It will only take a minute."

"I'm uncertain that's wise."

"It's the only way I can decide about my actions regarding Christian." He increased the pressure on her lower back and hurried to cross the street before a carriage rolled past.

She tried to pull away, but his hand snaked farther around her waist and tightened, drawing her closer to his side.

"I shall scream."

His steps didn't falter. She was bluffing. "You won't do that."

"I shall."

"You will create unwanted attention. People will talk." His voice softened. "Please, Miss Thompson. I will explain about what happened with Christian's mother."

Her resistance lessened, and she allowed him to lead her off the main road and onto a quieter street. The clapping of his boots on the cobblestones was the only sound until he pulled her into an alcove behind a flower shop.

She crossed her arms. "You have two minutes, so talk fast."

"You already know Christian is my son." Jacob stared into her eyes. "I was Johnny Raw, an inexperienced youth, not even out of university when I met Sarah—now the Duchess of Charlton. Her family inherited land near our country house and moved there for the fresh air in the summer. I was home on holiday. We both had demanding, aggressive fathers. We shared confidences and consoled one another. I thought I loved her."

As he relayed the tale of his unrequited love, Emily's expressions wavered between anger at his poor choices and heartbreak over the rejection he faced and the time lost with his son.

"I came to understand that what I thought was love was infatuation, but I was bitter. She refused to tell me where our son was. I set out to hurt Sarah the way she hurt me, so I attended parties and wore women on my arm like flashy jewels. Sarah saw, but so did the rest of the ton. I was branded a libertine, and the fast set flocked to me."

She shook her head. "You tried to fix a breakdown of virtue with another failure of virtue?"

"The consequences of a blackened reputation was a hard-earned lesson. My spite for Sarah dulled as my heart hardened. Nothing mattered to me. London's social scene bored me. It lacked meaning. I came to believe that there had to be more to life than parading in fancy attire to impress others. Yet frivolity was the aspiration of everyone around me. I grew dissatisfied and restless and started seeking thrills and entertainment—anything to get my heart to beat again."

The Home Office had noted his rogue ways and recruited him to woo the daughters of foreign political figures and wives of diplomates to extract information, but he couldn't admit as much to Emily. His explanations were flimsy because he couldn't explain that, at the time, he'd been on assignment to gather intelligence on Lord Benton. "A month ago, I was asked to join a night of drinking and card playing at Lady Benton's townhome, not realizing Lord Benton was out of town. Wine flowed, and Lady Benton offered her husband's bootlegged French brandy. I've never been much for spirits, but the others drank heavily, including Lady Benton, who became quite foxed.

"Looking back, I should have let the servants deal with her, but because of the honor instilled in me, I couldn't leave her lying on the floor next to her vomit. I scooped her up and carried her to her chamber, intending to let her sleep off the ill effects." Jacob swallowed hard through the tightness in his throat. "Lord Benton arrived shortly after I deposited her in her bed."

Emily gasped.

"I'm still paying the penance for my rakish behavior. My

reputation followed me here—along with Lady Benton." A cynical smile twisted his lips. "This was supposed to be my clean slate, an opportunity to start fresh and be a good role model to my son, but one's sins have a way of catching up with him."

∼

*E*mily bit her tongue. The Jacob she'd known since he arrived was a good role model for Christian. He was kind and cared for people. He gave of himself regardless of the consequences. But she dared not say her thoughts lest he decide he would make a good father and take Christian back to London with him.

"My brother Robert believes I have little regard for my life." He sighed. "Maybe he was right, but I've changed. The people of Sylvanwood have shown me what it's like to be content. They help each other and care about one another. I want to be part of that love because I care about Christian." He wrapped her hand in his. "And I care about you."

Emily's breath caught, her stomach somersaulting as if she rolled down a steep hill.

Why does he care about me?

Phoebe had the figure, the classic blond hair. She came from good stock. She dressed fashionably and offered a substantial dowry. She was the one who'd set her cap for Jacob and claimed to carry his child.

"But Phoebe—"

"I have not now nor have I ever held any affection for Miss Dorsham. Her attentions are misdirected." Jacob's expression darkened. "Miss Dorsham is walking a dangerous path. I was hoping you might talk some sense into her before it's too late."

Wasn't it already too late?

"I discovered her having a clandestine meeting with Lord Copeland."

"He's married." Emily gasped. "Are you certain?"

The intensity of his gaze strengthened. "Quite."

Phoebe's shrill voice rang in her memory. *You must finish my portrait early, for I'll be gone all next week. Mama and I have been invited to the Copeland house party.* Emily remembered Phoebe's exuberant face after their return. *The house party was lovely—a complete dream. I've returned no longer a girl but a woman.*

Emily's throat constricted. Phoebe couldn't marry an already married man. Was that why she'd been aggressively flirting with Jacob? To pawn off another man's child as his?

"I fear her choices will ruin her." Jacob shook his head. "I'm concerned because she's your friend, and I want to protect you from the scandal she may bring upon herself."

Why did she promise Phoebe she'd keep her confidence? She must confront Phoebe, have her stop this foolishness, and have her confess the truth to Jacob. If Phoebe didn't, she would —promise or no promise.

He cleared his throat, and the blue of his eyes darkened to a deep cobalt. "I care for you. You have upstanding character, gentleness, and goodness." His light chuckle danced in the air between them. "And splendid wit." He stepped closer. "My past isn't pretty, but I feel I've shed an old skin, and it's no longer a part of me. My future seemed dull, but now it's bursting with life and possibilities." He held her hand in his warm grip. "May I court you?"

Emily bit her bottom lip. Her heart screamed its sentiments, but she remained frozen. In her heart, she knew Jacob wasn't the father of Phoebe's child. He'd made mistakes, but since he'd been in Sylvanwood, God had been showing him the error of his ways and he'd repented.

Nevertheless, courtship wasn't possible. They were not suitable for each other. His blackened reputation would only darken the stigma she already carried of being baseborn, stamped upon her by her birth mother. She wanted to pretend the rest of society didn't exist and enter his world as she would dream of stepping into one of her paintings, but both were impossible.

Yet he looked at her as though all things were possible, as if she were a sought-after prize—that he'd tear down any wall, seize any territory, and defend her from any attack. Of all people, he should understand that all it took was one drop of mud to taint a clean glass of water, and impossible to separate once added.

Her emotions warred within her, and her knees wobbled. He cupped her elbows to steady her.

A tendril escaped her bonnet and swung down, brushing her cheek.

"The day you rescued me, I knew you were someone special." He gently toyed with the strand. "And the more I've gotten to know you, the more I understand what an amazing woman you are. You are talented and loyal. You are beautiful and smart."

He tucked the lock behind her ear, then traced the line of her jaw. His charm drew her like a magnetic pull.

The corner of his mouth turned up. "And you understand my humor. That's a rare find."

He seemed to look into her very soul as he pulled her into an embrace. The heady scent of lemongrass wrapped around her like soft, enticing currents, drawing her toward him until her eyes drifted close. His warm breath mingled with hers. The heat of his hands coursed through the fabric of her sleeves.

She waited, ready to welcome the feel of his lips over hers.

Someone sniffed—and not Jacob.

Mrs. Hayes had caught up with them.

Emily tore away from Jacob and turned her back. "I knew you couldn't change." She covered her burning cheeks with her hands, horrified at her wanton longings. Was she doomed to behave like her birthmother? "And neither can I."

Jacob reached for her. "Forgive me. I got carried away. I'm a fool. I didn't mean to—"

"Oh, there ye be." Mrs. Hayes rounded the corner. "I been looking all over fer ye. These ol' legs aren't as quick as you young'uns."

Emily dropped her hands and straightened.

Dear Lord, what did I almost do?

CHAPTER 17

"Mama, please, can we visit Lady Athol another time?" Emily and her mother rode in the carriage through Brownstone's wrought-iron gate.

"Emily, dear, what has come over you? Since when have you become opposed to visiting Lady Athol?"

Since her nephew attempted to kiss me yesterday, and I almost let him.

"She has been nothing but kind. The least we can do is call upon her and bring more jam and some of Mrs. Hayes's fresh scones as we usually do, especially since she threw a party in your honor. Besides, it's past time I reclaim the salon and we return the canvas to Brownstone Hall. Lord Warren's life-sized portrait keeps frightening Mrs. Hayes." Mama clicked her tongue. "She startles every time she walks in there, thinking there's a strange man in the house."

"Couldn't we have come tomorrow—when I'm to have a painting session?"

Mama flashed Emily one of her that's-enough looks. "If Lord Warren is home, I hope to speak to him. I want to hear more about what he told Papa. Find out his intentions."

Emily swallowed. As much as she wanted to learn Jacob's plans, it just seemed too soon after their near kiss to face him.

Once the carriage rolled to a stop, Emily lifted the hem of her cream-colored muslin walking dress and allowed the Brownstone Hall footman to aid her out of the conveyance. She would have preferred her sturdier frock, but Mama had insisted she choose one of her better dresses. She sighed. It would only encourage Jacob, but she couldn't exactly tell her mother that he'd asked to court her.

Lord Warren. I must stop thinking of him as Jacob.

Heat coursed through her veins. How dare he coerce her into a private meeting and attempt to kiss her? How dare *she* allow herself to get swept up by his charm and practically fall into his arms? Had she no self-respect? Had she no self-control? No strength to fight temptation?

Like her birth mother.

She tripped up the stone steps leading to Brownstone Hall's front entrance but gripped the railing to impede her fall.

Was that all it had taken for her birth mother? A single moment of weakness? A kiss igniting a passion that led to her assignation?

Mama glanced over her shoulder. "Do be careful. I don't want you spraining an ankle." She tapped the brass door knocker.

The sound of hammering and sawing rang in the background. The workmen had moved from the main house over to repair the stables and west wing.

Mr. Maslow swung the door open. "Good day to you Mrs. Thompson, Miss Thompson." His voice, as usual, was a few decibels too loud as he tugged on the sleeve of his brown livery waistcoat.

"Good day, Mr. Maslow. We've brought scones and jam for Lady Athol." Mama gestured toward the carriage. "And we're returning Lord Warren's portrait so that the finishing touches can be done in the original light. Might you have some footmen aid with moving it inside?"

"Indeed." He waved over two footmen and instructed them regarding the portrait before turning to Emily and her mother. "Lady Athol is awaiting your arrival. Please, follow me." He turned and shuffled down the hall.

Emily followed in a daze. The swoosh of blood rushed in her ears. No matter how hard she'd tried to live a godly life, she was susceptible to the same sins as her mother. Her insides felt like a fallen apple a worm had hollowed out. Her head hung. When it came down to it, she was as easily led astray as her mother.

Lady Athol rose as they entered the salon, her hands tightly clasped in front of her. A timid smile touched her lips, but her eyes sparkled with welcome. "Thank you for coming." She gestured to wingback chairs and sat herself. Her gaze settled on Emily, studying her.

Emily forced her legs to lower her onto the seat.

Mama asked about Lady Athol's welfare, and the women chatted. A shuffle of footsteps outside the door sent a surge of blood through her veins. *Please, don't let it be...* Her fingers dug into the armrests of her chair.

Mr. Maslow entered, carrying a tea tray.

Thank heavens. She didn't bother to examine the jolt of disappointment. What would she do if it had been Jacob—*er*—*Lord Warren*? She couldn't give him a cut direct or a slap across the face, which would be unspeakably rude in front of her mother and his aunt. Should she pretend nothing happened? Her mind drifted back to the feel of his warm hands on her arms, the nearness of him, his citrus scent overwhelming her senses.

I knew you were someone special...a rare find.

The memory of his words caressed her like the feel of silk.

Special. What tosh.

She'd always believed herself a strong woman. Samuel and Mr. Mathis had taught her to ride, shoot, and defend herself. But after what happened the day before, she knew she was weak—primarily where Jacob Warren was concerned. If only she could forget the man's existence, but she was tied to him because he was Christian's father.

God, make me strong again. Remove me from this awful situation or send Jacob back to London. Without Christian.

"I'm so grateful for my nephew." Lady Athol's voice cut through her thoughts. She passed a cup of tea to Emily.

Thanking her, Emily accepted the china cup with an Aynsley rose pattern.

Lady Athol sat back and sipped her tea. She inhaled a long breath, and her brow furrowed. "I'm certain you've heard, my husband was not a kind man."

Mama patted Lady Athol's wrist.

"Jacob has been a blessing. Because of his kindness and goodness, I've been able to hold my head up once again." She swept one hand out and glanced about her. "My home has been restored, and I can receive visitors for the first time in thirty years. I resisted at first. I'd lived in fear for so long, but Jacob coaxed me out of my confinement. He's taught me how to laugh again. Having him here has been good for these old bones."

Mama leaned in with a sympathetic smile. "We are delighted at the changes we've seen in you and Brownstone Hall. It broke my heart to think of you as a hostage here."

Lady Athol presented a sad smile. "Part of it was of my own making. I wonder if things might have been different if I'd sought help from the church community instead of barricading myself in my gilded prison."

The two footmen carried Lord Warren's painting past the salon's open door to be placed on the easel in the conservatory.

Lady Athol gasped and turned to Emily. "The portrait looks marvelous."

Mama eyed Emily with a proud slant to her lips. "God has blessed Emily with a wonderful talent."

"I must see it more closely." Lady Athol set aside her teacup and rose. "You don't mind, do you, Miss Thompson?"

"I guess not." *To see the painting—no. To roam the hall and perhaps be spotted by Jacob—yes, definitely.*

Lady Athol led the way, Mama and Emily trailing her. The corner of Lady Athol's shawl dragged along the floor, and Emily's fingers itched to lift and tuck it under her arm, but she didn't dare be so forward. She only wore one shawl today, and Emily couldn't remember her without at least two.

A door creaked, and Emily's gaze darted in that direction. A servant. She released a tiny sigh. She knew the route to the conservatory well. The door to the library hung open. She held her breath as she passed, but no sign of Jacob. A few books rested on the end table beside the sofa. One large tome, which appeared to be a Bible, lay next to a nub of a candle burned low. Was that the Bible Papa gave to Jacob?

Mama chattered about the renovations as they passed the door to the master's study. A stout man dressed in a brown cravat and matching coat sat at the desk, his head down, scribbling notes. He peeked up as she passed and nodded but returned to his writing. Was he waiting for Jacob? No one else was in the room. Something seemed familiar about the man. She'd seen his face before, but where? In town? At church?

Mama's voice bounced off the walls, and Emily wished she would lower her volume to a whisper so as not to draw undue attention.

Lady Athol rounded the corner into the conservatory and stepped aside with a genuine smile.

Mama entered the room and approached the canvas, which rested on its easel. "I do believe it's the largest portrait she's ever done." She grabbed Emily's hand and pulled her forward.

Lady Athol moved for a closer inspection. "You've captured

not only his form but his essence. It's the expression he wears when challenged just before he attacks with a witty remark." She clasped her hands at her waist. "After Jacob returns to London, I'll probably be sent to Bedlam for talking to the painting as if it were Jacob himself."

Had he set a date to leave? Jacob returning to London would save her from the temptation of his kiss. She should be overjoyed, but the knowledge only made her feel hollow. Of course, it did. She worried he would take Christian with him. That was all.

While the older women pointed out all the things they liked about the painting, she saw all the flaws. "I still have more detail to add to the hair, the face, and the clothing. I finished the background scenery at home." Emily fiddled with her thumbnail. "Initially, it's best to focus on the areas the—um—model must be present to paint. I need one more session of his lordship's time in the original lighting."

Lady Athol tilted her head. "Do you paint the clothes from memory?"

"My brother constructed a tailor's dummy, so I can borrow the original clothes and dress the wooden man in them so the subject can go about their day."

Lady Athol stepped closer. "The detail is incredible. Especially in his eyes."

Emily had seen that same glint yesterday, that maddening hint of arrogance, just before those blue depths darkened into a smoky gray. His steady gaze, laced with silent expectation, had seized her thinking ability.

Emily closed her eyes to shut out the tempting image of his lips hovering over hers, the sweetness of his words, and the tang of lemongrass haunting her senses. She itched to press her palms to her face and squeeze out the memory, but that would draw Mama's notice.

A baritone voice sounded in the hall, and Emily jolted. The

familiar clipping of Jacob's boots on the marble floors drew closer.

Mama and Lady Athol turned to face the door.

Emily slid partially behind her mother. Maybe, if she remained perfectly still, he wouldn't notice her. It was a farfetched plan, but she was out of options.

Jacob and the man she'd seen working in the study strode past, deep in conversation. The man handed Jacob a letter, and he tucked it inside his coat pocket.

He didn't notice. The tight muscles stiffening Emily's spine melted into a relaxed state.

The clipping of his boots stopped.

"Excuse me, Mr. Welsh. I need a moment."

The rich timbre of his voice vibrated through her. He backed up and halted in the conservatory doorway. His buckskin breeches clung to his muscled legs, and his dark umber coat enhanced the blue of his eyes, which panned the room and settled on her.

"Miss Thompson?"

She swallowed.

He stepped inside and bowed a deep, formal bow, addressing his aunt. "You didn't mention we'd be having company." He beamed one of his charming smiles at Mama. "Mrs. Thompson, jolly good to see you, and you, too, Miss Thompson." His assessing eyes lingered a tad too long on Emily.

She forced a smile, but the corners wobbled.

"I was going to pay you a call." His eyes held the same spark of hopefulness as when they almost kissed in the alley. "I have news."

Heat crept up her neck and settled in her cheeks.

"Good news, I hope." Mama clasped her hand to her bosom.

"Indeed." He moved closer and stood by his aunt's elbow. "I

heard back from Lady Kauffman, and she would like to see Miss Thompson's work. She wrote that if it's half as good as what I describe, she'd sponsor her for the academy."

Emily's breath caught. Lady Kauffman wanted to see her artwork? She deflated with an exhale. She couldn't go to London, nor be part of the academy. Someone would recognize her resemblance to her famously painted mother. Why did Jacob have to get her hopes up?

"That's wonderful news." Mama rounded on Emily with a broad smile. "You always wanted to be a member of the academy."

"Indeed." Emily forced cheer into her voice, then bit her lower lip. "But there are costs associated, and we have been saving for Christian to attend Eton."

Jacob raised a brow. "I'm certain something could be arranged."

"Speaking of Christian..." Mama straightened her shoulders, increasing her height by a half inch. "Since you're home, I would like to speak with you, Lord Warren. If you prefer, we can meet in private."

Emily swallowed.

Jacob appeared unfazed. "I'm assuming the vicar spoke to you about Christian?"

"He has." Mama laced her fingers and clasped them at her waist.

"My aunt is aware that I'm Christian's birth father, and Miss Thompson's astute eye began the conversation. It might be best if we all are part of the discussion."

"Agreed." Mama nodded.

"Please, have a seat." He gestured to the chaise lounge and surrounding chairs.

Mama and Emily perched on the chaise while Jacob and Lady Athol took the chairs.

A weary look creased Jacob's brow.

Mama didn't wait to address the situation. "So you are certain that you are Christian's natural father?"

"I am."

"I can see the resemblance. I'd like to know the story. My cousin, Sarah, spoke nothing of the father. We assumed a man had forced himself upon her."

Emily swallowed her gasp. Jacob wouldn't...

"My reputation might not be spotless, but I can assure you that I've never, nor would I ever, force myself upon a woman. I was quite smitten with your cousin. I'm not without blame, mind you. I've come to recognize my mistakes and to own up for my actions, especially my responsibility to Christian."

"Then why has it taken five years?" Mama's voice held a motherly reprimand.

Emily had never heard her mother be so forward.

Lady Athol opened her mouth, but Jacob quieted her with an upraised hand. He launched into the same story he'd told Emily—about his relationship with Sarah and how their friendship had grown to something deeper. About how much he'd cared for her and how brokenhearted he was when she didn't accept his proposal.

His expression grew somber, and his mouth set tight and grim. Despite Emily's misgivings with Jacob, her heart ached for him as he exposed his past mistakes. How many times would he have to bare his vulnerabilities for all to hear?

Would she have been able to endure such judgment?

At the mere thought, she wanted to cast up her accounts. All the more reason for her to be on guard. Another slip-up like yesterday's and she'd be in his spot, publicly professing her sins.

The only difference was that, for a woman, such indiscretions meant societal death.

If Phoebe didn't find a husband soon, she would face shame

and public shunning. Her parents would send her away and perhaps disown her.

"Ever since she disappeared to give birth to our child away from society," Jacob said, "I've been searching for him. With the help of an investigator, we traced him here." Jacob ended with his arrival in Sylvanwood.

Mama turned to Emily. "This is what he told you?"

"Almost to the word."

Lady Athol said, "The very same."

"It is also what my husband relayed to me." Mama released a long breath. "Our sins don't have to define us. It speaks to a person's character when they genuinely repent."

"I can't change what I've done." Jacob rubbed his hand over his mouth as if controlling his emotions. "I want what's best for my son."

Mama leaned forward and patted his knee. "Greatness doesn't demand perfection. It demands we take responsibility. Even King David, God's beloved, struggled with sin. He had an affair with Bathsheba and had her husband killed, but David repented to God, saying, 'Against Thee, and Thee only, have I sinned, and done this evil in Thy sight.' God forgave him. If you ask God, He will do the same for you."

"But there are so many wrongs." Strain lined his face.

Mama flashed a sympathetic smile. "God is aware of all of them. You can't hide anything from an omnipotent father."

"So I should pray...for forgiveness?"

Mama nodded.

"Prayer seems to be the answer to a lot of things."

"It doesn't mean the problem will go away, but a burden will be lifted."

Lady Athol squeezed her nephew's hand and smiled.

"I've been praying for wisdom and reading the Bible as the reverend suggested."

"And what has God shown you?" Mama asked.

Jacob shifted to lean on the chair's arm and stared out the window. "I'd always pictured God to be like my father—a tyrannical ruler judging and condemning people. But the more I read"—he blinked and returned his gaze to Mama—"and prayed, the more God seemed merciful, gracious, and forgiving." His eyes shadowed. "My father attended church every Sunday faithfully. We even have our own cushioned pew, but the man the world saw was very different from the man at home. He was often in his cups, and when he was..." Jacob's voice tightened. "He'd lash out in a vile rage at Mama or me or my brothers."

Emily pressed a hand to her stomach. *Poor Jacob.*

Lady Athol closed her eyes, and tears cascaded over her cheeks.

Mama sandwiched one of his hands between hers. "It's best not to judge Christ by those who claim to be Christians. We are human and therefore fallible. I ask that you judge our faith by the Creator, who will leave the ninety-nine to go after the one lost sheep."

Jacob blinked and leaned back in his chair, rubbing a hand over his eyes.

Emily had never wanted to throw herself into a man's arms. Yet everything within her wanted to cling to Jacob and weep. She gripped the side of her seat to stay in place.

"In your time with God," Mama asked, "has He given you any direction for Christian?"

This man, who always seemed to have something to say, fell silent. Mama watched him, waiting. A stranger wouldn't notice it, but Emily saw the lines of strain around her mouth and eyes. She saw fear there.

Seconds passed, and still Jacob didn't speak.

Even the birds chirping outside quieted.

Jacob's lips parted, but he frowned and shook his head.

"God told him to purchase a toy boat to sail with Christian."

The words blurted out of Emily's mouth. Her eyes shifted from Mama to Lady Athol and froze on Jacob, whose gaze snapped in her direction. "So he could spend more time with Christian and get to know him."

What was she doing? Advocating for Jacob to take Christian away from her? She bit her tongue. She may be sympathetic to what Jacob was going through, but she needn't aid him.

"A lovely idea," Mama said. "I, too, have been praying and wrestling this out with God. I believe God has impressed the same on my heart as a next step." Mama paused. "Well, maybe not the toy boat precisely, but that you spend time with Christian."

"Then what?" Emily couldn't mask the panic in her voice.

Mama eyed her, love in her gaze. "We wait and continue to pray until God reveals the rest of His plan." She turned back to Jacob. "In the meantime, you may drive Emily home after your painting session tomorrow. Christian will be finishing his lessons then. He'll be delighted to see you."

Lady Athol straightened her shawl. "Jacob, why don't you and Emily take some air while I talk a bit more with Mrs. Thompson?"

Alone with Jacob? Absolutely not.

"You can show her all the plantings you've done by the pond," Lady Athol said. "Stay in view from the conservatory window."

Emily glared at her mother trying to impart her message. Wouldn't she want to censor their conversation?

"Lovely idea," Mama said, and Emily had to clench her teeth to keep her mouth from falling open. "The weather is beautiful today. I believe spring might be on its way."

Jacob rose and offered his arm to Emily. "Shall we?"

Emily sent up a please-save-me prayer to God before she stood and accepted Jacob's arm.

~

*J*acob strolled in the warm sunlight, Emily's graceful hand tucked neatly in the crook of his elbow as if she was meant to be on his arm. He hadn't realized how heavy a burden his secrets were to bear until confessing the truth lightened him. Now that she knew his past, would she be willing to be part of his future? She, too, felt the pull between them. He had seen it in her eyes yesterday, but he'd sabotaged the progress he'd made in explaining his heart when he attempted to kiss her. This morning, she'd appeared tentative, but then she had advocated for him after he hesitated on saying he'd heard from God.

His day had been full of pleasant surprises. He'd stolen a moment before he met with his steward to read a missive that arrived from Lieutenant Scar. Lord Benton had indeed been spotted in Bath, and the confirmation of his assailant being a day's ride away allowed Jacob to relax. At least he needn't wonder if a bullet would hit him while his back was turned. At least not today.

The still-murky pond water reflected his and Emily's linked silhouettes. A red-breasted robin hopped on both feet in the yellowed grass, stopping to pluck a juicy worm from the earth. Jacob pointed to the winter aconite, which had started to bloom with a spray of yellow flowers, a sign that life would begin again after a long winter.

His heart lightened from Mrs. Thompson's words. He could be forgiven. There was still hope he could change—perhaps be a father to his son. Maybe even settle down and find a wife.

After Sarah's betrayal, he'd never longed for a wife. Women had only caused him problems. But his aunt proved not all women were conniving like those in Jacob's social circles, and Mrs. Thompson was a lovely woman who didn't shun him for his past, but instead had been nothing but kind and understanding. Maybe there were women whom he could trust with his heart. The idea had planted in the desolate soil of his heart the moment he woke to find Emily had risked her life to save him. Further encounters with her continued to water the belief that she was different. He glanced down at the timid beauty beside him.

She could be trusted with the intimacy of his heart.

Was this what it would feel like to stroll with Emily as his wife? She already knew and loved Christian. Did they have a chance of becoming the family he'd dreamed of but never believed possible? He was comfortable in Emily's presence. He didn't have to maintain appearances or use witty quips as a sword to bolster his defenses. She knew the truth about him and had yet to run away—well, maybe at the mercantile, but she was here with him now.

Only her fingertips rested on his forearm. Instead of brushing against his shoulder or hanging on his arm as most women did, she kept a distance of several inches.

By Jove, she wanted to run.

His steps slowed. Inside, Emily had defended him, and when he'd regarded her, she'd appeared so compassionate. She melted his heart and stirred a protectiveness within him he hadn't felt for any woman except his mother. But what he felt for Emily was different. He longed to hold her, tuck her head under his chin, and rub his thumb against the soft skin at the nape of her neck. He desired to make her smile and hear her laughter.

Meanwhile, she was withdrawn and ready to bolt.

She glanced his way and caught him staring. "What is the matter?"

"Nothing."

She pursed her lips. "Something's bothering you. I can tell by the deep crease between your brows."

Blast, she was observant. He rubbed his forehead with his thumb and index finger to relax the muscles.

"Are you upset by what Mama said?"

He shook his head.

"What I said?"

"Of course not." He sighed. "It's...it's how you're acting."

She frowned. "How am I acting?"

"As if you want to flee."

She paled.

A loose tendril of hair fell, dangling between her eyes. He reached for it, and she stepped back.

"Did I imagine the feelings between us yesterday?" he asked. "You didn't force distance between us then. What changed? Was it something I said inside?"

"No." She licked her lips and tucked the errant strand behind her ear. "I'm not like other women."

"That's what I like best about you."

She turned away. "We are of a very different class, you and I."

"You're the vicar's daughter." He stepped around to face her. "Born and raised in a genteel manner by a gentleman. You are well respected within the community. I might have been born into the peerage, but I'm a third son. I hardly think anyone would bat an eye at our courtship."

"I have a reputation to uphold."

"I see." His stomach twisted into a tight knot. "You're ashamed to be seen with me." He stepped back, and her hand fell from his arm. "God will forgive my past, but you won't." He forced a calm tone through his tight jaw. "In that case, I'll leave you to finish the walk on your own."

She stayed him with a hand on his arm. "It's not that."

"What is it, then?" Emily's beautiful face was suddenly blurred by the image of his father, the man's disappointment falling upon him like a heavy yoke.

"I'm scared." Her lower lip quivered.

Scared? She was afraid—of him?

His anger melted away, and he stepped closer. "I would never hurt you."

"Not intentionally." She drew back and closed her eyes. "Please don't look at me that way. That is how it begins, and I can't allow it to happen."

He shook his head as though a good shake would add understanding in the gaps her words failed to fill in. "I'm not following."

"Sin. I can't fall into sin." Her chest rose and fell with her quick breaths.

He raised his palms to catch her if she swooned.

"I almost let you kiss me." Her eyes opened, pools of amber glistening with unshed tears. "I wanted you to."

Oh. A smile tugged at the corners of his lips, but he worked hard to keep it from blooming on his face. The temptation to pull her into his arms stole the breath from his lungs.

"I can't. I'll become like my mother."

He glanced at the window behind which Mrs. Thompson sat with his aunt.

She spun on her heel and dashed back into the house.

"Emily. Wait." He jogged after her, but she didn't stop until she was next to the house entrance.

He joined her there. "Explain what you mean."

She didn't—merely slowed her breathing and squared her shoulders, behaving as if what she'd just said made sense. But as far as Jacob knew, Mrs. Thompson's character was beyond reproach.

He didn't understand.

CHAPTER 18

"*Y*ou lied to me." Emily crossed her arms and blocked Phoebe from getting down from her phaeton and darting into Brownstone Hall, where their discussion would end.

"Whatever are you talking about?"

Emily dropped her gaze to Phoebe's stomach and then resumed eye contact. "You know exactly what I mean. You're my closest friend. We've shared confidences, and you know my secret. Why lie, especially to me?"

Phoebe glanced back at her snoring companion. "I had no choice. I needed—still need—your help to snare Lord Warren."

"You mean *trap* him." Emily pursed her lips. "It's not his child."

Phoebe's lips curled and nose wrinkled. "I can't believe you told him."

"I didn't."

"No one will have me"—Phoebe spoke over her—"if word gets out. I'll be ruined. My parents will send me away. Is that what you want? So you can keep him for yourself? Don't you think you're overstepping?"

"Did you not hear me?" Emily struggled not to raise her voice and draw attention or wake Ms. Neves. "He told me."

Her friend blanched. "He knows? How?"

"I don't have the foggiest."

Phoebe grabbed Emily's arm and jumped down from the Phaeton. "I'm doomed unless I can convince Lord Warren to marry me. Would you truly let one wrong decision ruin me? Please have compassion"—her eyes pleaded—"like your mama who took in your birth mother when she was in trouble. And Christian's mother. Doesn't my child deserve a good life like you've had?"

God had blessed Emily with a wonderful family when she could have been tossed in an orphanage or raised crushing bones in a workhouse. The child was innocent of wrongdoing, and Phoebe was right in that her baby would fare better under a mother and father's protection. Emily's near-kiss with Jacob proved how easily one could slip into sin. Should she be so tough on Phoebe for falling into temptation? Emily wavered.

"Please, Em."

Emily had never heard such desperation.

I care for you. Jacob's sentiments rang in Emily's ears.

Encouraging him to marry Phoebe still seemed wrong and an unlikely feat, but at least Jacob knew Phoebe was having another man's child. "You're going to do what you want to do. I'm not going to stand in your way, but I will not be part of any deception."

Phoebe accepted Emily's statement as agreement and nudged Miss Neves awake. Threading her arm through Emily's, Phoebe strode toward the entrance to Brownstone Hall, exuding confidence.

Which Emily did not feel.

~

*P*raise God. This would be their last session. Emily added the last details to Jacob's face in the painting, including a little highlight to emphasize his full lower lip. She picked up a different brush and blended a deeper purple into the lowlight at the bottom of his cheekbone just before his ear.

A book dropped with a loud bang on the marble floors. Emily startled at the sound, smudging purple paint on the canvas. *Drat.* Now she'd have to wait for the paint to dry before fixing the smear.

"Oh dear, dreadfully sorry." Phoebe leaned over to retrieve her book, and Emily blushed at the glimpse it afforded from the low-cut gown.

Jacob's glance flicked in Phoebe's direction but didn't linger.

Phoebe's nostrils flared as she glowered at his profile. Her attempts at turning Jacob's eye had transformed from flattery to degrading displays of seduction. The only exception was when his aunt joined them for tea. Then she behaved as a respectable lady of her station.

Phoebe's desperation showed. It was her last week to wring a proposal out of Jacob before she headed to London for the Season, and it turned Emily's stomach to watch her friend belittle herself in such a manner. Several times, Emily had explained that such displays wouldn't attract Lord Warren, but Phoebe had only laughed and said, "You don't understand the ways of flirtation and how ladies of the ton go about it."

Perhaps not, but it was as clear as the smudge of purple on her canvas that Jacob wasn't impressed as Phoebe flaunted her figure.

Jacob's jaw was tensed, and the crease between his eyes had only deepened in the previous few minutes.

Phoebe monopolized the conversation, which allowed Emily to focus on her work. She found a way to blend the purple smudge into a crease in Jacob's jacket and added a few highlights and lowlights elsewhere. Yet whenever Emily studied Jacob's face to add the final details to his features in the painting, he issued her a we-have-much-to-discuss look.

She stepped back and examined her work. Jacob's eyes still held his initial mocking laughter, but she'd layered a serious undertone in their depths, which she'd seen more in his recent poses, adding to his cheeky rogue mystique.

"I'm not certain of which I am more excited, my send-off ball or my coming out." Phoebe paced in front of Jacob.

Emily worked around the interruption. She'd given up informing Phoebe that her sauntering back and forth blocked Emily's view of her subject.

"I hope those highwaymen don't scare off my guests." Phoebe sighed. "We've instructed our coachman to keep his weapon ready and allotted for an extra footman after Lord Copeland's coach was raided."

A vertical crease formed between Jacob's eyebrows, but she didn't scold him since she'd finished his forehead already.

"They stole Lord Copeland's pocket watch and emerald cufflinks and Lady Copeland's emerald earbobs, bracelet, and necklace. Their driver took a blow to the head, which knocked him out, and the highwaymen got away." Phoebe fanned her face. "To think, I'd been at the same party and left minutes after Lord Copeland and his wife. The thieves could have stolen my sapphire pendant if we'd taken the long way home. I do hope the bandits are caught before two weeks hence. The entire town will be in attendance to usher me into—" Phoebe stopped her pacing. Her face tinged chartreuse green, and her lower lip quivered. She whispered, "Pardon me."

She strolled from the room, but after she turned the corner, Emily heard the soft footfalls of her slippers as she dashed down the hall. She was sick, no doubt a symptom of her condition.

Lord help her.

A rush of air passed through Jacob's lips, and his shoulders relaxed. "It amazes me that you two are friends." He quirked a lopsided grin. "There have never been two women so different."

A weight pressed on Emily's heart. As children, they'd been inseparable. She and Phoebe had shared the same schoolroom, dreams, and hopes. They shared a history. No one knew her like Phoebe did. Recently, her friend had changed.

Emily lowered her brush. "We may differ in appearance and social ranking, but when that is all stripped away, we are very much the same."

Jacob raised a single brow. "I find that hard to believe."

Perhaps he'd appreciate her friend's inner qualities. "Phoebe is a passionate, caring person who simply wants to be wanted." Emily wiped her brush clean. "Her parents show her off like a jeweled brooch but don't show their love unless she's performing. That is all she knows. She may parade around as though she's the heir apparent, but deep down, Phoebe fears being found lacking. One of the things I admire about her is her boldness to go after what she wants."

"Like a tigress ready to pounce on its prey."

Emily ignored his comment. "She fearlessly follows her heart. A man would be lucky to have such a passionate woman by his side."

His face darkened. "Problems arise when desire is mistaken for love."

As he had with Sarah? Emily cleared her throat. "Phoebe is a beautiful woman of means and quality, a woman society and your family would approve."

Jacob shook his head. "I've seen what a loveless marriage can do. My father feels nothing but disdain for my mother, and my mother fears my father. They make each other miserable. Call me a romantic, but I want something more."

He broke his pose and walked toward her, stopping beside the canvas. "Is it wrong to hope for someone who at least sees potential within me? Someone capable of returning my love—maybe not now, but in the future? Someone who doesn't rush in like a fool but carefully weighs her decisions. Someone who is loyal to a fault? Someone like you."

Blood rushed into her hands and feet, causing them to tingle. "Like me?"

"Emily." He rubbed his hands down her arms.

A shiver ran over her skin. Walk away. *Run.*

"Precisely like you." He stepped closer. "Someone who notices the little things about me. Someone who cares and loves deeply."

The intense, radiant blue of his eyes bore deep into her soul.

He cupped her elbows in his hands, and she could feel the support of their rugged strength. Her knees had turned to water. His warmth draped around her like a dressing robe filled with his familiar lemongrass scent. She swayed toward him.

"What is going on here?" Phoebe's voice sounded from the doorway.

Emily snapped her gaze that way.

Jacob's hands dropped to his sides, and Emily stepped back.

Color had returned to Phoebe's pale face. The greenish tint had been replaced by pink, quickly turning red.

Emily swallowed at the accusatory glare in Phoebe's eyes. She'd meant to persuade Jacob's affections toward Phoebe, not become swayed herself. "We were discussing you."

Jacob moved back into position to resume painting.

Phoebe raised her chin. "It must have been a very intimate discussion."

"I...we...it was merely...nothing." Emily moved toward her. "Truly."

Phoebe stood stock still, her hands clasped tightly in front of her. "It seems *my friend*"—bitter betrayal stung her words—

"can entertain you just fine without my help." She stirred Miss Neves. "I must be going. There is much to do."

The woman roused and stood.

Phoebe stepped back, tugging her gloves up on her arms. "There are details to attend to for my farewell party—decorations, food, refreshments, and the like." She shot Jacob a frigid smile. "I shall see you next Friday evening. Good day, my lord." She bobbed a dainty curtsy and swiveled her head toward Emily with an icy glare. "Emily."

With a swish of her skirts, she turned and left the room. "Come, Miss Neves."

The woman hurried to follow.

"Phoebe, wait." Emily started after her, but Jacob caught her wrist.

"Let her go."

Emily whirled on him, breaking her hand from his grasp. "She's my friend. I have to explain."

Jacob held her gaze. "By the way your friend treats you, I'd hate to meet your enemies."

Lady Athol strolled around the corner and peeked in on her nephew. "Miss Dorsham left in a huff. Is everything all right?"

Jacob stuffed his hand into his pocket. "Miss Dorsham decided there was much to be done before the party."

She stepped into the room and spied the painting. "Oh, Miss Thompson, it is coming along famously."

Emily eyed the door, still tempted to chase her friend. How much had Phoebe heard? Would she forgive her for falling for Jacob? Wasn't there an unwritten rule of the friend honor code —thou shall not fall for the man upon whom thine's closest friend had set her cap?

"It appears to be finished," Lady Athol said. "Is it not?"

Emily turned her attention to the portrait. "There is more to be done with the clothing."

She paused, knowing what needed to be said but wishing it

weren't so. "I no longer require your presence, my lord. If you could have your footman deliver the canvas to my home in a couple days after the paint has dried, I can finish the work there."

Jacob's gaze locked on hers.

She swallowed, surprised by the tears clogging her throat.

His brow furrowed.

"I will need to borrow your shirt and pants."

He drew back. "Pardon?"

She ignored his grin. "A servant can model for me, or I can use my tailor's dummy."

"Why would you want to do that when you can have the real thing?"

"I do not want to take any more of your time away from the hall's renovations."

"I can manage."

Lady Athol tilted her head. "The renovations are coming along quite nicely. The new steward Jacob hired has freed much of his time." She glanced out the window. "It is such a pleasant day. Why don't you two take in the air?"

Hot tears pressed on the back of Emily's eyelids. Being alone with Jacob was the last thing she needed. She couldn't trust herself not to jump into his arms. She couldn't cling to false hope. Phoebe would have taken full advantage of the moment, but Emily wasn't Phoebe, and she wasn't a maiden in a fairytale.

Was romance supposed to be so complicated? She'd let down her friend and only encouraged Jacob. Jacob's family, especially his father, would want him to make a better match. How disappointed they'd be if they knew he believed himself in love with the adopted daughter of a country vicar. And then there was the fact that Jacob was Christian's father.

"I'm sorry. I must be going."

"Your brushes need cleaning," Lady Athol said. "I'll have

Maslow see to them while you stroll the grounds." She swept from the room.

Emily called after her retreating form. "I can take care of them at home."

"I see." His jaw tightened.

No, he didn't see. She wasn't rejecting him. Despite any feelings they held for each other, this was an impossible venture. "It's challenging to wash oil paints with water. You need the proper mineral spirits."

"Indeed, oil and water do not mix."

"Rightly so." She swallowed around the lump in her throat. "If the paint sets, the brush will be ruined. All you can do is discard it."

"I'd like to think, if given the proper treatment, the brush can be saved. One must have the patience to work it out."

She had the distinct impression they weren't talking about brushes anymore. "Some things are too far gone."

"Like me." His jaw tightened. "You have grace for your friend, just not for me."

"It's not about you." She pressed her fingers to her temples even though she'd probably leave a paint smudge. "It's extending grace to myself that I can't do."

"You're so fearful of sinning that you refuse to feel? You'll marry a man like Mathis, who you don't love and never will, in order to avoid deep attachments?"

No. Of course not.

Except...was that what she was doing?

Her hands fell back to her sides. She liked Mr. Mathis in the same way she liked her brother. That was a good place to start, wasn't it? He'd be a good provider.

Everyone expected her to marry him.

But did she love him? No, not as a wife should love her husband.

Could she, in time? Perhaps. But could she ever feel for him what she felt for Jacob?

Did it matter? Mr. Mathis was safe. Jacob was...dangerous. Everything about him was reckless.

"Is that God's best for you?" Jacob no longer looked hurt. He stepped toward her, head tilted to one side, eyes filled with curiosity. And maybe something else.

He didn't understand.

I'm tainted, unworthy of God's best.

The tenderness and determination in Jacob's eyes awed and frightened her.

A voice from her heart whispered. *If God has redeemed Jacob, then you, too, can be redeemed.*

She wrapped her brushes in a rag to wash later. "I must go."

"Maslow will have a carriage brought around." He aided her in packing her belongings. "I promised your mother I would see you home, and I want to remind Christian of our race tomorrow."

Tomorrow. It seemed no matter what she did, she was destined to see Jacob.

He rang for his valet while she finished packing her paints. She accompanied Jacob to the curricle, and a footman passed her a laundered shirt and breeches.

"We have more to discuss." Jacob eyed her and snapped the reins.

Discuss or persuade? "I need to sort my thoughts. I suggest we wait." *For a week, a month, maybe never.*

A crooked smile brought the taunting spark back into his eyes. "I'm open to suggestions"—he raised her paint-stained hand to his lips and kissed the back—"just not taking them." He squeezed her fingers before releasing them. "But I'll give you until tomorrow."

Argh! If only she had a fifth of his confidence.

CHAPTER 19

The following afternoon, the mantel clock chimed the three o'clock hour as Emily curved the paintbrush bristles around the rolling clouds of a landscape she'd painted to quiet her roaring thoughts. Jacob and Christian would return from the stream at any moment. She wanted to make herself scarce and retreat to her bedroom because Jacob would surely seek her out to finish their discussion. But she'd mixed too much paint, and it would go to waste if she cleaned up now.

Perhaps she could complete the lowlights. She added a liberal amount of darker gray to her brush and swept another line parallel with the horizon and a couple more lines on the pond's reflection underneath.

She'd successfully avoided Jacob earlier. Guilt had eaten at her as Christian and Jacob waited for her in the side yard. Eventually, she'd sent Samuel to them with an excuse about her heel getting caught in her gown lining and tearing it, advising them to go on without her. It wasn't a lie. Her heel had gotten caught in her dress—a couple of days ago, but she'd already mended it.

God forgive her. She couldn't face Jacob yet. Her feelings had fallen into a mixing bowl and were whisked into confusion.

She wanted to separate herself from him, keep him at a proper distance, merely a portrait subject and nothing more. But her mind feared what her heart seemed to already know.

Those eggs couldn't be unscrambled.

How could Jacob endearing himself, not only to her but also to Christian, end well? Their hearts would break when Jacob returned to his ostentatious life in London. She couldn't fathom the pain if he took Christian with him.

This morning, she'd awoken early to watch the sunrise and pray. But a barrage of questions distracted her time with God. God wouldn't allow Jacob to take Christian away from them, and Jacob wouldn't dare take Christian back to London. If he did, Christian would be branded as illegitimate. He'd be an outcast—shunned from society. Jacob wouldn't do that to him, would he?

And why would God allow her to have feelings for Jacob? She could never go to London, never live as Jacob's wife there. God knew her mother's reputation and how her partially nude image also hung in Carlton House, the prince regent's home. It would have been simpler if she could have loved Mr. Mathis and Jacob had fallen for Phoebe. That would have solved Phoebe's problem.

But Jacob would have been deceived into believing Phoebe's child was his.

All the hypotheticals would drive her mad and still leave her with a broken heart.

"Emily! I won. I won!"

Christian charged into the converted art studio, waving his toy boat above his head, and circled her easel.

"Careful around the painting."

"*Pirate Catcher* won. It beat out Lord Jacob's boat by at least two yards."

"I'm demanding a rematch."

She tensed at the sound of Jacob's voice. Why hadn't she

cleaned up earlier? How much would the wasted gray paint have cost her? She turned to face her punishment.

Jacob leaned against the door frame, his arms crossed and a smug grin lifting one side of his mouth. His gaze dropped to her hands, and his smile faded.

She followed his line of vision to a spear of red paint near her wrist.

He paled.

"Wait!" She grabbed a cloth. "It's paint." She wiped the paint away. "See?"

He sucked in a ragged breath. "Phew. We didn't need another ship sinking today."

Emily gasped. "Your ship sank?"

"No, but Christian didn't warn me that the *Shark Hunter* could run aground on a reef." He arched a brow at Christian. "Don't worry. I don't hold grudges. I merely remember things for a long, long time." He winked, ruining the stern effect.

Christian returned a similar arched brow—a mirror image. "You got stuck in the reeds. Creeks don't have reefs to run aground on."

"I had you beat."

"That's because you released the boat before Samuel said 'go.'"

"Did not." Jacob's petulant tone almost had Emily forgetting to fret.

She tended her brushes as they recounted the match. There was no question that Christian was Jacob's son. Perhaps Christian would be better off knowing his true father. She'd sacrifice her own life for Christian's happiness, but would that mean letting him go?

Surely, her parents wouldn't allow it, but they kept saying it was in the Lord's hands and to pray to understand His will. *God, I promised to protect Christian.*

"Did you see the *Pirate Catcher* almost tip over as it rounded the bend?"

"I thought it was a goner for sure." Jacob ran a hand along the back of his neck. "It was strange how my boat changed direction. It was on a direct path to the finish line."

Christian giggled. "That frog knocked it off course and drove it into the reeds."

"What frog?"

"You didn't see it jump off the lily pad?"

Jacob scowled, and Christian laughed louder.

Emily gathered her brushes in one hand to take to the sink.

"Confound it," Jacob said. "A frog? Really? Those creatures are the bane of my existence."

Emily recalled Jacob's tale of the happy little frog's croak, nestled in his mother's bosom, and a burst of laughter exploded from her lips. She raised her arm to cover her mouth since her fingers were smeared with paint.

"Go ahead and laugh at my expense"—Jacob cocked an eyebrow—"but don't be surprised if you one morning wake up to find frogs stuffed in your slippers."

She eyed Jacob and Christian with a look she hoped communicated, *don't you dare*.

"Let me help you with the brushes." Jacob moved to her side and wrapped his warm hand around hers.

His nearness drew her nerves tighter than a bow string, and the heat of his touch sent her skin up in flames. She didn't remove her hand. "I don't want you to get paint on your clothing. The stain will not come out no matter how often you wash it."

"The gentleman inside me cannot stand idly by."

She tugged on the brushes, but his grip tightened.

"I insist."

His gaze flowed into her with the intensity of a river current after a heavy rainstorm.

She released the brushes. "They must be taken outside and soaked in mineral spirits."

He issued her a curt nod. "Lead the way."

Christian played a game of pretend pirate adventure with his boat as they left the room and strode into the kitchen.

She gestured at a small basin on the counter, and he set the brushes inside while she retrieved a bottle of mineral spirits and a cloth for Jacob to wipe paint off his hands. She picked up the basin with the brushes, but Jacob took it. He *was* a gentleman, and she appreciated his noble gesture. She showed him outside to a small table where the powerful turpentine scent wouldn't seep into the house, poured the solvent onto the brushes, and worked the paint from the bristles.

Mrs. Hayes was nearby, hanging the wash out to dry. A gentle breeze ruffled the sheets already pinned on the line.

Jacob's gaze flicked between Emily and Mrs. Hayes.

He wanted to speak to Emily, but Mrs. Hayes stilled his tongue. *God bless the dear woman.*

A comfortable silence fell between them as Emily worked.

Jacob covered a yawn.

"Am I boring you? There's no need for you to stay. I appreciate your assistance, but I can take care of this."

"I'm not bored." He leaned against the house. "I could watch you work all day."

"Is that a threat?"

He chuckled. "Pardon my ill behavior. I woke early and watched the sunrise."

"It was rather colorful this morning with pink streaks and indigo clouds." She swished the brushes, muddying the clear mineral oils.

"I thought the sky was more violet than indigo."

"Truly, there's not much of a difference." Emily massaged the paint from the brush and glanced his way. "Was there a reason you watched the sunrise?"

"I do every morning. I look forward to it. It's the most peaceful part of the day, before the staff awakes and bustles about. The morning holds the most promise." He shrugged. "Unless it's raining, of course."

She paused and stared at him. "I didn't know that about you." Did he know that she, too, got up every morning to enjoy the sunrise and pray?

"Keep this as our secret. I try to uphold a tough image." He pushed away from the house. "I thought you'd understand, being God's canvas and all that." He waved a hand.

Mrs. Hayes ducked around a sheet and bobbed a curtsy before slipping back into the house.

Jacob didn't hesitate. He stepped so close that it would have been rude for Emily to continue her work. Their gazes held. "There's a connection between us. I've felt it since you rescued me."

His eyes darkened like storm clouds, and his nearness sent a shiver of anticipation over her skin.

Mrs. Hayes returned with more clothespins.

Jacob drew back but didn't step away.

Mrs. Hayes eyed them, and her steps slowed. She patted her skirts and mumbled about forgetting something before retreating into the house.

Jacob leaned in again. "I knew my world wouldn't be the same after we met. You've helped me see life differently because you hold no pretenses, no airs. With you, I can be my true self, no guarded walls or secrets. I want to court you not like I used to woo ladies, but with marriage intended. I trust you, and I haven't been able to say that about many people. I no longer want to return to my old life. More than ever, I want to lead a life pleasing to God"—he took her hand, ignoring the mineral oil that covered it—"and to you."

His words filled the dam of her heart to nearly overflowing. Never had she wanted to hear something so badly—but at the same time, it wasn't true. She wasn't to be trusted. She wasn't a vicar's daughter. She was the bi-blow of an opera singer and could never step foot into his life in London without being recognized. Nor had she been honest with him about Phoebe due to her promise. She longed to open the floodgates and let herself absorb the sweet bliss, but Jacob mingled with lords and ladies in London. He was expected to marry the likes of Phoebe, and Emily was supposed to marry the likes of Peter Mathis.

What her heart wanted was too risky. Why couldn't Jacob see that?

A white cap peeping above the window caught Emily's attention before it ducked away.

"Please, allow me to escort you to the Simmons' dance. It's a small venue, but I want others to see what a rare and brilliant woman you are, and I want you by my side. You're worth risking my heart for, and I'd be a fool to let you get away." He leaned in farther. "I know you feel the same way. I can see the tender affection in your eyes. The pull between us in the alley and again in the solarium before Phoebe interrupted us was over-powering." He ran his thumbs over the back of her hands. "There's something uniting us. It's real, tangible. Undeniable."

Tears filled Emily's eyes. She didn't dare blink, fearing she'd send them cascading down her cheeks.

"You don't have to say anything. I know you need time to consider what I'm proposing."

"Don't you see?" Tears blurred her vision. "You told me your father believes you to be a failure? Think of how disappointed he'd be in me."

"I've learned not to weigh my father's opinions heavily."

"He'll hate you even more when he finds out. Everyone will know. I'll be scorned."

"Because of me?" His brows drew together. "I'll change. I'll make them understand."

Her head shook violently. "No, because of me. Because of who I am."

"You are wonderful. Everyone will love you as I do."

"You don't understand."

"Then help me."

"I'm..." She choked on the word. "I'm...adopted." Her body recoiled against the sound. *And baseborn.*

"Like Christian?" He paused, but his eyes jumped as if creating a mental checklist and refuting items.

A thousand knives dug into her heart and twisted. She stepped away from his hold and paced as though she could shake off her torment. "I received information regarding my birth mother—a well-known opera singer. There is no denying I'm her daughter."

Jacob's face was a stone mask as he sorted the new information. He reached for her. "I don't care."

She angled out of his reach. "I do. I have to. I must think of my family and what pain a poor reputation would cause them. I must think about Christian's future employment and marriage prospects."

"No one will know. The Thompsons raised you as their own."

"I must remain in Sylvanwood, where people won't recognize the resemblance between my mother and me. She posed for paintings...nude paintings." Heat flooded her cheeks. "My family means everything to me. For them, I'll sacrifice my dream of going to London to study at the academy, and for them, I must sacrifice my feelings for you."

"Don't you think God will provide a way?" Jacob stepped closer, looking more confused than hurt. "Can't we trust Him to cover the sins of your parents as He's forgiven the sins of my past?"

Her heart told her *yes*. God was all-powerful. He was

merciful and forgiving. But her flesh screamed, and her logical side shouted, *I'm not worth the risk.*

"Shouldn't we trust God with this situation—with our futures?"

In her torment, she couldn't find words to respond. Tension electrified the air between them as he waited for her answer.

Mrs. Hayes returned, sneaking around the corner as if hesitant to intrude upon their moment but unable to dally in her duties any longer.

Emily wilted inside as he waited for an answer. When she remained silent, his gaze flickered with pain, and his expression fell.

He was disappointed in her, and it stabbed her heart.

"I don't need an answer now. Pray about it." He bowed and excused himself.

Her heart crushed under the image of his normally confident posture sagging as he walked away.

Oh God, where is my faith? And when did Jacob's become so strong?

CHAPTER 20

"*H*ave a seat, Emily." Papa gestured to the chair in front of his desk.

It creaked when she sat, and she felt the wooden slats through the well-worn cushion.

"Peter Mathis has returned from London."

"How splendid." She forced the words to sound more enthusiastic than she felt. Her stomach didn't swirl, nor did her heartbeat quicken as it did at the mention of Jacob's name.

"He visited me at the church office."

"Oh?" The pastry she'd eaten for breakfast turned to stone.

"He's asked for your hand."

Her head ached as if her blood had thickened into sludge. Jacob's voice pressed through. *You are worth risking my heart for. There's something uniting us. It's real, tangible. Undeniable. Can't we trust God to cover the sins of your parents as He's forgiven the sins of my past?*

Papa studied her face. "Do you want to marry Peter?"

She swallowed. Wasn't that what was expected? Mr. Mathis was the safe choice. With Jacob, there were so many insurmountable obstacles. Could she take such a risk with her future?

Papa awaited her answer.

"Er—yes. Of course."

His brows sloped together. "Are you certain? You don't sound—"

"Mr. Mathis is the best option for me. We've grown up together, and he plans to remain in Sylvanwood. He's a God-fearing man with an upstanding reputation, and I shall not lack for anything. I'd be fortunate to be his wife."

Papa laced his fingers and leaned over his desk. "Have you prayed on it?"

Had she? Until she'd met Jacob, marriage to Peter Mathis had seemed like a foretold event, but now?

Don't you think God will provide a way?

"Seek God's will in this matter," Papa said. "Ask for His wisdom, and He will provide." Papa reached across his desk and squeezed her hand. "Sleep on it and let me know tomorrow."

Emily swallowed. Papa was right, but was she brave enough to heed God's answer?

~

*M*athis had returned.

Jacob overheard Miss Dorsham saying as much to her mother as she climbed out of the carriage along-side Miss Neves in Fairford, where Lady Simmons hosted a pre-season soirée. After they'd alighted and entered the manor, alive with music and chatter, he snapped the reins, and the horses trotted toward the stables to park and be watered.

Jacob joined other coachmen, except this time, instead of driving near the center of other carriages to eavesdrop, he stopped along the outskirts so he could sneak into the party as a guest.

Emily had come by and finished the painting while he'd been calling upon Lord Copeland to question him regarding the events on the night of the highway robbery. He'd hoped she would change her mind regarding his invitation, but she had not.

With Mathis back to lay claim upon Emily, Jacob wanted to get this night over with so he could finish wooing her before she married the wrong man.

To add to his problems, he'd received a letter from Lieutenant Scar informing him to take caution. Lord Benton had returned to Sylvanwood to reunite with his wife, and most likely, to seek out Jacob for retribution.

Jacob had to ensure Mathis didn't propose to Emily, identify and root out the jewel thieves, avoid falling into Miss Dorsham's marriage trap, and watch his back for the bullets Lord Benton would surely implant there if given the chance.

After a young groom approached to water the horses, Jacob left his driver's hat on his seat and snuck around the stable, ducking under the window to remain unnoticed even though twilight had fallen. He shrugged out of his driving overcoat and hid it among the branches of a nearby maple tree. He checked his cravat to ensure the knot was straight and tugged on the bottom of his kerseymere jacket before reaching into his pocket and pulling out his invitation. With a brisk stride, he dodged a passing carriage and scooted behind a boxwood hedge, peeking to ensure no one was watching. He rose and jumped over the low stone balustrade railing, sauntering up the steps to the footmen at the front entrance. Between two fingers, he flicked out the invitation for the butler, who led him through the gallery foyer.

With Benton's arrival in town, it was for the best that Emily hadn't accepted his invitation to accompany him to the party, but what he wouldn't give to look upon her face as the footman opened the double doors to the ballroom. He could imagine Emily's joy at the explosion of colorful gowns. She'd be memorizing the scene, absorbing every aspect to capture on canvas later. And while she painted, he'd have the excuse to visit and aid her in remembering details, such as how Lord Grimwold smirked or how Lady Simmons raised her hands as if conducting an orchestra.

As he stood in the ballroom's entrance next in line to be announced, stuffy heat wafted the aroma of expensive perfumes and colognes through the air. Music drifted down from the second-floor mezzanine, where the orchestra musician played a quadrille as guests danced below. People mingled around the dance floor's edge as servants carried drinks and silver platters of finger sandwiches to a refreshment table in the corner. In a row under tall, corniced arches, the terrace doors stood open, but the chilly night air did little to cool the room.

The butler announced Jacob's arrival. "Lord Jacob Langford Warren."

Two women swiveled in his direction—Miss Dorsham and the Duchess of Charlton.

Miss Dorsham flashed him a smile less enthusiastic than usual. Still, her gloved fingers moved to her chest, where a low-cut bodice exposed a broad expanse of skin and displayed a sapphire-and-diamond pendant on a thick gold chain. Her cloak had hidden the jewelry earlier, but now, desperation for a husband clung to her in the form of a statement piece necklace.

At Miss Dorsham's side, the duchess, Sarah, eyed him with cool reserve. She was the perfect person to give Miss Dorsham fortune-husband-hunting advice.

Jacob was new to prayer, but he quietly asked God to help him with his unforgiveness toward Sarah and for the strength not to fall back into his old libertine ways. He greeted his host and hostess, who asked about his brothers.

Jacob was glad for the diversion. "Alex is on a trip to Prussia, and I've received word that Robert and Nora shall visit my aunt and me in Sylvanwood soon."

"The duke and duchess?" Mrs. Simmons fanned herself. "I do hope you are throwing them a party. It would be well-attended—the event that starts the season."

If his aunt were here, she'd swoon at Lady Simmons's suggestion. "I'm afraid they will be visiting more for business than pleasure. My brother intends to check on the progress of Brownstone Hall."

"Then, I shall call upon the marchioness while she's in town." Lady Simmons said.

"I plan to convince them to attend Miss Dorsham's coming-out party for her kickoff of the season." Emily would have no choice but to be present at her closest friend's party. He would use it to be seen with Emily and show Sylvanwood his intentions toward her. Mathis was long overdue for some competition, and Jacob would bring his all to the ring in this match.

"How splendid." Lady Simmons perked up. "I plan to be there." She tapped her index finger on her cheek. "But now I must rethink my choice of gown."

He stopped next to a marbled pillar with a bust of Lord Simmons's father and searched for Benton or anyone who seemed unduly drawn to jewelry and other baubles of the wealthy. The highwaymen's attacks hadn't been random. The leader must have inside knowledge of high societal events and chose the carriages of those bedecked in jewels to rob. If Jacob had to guess, one of the bandits was a member of the *ton*.

A familiar face caught his eye. Jacob strolled to the perimeter of the ballroom to stand shoulder to shoulder with his handler.

Lieutenant Scar wore black except for a snowy white cambric shirt and cravat. He leaned against a pillar and sipped a drink, watching his wife converse with a group of ladies.

Jacob kept his voice low. "I didn't expect to see you here, Lieutenant."

"Tonight, it's Lord Scarcliffe." He nodded to his lovely wife. "Abby desired to attend, and I conceded, knowing someone should be here to guard your backside." He issued him a sideways glance. "On your ten."

Jacob gazed to where Lord Benton stood red-faced with a half-empty glass in his hand. A nearby footman collected three empty glasses from off the table. Benton was well on his way to getting foxed.

"And the missus?"

Lieutenant Scar gave the slightest tilt of his head to the right. "On your two."

Lady Benton clung to the arm of a young buck, laughing as if the man were the cleverest fellow in the land. They strolled onto the terrace. The night breeze caught her skirts and curled them around the bloke's legs like a lover's embrace. Hopefully, the young fool understood the consequences of the path he treaded.

"Any leads?" Scar sipped from the glass he held.

"Nothing conclusive, but I'm narrowing the suspects."

"Indeed."

Jacob glanced to make certain no one was within hearing range. "Whoever it is walks among us or is tipped off by a guest. They seem to have inside knowledge of who is wearing the family valuables."

Scar rubbed his chin, and his gaze roved the room.

"From eyewitness accounts and hearsay," Jacob said, "it seems we're looking for two or three men. They're skilled riders and use the heath or forest to take a driver by surprise. One of them is of small build, around five foot five, but he stays on his mount and points the pistol at the coachman while the other, who's taller at five-foot-nine or -ten with a local accent, collects the goods. Recollections were hazy on the third, a shadowy figure lingering in the woods that may or may not have been their imagination. They mask their faces. Copeland thinks he saw a lock of blond under the bandana but wasn't certain when pressed. It was dark, and it could have been a trick of the moonlight."

"A short, potentially blond local man." Scar exhaled. "Not much to go on."

"I've been posing as the Dorsham driver, and guess who draped herself in the family valuables tonight?"

"By your bidding?"

Jacob shook his head. "Of course not. Miss Dorsham is in want of a husband."

"I see." He scanned the room until he found the young woman. "Indeed, that would be tempting. I've posted lookouts on the post road in Bibury."

"Good. The moors there offer bandits plenty of hiding spots."

Scar nodded. "I'll also trail you a few minutes behind."

"But your wife?"

"Laurel House isn't far from here. Her brother will see her home."

The orchestra struck up a country reel.

"How's your son?" Scar sipped his drink.

Jacob couldn't stop a grin from spreading. "He's like me—an adventurer. Christian loves racing toy boats and adores horses. He's not afraid to get muddy and not shy of adults." His smile fell. "He's been raised well. The Thompsons are good folk."

"But...?"

"No buts. They're tremendous, which is why I haven't yet told my son I'm his father. I'm still praying about the best course of action."

"Praying? So you've become religious?" A spark lit Scar's eyes.

"I told you they're good folk. Mr. Thompson is the local

vicar. He's got me repenting, praying, and desiring to mend my ways."

Scar chuckled. "God will do that to you."

"He has a daughter, Emily. She's the one who put an arrow in Benton's shoulder. She saved my life. She has the face of an angel and makes me want to better myself, the kind of person she'd set her cap for."

The lieutenant jerked back his chin. "You're besotted?"

"I am."

Scar grabbed a drink from a passing footman's tray and handed it to Jacob. "Cheers to a better man."

They clinked glasses and drank. Scar's voice lowered after he swallowed. "Marriage mart mama on my twelve."

"Lord Warren." Lady Dorsham's voice boomed.

Jacob cringed.

"And Lord Scarcliffe. What a delightful evening. Lord Warren, I know you're acquainted with my daughter Phoebe, but I don't believe Lord Scarcliffe has had the pleasure."

Scar bowed his head to Miss Dorsham, who trailed her mother. "Delighted to meet you, but please excuse me. My wife beckons."

Jacob pinched his lips tight to hold back the word *coward*, shooting the lieutenant a look he hoped conveyed the sentiment. Lady Scarcliffe seemed surprised yet pleased when he grabbed her hand, excused her from an ongoing conversation, and led her to the dance floor.

Abandoned to face the Dorsham ladies alone, Jacob relaxed his jaw and attempted to put on a good face. "Rather a crush of a party, don't you think?"

Miss Dorsham fanned her face. "Indeed, it's made the ball insufferably warm."

Her mother's eyes sparkled. "Why don't you two take a turn about the room or take in the air on the terrace?" Lady Dorsham shooed them away. "Run along now."

Miss Dorsham tucked her hand in the crook of his arm, leaving Jacob with the choice of giving her the cut direct, offending Emily's friend and causing a scene, or strolling the room with her on his arm.

He accepted the latter option but strode the ballroom's perimeter at a quicker pace than considered acceptable, desiring to get the obligation over.

Miss Dorsham tugged his arm. "You needn't run, Lord Warren. I hold no designs that you have any sentiments for me. You've made your intentions clear, but I must continue to play the game for Mama's sake or she'll begin to question."

He forced himself to slow down and said in what he hoped was an apologetic tone, "Forgive me, Miss Dorsham. I didn't realize how quickly I walked."

Lord and Lady Copeland passed nearby. Lord Copeland's gaze swept over them, but he quickly diverted back to his wife.

Miss Dorsham tensed, and for the first time, Jacob felt sorry for the chit. "What are your plans for the season?"

"To make a catch." She grinned, but it didn't reach her eyes. "My coming-out party is less than a week away. After that, I will leave for London, where I will hope to make a splash and receive several offers of marriage."

And if you don't?

The silent question weighed the surrounding air, but Miss Dorsham didn't know he was aware of her condition.

"You love her, don't you?" Miss Dorsham flashed him an askance look. "Don't answer that." She shook her head and closed her eyes as if irritated. "I can see it on your face whenever you look at her. I just want to know why. Why her and not me?"

"You are a lovely woman." The kind his younger self would have been attracted to, and he would have matched her flirtatious nature and added her to the list of women who'd succumbed to his charms.

What he felt for Emily was different. There was nothing self-serving in it. He wanted her to feel adored, loved, and valued. He desired to make her smile more, laugh more, live more. If she wished to be a member of the Royal Academy, he'd use his influence to give her the greatest chance possible, and if she wanted a simple life in Sylanwood, he'd send for the rest of his things and become a gentleman farmer. Now, when he envisioned his future, she stood by his side. She made him a better person.

He slowed his steps, peering at Miss Dorsham. He would explain, but bitterness was etched in the tight lines around her mouth. Emily had done nothing to deserve her friend's resentment. Pure jealousy drove Miss Dorsham.

"Why can't you be happy for her?" He probably should have kept the question to himself, but his desire to know overwhelmed his training as a gentleman.

Her nostrils flared. If he'd expected any softening in her eyes, he'd have been disappointed.

"Must you always cast her in the shadows? She's been a good friend and stuck by your side when you haven't deserved it."

Her eyes flashed, but the anger fizzled. She lowered her chin. "I don't know why I treat her so. I guess I'm jealous, even though she's a penniless bi-blow." Miss Dorsham clasped a hand over her mouth. "I shouldn't have said that."

By the look on her face, she'd said exactly what she meant, hoping to give away her friend's shameful secret.

This walk couldn't end fast enough.

"Miss Thompson confided in me, but that is *not* something you should mention unless you intend to harm the person you call your friend." He turned to leave, unable to tolerate her presence any longer.

Miss Dorsham clung to his arm. "That's just it. She's good.

Emily would take my secret to the grave." She blinked rapidly. "I can't be good."

Jacob sighed and pulled a handkerchief from his pocket, passing it to her. "I believed I couldn't be good either."

She wiped her tears. "That's why I thought we'd make a brilliant match. We're alike."

He gave her a moment to regain her composure. When she did and faced him again, he explained. "But Emily and the Thompson family have shown me I can have a second chance to redeem myself. They act as though my past doesn't define my future. They believe that, despite my mistakes, God still loves me."

A sob tore from Miss Dorsham's lips.

Several people glanced their way, including Sarah, who eyed him with a stern look.

He ushered Miss Dorsham out the French doors onto the terrace.

"My parents see me as a pawn to make connections and gain entrance to more of the *tons's* parties, drawing rooms, and events. I tried—" A sob choked her voice. "But you're right." Tears streamed over her cheeks, and she wiped them away, soaking his handkerchief. "Emily never has treated me that way. She's loved me despite my faults, and how I've hurt her."

"Miss Dorsham?" Sarah's voice approached them from behind. "I do hope Lord Warren is being a gentleman."

Jacob turned to defend himself. Sarah had become even more beautiful with age, shedding the softness of youth for a more mature look, but the malice that had flashed in her eyes as a young girl now held steadfast.

Miss Dorsham swallowed. "We were merely talk—"

"Why don't you run along and freshen up before rumors spread about why you cry so easily?" Sarah arched a sculpted eyebrow.

Miss Dorsham paled, the moonlight tinging her face a cornflower blue. After bobbing a curtsy, she left, and Jacob inwardly grunted. *Cornflower blue? Indigo versus violet?* Emily was rubbing off on him.

"I came out here to save you." Sarah ran her fingertip down the lapel of his jacket before striding to the railing, presuming he would follow, as he always had. Should he engage in conversation or walk away? His curiosity won out, and he moved to stand beside the balustrade but maintained a safe distance between them.

Sarah faced him. "I know we've had our differences, but since you were my first, I still hold you in high regard."

First love? She'd never returned his sentiments.

"I admit the physical attraction between us has always been strong, and I was disappointed when you declined my offer."

To warm a married woman's bed? Even the rake he used to be had set a boundary line there. "You were married."

She snorted. "All you cared about was finding your son."

Our son—but he'd stopped correcting her long ago. "What do you want, Sarah?"

"To warn you." She turned and leaned against the railing. "You're being manipulated. Miss Dorsham plans to trap you into marriage at her coming-out party."

"How so?"

She shrugged. "I don't know the details, but I'm assuming by someone discovering the two of you alone. She's desperate to wed and pawn off another man's bi-blow as your own."

"I'm aware."

Had Sarah's eyes widened in the lamplight? Was she surprised he already knew?

"But are you also aware"—her gaze narrowed—"that Miss Thompson has been aiding her?"

CHAPTER 21

*J*acob fought to keep his expression neutral. The denial of Sarah's pronouncement pressed against his teeth, demanding release, but Emily's voice rang in his memory. *Phoebe is a beautiful woman of means and quality, a woman of whom society and your family would approve. A man would be lucky to have such a passionate woman by his side.*

Sarah studied his face as if feeding off his pain.

His heart writhed in his chest, but he shrugged and stalked past her. "Don't worry about me. Since I met you, I assume all women are trouble."

Jacob stepped aside as the French doors opened and another couple exited. He held the door and re-entered the stuffy room.

Scar locked gazes with him with questions abounding, the guests' laughter stung Jacob's ears, and the swirling dancers left him sick to his stomach.

Miss Dorsham appeared the same as he felt, for she pressed a hand over her mouth and dashed toward the ladies' retiring rooms.

He sought solace in the opposite direction, ducking into the men's cardroom.

The thick smoke of cheroots muddied the air. An open seat at a high-stakes table called to him, but a warning sounded in his head. He didn't want to return to his old ways. Would he get another chance at redemption if he blew this one? He wanted to believe what Emily said, that he could become a new person. But if she'd deceived him, who could be trusted?

A curse split the air, and Sarah's husband tossed his cards on the table as Lord Dorsham scooped all the chips. The Duke of Charlton had lost big.

Jacob couldn't remember the duke winning much, but he gambled frequently. If Jacob's mood had been better, he would have found irony in Sarah choosing him for his money. If he kept gambling at this rate, he'd land them both in the poorhouse.

Jacob exited and strode down the hall to the men's retiring room, pushing the door open a little too hard. It bounced off the wall and startled the room's only occupant.

Lord Benton tipped back the rest of his drink and set the glass down next to a half-empty bottle of scotch. He rose on unsteady feet.

Blast.

Jacob berated himself for forgetting protocol to scout an area first. He checked the small pistol stashed in his pocket, aiming it at Benton in case he tried shooting again.

"It's you." Benton's scathing voice spewed like venom. "You know what your problem is?"

Jacob had reached the limits of congeniality tonight. He laced his words with sarcasm. "I've longed to hear your take on it."

If Benton comprehended the mockery, he didn't show it. He wagged a finger at Jacob and sank back into the low-backed chair. "You just won't die."

Jacob snorted. The man was clearly foxed—but he wasn't wrong. And he had no intention of letting Benton win.

"I tossed you out a window and tried to put a bullet in your skull." His nose wrinkled in a snarl. "I even kicked you face down into a creek hoping you'd drown but, confound it, you survived. How?" He waved his hands. "Why?"

"God still has a plan for my life?" The sentence formed as a question, but hearing the words changed them into a statement in his heart. God did have a plan for him, and it didn't include becoming a wastrel or a pawn to be used by others. He had a purpose—to be a father to his son and teach him how to avoid the traps he'd fallen into.

"I despise you." Benton spit the words, and droplets of saliva sprayed the air with the scent of spirits. "But it's good you didn't die. That's what *she* would have wanted."

"Why?" Jacob furrowed his brow.

He chuckled, a hollow, bitter sound. "If I danced from the hangman's noose, she'd celebrate. I know my wife is a light skirt. The gall of that woman cuckolding me, making me out to be a fool. My valet explained why you'd been in her chamber." He shook his head. "Of all the men she's lured in her bed, who'd have thought you'd be the one with good intentions?" He refilled his glass with scotch and downed it in two gulps before refilling it again. "She's the mastermind. Lucile has no qualms. No morals. Got me all roped in and tangled up, and now I'll probably hang on the rope of her making."

Jacob struggled to make sense of the man's rant.

"At least I won't hold your death on my conscience." He pointed at him with his glass. "They do her bidding."

"Lady Benton's?" Had he missed her involvement in the jewel thieving ring?

"They adore her." Benton swallowed another gulp from his glass. "But not you. How are you immune to her wiles?"

Ah, the man was referring to his wife's lovers.

Benton didn't wait for an answer. Instead, he jabbed his index finger in Jacob's general direction. "Do you believe in love at first sight?"

He thought of Sarah, how their relationship ended, and then Emily and her betrayal. "I believe in annoyed at first sight."

Benton snorted a laugh and saluted him with his glass. "Lucile's an odd combination of gentlewoman and a mad-as-a-hatter demon."

"You two are perfect for each other."

He scowled but then sobered. "I wish..." His head bobbed, and he blinked. "I wish I never laid eyes on her."

The door swung open, and a young dandy entered. "Pardon me, gents." He brushed past into another room to relieve himself.

Jacob caught the hallway door with his hand before it closed. "Well, Benton. I believe we've had a moment."

The man nodded but struggled to keep his eyes open.

"True bonding happens when you're angry over the same thing."

"I'll be beggared," Benton mumbled with his chin resting on his chest until the words drifted into snores.

"Good talk." Jacob slipped out of the room, hoping Miss Dorsham hadn't feigned a headache and decided to leave while he wasn't at his post.

~

"*E*m?"
Christian's whisper woke Emily from a restless sleep. She sat up in bed and lit a candle. "What's the matter?"

"I couldn't sleep." He tiptoed over and sat on the bed next to her. "I overheard Mama and Papa talking downstairs."

"You shouldn't be eavesdropping on adult conversations." Emily's reprimand held a mothering tone.

He peered up at her with innocent blue eyes. "Is Lord Warren my real father?"

Her breath caught.

Oh, no.

What should she say? He was too young to understand why his mother left him to be raised by another family.

"Please, Em." He crawled onto his knees and placed his hands on her cheeks. "I want to know the truth."

She swallowed and nodded. "He is your father by birth."

Christian blinked but remained still as if processing the information.

"But Papa and Mama love you. You are their son."

"I know." Christian nodded and dropped his hands back to his sides.

"And I love you. You are my brother, and I'd do anything for you."

"Is Lord Warren your real father too?"

"No." The word flew from her mouth, and Christian's brow wrinkled. "I mean, I was also adopted like you, but my parents live in London."

"Did they come to find you like Lord Warren found me?"

"No."

"Oh."

A mournful silence fell over the room.

"But Samuel wasn't adopted." Christian shifted so that his bare feet hung over the bedside again.

"Mama had Samuel during her first marriage, but Samuel's papa died when he was very young. In a way, we're all adopted."

Christian sighed. "Don't they deserve to have a real son?"

"They have two real sons." She patted his knee. "I don't think it matters to them whose blood runs in your veins. They love us just the same as they would their own children—with their whole hearts."

She allowed him the space to consider that.

"I like Lord Warren." Christian said after a moment. "I want to play with him more. Go to his house."

Her heart screamed. She didn't want to lose Christian.

"You could come with me." He released a wide yawn. "Lord Warren likes you too. Almost as much as he likes me."

Emily couldn't resist smiling at his innocent remark.

"If you married Lord Warren, we could live at Brownstone Hall together and visit Mama and Papa every day. Wouldn't that be grand?"

She pictured Christian bounding into the chamber, jumping on the bed, and waking her and Jacob. He'd scoop Christian up and tickle him until Christian begged him to stop. Then Jacob would lean over with his boyish smile and kiss her good morning.

Emily pushed the indecent thought away. "Life is complicated."

Christian jumped off the bed and turned to face her. "What's so complicated about it?"

Truly, what was?

Jacob had feelings for her, and she for him. She'd never have to worry about him taking Christian away if they were to marry. They could be a family.

"Hmm?" Christian stuck out his chin and raised both eyebrows.

"I don't know."

"All right." He gripped her hands. "Let's pray to God for it, then."

"Christian—"

"Heavenly Father. Please marry Lord Warren and Em so that we can be a family. Amen." He grinned and released her hands. "Good night, Em." He skipped to the door but paused with one hand on the knob. "One more thing." He folded his hands and bowed his head. "And Lord, I'd like a younger brother, too, please. Amen."

He disappeared down the hall, leaving Emily an all-too-clear picture of what her life could be.

CHAPTER 22

*J*acob left the party through a side door and eyed a servant shirking his duties outside.

Was he a servant? He wasn't dressed in the Simmons' livery. Jacob looked again, but the man rounded the corner of the house toward the gardens. Jacob moved to chase him but paused. Truly, he had no time. He needed to get into position.

He skirted the perimeter to the tree where he'd hidden his driving coat, which remained hung on the tree limb where he'd left it. He donned it, strode to the Dorshams' carriage, and climbed into his driving seat.

"There you are." A footman rounded the back of the conveyance. "I've been searching for you. Lord and Lady Dorsham are ready to depart. Snap to it and be quick about it. I've got other coachmen waiting in line."

Jacob plopped on his hat and snapped the reins. He drove the team to a stop beside the Simmons' mounting block near the front entrance, where Lord and Lady Dorsham waited with their daughter.

"...lovely party," Lady Dorsham said. "I'm only disappointed

Lord Warren didn't ask you to dance." She harrumphed as if Miss Dorsham were to blame. "At least you two took a turn about the room."

Jacob sank into his driving coat and tipped his hat lower.

The Dorshams climbed into the coach, and Jacob turned the team and headed down the lane toward home. Moonlight filtered through the clouds, casting shadows along the dirt road. If he'd been correct and one of the highwaymen mingled among high society, then the chance of the Dorsham carriage being raided tonight was great, thanks to the brilliant display of jewels strewn across Miss Dorsham's neck.

The raspy barking of foxes died as the carriage rumbled past the heath, and a screech owl cried its warning.

Jacob released one hand from the reins to check for the blunderbuss he'd tucked under the driver's seat earlier. The weight of the pistols he'd hidden in his driving coat and his jacket's inside pocket reassured him of their presence.

He strained to hear any sound above the pounding of the horses' hooves and the crunching of the wheels. Despite the cool night air, perspiration beaded on his forehead as they approached the canopy of trees. He'd forgotten how dark this section of the road was at night—the perfect cover for someone seeking to accost a passing coach. Scar's men were posted along the road in Bibury, but it was a good distance away. The damp forest air hung with the smell of earth and moss. His palms tingled, and his grip tightened on the reins. He nudged the team faster.

The break in the forest beckoned in the distance, but so did a sharp turn where he'd have no choice but to slow the horses. If they made it past the turn, he and the Dorshams might return home tonight without any scuffle. He wanted to crack this case, but he also desired to return the Dorshams home safely and for him to have a chance to see his son again. His career had aided him in locating his son, but now that he'd found Christian, he should give up his position. He shouldn't risk his life or his future as Christian's father. Provided he stayed alive, the funds he'd earned would allow Christian to attend Eton.

Two shadows emerged from the trees.

He'd been right, but it offered little solace as cold tingles spread to his toes. He tensed for a fight.

The single riders could outpace the cumbersome coach and doubtless had chosen this spot because driving the team through the sharp turn forced the driver to keep both hands on the reins.

One rider passed him, and Jacob strained in the dark for a good look, but all he could discern was that the man was small, like a lad.

The second rider approached from behind, most likely with a gun pointed at Jacob's head.

Jacob fought the urge to glance over his shoulder. Best to let them think they held the element of surprise.

The small rider turned his mount, nudging the team off the road.

The horses balked, trapped between the single rider and the tree line.

Jacob struggled to keep them from rearing.

"Halt." The click of a gun's hammer pulled back froze Jacob. He slowly shifted in his seat to peer down the barrel of the taller highwayman's pistol.

The man nodded to his accomplice, and after the lad stopped the team, the smaller man pointed his weapon at Jacob's head.

The larger rogue dismounted and pounded on the carriage window. "Stand and deliver your purse and jewels."

Jacob scanned for additional thieves hiding among the trees, but it seemed there were only the two riders.

The taller highwayman ripped open the carriage door.

Miss Dorsham screamed.

"Now, see here..." Lord Dorsham's voice rang out.

The highwayman stuck his blunderbuss and his open palm into the conveyance. "Give it over quick, and no one will get hurt. More men await my signal. They'll come if you give me trouble."

Were there footpads waiting in the woods? If so, he and Scar would be at a grave disadvantage. It had to be a Canterbury tale. Jacob saw no sign of other robbers. Definitely not other horses.

Miss Dorsham's soft crying followed the clink of jewels and money purses being handed over.

Jacob glanced back at the carriage, nervous for the Dorshams. He reached for his weapon. Timing was everything. If the taller rogue lowered his gun—

"Get your hands where I can see them."

Jacob jerked back to face the smaller thief and raised both hands in the air. His gaze honed in on the slight figure. The blackguard disguised his voice, but he didn't sound like a lad.

The taller rogue stuffed a handful of jewels into his pocket and returned for more. "Give the rest over. Now!"

Miss Dorsham's wailing increased, and a coin purse and other loot jingled while being handed to their assailant.

The sound of an approaching rider had both rogues craning their necks. Was it Scar or one of their accomplices?

The taller kicked the carriage door shut.

Jacob sprang from his perch onto the smaller rider, reaching for the weapon. His forearm hit the thief's neck before the rest of his body knocked the bloke off his horse.

The bandit's foot caught in the stirrup, and he released a cry of pain as they swung through the air.

Jacob slammed into the ground. Pain shot across his shoulder and back. He wrestled for control of the gun, rolling to wrench the other man's leg, still stuck in the stirrup. Jacob yanked hard on the weapon, seizing it. He pointed the gun at the taller bandit.

The larger thief swung his weapon in Jacob's direction while the smaller reached to dislodge his foot with an angry groan.

"You fool! What have you done?" The tall brigand shook his weapon at Jacob, and his eyes grew wild in the dim light.

Leg free, the smaller bandit sat up.

The hoofbeats of the approaching horse grew louder.

Jacob winced at putting weight on his injured shoulder but rose, staying low.

"I'm going to kill you for hurting her."

Her?

The small-framed person he'd wrestled hadn't been a boney, skinny boy.

A female highwayman was unheard of. He'd read Alexander Smith's accounts of the infamous, wicked Katherine Ferrer and her robberies, but she'd lived over a hundred years before, and her story read more as myth than legend. A mask covered this robber's face, but the chin was pointy, and a long wisp of hair blew in the night breeze. Her bulky overcoat made it impossible to detect any feminine curves. Which would be the point.

She rose, staying close to her horse's side. The larger bandit stepped toward Jacob.

Jacob removed his other pistol from his coat pocket with his free hand and pointed it at the woman's head, standing between the two assailants.

She gasped, and the other bandit drew back.

"Drop your weapon!" a man yelled. It sounded like Lieutenant Scar. His handler barreled toward them, pistol extended and black cape whipping behind him.

Thank heaven.

Pain shot through Jacob's groin.

She'd kicked him.

He dropped to his knees and fought to keep his weapons pointed at the bandits. Through the pain blurring his vision, he saw the woman climb onto her horse.

A shot rang out, and the male thief stumbled.

The woman screamed, and her horse charged toward Jacob. He dove into the grass to avoid getting trampled, twisted, and raised his pistol. But didn't fire. He didn't have it in him to shoot a woman.

She clicked her heels and darted into the woods.

Her companion used the carriage as a shield, emerging on his horse, and chased her.

Jacob aimed and shot, but his target gave no indication he'd been hit.

The brigands drove their horses deeper into the woods.

"Are you hurt?" Lieutenant Scar reached him and slowed his horse.

"I'll live." Jacob rose onto one knee with a grimace. Whether he could walk yet—or sire another child—was still to be determined.

Scar reloaded his weapon and spurred his horse into the woods after the thieves.

Jacob would follow and provide backup, but he had no horse. Unless he unhooked one from the team and rode bareback, but that would take at least five minutes. By the time he caught up, the action would be long past. Assuming Scar even found them.

The carriage door cracked open, and Lord Dorsham peeked out.

"Get inside and stay until I say it's safe," Jacob yelled. No sense in blowing his cover.

Lord Dorsham recoiled, slamming the door.

The moonlight outlined a dark shape resting in the road. Jacob drew closer and picked up the hat the woman had worn.

It must have been knocked off during the fall. He held it up to the carriage's lantern. It was an ordinary clericus hat with a low profile and slopped brim. Inside were three long strands of hair. He'd need better lighting to be certain, but they appeared blond against the black fabric.

Lady Benton had blond hair. For that matter, so did Sarah, Lady Copeland, Lady Simmons, the party's hostess, and countless other guests. Even Miss Dorsham had blond hair, though she could be ruled out, since she was in the carriage.

But now he knew one of the robbers was a blond woman. That narrowed the suspects. The woman had a slight build, around five-and-a-half-feet tall, and a male companion who appeared to be of a similar height and build to Jacob. He had a local accent.

Hoofbeats approached.

Jacob ducked behind the carriage and drew his weapon.

Lieutenant Scar reined his steed to a halt, and Jacob tucked his gun back in his pocket.

"They got away." He dismounted and faced Jacob. "They know these woods well."

Jacob nodded. "The man is local."

Scar's eyebrows rose. "The other was female? I thought it was a lad."

He held out the inside of the hat, pointing to the hairs. "A blond lady of the *ton*, I suspect."

"Interesting. Do we have our own Wicked Lady? They didn't take their lesson from Lady Katherine Ferrer's death?"

"Wasn't her highway-thieving mere hearsay?"

"Sometimes all a mimic needs is to believe in a legend."

Jacob tried to recall the gossip. According to legend, Lady Ferrer had been a wealthy orphaned heiress, forced to marry a sluggard who spent her family's fortune. She'd taken up thieving with her lover to keep the coffers filled but got shot and died inside her childhood home. Her bloodied male clothes had been stashed by a secret entrance.

Was their current female highway thief leg shackled to a sluggard? It didn't rule Lady Benton out.

"Have you questioned your charges?" He inclined his chin toward the coach.

Jacob shook his head.

"I'll handle it. You climb up and take a moment to remember the events."

He did what Scar requested.

Ten minutes later, Scar rode away and Jacob drove the Doshams back to their manor before wearily climbing on his horse and returning to Brownstone Hall.

Thank goodness Jacob hadn't brought Emily. She might have wanted to ride with Miss Dorsham. The fear she would have endured. He enjoyed the thrill and challenge of espionage, but he'd just found Christian and wanted to know his son—more than anything. After tonight, his decision was made. He'd resign from his position once the jewel thieves were caught.

Could he afford to leave the Home Office and still provide the lifestyle he desired for Christian? As much as he hated to admit it, Christian might be better off without him in his daily life, but Jacob couldn't bear seeing his son only on holiday or special occasions.

Had he been mistaken about Emily? He'd believed there was something between them, but she'd pushed him away at every opportunity, and now, he was fairly convinced she'd tried to coerce him into marriage with Miss Dorsham. Was she bent on ridding him from Christian's life? Perhaps she figured if she pawned some other man's child off as his, he'd forget about the son he'd searched five years to find.

Was Emily Thompson different or just like all the other women who'd betrayed him?

He rode through Brownstone Hall's iron gates, up the drive, and into the stable. He woke a sleepy groomsman to rub down his mount but stopped beside a horse still saddled in its stall that hadn't been cooled off and brushed. "What's this?"

The groom peered over the stall door. "I don't rightly know, milord." He lifted his hand and scratched his head. "I didn't saddle this one nor hear its return."

Jacob entered the stall, noticing the dirt and sweat covering the horse's coat and a dark stain near the saddle. He touched it and held the red sticky substance to the light.

Wooziness overwhelmed him.

Blood.

He stumbled against the stall and inhaled some deep breaths to fight the darkness trying to swallow him. *Focus on the task at hand. A good spy can't faint at the sight of blood.*

Could the highwayman Lieutenant Scar shot be living under Jacob's nose? Or was this a coincidence? He grabbed a lantern from off a wall hook and held it up, asking the groom to scan the dirt and hay for other blood splatters.

The groom pointed a few feet away. "Over here."

For the third time that day, Jacob removed his gun from his pocket. People, like wounded animals, lashed out when cornered.

The groom followed the splatters out of the barn and up the crushed-stone path. "It looks as though it leads to the steward's lodging."

Jacob moved in front of the groom. "Follow me but stay back a bit."

He led the way to his steward's house.

Blast.

The steward's door stood wide open, and a low moan resonated from inside.

"Welsh?" Jacob peeked through the window into the

sparsely furnished room before crouching low and moving to the door, carefully checking his blind spots.

"Here." The raspy reply came from a shadowed corner.

Jacob found Welsh slumped in a chair. The scarf that had hidden his identity earlier hung around his neck. His pale face contrasted against the darkness, and his hand covered a wound in his stomach. The dim light hid the sight of blood, but Jacob's knees wobbled, anyway. He gripped the door frame and turned to the groom. "Take a horse and fetch the physician. Hurry!"

The groom's feet kicked up stones as he dashed back toward the stable.

Jacob removed his coat and held it out to block the sight of blood. If he didn't need to interrogate Welsh, he would have gone for the doctor and left the groom to care for the injured man. He forced his shaky legs to move to his steward's side and wadded his jacket over the wound, applying pressure with his hands.

A wheezing chuckle with a bit of spittle emitted from Welsh's mouth. "You should have sent him for the coroner."

"You've held on this long. You can hold on a bit longer." As Jacob knelt, the metallic scent of blood filled his nose. Queasiness washed over him, but the bleeding must have slowed because no liquid seeped through. The man had little time left. Jacob needed to get him to talk. "Why'd you do it? Why a life of stealing?"

Welch's lips twisted in a wry smile. "You were right." He paused as though summoning the energy to continue. "Women are nothing but trouble."

"Who is she?"

Welsh's eyes closed, and Jacob patted his cheek to keep him awake.

"What's her name?"

"She used me. Took the jewels and left me to die like a dog." His voice cracked on a sob. "I love her. Did this for her."

"Who?"

He whispered something Jacob couldn't make out, and his eyes closed. Jacob smacked his face a bit harder and leaned in to hear.

"I'll see her again." On a long exhale of breath, Jacob thought he heard him say, *in hades*. Welsh's head lolled to the side.

"Stay with me. Help is on the way." He shook Welsh's shoulders, but the man didn't rouse again. He checked for a pulse in his neck.

Welsh was gone.

Jacob stood and ran a hand through his hair.

Thunder and turf. His own steward? To think he'd brought the hoodlum into his aunt's house. When she found out, he wouldn't be surprised if she told him to leave and locked the gate after him, never to allow another visitor. Blast. He'd come to love it here, and she'd made such progress.

He felt Welsh's pockets where he'd witnessed him stash the Dorsham jewels. Nothing.

He removed a tablecloth and draped it over the man's body before turning up a nearby wall lantern. The man didn't bring much in the way of possessions, other than the furniture already provided—a few books, a spice rack, a homemade quilt folded over the bed in the corner, and a stack of letters. He'd review those later.

Best to pen a missive to Lieutenant Scar to apprise him of the latest event while he waited for the physician. He sat at the roller desk and removed a sheet of paper.

Jacob paid Welsh a good salary and provided a roof over his head. Jacob had done his due diligence on Welsh before he hired him. His steward hadn't been in any debt or need of money. Why the life of crime?

His words haunted him. *I did it for her.*

Who was she?

Had he been suspecting Lord Benton when he should have been focusing on the man's wife?

CHAPTER 23

"Are you certain it's wise?" Emily stopped kneading the bread dough while thoughts whirled in her head like a disturbed nest of bees. Allow Christian to spend a week with Jacob? How could her parents be all right with this? Did Jacob know how to care for a five-year-old? What if Christian scraped his knee? Jacob would need to tend to it, not fall into a faint. What if Christian had a nightmare? Would Jacob know what to pray with him?

What if Christian enjoyed himself so much with Jacob that he wanted to live with him?

She pressed her lips together to hold back her trembling and punched her fist into the bread dough, mixing the yeast.

"It's natural for Christian to want to know more about his father." Mama finished chopping vegetables and scraped them into the soup pot while Mrs. Hayes polished the silver. "Your papa and I have discussed this at length. It's only for a week. Christian will be back before church on Sunday. It's honorable that Lord Warren wants to be a part of his son's life."

Emily forced measured breaths even though she felt far

from calm. "But what if he wants to take Christian from us? Aren't you worried?"

"Of course, but we must be obedient to the Lord's will and trust Him. Just as Abraham did when he was told to sacrifice His son, Isaac. Abraham was tested, but he trusted God would make a way, and God provided a ram to take Isaac's place. God intends the best for Christian."

Mama was right, but it didn't ease the urge for Emily to pound her fists and rile at Jacob for interfering in their lives.

"And it's commendable that Lord Warren wants to learn more about his son." She stirred the soup. "I don't understand why you're so opposed to this. I thought you were taken with Lord Warren, and he with you?"

"Taken?" Emily froze mid-knead, and heat rushed to her cheeks. "What gave you that impression?"

"I have eyes, my love." Her mother smiled at her. "But you keep fighting the feelings God has placed inside you as if you've condemned any attraction as a sin."

Emily drew her chin back. "Mama!"

"Attraction is part of loving someone. God put the feeling in us to draw us into a deeper relationship with others." She shook the stirring spoon at Emily. "However, we are not to act on foolish impulses. Passion is kept for the holy sacrament of marriage."

The tips of Emily's ears burned as though they'd caught fire. She focused on pounding the dough.

But Jacob's dashing physical features weren't the sole reason for her attraction. Peter was considered very handsome, but she'd never felt a pull between them, not as she did with Jacob. She loved Jacob's witty banter, how he played with Christian, his desire to become a better father and person, and his hunger to know more about the Lord.

And how he made her feel as though she was someone

worth pursuing—like a precious treasure he'd search any length to find. Much as he had for Christian.

She gasped and raised her hand to cover her mouth, stopping before sticky bread dough touched her face.

She loved Jacob.

Her hands shook as she placed the dough in the bread pan and covered it with a cloth to rise.

Mama chatted with Mrs. Hayes as Emily washed up in the sink. She shook off the excess water and dried her hands on her apron before stepping outside into the sunshine.

Christian was chasing a runaway sheep back into the pen. Hopping up on the gate, he rode the swinging door closed.

His prayer from last night echoed in her mind. *Lord, please marry Lord Warren and Em so we can be a family.*

She pressed her apron to her face. *Oh Lord, was that her prayer too?*

Her heart screamed a resounding, *Yes!*

～

a lump had wedged in Emily's throat, making swallowing a challenge as she guided Christian through the open gates of Brownstone Hall. Papa had spoken with Jacob and arranged for Christian to stay the week with Lord Warren. Her grip on Christian's hand tightened. "You're going to have a splendid time."

"I know." Christian skipped beside her.

She'd awoken this morning before sunrise, feeling as though the picture she'd carefully drawn of her life had become a blank white canvas. She had the paints and brushes, but did she dare try the bold, vibrant colors that she longed to see or stick to the browns and earth tones people were used to?

God had answered with a bright and brilliant sunrise.

She would allow Jacob to court her. She'd tell him so today.

Christian rambled on about the things he was going to do with his father as he skipped down the drive, but before they reached the front steps, he paused and peered up at her. "Can I call him Papa?"

"Not yet." Gossip could spread that would hurt Christian's future. "Let's think of these next couple of days as an apprenticeship, like how Samuel is apprenticing to be a vicar. That way, we can all be certain what path to take."

Christian frowned. "You told me God doesn't make mistakes."

"He doesn't." Emily lowered the knapsack she'd been carrying for Christian and crouched level with him. "His ways are perfect."

"God brought Lord Warren to Sylvanwood." He placed a hand on Emily's shoulder. "So everything's good. You can stop worrying."

She chuckled. "How did you become so wise?" Rising, she gripped his hand. "You're right. I need to trust in God's plan."

Inhaling a deep breath, she slung the knapsack over her shoulder, climbed the steps to the main entrance, and rapped the heavy brass knocker.

Inside, the elderly butler's snore resounded even through the thick oak door.

She rapped again, and the snore broke with a sleepy grunt. Shuffle steps approached, and Maslow cracked the door open, peeking at them down his aquiline nose.

"Good morning, Maslow." Emily raised her voice to a half shout for the near-deaf butler.

He swung the door wide. "Good morning, Miss Thompson and Master Christian. His lordship is expecting you. Follow me."

She trailed the man, who walked with a shuffle step. Christian glanced at her with a can't-he-go-faster look. She twisted her lips into a half smile that she hoped conveyed the need for patience.

Maslow guided them down the hall and past the solarium, where Jacob's painting stared back at them, finished but still on the easel. He stopped at a door on the left and gestured for them to enter.

Emily swallowed and entered the room, gripping Christian's hand.

Jacob sat behind a large mahogany desk with several ledger books open.

Her breath caught, seeing him in his white cambric shirt, knotted cravat, and dark-gray waistcoat, looking serious and very much like a meticulous, landholding gentleman.

He jotted a number before setting the quill back in the inkwell and peering up at them. His gaze met hers, and something flashed in those blue depths. Anger? Disappointment? Disapproval? She couldn't decipher, for it passed quickly, but it was certainly not delight to see her.

Anxiety swirled in her middle. Had she done something to displease him? Had she lost her chance?

"Good morning." Jacob rose, and his gaze lowered to Christian. His familiar smile quirked one side of his mouth, and he saluted. "Good to see you, Captain."

Christian returned the salute. "And you, Captain."

He rounded his desk and rang the bell pull. Leaning his hip on the corner of the mahogany wood, he crossed his arms. "Jolly good idea to come and stay for a bit. I'm delighted and have cleared my schedule so we can make the most of our time together. Just you wait for what I have planned."

Christian wiggled out his excitement and did a little hop in place.

"Lady Athol is also thrilled to host such a special guest." He nodded to someone in the hall, and Emily turned to spy Lady

Athol and a servant standing in the doorway. She greeted Lady Athol with a curtsy and their usual wave.

"Before we can begin, I must first speak with your sister. Lady Athol, my aunt and your second cousin, will give you a tour of Brownstone Hall and show you your bedchamber."

"Pleased to meet you." Christian bowed and Lady Athol curtsied.

The servant extended her hand, and Emily passed the woman Christian's knapsack.

"Make the kitchen the last stop," Jacob said, "and see if you can pilfer a few muffins as they come out of the oven. He'll need to eat before we ride."

"Ride?" Christian jumped in the air and pumped a fist. "Huzzah!"

Lady Athol gripped his hand, and Christian skipped beside her down the hall.

Emily turned to Jacob. "I have something I wanted to tell you too."

His smile faded, and his face hardened into granite. He returned to his chair behind his desk and gestured to her. "Be seated."

She lowered into the chair. He was definitely angry. But why?

He closed the ledgers, setting them aside, and laced his fingers, leaning forward over the desk. His stern gaze locked on her. "When did you know Miss Dorsham was in a family way?"

~

Jacob had interrogated plenty of guilty parties, and Emily Thompson squirmed like the worst of them. She pressed her palms into the chair cushion, pushing herself farther upright, but her gaze no longer met his. Instead, she focused on his shirtfront.

Her lips parted as if to speak but closed again. She swallowed, and her lips trembled.

He read the guilt on her face before she even spoke. She was an easy read and should stay away from the gambling tables.

"She told me after our first painting session."

His jaw clenched. "You knew and still tried to convince me to pursue her?" He leaned back in his chair and crossed his arms. "You tried to deceive me, hoping to pawn off another man's child as my own."

"She told me the baby was yours. I didn't know otherwise until our last session." She shook her head with enough vehemence that a loose lock of hair whipped back and forth.

"Yet you still tried to convince me of her attributes. 'Phoebe is a beautiful woman of means. A woman society and your family would approve of.'

"I would have told you."

"*When* would you have told me?" He pounded a fist on the desk, startling her. The memory of his mother jumping at his father's shout should have reined in Jacob's temper, but he didn't want to control it. He'd given Emily his heart, and she had betrayed him. "After your father pronounced Miss Dorsham and I man and wife, or the morning after we'd consummated the marriage?"

"I didn't fear that would happen because you showed no interest in Phoebe."

"Did you think a baby and another family would distract me from Christian? Do you not know me? I've searched the whole kingdom to find him. Do you think I'm not a good enough father for him? If so, I'm surprised you didn't talk your parents out of this visit."

Tears pooled in Emily's eyes. She looked to the side and shook her head. "I was frightened you'd take him back to London with you, and we'd never see him again."

Her confession blew away the heat of his ire. He'd been devastated when Sarah ran away with their child. Wouldn't the Thompsons feel as upset if he'd run off with Christian, even more so since they'd had a chance to know and raise him for five years?

Emily bit her lip and wiped her tear-stained cheeks with the back of her gloves. "I promised Phoebe I wouldn't reveal her condition, but I was uncomfortable with what she was trying to do. I'd planned to tell you if you showed an interest in her. Phoebe pleaded for my help, but I never thought her plan would work. She must marry and quickly, or else she'll be ruined."

"What about the poor chap she'll fool next? Doesn't he deserve to know? Shouldn't Phoebe face the consequences of her actions? If she doesn't, what will keep her from further indiscretions?" Lord Copeland's desperate voice rang in his ears. *I made a mistake. I was hurt and lonely. What would you have me do?*

Should the babe's father get away without punishment?

"The child is innocent. Christian and I were fortunate that the Thompsons took us in. Most orphans end up in work-houses or as street urchins, picking pockets to stay alive. What if the child could have a chance to lead a normal life?"

Jacob puffed his cheeks and exhaled a breath. He was uncomfortable allowing trickery, but he knew in his bones that Emily was too. She'd worked to earn a pristine image and undo the tarnish her mother's actions created. But if her mother hadn't fallen from grace, would Emily have even been born? "I guess we'll need to trust God to determine what is best in this situation."

Emily bit her bottom lip and nodded.

"Life is messy." He grunted. "People are messy. We make mistake after mistake, failing God in many ways, but He pulls us out of the mire and cleans us off, anyway."

Emily stared at her hands, picking at a bit of paint staining her wrist above the glove line.

Christian ran into the room. "Em, have you seen this place? It's huge." He held both arms stretched out wide. "They have a pond and a big stable under repair, but it has eight horses and more to arrive. We're going to have the best time ever."

"Indeed." He tussled Christian's hair. This week he'd focus on getting to know his son better. No distractions.

⁓

*E*mily swallowed around the lump in her throat. Earlier, she'd been nervous but hopeful, but after Jacob's accusations, she felt like a tulip whose petals had blown off. Nothing but a naked stem remained. She reminded herself that God was in charge, and His ways were higher than her ways. Even tulips would re-bloom again year after year. Still, she couldn't shake the feeling that she'd squandered her chance at happiness.

She kneeled in front of Christian, straightening the lapels of his tiny jacket. "Now, you be good for Lord Warren. Remember your manners, and be on your best behavior. No running off, and no complaining if you don't like something on your plate."

Jacob approached and placed a hand on Christian's shoulder.

Christian leaned in and whispered in Emily's ear. "But what if they serve Brussels sprouts?"

Jacob chuckled. "No worries, Cap. I've banned the cook from making them."

A burst of weak laughter spilled from her lips. She blinked away the sting of tears that burned the back of her eyes. "Sometimes he has bad dreams."

Jacob nodded. "I did, too, as a lad."

"And he has tutoring with the Danburys' youngest son on Wednesday."

"I'll mark it on the schedule."

"Well, then." She exhaled. "I guess I'll be going."

Christian wrapped his arms around her waist. "Bye, Em. I love you and Mama and Papa too. Don't worry. I'll be back."

She hugged his blond head. "I love you too."

He dropped his arms, and she reluctantly let go, choking back a sob.

"Why don't we see your sister to the door?"

Christian nodded. "That's what gentlemen do."

Jacob raised his elbow, and she looped her hand through it. They exited the office and strolled the hallway. "You have my permission to come by at any time."

"Thank you." She sniffed and blinked up at the ceiling. "Leaving him is harder than I expected."

He patted her hand. "I understand."

Maslow swung the door wide.

Jacob paused. "Would you like to take my carriage home?"

"I'd prefer to walk. I have a lot to consider." She released his arm but turned to him before stepping out the door. The words stuck in the tightness of her throat, but she forced them out. "I'm sorry. I never meant to deceive you."

He nodded with a grim twist to his mouth. "Good day, Miss Thompson."

She ran a hand alongside Christian's face. "Have a lovely time."

Turning before they spotted her tears, she trotted down the front steps. Every muscle in her body locked up tight to hold back her emotions. Christian would be back at week's end, and she and Jacob...

Things hadn't gone as she'd hoped, but at least they could be friends.

"Hey, Em!" Christian yelled.

She pivoted to find Christian and Jacob on the front steps.

Christian cupped a hand around his mouth. "Don't give Papa an answer about marrying Mr. Mathis. I'm still praying."

Jacob's head snapped in Christian's direction and then in hers. His eyes widened, but he said nothing.

A long, awkward moment passed, with the two of them staring at each other. What did she expect him to do? Run after her and beg her not to marry Mr. Mathis but to marry him instead? Really? After their argument over helping Phoebe trick him?

She forced herself to turn and walk down the lane but allowed her tears to fall.

CHAPTER 24

*J*acob stood in the foyer under his portrait as the footman finished hanging it.

Christian would be at tutoring for the rest of the afternoon, giving Jacob a rest. Who knew playtime could be so exhausting? A pony had been delivered the first day, and he'd taught Christian how to ride. They'd raced boats in the creek, played blind man's bluff with his aunt and the staff, and held every sort of competition he could think of, including who could fall asleep the fastest.

Jacob had won that one.

He stood back, admiring the artwork, and couldn't help but chuckle at the mischievous eyes and hint of a cheeky smile that would meet all newcomers as they entered. The likeness impressed him, but he thought of the artist every time he passed the portrait. Also when he woke, spoke, or moved. He'd see a unique color and wonder what name Emily would call it. He'd think of a witty remark and ponder what clever comeback she'd fire back. Christian would need a mother's touch, and he'd wonder how Emily would handle the situation.

He was sad the painting sessions were finished. Emily hadn't been by since she'd dropped off Christian.

Was she too busy preparing for her wedding to Mathis?

His heart clenched. He should have run after her, begged her to marry him instead.

Now it was too late.

He glanced at Maslow and clapped his shoulder. "Wait until my brother sees this."

The carriage wheels crunched over the rocks in the drive, turning Jacob's attention to the window.

Had Lieutenant Scar received his missive regarding Mr. Welsh? Had he come to search for clues as to the woman's identity?

Jacob had scoured the steward's residence and the man's office inside Brownstone Hall. In order to not interfere with his time with his son, he did his sleuthing in the evenings after Christian had fallen asleep, but searching by candlelight wasn't ideal. All he'd discovered was an unfinished love letter in which Welsh poured out his devotion to his dearest beloved. Apparently, their thieving had paid down her debts significantly. They'd planned for two more heists to obtain the funds to travel to Italy, where they would purchase a villa.

Things hadn't gone as they'd intended.

"Were you expecting company?" Maslow shuffled to the door.

Jacob pulled back the curtain and snorted at the gold crest on the carriage. It wasn't Lieutenant Scar. "Indeed. Eventually." He straightened, letting the curtain drop. "My portrait was hung just in time." He rubbed his palms, eager for what was about to happen. "Inform my aunt that her second-favorite nephew has arrived. Also, tell the housekeeper to prepare a room and have tea and scones prepared for the duke and duchess."

Maslow bowed and hailed the housekeeper, moving faster than Jacob had ever witnessed the butler go.

Jacob glanced up at the high-hung portrait and assumed a similar position beneath it.

Maslow returned and swung the door wide, standing erect with chest puffed out and chin high. "Welcome, Lord and Lady Sudbury, to Brownstone Hall."

Through the open door, Jacob watched Robert survey the exterior façade's changes before escorting his wife, Nora, through the front entrance and into the foyer, still inspecting his surroundings.

Aunt Louisa peeked around the upstairs corner.

Jacob caught her out of the corner of his eye and waved her down. She'd had some setbacks since learning she'd sheltered a highwayman and hesitated before moving to the stairs and grasping the railing. Thankfully, Christian was a good influence on her, and she'd already started to rebound.

Nora smiled at Jacob and extended her hands to greet him. Her gaze rose to the portrait above, and she drew up short.

Her sudden stop drew Robert's attention to her face. Nora clasped a hand over her mouth, but an unladylike giggle escaped.

With a questioning look, Robert followed her gaze.

"Truly?" He shook his head, but his lips twitched as he struggled to contain a grin. "I can't leave you unsupervised for a single moment."

~

While Nora and Aunt Louisa had tea, Jacob walked Robert around Brownstone Hall, explaining the prior condition, what renovations he'd completed, and what remained to be finished.

"The place is coming along quite nicely. I wasn't sure you had it in you, but you've proved me wrong."

Jacob hadn't known that he had it in him either, which made his brother's praise all the more enjoyable.

As they walked the perimeter of the property, heading back to the main hall, his brother flashed him another askance look —the third one in the past ten minutes.

Jacob stopped and propped fisted hands on his hips. "What? Do you not approve of the stable's renovations?"

"The stable is coming along famously." Robert resumed their walk at a slower pace. "It's nothing." He waved his hand. "Merely that you've changed. There's a peace about you—a contentment. I wouldn't have thought you'd be taken with the rural countryside."

Jacob snorted. "Sylvanwood is lovely, but it's what resides in the country that makes me look forward to each day."

"Let me guess. The women?"

"Not this time. Well, one, yes." Emily's warm amber eyes teasing him over his fainting spell floated through his memory. He imagined her waiting for him and Christian on the back portico as they returned from a ride.

But Mathis nudged his way into the picture, sliding a proprietary arm around her.

The heavy grief of what could have been weighed Jacob's body and soul. "I fear I lost my chance to claim her." He clasped his hands behind his back to hide the slump of his shoulders.

Robert drew up short. "Marriage? That's the first time I've heard you consider the institution. She must be special to break through the fortifications you've built around your heart."

"She's good and pure—a vicar's daughter who thinks a redeemed rake isn't the wise choice for a husband."

"Then the vicar's daughter doesn't know her Bible."

"What do you mean?"

"Moses killed an Egyptian. Abraham lied. Noah got drunk.

Saul persecuted Christians. David had an affair and sent the woman's husband to die. Seems to me God uses imperfect people to accomplish His will."

Huh. All those Bible heroes had made mistakes, some worse than Jacob's. He could be used by God.

"But you said a woman wasn't why you look forward to each day." Robert started strolling again.

Jacob fell into step with his brother. "I found him."

Robert's gaze snapped to Jacob's face. "Your son?"

He nodded. "His name's Christian Thompson."

"You did it." Robert clapped his brother on the shoulder. "When do we get to meet him?"

Jacob flipped open his pocket watch. "He'll be returning from his tutoring any moment. You're going to love him. He's just like me."

"Lord help us. I can barely handle one of you." The teasing twinkle in Robert's gaze showed he was excited to meet his nephew. "I'm an uncle."

Jacob stepped onto the terrace, and a footman opened the French doors. "Master Christian has returned, milord."

"Splendid."

"He's with Lady Alton and Lady Sudbury in the back salon." The footman stepped aside for them to enter.

Jacob followed the excited chatter to the salon with Robert in tow.

"What, then, is twenty and four plus thirty and six?" Nora's voice posed the sum before he slipped into the room.

Christian faced the ladies, chest puffed, with his back to Jacob and Robert. "The answer is sixty."

"Very good." Lady Athol clapped her hands before peering at Jacob. "He's a bright boy."

"Indeed." Jacob nodded.

"Papa!" Christian spun. "I mean, Lord Warren." He hugged Jacob's legs.

Jacob's chest swelled at the reference, and he longed for his son to call him *Papa*, but not yet. Not when society would shun a child born out of wedlock. Robert hit Jacob with another askance look, which meant his brother had questions.

"Can we go riding?" Christian tugged on Jacob's pant leg. "I want to show Lady Sudbury how I can ride a pony."

"There will be plenty of time tomorrow." He patted Christian's back even though the lad's shoulders slumped. "You need to wash up before the evening meal, but first, I want to introduce you to my brother, Lord Robert Warren, the Marquis of Sudbury."

Christian straightened and folded his body into a stiff, low bow. "Pleased to make your acquaintance, my lord."

"The pleasure is all mine, good sir." Robert bowed in return.

Jacob gestured to Nora. "And I see you've already met my sister-in-law, Lady Nora Warren, Marchioness of Sudbury."

"Not formally." Christian hop-stepped to stand in front of Nora and extended his palm. She placed her gloved hand in his, and he bowed low over her knuckles. "A pleasure to meet you, my lady." He righted. "I always thought my sister, Em, was the most beautiful woman in the world, but you are quite lovely too."

Robert nudged Jacob with his elbow and said in a low voice, "He's definitely your son."

"Show the marquis how smart you are," Aunt Louisa said. "Sum fifty and two plus thirty and six."

Christian scrunched up his lips and peered at the ceiling. "Eighty-eight."

While the ladies continued to challenge Christian, Robert leaned close to Jacob's ear. "What are you going to do about him?"

"I'm still waiting on God's direction."

He received another side glance from his brother at the

mention of God, but if Robert thought his finding religion odd, he didn't mention it.

"If you bring him back to London as your son, he'll be shunned by the Quality." Although his words were a warning, his tone held a note of sadness as though wishing it weren't so.

"I plan to stay here. Take up employment as Aunt Louisa's steward."

"You'd leave your life in the city?"

Jacob gazed at his son. "My life is here now."

Nora rose and moved to her husband's side, smiling at Christian. She placed a hand on her stomach. "I said I hoped for a girl, but I've changed my mind. I want a boy."

It was Jacob's turn to flash his brother a questioning side glance.

Robert drew his wife closer, and she peered at him with a look of love that elicited a deep ache from Jacob's heart. Would Emily ever look at him the same way?

"God knows what we want but also what we need." Robert pressed a gentle kiss on Nora's temple. "We'll be blessed by whichever He gives us."

~

*E*mily tugged at an errant string on the puffed sleeve of her gown but quit before damaging the stitch. As of late, her emotions were so tightly wound, she was afraid if she pulled the wrong string, her entire life might unravel.

Mr. Mathis placed a hand on her lower back and ushered her into the Hinwick Manor ballroom. The air warmed as townsfolk filed into a receiving line that formed along the edge of the ballroom to greet their hosts, Lord and Lady Dorsham and Phoebe for her send-off party. All the chairs had been pushed back or taken elsewhere to clear the floor for dancing. A five-musician orchestra sat on the far side of the room, playing a soft melody to allow for conversation before the dancing began.

Samuel would join the party later. He had been summoned to pray over a parishioner's ailing grandmother.

Mama and Papa stood before her and Mr. Mathis in line. Mr. Mathis had insisted he escort her to the party even though she'd asked for more time to pray about his offer of marriage. He'd remained quiet the whole carriage ride, and when Emily tried to converse, he kept his responses curt, pouting because she hadn't enthusiastically accepted his offer.

Emily took in the home where they'd spent much of their childhood. The high-ceilinged ballroom didn't appear as expansive as it had when she and Phoebe used to play pretend ball and dance around. If anyone inspected the oriental vase in the corner, they'd discover a fine crack where she and Phoebe had bumped into the pedestal and broken the vase. Phoebe had convinced a maid to glue it back together and swear she'd never tell Lady Dorsham.

Mr. Mathis peered up at the chandelier, and for the first time that evening, the corners of his lips twitched into a smile. "Remember when Phoebe dared us to jump from the orchestra balcony to the chandelier and then land on the sofa below?"

"I remember none of us thought the challenge a good idea, so Phoebe decided to prove us wrong." Emily shook her head. "I couldn't watch. I still can't believe she made it to the chandelier."

"Only to dangle there because she was too frightened to let go." He snorted.

Emily chuckled. "Samuel and I rushed to get a blanket to hold and break her fall, but her grip gave way, and you caught her before we could get there."

"And thank heaven because with the chandelier swinging, she would have missed the sofa and hit the floor."

"She was never afraid to go after what she wanted." Emily's

gaze drifted to Phoebe, looking lovely in her best gown. "This is Phoebe's big night, and I want it to be special for her."

"Indeed." His smile fell. "These events remind me of a horse show, where the owners, in this case the parents, show off their filly." He stiffened. "I'm here to protect Phoebe from the rake-hells who prey on innocents."

Emily frowned. Specifically Phoebe?

He glanced down at her. "Er—and you, too, of course."

Did he say that because of the rumors regarding Jacob? Or had gossip spread about Phoebe's condition? Was he being surly because he didn't like that Phoebe was moving on without them?

Or, all this time, had Emily been oblivious to Mr. Mathis's feelings toward their mutual friend?

The couple in front of them in the reception line swept away toward the refreshment table.

"Welcome, Reverend and Mrs. Thompson." Lord Dorsham smiled at Emily's parents. "So happy you could join us for Phoebe's send-off. Mr. Mathis and Miss Thompson too. Phoebe, I'm sure, is delighted you're here. Aren't you, dear?" He elbowed his daughter.

Phoebe's smile wobbled. "Indeed. Thank you for coming."

"I came by twice to see how you were faring after the robbery," Emily said, "but you weren't at home. I do hope you're all right."

"I'm fine." Phoebe refused to look at Emily. Her face was paler than normal. Phoebe would normally be basking in the attention afforded her by a ball in her honor. Was she still shaken from the robbery last weekend? Phoebe extended a warm hand and graceful curtsy to Mr. Mathis. "Please help yourself to some refreshments. The dancing should start shortly."

Was she still feeling betrayed after finding Emily and Jacob standing so close? Emily never meant for any of this to happen.

Emily touched her friend's sleeve. "We need to talk."

"Excuse me one moment." She turned green. "I need to freshen up." Her friend turned in a swirl of skirts and scurried in the direction of the retiring rooms.

"Oh, dear." Lady Dorsham watched her dart off with a frown. "I fear she's a bit under the weather tonight. All the strain over planning the ball must have been too much for her."

Emily gripped Mr. Mathis's sleeve. "I should go check on her."

He clasped a hand over hers to keep her at his side. "No need. She'll be back soon. Nothing could keep Miss Dorsham from missing her own party."

Emily didn't miss the look of concern that passed over Mr. Mathis's face. He guided her along the perimeter of the dance floor, following her parents, who stopped to speak to the Danfords.

Mr. Mathis excused himself, murmuring about needing to speak with the magistrate, and left her with her parents.

"Good to see you, Mr. Danford." Papa clapped the lanky, bearded man on the shoulder. "How's young William coming along with picking up his new trade as a colorist?"

"He's taken to it like a natural. Truly enjoys his work."

Emily tracked Mr. Mathis. He paused by the magistrate who was deep in conversation with another guest, but then her escort turned and slipped out a side door into the hallway. Where was he going?

"My daughter, Emily, will be a frequent customer of his shop when she's in London painting for the academy."

What? Emily returned her focus to the conversation. She must break it to Papa that she wouldn't ever be going to London.

Mr. Danford's gaze flicked to Emily. He scratched his beard with one finger and ran it along the inside of his collar.

Emily swallowed a sense of unease.

Mr. Danford's ears reddened, and he blurted out a change in topic. "So I heard the parish wants a new organ?"

Emily sidestepped to her mother. Why was Mr. Danford looking at her as if she carried the plague?

"I'm so grateful no one was hurt. Jewels can be replaced, but people cannot." Mama smiled at Mrs. Wilcox, the baker's wife.

"But that necklace cost more than the price my apple dumplings brought in this year." Mrs. Wilcox clicked her tongue.

"Did you get to eat one?" Mama asked Emily.

She shook her head. "Sadly, no. Samuel devoured them all. He raves over them."

Mrs. Wilcox's face drained its color. "How kind." Her eyes darted left and right before she excused herself, murmuring that she hadn't seen Mrs. Archer in an age, even though Emily knew they'd sat next to each other in the pew this past Sunday.

The hairs on Emily's neck prickled. *Something's wrong.*

Her parents settled into conversation with the barnstable and his wife.

Emily stood off to the side. Guests milled around, taking turns about the room or sipping lemonade. A group of women whispered behind fans to each other, a couple glancing in her direction.

Emily peered left and right, but no one besides her stood in the corner. Were they whispering about her?

The dancing commenced, and Phoebe returned to partner with John Wesley Thurgood, who had been considered Sylvanwood's most eligible bachelor and best catch before Jacob arrived.

Emily searched the room for Mr. Mathis, who usually asked Emily for the first dance, but he was nowhere to be found. No matter. She'd sit this one out.

Preston White, a gentleman farmer, often led her out for the second dance. Although Mr. White's lack of rhythm left her toes bruised, he was a sweet young man with a shy demeanor, and Emily enjoyed any opportunity to dance.

An image of Jacob's jaunty smile flittered through her mind. He would be a superb dancer, but would he ask her to dance after their falling out? She wished she'd refused to help Phoebe. If only her birth family had truly been the Thompsons. If only Jacob's family would accept a country vicar's daughter for their son. If only her heart didn't crave to be in Jacob's arms.

Why couldn't she just settle for Mr. Mathis, as she'd always planned to do?

The orchestra played a catchy tune, and Emily's toe tapped the rhythm. The music inspired her. If she closed her eyes, she could imagine color in every note, exploding into artistic creations.

The first set ended, and the dancing couples reshuffled their partners. The merchant's son asked Phoebe to dance, and to Emily's surprise, Mr. White led Miss Cantor onto the floor.

Emily forced her chin up. Good for Mr. White. Miss Cantor would make an excellent match. She should feel blessed to witness young love in the making. Where was Mr. Mathis?

Loneliness swept over her, but she shook it off. She, Phoebe, Samuel, and Peter had always stuck together at these events, but they were growing older and apart. Phoebe would attend the London season and marry the first gentleman who fancied her. Samuel had shown interest in Miss Beatrice Michaels. Mr. Mathis...he deserved better than a loveless marriage. And if this evening were any indicator, she'd be painting.

The air in the room suddenly felt charged with electricity. She sensed Jacob's presence even before the husky tone of his voice sounded in her ear. "Tell me you haven't agreed to Mathis's offer of marriage yet." His voice was a whisper, a breath in her hair. "I spoke with your parents, but I need to hear it from you."

She turned and looked up at him. "A wise man informed me I was so fearful of sinning that I refused to feel. He scoffed at me marrying someone I didn't love."

Hope flickered in his eyes.

"God showed me through that man that I was refusing to love because I thought punishing myself would atone for the sins of my parents." She fought to not hang her head.

His gaze softened. "And?"

"I'd believed I was tainted, stained, and ugly. I figured if I could live a sinless life, and if I created beauty through my paintings, I could cover my stain through works."

"What did God say?"

She inhaled until her chest swelled. "Redemption is a gift, but I have to open it, not try to recreate it."

"Dance with me."

His words jolted through her being. It wasn't so much a question as a statement, and he didn't allow her the opportunity to decline, for he gripped her hand and gently pulled her onto the dance floor.

"You've forgiven me?"

He chuckled. "Who am I to withhold forgiveness after all that's been forgiven me?"

Couples lined up for the quadrille.

Jacob's fingers slid along her lower back. She'd attended over a dozen country dances, danced with a myriad of men, yet his touch felt intimate. The warmth of his hand spread through her body, igniting a tingle of excitement. He stared at her with a possessive indulgence that quickened her pulse.

"Christian fared well?" she asked as he led her into a turn.

"Better than I. He's a ball of energy."

Emily laughed but quickly subdued it. People would notice. They would wonder about his boldness and her outrageous outburst. She should care and avert her eyes. But the room faded along with their pasts. She wasn't doing anything wrong by dancing with Jacob. Many other women in the assembly hall would do the same, but he'd chosen her first.

No one else could claim that tonight. A little thrill lifted the hairs on her arms.

Jacob's timing and footwork were excellent, as she had known they would be. Only this moment mattered, not his reputation or her parentage. She'd enjoy the freedom of this dance. It was a gift from God, one of the rare moments she could let her guard down and enjoy herself.

His gaze remained steadfast upon her as they danced the figure, even during the partner exchange. Emily soaked it in like a flower, raising its head to the sun.

They stepped aside to afford the other couples their opportunity. She found herself unable to contain the bubbling spring inside her. Fiddle on what others thought of her grinning like a fiend.

"You look radiant tonight."

A wave of heat washed over her, and it wasn't due to the dancing.

"Although, I'm used to seeing you with more color."

She raised a questioning brow.

He raised a finger. "Indeed, I'm used to a smudge of color here." He brushed a knuckle down her cheek. "And a dab of color here." He ran his thumb across her chin.

She grabbed his hand and held it in proper dance form, hoping the others didn't notice his intimate touch. He always pushed propriety to the line. "The world looks better in color, and so do I."

The humor in his blue eyes sobered. "You give the world color."

Her heart exploded into a thousand sparkling embers. She longed to melt into his embrace, to feed off his confidence. She wanted to believe they could be together.

He led her into the next figure. Dazed, she allowed him to

usher her through the movements, though her feet hardly touched the floor. The music ended, and he whirled her back into place, where they bowed to the other couples.

He guided her back to her parents, but his long strides slowed significantly. She also didn't want their time to end.

A murmur sounded amongst the guests, and all eyes shifted to face the entrance. Emily craned her neck to glimpse what was causing the stir.

And then Jacob said, "There is someone I'd like you to meet."

CHAPTER 25

*E*mily was confused. Who would he know in the small town of Sylvanwood that she didn't?

As Phoebe curtsied low, a sightline emerged of a finely dressed couple, her in a gold brocade gown with a shimmery gauze overlay and him in a well-tailored jacket and snowy white shirtfront. The way they carried themselves and how the crowd gaped in awe signaled that the couple belonged to the upper echelons of society.

Emily hesitated, and Jacob focused on her. "What's the matter?"

"Who are they?" Her hand squeezed Jacob's arm tighter.

One side of Jacob's mouth curved upward. "My eldest brother and his wife—come to Sylvanwood to ensure I haven't gotten into trouble."

"The marquis and marchioness?" Emily felt the blood leave her face. "I-I can't meet them. I'm not dressed properly." She had worn her best gown, but to meet nobility, shouldn't she be wearing the latest fashion from a French dressmaker?

Jacob snorted. "You look beautiful. Besides, they came tonight specifically to meet you."

"Me?" Her voice squeaked.

"I quote," Jacob said. "'We must meet the artist who depicted you so accurately.'"

The painting. Of course. Even so, her steps slowed.

"I assure you they don't bite." He shrugged. "At least not Nora. She's an angel. How she puts up with my brother is beyond me. They are truly a love match." Jacob pulled lightly on Emily's arm.

She patted her coiffure before exhaling a shaky breath. Leaning heavily on Jacob's arm for support because her knees refused to cooperate, she stumbled to where the couple stood by the entrance.

Lord and Lady Dorsham gushed over the Marquis of Sudbury, creating an awkward display. Phoebe had to excuse herself, rushing to the ladies' retiring room once more.

Emily didn't miss the relief on the marquis's face when he spotted his brother.

"Jacob. Good to see you." The man bowed, excusing himself to Lord and Lady Dorsham, and skirted away even though Lady Dorsham continued to speak to his back. His grip tightened on his wife's arm, pulling her along in his wake.

She excused herself to Lady Dorsham over her shoulder. The Marchioness of Sudbury smiled at Jacob. Her gaze drifted to Emily, and a spark of interest lit their depths.

"Robert." Jacob clasped his brother's arm. "I knew you had arrived when I saw women fainting in the wings."

"Merely an occupational hazard of the title. In my opinion, it's better than men reaching for their weapons and naming their seconds, as when you walk in the room."

"My favorite opinions are the ones people keep to themselves." Jacob pushed back one side of his jacket and hooked his thumb in his pant pocket, but his eyes danced. "Ah, the perils of being the handsomer brother."

The marchioness locked eyes with Emily. "Do not fear.

They love each other dearly. This merely is how they express it."

Lord Sudbury's arm slid around his wife's waist. "And who do we have here? Is this the lovely and gifted artist who painted the portrait?"

Jacob ushered Emily forward a step. "May I introduce Miss Emily Thompson, talented artist and daughter of the local vicar?"

"Miss Thompson is the vicar's daughter?" Lady Sudbury covered her surprise with a cough. She glanced at Jacob, her eyes twinkling. "You neglected to mention that part. My, how your tastes have changed."

"Miss Thompson," Jacob said, "may I present my brother Lord Robert Warren, the Marquis of Sudbury? And his much too beautiful wife for such an ugly beast, Lady Nora Warren, the Marchioness of Sudbury."

Emily curtsied, and Lady Sudbury followed suit but shook her head at Jacob as if to say, *what shall I do with these brothers?*

The two men continued to taunt one another, but Lady Sudbury ignored their antics and focused on Emily. Her expression glowed. "I am amazed at your talent. I had to meet you after seeing such a lifelike rendering."

"You are too kind."

Her voice lowered, and she leaned in closer. "You captured the tease in his smile and the humor in his eyes but also a trace of vulnerability." Her eyes held Emily's as if searching. "You must be an especially gifted woman to recognize that in him in such a short time."

Emily swallowed, wondering what she was implying.

"Jacob may appear cavalier, but those who see beyond his ruse find a kind and, I daresay, noble heart."

Jacob chuckled at something his brother said, and a carefree smile illuminated his features. Flashes of him playing pirates with Christian by the stream swelled her heart.

"He had your painting hung in the entranceway of the Brownstone Hall before our arrival. Jacob's smile greeted us in more ways than one when we arrived."

"Lord Warren intended the painting as a jest to irk his brother."

"Indeed. It worked brilliantly, for it's too wonderful to take down and has left his lordship in a conundrum." She issued a loving sideways look at her husband, who rubbed the back of her glove with his thumb. "Is that how you met? By Jacob seeking an artist to commission for a painting?"

Emily hesitated. "Not precisely."

"Oh?"

Emily launched into a brief explanation of their first encounter, when she discovered him held at gunpoint.

The men quieted until Lord Sudbury crossed his arms over his chest. "It was Benton, wasn't it?"

His scowl caused Emily to back up a step.

Jacob confirmed with a curt nod.

"Don't you have a care for your own life?" The marquis's glare shot sparks. "I'll have him brought before the House of Lords."

"And create a scandal? I think not."

"As I recall, you've already done that." The marquis arched a brow, which must be a family trait.

"I can handle Benton. He has licked his wounds at his paramour's in Bath and is most likely returning to London soon."

"How can you be certain?"

Jacob hesitated.

"Because Lady Benton said as much." Lady Sudbury answered for him. "She called upon Brownstone Hall the minute she heard of our arrival."

Lady Benton? The fancy woman Emily had met in town? Her husband was the highwayman Emily had pierced with an arrow? She met Jacob's gaze, but he glanced away.

"We can discuss this matter another time." Jacob held his arm out for Lady Sudbury. "The dance floor awaits, Nora. Shall we?"

Lady Sudbury accepted Jacob's arm.

Lord Sudbury offered his arm to Emily. She accepted with a silent prayer that she wouldn't dance like a green country chit and followed them onto the dance floor.

Lord Sudbury was, like his brother, an excellent dancer. In many ways, he reminded her of Jacob. They held the same frame and similar features, yet he carried an air of responsibility and bore the creases in his forehead as scars from its weight. Heaven knew having Jacob under his care would warrant it. He kept his questions casual, asking about her family and issuing lighthearted jabs at his brother. As the dance sets progressed, Emily found Lord Sudbury to be a delightful fellow.

He promenaded her through a turn, and she felt Jacob's eyes on her. Their gazes met, and the affection communicated in their depths sent her heart racing.

"Ah, the night becomes even more interesting."

She followed Lord Sudbury's gaze to the entrance but couldn't see over the revelers.

"Lady Benton is here."

Emily faltered a step, and Lord Sudbury's pressure increased on her lower back.

"Do not fret. Lady Benton rarely attends events with her husband."

"That is all and well, for I didn't bring my bow and arrows with me this time."

A wide, sweeping smile framed the marquis's evenly lined teeth, and the creases in the corners of his eyes deepened. "Quick-witted. No wonder Jacob speaks so fondly of you."

Did he?

Emily swallowed, unsure how to respond to such a

comment. How was it that her wit chose to come to her aid and then evaporated when she was still in need?

~

*L*ady Benton was the last woman Jacob wanted to see, even if she'd become his prime suspect. Not only did she have blond hair, but she was known to gamble, which could have caused the debts that Welsh mentioned in his letter.

The woman, like his past, haunted him, showing up when he least expected it, drawing suspicions, and causing trouble. He especially didn't want to see her now that Emily knew it was Lord Benton who'd nearly taken Jacob's life. He ground his teeth. The last thing he needed was for Emily to be reminded of his past libertine ways. She had begun to trust he'd become a changed man. He'd seen the regard in her eyes when they danced.

As if Nora could read his thoughts, she squeezed his arm and said, "I like Miss Thompson. She seems like a bright and intuitive woman, the kind who sees a person's true heart."

"Indeed." He grimaced. "She also puts a lot of stock in her family and their reputation."

Sympathy filled Nora's eyes. "But you've changed so much."

"I'm not certain it will be enough."

Nora shook her head. "It's not."

Jacob fake-clutched his chest as though she'd wounded him.

"None of us are good all the time. Try as we might, all of us, at some point, will fall short." She glanced at Robert, and a warm smile spread across her face. "Love is about relationship, knowing each other deeply, our hopes, dreams, fears, and mistakes."

Her words resonated. It hadn't been enough for him to

know Christian was alive. He'd never be content to stand at a distance and merely send him money or gifts. He wanted a relationship with his son.

Like how God wanted a relationship with him.

The Father-son dynamic illuminated Jacob's life in a new light, and a verse floated in his memory. *We love Him because He first loved us.* God knit Jacob together in his mother's womb. He knew him inside and out, good and bad, and loved him, anyway. God desired a relationship with Jacob.

Jacob glanced up at the chandelier, though his focus was far higher. *Lord, I want You to be part of my life, and with Your guidance, I want to be part of Christian's life.*

Robert said something to make Emily laugh, and Jacob caught the lighthearted joy in her expression.

And Emily's life.

The song ended, and Jacob guided Nora to meet Emily's parents. His brother and Emily joined them. Politeness required that he dance with Miss Dorsham and Lady Dorsham, since they were their hosts and of a similar status. If he didn't, it would draw attention in such a small town. Jacob snorted. Since when did he care about maintaining appearances?

But the answer was clear. Since God had sent an angel to wake him from a dark, sin-filled sleep. He stole a glance at Emily's rosy cheeks and eyes that sparkled with festivity. He'd dance with a clubfoot dowager if it meant he could enjoy one more dance with Emily.

He excused himself and sought Miss Dorsham to fulfill his obligation. He found her near the refreshment table.

"Miss Dorsham, may I have the next dance?" He bowed.

She flipped open her dance card and trailed her index finger down the names. "Oh yes, there you are, squeezed in between Sir Kenneth Pembrook and Mr. Mathis."

He'd signed her dance card when he arrived—she'd seen

him do it. If she was going to be petty, then he, too, could be difficult. Instead of offering his hand, he crossed his arms.

The corners of her mouth tilted into a tiny frown, but she rounded on Sir Kenneth with a wide smile. "Thank you for partnering with me." She stepped closer and whispered something to him behind her fan.

The man blushed the colors of a sunset.

"Please excuse me," she said to Sir Kenneth, who, with a nod, backed away. She tucked her gloved hand around Jacob's elbow, and he led her onto the dance floor.

"You are playing a dangerous game."

She shrugged one shoulder.

He gave her a little shake, encouraging her to look at him. "You think you're in control, but things get out of hand quickly. Your new friends, Lady Benton and Lady Charlton, use others to get what they want. They don't care about you."

She snorted and scanned the ballroom. "Neither do you."

"You're wrong." He wanted to strangle her, but Emily's words echoed in his mind. *Phoebe is a passionate, caring person who simply wants to be wanted. Her parents don't show their love unless she's performing.* Hadn't he done much of the same? Acted out to get his father's attention, and then Sarah's after she'd rejected him?

The waltz started with a promenade, and he led her through the steps. "I care because Miss Thompson cares."

She stiffened and turned her head away.

"Listen." His stern voice drew her attention. "Miss Thompson considers you a good friend, and she sang your praises despite the contradictory actions I've witnessed in you. You are blessed to have such a loyal friend, especially considering you treat her poorly."

"I have done nothing of..." Miss Dorsham faltered a step, and he helped her recover. Her gaze flicked about the room until it landed on Emily, and her lower lip trembled.

Emily stood alone against the wall with her hands folded in front of her. Why? Why had no one asked Emily to dance, even though the men outnumbered the women?

She was too lovely, respected, and witty to be a wallflower.

His grip tightened. "Why is no one dancing with Emily?"

Miss Dorsham chose to stare at his waistcoat.

Jacob wanted to rush to Emily's side. But he needed intel, and Miss Dorsham had it. "What have you done?"

"Nothing." She tried to brush off his question and focus on her footwork, but Jacob would have none of it.

"Tell me the truth, or I'll disgrace you by leaving you here on the dance floor."

Her eyes widened. "You wouldn't."

"Not only that, but I'll leave the party and take the marquis and marchioness with me." He broke their dance hold.

"No, please." She clung to his jacket.

He stared her down.

"I was angry because she'd stolen you. She knew I'd set my cap for you."

"What did you do?" He hadn't meant the words to sound menacing, but there was no taking them back.

"I slipped and told Lady Benton that Emily's real mother is an opera singer. I didn't mean to. The gossip spread like wildfire."

Jacob's stomach clenched. "You need to fix this."

Phoebe bit her lip, and lines of remorse marred her pretty face. "I don't know how. It's out there, and there's no way of putting the milk back in the cow."

He'd pressured criminals to confess, but this was different. Should he use the intelligence he'd gathered as their coachman? He glanced at Emily, holding her head tall despite being ignored. It wasn't for personal benefit. It was for Emily. He narrowed his gaze on Miss Dorsham. "A secret for a secret, then?"

Miss Dorsham gasped loud enough to turn heads. "She told you?"

"Not Emily." He led her through a turn.

"*He* told you?" She blanched whiter than the pearls encrusting her gown.

"Let's merely say I overheard a conversation not meant for my ears."

"It was you. You were pretending to be our coachman the night of the Simmons' party." Miss Dorsham's voice lowered to a horrified whisper. "The night by the river." Her grip tightened on his sleeve. "You wouldn't. I'd be ruined."

"Isn't that what you did to Miss Thompson?"

Miss Dorsham looked as if she might get sick. The song ended, and he walked her the long way around the dance floor. They needed more time before he returned her to her parents.

"I didn't think." Phoebe's lip trembled. "I was angry."

"Did hurting your only true friend make you feel better?"

"No." Her chin lowered, and she walked in silence for a moment. "What do I do?"

"Tell Emily the truth and ask for her forgiveness."

Miss Dorsham wavered as if she might faint, but he wouldn't let her fall into hysterics.

"Next, you need to spread the truth, that the rumor had been spread out of malice and that Miss Thompson is a reputable young woman and a good friend." He led her straight to Emily's side.

"I believe the two of you need to talk." He bowed, spying Peter Mathis eyeing him with a jealous scowl from behind a nearby pillar.

"*Y*ou look pale. Is something wrong?" Emily cupped Phoebe's hand between her own.

"I'm going to be sick." She ran from the room.

Emily waited, her concern for her friend in her condition overriding her wariness of the impending conversation. She'd already suspected, by the way people treated her, either Phoebe or Lady Dorsham had let the truth slip about her birth mother.

Phoebe returned looking weary and pale and dabbing at the corner of her mouth. "Why are you being nice to me when I don't deserve it?"

She wanted to rile at her so-called friend, but Scripture rang in her heart. *Forgive each other as the Lord has forgiven you.*

Phoebe blinked, clearing the glassy look in her eyes. "I know you've already figured out what I did. You were always the smart and talented one." Her chest rose and fell with a heaved sigh. "I'm sorry. I was hurt that Lord Warren's affections were for you and not me. And I'm so frightened that I won't be able to pull off a wedding"—her voice squeaked—"in time." She hung her head. "If I were you, I'd never forgive me."

She should worry about what her secret, revealed to the whole town, would mean for her future, her parents, and Christian, but Jacob's words rang in her ears. *Don't you think God will provide a way? Can't we trust Him to cover the sins of your parents and the sins of my past?*

Jacob was right. As a vicar's daughter, she should have known that. She located chairs near a pillar and gestured for them to sit. "What you did was wrong and hurtful, but Jacob has taught me that God will make a way in the wilderness and wastelands."

From her seat, Emily tracked Jacob to where he stood next to his brother. The marquis was handsome, as the gossipmongers had stated, but Jacob even more so. Next to his brother, Jacob was at ease. He could speak to anyone and make them comfortable and wasn't afraid to take on a challenge like Brownstone Hall. He was observant and amusing, confident and humble.

"You love him, don't you?"

Emily's gaze snapped from Jacob to Phoebe's blotchy, tear-stained face. "I—"

"We all thought you'd marry Peter, even Peter."

"He told you I haven't accepted his proposal?"

Phoebe nodded. "I ran into him at the market and again tonight in the hallway. We spoke, and he truly listened to me."

"Mr. Mathis is a good friend. He's the logical choice for me to marry."

"Why?" Phoebe gave her a funny look. "You don't love him." She tapped her chin. "I don't even think you enjoy his company —at least not in the way you enjoy Lord Warren's." Her gaze drifted to the wall above Emily's head. "Peter is too strict, too controlling for you. I'm the one who needs someone to tighten the reins. You'd be miserable marrying him." She frowned. "But that's the idea, isn't it? You feel the need to punish yourself because of your mother's mistakes. As though you don't deserve love. But what about all that redemption your father preaches?"

Phoebe peered hard into Emily's eyes as if desperate for the answer, but Emily had no words.

"Am I forever unlovable because of my mistake? Is my child doomed for my sins? I realize I must suffer the consequences, but has my mistake made me worthless? Will God toss us away like trash, much like society will do when they find out?" She scooped up Emily's hand. "Does suffering earn God's love?"

"Of course not." Emily shook her head, but Phoebe's words hurt like a finger pressing on a bruise. "Jesus paid the price. While we were still sinners, Christ died for us."

Phoebe's brows lowered. "Then why are you still trying to

climb on the cross and pay for your sins and that of your mother?"

How had everyone else seen the truth before she did? "You're right. The stain of sin is gone." Emily placed her other hand over top of Phoebe's and remembered Jacob's words. "I can forgive you, my mother, even myself because so much has been forgiven me."

Phoebe glanced across the room. "Lord Warren can't take his eyes off you. He loves you. It's time for you to tell him you return his sentiments."

"I couldn't." Her breaths quickened. What of Jacob's father and Jacob's life in London? "I fear—"

"If it's God's will, then wouldn't disobedience be a sin— especially when Lord Warren loves you and you love him back?" Phoebe held up a finger to stay a gentleman coming to ask for a dance. "Peter helped me understand I've ended up the way I am because I wasn't putting God at the center. I placed what I wanted above God's best for my life. But you've been living out of fear, which is also not God's best. Haven't you read Song of Solomon? You and Jacob have that kind of love, and if God has blessed you with such a gift, why would you turn it away?"

"I—"

Phoebe pressed her hand over her mouth and gripped Emily's hand.

"Are you all right?" Emily prepared to escort her friend to the closest chamber pot.

Phoebe closed her eyes and waited a moment. She opened them and inhaled a deep breath. "I can't go to London. My plans are ruined, and so am I."

"Whatever do you mean?"

"I can't keep any food down." She slumped in her chair. "I can't go to London for the season and be sick the entire time.

People won't want to be around me." She choked on a sob. "They'll suspect."

"Oh, Phoebe." Emily wanted to put her arm around her friend, despite all the hurt she'd caused, but it would draw attention in front of the guests. Instead, she patted her friend's hand. Would Phoebe's parents send her away? Disown her and their grandchild? Their family name would be tarnished. They'd never be able to appear at another gathering of the ton. All the Dorshams' connections and ambitions would be for naught.

Peter Mathis appeared from around the pillar, his expression stern.

Merciful heavens. What had he heard?

Emily shrank against the wood chair as his form shadowed the light from the blazing chandelier.

"Miss Thompson, I must beg your forgiveness for misleading you." His Adam's apple bobbed. "I had every intension of marrying you out of duty to your family and our friendship, but I've been in love with someone who's been out of my reach. Until now." Mr. Mathis looked at Phoebe, who covered her face with her gloved hands.

"How could this night get worse?" Phoebe murmured against the satin fabric. "Emily's in love with Lord Warren and now Peter confesses a secret love. All my friends shall marry, and I'm destined to be desperate and alone."

Mr. Mathis pulled Phoebe's hands away from her face and knelt in front of her. "Phoebe, I've been in love with you for years. It's always been you, but you were above my station with grandiose plans. You would have despised being the wife of a gentleman farmer, but now..." He dug into his pocket and glanced about to ensure no one else watched. He pulled out a sapphire ring. "Will you accept the protection of my name?"

"What?" Phoebe blinked. "You would have me?"

He nodded.

Phoebe leaned in and whispered. "You'd raise someone else's child as your own?"

"I will raise *your* child as my own."

Phoebe stared at her hands, her chest rising and falling with quick breaths. Time seemed to stretch into a long moment, but then a wide smile broke across her face. "Yes. Of course, I will marry you. You've always been more than a friend to me, the man who I've needed."

Mr. Mathis slid the ring on her finger. "We'll need to speak to your parents posthaste."

Phoebe blanched, but Mr. Mathis stood.

"Miss Dorsham?" He held out his hand. "May I have the next dance?"

The glow returned to her face. "Most definitely."

Wow.

Emily watched as Peter and Phoebe stepped onto the dance floor before scanning the room for Jacob. Her gaze met his above the crowd gathering to speak to the marquis and marchioness. The tenderness in his eyes wrapped around her like a shawl, and the pull between them grew stronger with each passing second.

Lord, Your ways are higher than our ways. I'm trusting You.

CHAPTER 26

*J*acob couldn't cross the room fast enough. The loving look in Emily's eyes and his curiosity over how her interaction went with Phoebe lengthened his strides.

"Lord Warren, I beg your pardon."

The Dorsham butler intercepted him halfway. Jacob wanted to ignore the man, but an unsettled inkling caused him to stop. He leaned in to hear better over the music and hum of the crowd.

"Your butler is here, my lord. He claims it's urgent."

"Urgent?" The warmth seemed to flow from the room, leaving him cold.

"I shall have you hear it from him directly, my lord. Follow me."

Jacob shot Emily an apologetic glance and followed the butler toward the foyer.

Had something happened to Christian? A fall down the stairs? Thrown from his pony? No. It was too dark to go riding.

God, please let him be safe.

The crowd near the door had parted to let the butler and Jacob pass.

Maslow stood near the double front doors. His hands rested stiff by his sides, and a look of grave concern lined the butler's normally stoic face.

Lady Athol was nowhere in sight, but her butler's voice carried. "Lord Warren, come quick. Something terrible has happened."

Not to Christian. Please, Lord, not Christian. The room fell out of focus as Jacob reached the butler. The music from the ballroom sounded off rhythm, and the rumble of the guests lowered to a muffle. He focused on Maslow's voice, but it came across slow and garbled. "Master Christian and Lady Athol have been abducted."

"Abducted! How? By whom?"

"What?" Emily gasped and skidded to a stop by Jacob's side.

Jacob hadn't known she'd followed him. He hooked her arm, drawing her close to his side like a bulwark as the room's sounds returned to normal. They faced Maslow together.

The butler's hands visibly shook. "The woman was dressed in men's garb. God bless Lady Athol. She tried not to let her take him. Volunteered herself in exchange, but the woman only wanted young Master Christian."

Jacob gripped Maslow's elbow. "What happened? Where is he?"

"He and Lady Athol were returning to the stables. The woman rode over and scooped up Master Christian, setting him on her horse. But Lady Athol stalled her, getting her to talk. The woman said you killed the man she loved, and she would take something that you loved."

Jacob leaned on Maslow, for his knees couldn't support his weight. The elderly butler gripped Jacob's arms, holding him up.

"Who was killed?" Emily rounded on Jacob.

Jacob released Maslow. "Mr. Welsh, my steward, was shot robbing the Dorsham coach. His accomplice was a woman. She must have recognized me"—he swallowed and broke the first rule of espionage—"undercover as the Dorshams' driver."

He couldn't focus on Emily's reaction, not when Christian was in peril. He'd deal with the repercussions later.

But how did Lady Benton know about Christian? Had she been spying on him? Nora said she'd come calling, but it wasn't like Nora to give away a family secret. She knew they weren't announcing that he was Christian's father.

"Undercover," Emily whispered and peered at him dazed. "And she kidnapped Christian." The pitch of Emily's voice rose with each word.

"And Lady Athol," Maslow added. "She made the woman take her with them."

Jacob stepped back, raking both hands through his hair. *Lord, not Christian. Protect him. He's a little boy.* "Where did she take them?"

"They headed east."

"Did anyone try to follow?"

"The head groom, but he stopped when the woman started shooting at him."

Emily clasped a hand over her mouth.

"What's going on?" Robert stepped into the foyer.

"Christian and Aunt Louisa have been kidnapped."

"Thunder and turf!"

"I will find them." Jacob spoke the words, solidifying his resolve. He'd search every corner from here to London and farther if need be. He'd find his son, but the sooner they acted, the better. Clues can be accidentally erased and details forgotten, as he knew all too well from his job and past search for his son.

"Take my coach." The marquis gestured to the door. "Go. I'll inform the magistrate and gather Nora and Christian's parents. We'll ride in their carriage. We'll be right behind you."

Jacob aided Maslow out the door. "I'll need you to give me more details on the way."

"I'm coming." Emily didn't give him a chance to say no. She scooted around them and instructed a footman to have the carriage brought around.

The team of horses arrived, and Jacob aided Emily inside the coach. "Maslow, ride with us."

"But my lord, it's not my station, and I rode a horse from the Athol stables."

"I need you to recall everything in detail." Jacob helped the butler into the carriage. "Send a groom for the horse later."

Jacob climbed in and settled next to Emily. Maslow relayed what happened once more.

Emily crossed her arms and hugged herself. "I keep picturing Christian hopping on the fence rail to watch the horses, cheering and shouting huzzah as his toy sailboat won the race." A sob escaped her lips. "And his little cherub face as he prayed to God to make us all family."

Jacob wrapped an arm about her shoulders and drew her to his side. "I will find him." The strain in his voice didn't hide his intensity—the vehemence of a father's love.

She shifted to face him, and he felt the surety in her gaze. "I know you will." She cupped his cheek. "You'd sacrifice everything for him. You're his father, and you're a good one."

A good father? He never should have left Christian alone. He should have skipped the party and stayed by his side, especially after the Dorshams' carriage robbery. What kind of father put his son in danger—got him kidnapped? A tremble ran through Jacob.

"You turned over every stone to find him the first time. I've no doubt that you'll move mountains to find him again. But this time, you're not in this alone. Christian is my brother, and he's God's son too. We'll find him together."

Jacob's arm tightened, crushing her into his chest, and he pressed a kiss to the crown of her head. In a choked whisper, he repeated, "Together."

She clung to him for a long moment, and he drew from her strength, savoring comfort, and willing the coachman to drive the team faster.

"Mr. Welsh!" Emily shouted the name into his shoulder before pulling back. "I remember now where I recognized your steward. The woman said you shot the man she loved. I drew his picture. He was besotted with Sarah." She blinked at Jacob. "I sketched a picture of Christian's mother before she birthed Christian. She didn't know I was hiding in the tall grass peeking between the two tree trunks. She and a Mr. Welsh sat on the bridge." She clasped her hands to her chest. "I saw him with you at Brownstone hall but couldn't put my finger on where I'd seen him."

"Welsh." Jacob spit the name and fell back against the coach's cushions. "Sarah has Christian."

It made sense.

Who else would know about Christian? Sarah had blond hair. But highway robbery?

What would possess her to do such a thing?

She was married to a duke. Jacob knew about the Duke of Charlton's long nights at the gambling table, but the Charlton coffers were vast. If he was in that deep, the news would've been whispered all over town. Gossip like that had a way of spreading.

Had the duke wasted the family fortune? Had Sarah faced creditors and turned to Welsh to aid her in thieving?

The horses pulled through the gate of Brownstone Hall, the place where Christian and his aunt had been abducted. If he could find a set of tracks, he might be able to overtake them before they located a place to hide or someone got hurt. He prayed for Christian and Aunt Louisa's safety. The thought of Christian afraid, injured, or worse nearly destroyed him.

The small staff gathered on the front steps. Jacob threw open the coach door before the carriage came to a complete halt and yelled for two horses to be saddled. Time was of the essence. He couldn't wait for his brother or the magistrate to arrive. He aided Emily and Maslow from the coach, addressing Maslow. "She'll surely send a ransom note. When it arrives, give it to the marquis and do what he instructs. We're going to take advantage of the element of surprise while we have it." He turned to the staff. "The marquis, marchioness, and the rest of the Thompson family aren't far behind us. Prepare for their arrival and arrange a vigil to pray for your mistress and Master Christian's safe return."

Jacob jogged past them into the house and down the hall to his office. He patted where he'd tucked his pistol away in his coat pocket and removed a blunderbuss from his side drawer, checking to ensure it was loaded, before tucking a few spare lead balls in his pocket. He rounded the corner, slamming into Emily, and gripped her elbows to steady her.

She scurried alongside him back down the hall and into the drive.

He grabbed a lantern. "We'll need to search for tracks to see which way they went." He set the lantern aside to help her mount her horse before lifting the lamp again.

"The Duke of Charlton has a holding in the northern Cotswolds, but I can't imagine Sarah would take them there." Maslow had said they'd been returning to the stables. He gripped his horse's reins, and holding the lantern out, he examined the ground for prints.

"Can you make out anything?" Emily asked.

"There's been too much activity here. I think this might be Aunt Lousia's boot. It appears fresh." He waved her forward.

Passing through the gate, Jacob stopped to look left and right. "Maslow said they turned east." Sure enough, a fresh dent along the roadside confirmed their direction. "I found their tracks." Jacob mounted his horse, and they rode until the path forked.

He jumped down and searched the ground, but the dirt was hard-packed.

Emily remained on her horse and bowed her head. He heard her whispered prayers for God's wisdom and silently sent up one of his own. The well-traveled ground offered little information. *Please, Lord. I need You. Christian and Aunt Louisa need You.*

A gentle breeze whispered through the underbrush, and something caught Jacob's eye. A tiny thread danced on an elderberry branch. He marched that way and picked it off to examine. God bless Aunt Louisa. Holding it up in triumph, he returned to the horses and showed Emily. "It's from my aunt's shawl." He pointed to the north. "They went this way."

"That's the road to Chipping Norton." Emily spurred her horse.

About a mile later, the path split once more. The tracks headed back toward town, but this time, there was no shawl string to confirm. Why that direction? Was Sarah misdirecting them? Blast. She knew he worked for the crown. She'd seen him posing as the Dorshams' driver. He might have fooled the Dorshams, but Sarah would have recognized him.

"This is all my fault." Jacob slowed to determine if they were following the right tracks. He rubbed his chest, unable to lessen the tightness.

Emily pulled her horse close, her thigh brushing his. The innocent touch offered him comfort, but guilt weighed his heart.

"You are not responsible for Sarah's actions. She is a broken woman. I overheard Mama telling Papa how Sarah's father treated her."

Pointing to an imprint, he said, "I don't see any other tracks, so we might as well keep going." He spurred his horse to a gallop but couldn't ignore the niggling that they were going the wrong way. Emily stayed on his flank.

Jacob had seen the bruises on Sarah. She'd been physically abused, and Jacob hadn't been the first person with whom she'd been intimate. He suspected she'd been violated by her father—the man who was supposed to protect her—but Jacob hadn't dared to ask. He'd been so afraid that Sarah would push him out of her life. In the end, she'd shut him out, anyway.

He slowed once more, checking the direction of the hoof prints, but the tracks blended in with others.

Secrets were relationship-killers, and if they were to have a life together, it was past time he disclosed the full truth. "I'm an agent for the Home Office."

She nodded, but unspoken questions lingered. "Undercover."

"I joined for access of the crown's resources to locate Christian, but now my job has jeopardized him. I was assigned to stop the highwaymen. I was working undercover as the Dorshams' driver when they were robbed. Sarah saw me. My associate shot Welsh."

Emily's lips parted, and she exhaled a breath. "Then I thank God that He has given you the skills to locate Christian and bring him home safely."

By Jove. He loved this small but mighty woman beside him, but time was wasting. He must focus. "Sarah might have tried to get us to lose the trail by leading us in the wrong direction. The last tracks we saw were headed back toward town, but where, exactly?" He closed his eyes to think.

"We saw Sarah, Lady Benton, and Miss Dorsham at an inn."

"The Rose and Thistle." He looked at Emily and she nodded. "If they're not there, perhaps we can get information."

He spurred his horse to a gallop and glanced back to ensure Emily could keep up, but she stayed on his horse's flank. As they approached the center of town, he slowed their pace as to not draw attention. He rapidly formed a plan.

They stopped in front of the inn.

He helped Emily dismount and pressed a coin into a groom's hand to take care of their horses. "Tell me, young fellow, did you happen to see two women and a young boy, age five?"

The groom shook his head jostling his cap. "Sorry, guvnor. I just returned to my post."

Jacob tucked Emily's hand into the crook of his arm and strolled into the inn as though they were man and wife.

The innkeeper's brows raised at Emily. Did he recognize the vicar's daughter? It didn't matter. If all went according to plan, they'd get Christian and Aunt Louisa back, and he'd get a special license to marry Emily posthaste. "We're here to visit a guest of yours. Which room is Lady Charlton's?"

The innkeeper's jowls lowered as he frowned. "I'm afraid the duchess checked ow-oot of her room several days ago." The man spoke with a thick Scottish brogue.

Jacob stifled a curse. Something Lord Benton said in his drunken state bubbled to the surface. *Lucile's the mastermind. They do her bidding.*

"I apologize." He shook his head and flashed the innkeeper an I'm-sorry grin. "It's Lady Benton we seek."

"Och. Lady Benton has also left us. Packed up and left all dressed for the evening, but she's paid her bill and tab in full."

Blast.

Emily's shoulders drooped.

The rumble of a cheer rang in the back hall. "Is the back room open?"

"Indeed, my lord." The owner gestured. "You know the way."

He felt Emily's questioning gaze and patted her arm to reassure her as they strolled the back hallway. He drew aside the curtain and scanned the three round tables filled with cards and piles of coins. The patrons he sought sat at the table closest the bar.

Emily stiffened. "We don't have time for games."

He leaned and whispered in her ear. "This is how I gain information."

A chair opened up at the table next to Lady Anne. This was his chance. He strolled over with Emily on his arm and tossed his change purse onto the table. "Mind if I bring my luck to the table?"

The patrons glanced up from their cards and eyed the coins spilling from his bag.

Lady Anne leaned to the man frowning to her right, "He's the brother of the marquis, with large pockets to let."

"We'll be happy to take your money." Mr. Klay, the same man who'd been seated next to Lady Benton the first time Jacob had entered the back room, chuckled and gestured to the open chair. "Sit wherever you like. The game's Macao." He nodded to the dealer. "Deal Lord Warren in."

Jacob sat and Emily positioned herself behind his elbow. Cards flew across the table and high stakes were placed. He pushed a stack of coins toward the center of the table and heard Emily's quick intake of breath. He gestured her closer and whispered, "Don't look at my hand. Your expressions will give us away."

She nodded and straightened.

The bar maid brought drinks to the other players, but Jacob declined. He forced a casual pose although his mind couldn't relax. He drew Lady Anne on his right into conversation, getting her laughing and setting her at ease. "I'm surprised you're not with Lady Benton."

"Nay." She reached for her glass of gin and drank it with one gulp. "I've had my fill of country parties. I'm ready to return to the city."

"When will you see her again?"

"A few days. She's organizing a hunting party at some place in Chipping Norton, but I'm invited to her next soiree this weekend in London."

Emily shifted at his side, and he willed her to be patient.

Mr. Klay drew a card and cursed under his breath. "I enjoy a good hunt, but Lady Benton told me I wasn't invited. I guess I'm too common for the duke's lodge."

That was it. The Duke of Charlton's hunting cabin in Chipping Norton. It had to be where Sarah had taken Christian and planned to meet up with Lady Benton. Jacob stood and tossed his only card into the pile, winning the round. "I'm afraid I must be going." He hooked Emily's arm. "That was an enlightening game. Keep the winnings."

He and Emily exited the room, strode down the hallway, out the entrance, and toward the stables.

Jacob removed another coin from his pocket and flipped it to the stable groom. "Here's another shilling. Run to Brownstone Hall and tell the marquis and magistrate Lord Warren is at the Charlton's hunting lodge in Chipping Norton." He and Robert had been invited on a hunt there a few years back, so Robert would know exactly where to go. "Understood?"

The boy stared at the shiny coin in his palm and nodded. "Yes, guvnor."

"Be quick about it."

He handed them the horses' reins and sprinted down the road.

Jacob gave Emily a leg up onto her horse. "What you saw in there—that lifestyle was the old me, but it's gone."

She cupped his cheek. "God turns things around for His good. Let's go get Christian."

He kicked a leg over his horse and slid into the saddle, spurring his steed to a full gallop. They raced in silence the twenty minutes to Chipping Norton, stopping only to give the horses a short rest. He signaled for Emily to slow as they drew near the rustic cabin and dismounted. Emily did the same with his aid, and they led their horses into the woods and tied them to a tree as to not be spotted.

Jacob instructed Emily to crouch low and stay behind him as they skirted the tree line toward the lodge. A lantern burned in an upstairs window. From what he could remember, it was the duke's chamber. He tried not to rush into the cabin, but his son was in that room. He knew it.

They needed to be careful. Pausing, he surveilled the premises for danger. Only two horses were in the stable, one for Sarah and the one Aunt Louisa rode. The rest of the house other than the front bedchamber remained dark. He couldn't allow Emily, Christian, or his aunt to get hurt. He whispered for Emily to stay put, but she shook her head.

"I'm going. He's my brother, and I promised to protect him."

He handed her his pistol. "Do you know how to use this?"

"I do."

Of course. If her brother had taught her to wield a bow and arrow like Robin Hood, he'd surely taught her to use a gun too. He pressed a finger to his lips, telling Emily to remain quiet as they approached and entered the cabin through the servants' entrance.

The kitchens were dark except for the light the moon provided. He tread lightly into the back hall and up the back servant stairs.

Upstairs at the end of the hall, light fanned from under the cracks in the door, and a mumble of female voices could be heard.

A narrower door stood before the last one. He opened it and discovered a linen closet.

"Stay here until I say it's safe to come out," Jacob whispered, guiding her inside.

Emily shook her head. "I should go with you."

"I need to protect Christian and Aunt Louisa. My focus must not be divided." He gave her forehead a quick kiss, prayed for her safety—and that of the others here he loved so much—and then backed into the hallway. "I hope to only be a moment." He closed the door to a mere crack.

With his back to the wall and his blunderbuss at the ready, he moved to stand beside the door.

Emily remained quiet inside the closet, but she peeked through the crack.

He shook his head, telling her to inch away.

She did, as though she read his mind.

Voices carried, and Jacob leaned his ear closer to the door crack. Aunt Louisa spoke. "Please let us go. Another wrong doesn't make a right. I understand what you've been through. I suffered greatly at the hands of my husband."

Sarah's bitter laugh followed. "Men are egotistical, irresponsible brutes. Every man who was supposed to protect me did the opposite."

The dagger of her words pierced his heart.

He should have shown more restraint. He should never have taken advantage of her as he had. He'd fancied himself in love, but if he'd truly loved her, he wouldn't have bedded her. He'd have honored and respected her.

He'd failed.

His offer to provide for her under the protection of marriage had come too late in Sarah's mind because he'd already wronged her.

"I know Lord Charlton hurts you," Aunt Louisa said. "I see the signs—the high collars, the long sleeves, the skin-colored creams, all methods to hide the bruises. There were more days than not when I couldn't show my face, lest the town know my situation. It was only by the grace of God that I survived."

"God." Sarah scoffed. "He doesn't exist."

"I've been in your position," Aunt Louisa said. "I know you feel alone, but I can help you."

"I've learned to help myself." Sarah snorted. "And speaking of such, I'm famished and going to see what the duke has stocked for rations. Stay put."

Jacob jerked back and pressed flat against the wall.

Sarah flung the door open.

Jacob swiveled and pointed his gun at her chest.

She gasped and backed into the room, swinging the door to close it. But he caught it with his foot.

Sarah wore men's garb—as she had the night she'd robbed the Dorshams' coach. Aunt Louisa was seated in a chair with her hands tied on the left side of the room, and Christian lay asleep on the bed in the far right corner.

"Are you and Christian unharmed?" Jacob asked his aunt, flicking his gaze between her and Sarah.

"We're fine." She issued him a stiff nod.

Sarah's face crinkled with malice. "Of course, you'd come for *him*." She gestured to Christian, who stirred and opened his eyes. "You never cared for me, only for him."

"Papa?" Christian rubbed his eyes and blinked.

Jacob held his hand up, palm out. "Stay there, son. Don't move."

She lowered the pitch of her voice, mimicking Jacob in his most desperate moments. "'Where is he? I want to see him.'" Sarah's lips curled into a snarl. "Men are all the same. You want what you want and will stop at nothing to get it."

"I wanted us to be a family."

"You couldn't support a family, and I would have been cut off."

"I would have found a way."

"Scraping for pennies?" She side-stepped toward the bed. "While I'd be stuck with a brat in some London rookery."

"Don't move." He jabbed the gun in her direction.

She slid another half step toward Christian. "I needed a better option."

"Sarah." He growled her name as a warning, not wanting to hurt her, especially not in front of Christian. She was still his mother, but he couldn't risk endangering Christian or Aunt Louisa. Despite all Sarah had put him through, he still saw the wounded young woman he'd held in his arms. His romantic feelings for her died long ago, but God still laid compassion on Jacob's heart. If he could change, then there was still hope for Christian's mother. Perhaps he could stall until help arrived. Keep her talking. He inched closer toward Christian to try to block her path. "And being a duchess was the better option?" Even so many years later, he couldn't keep the biting tone from his voice. *God forgive me.*

"No one pities a poor duchess. Oh, the irony." She spit the word with disdain, and her eyes flared like blue fire. "The duke not only lays hands on me, he cut me off. I have no funds— aside from what he provides when he wants to parade me around like his show pony."

She pulled a pistol from her pocket and lunged onto the bed, scooping an arm around Christian and jerking him to her side. She sat on the mattress's edge and pointed the barrel end at his temple. "I'm still fighting to survive."

Christian stared at Jacob, bottom lip quivering, eyes wide.

"Be brave, son." He held Christian's gaze but concentrated on Sarah. Could he shoot her before she shot Christian? Too risky. He should have pinned her to the floor when she first opened the door. Why hadn't he? *You're a failure, that's why.* His father's words rang in his head, but the memory of what Emily said countered them. *You're a good father, and I thank God that He* has given you the skills to locate Christian and bring him home safely.

A sureness filled him. *Lord, You trained me for this moment. Guide my words and actions.*

"Sarah, you don't want to hurt your own child."

"Lower your weapon and kick it over." Her voice was cold. When he didn't move fast enough, she pressed the metal against Christian's head, wrinkling his skin. "Do it!"

Christian whimpered.

"All right." Jacob raised his fingers but kept the blunderbuss in the curve of his hand. He laid the gun on the ground and kicked it purposefully. The weapon slid across the floor and under the bed where Christian and Sarah sat.

"What have we here?"

Jacob recognized Lady Benton's voice but didn't dare take his gaze off Sarah and Christian. "A family reunion. How sweet."

With his hands up, Jacob pivoted to see Lady Benton and the shiny gleam of the pistol she pointed at him. He willed Emily to stay in the closet until the situation was under control. Or the whole thing was over.

What would that look like?

He didn't want to think about it, especially witnessing the spiteful pout on Sarah's face and the wicked twist to Lady Benton's lips.

Lord, I need You.

Lady Benton glanced toward the corner, where Aunt Louisa sat tied. "Lady Athol? What a surprise. I didn't think you left Brownstone Hall. I'm honored to be part of your first and last appearance in public." She frowned at Sarah. "Can't you do anything right? First, you get your accomplice killed, and now you've brought more witnesses who can identify us."

"It was your plan." Sarah's grip on Christian tightened.

"I instructed you to bring Lord Warren and his son to me. That was all."

Jacob needed to keep her talking until he could devise a plan. "I know you can't get enough of me, but why Christian?"

"Oh, I will have my fill of you. Or rather, you of me." Lady Benton's scathing look told him she didn't just mean in bed. "Your son's going to come and live with me as my ward." She smiled at Christian, who pressed farther back into the pillow.

Jacob shook his head. "He's not—"

"I wasn't finished!" Her shout made both Christian and Sarah jump. "You, Lord Warren, will be my inside man at the Home Office. You will get me whatever intelligence I request, and"—her gaze roved over the length of Jacob's body and back up again—"anything else I might desire. Otherwise, your son will disappear again. Maybe forever."

Jacob's heart slammed into his throat, choking out his ability to breathe. Not Christian. He'd do anything to keep him from harm. That was the problem.

And Lady Benton knew it.

"I want my share." Sarah raised her chin and stared Lady Benton down. "I'm leaving on the next ship to the continent. I want my money now."

A snide chuckle passed through Lady Benton's lips. "You've lost your usefulness to me. It won't be long before you're identified. I have word that Welsh confided to his sister about his love for you and your plans. You, darling, are a liability."

Lady Benton aimed her weapon at Sarah.

"No!" Jacob launched himself at the bed, covering half of Sarah and pushing Christian out of harm's way. A shot blasted, and pain seized his shoulder.

He let out a growl of rage.

He pushed up, refusing to look at the wound for fear he'd faint.

Christian muffled a cry against the bedside, but he was

alive. *Thank You, Lord!* Jacob cupped his face, said, "Be of good courage," and pushed him under the bed.

A metal object clattered to the floor—Sarah's gun. Jacob twisted to look at her. Her face was pale, her eyes wide and filled with confusion and pain.

"You jumped in front of me. After all I did to you, you tried to save me." Her hand gripped her chest, and blood seeped through her fingers.

Jacob's shoulder pulsed with pain, and he realized what must've happened.

The bullet had grazed it.

And hit Sarah.

He'd tried to save her. Once again, he'd tried to do the right thing—and failed.

Wooziness washed over him. He was going to faint. He pressed his hands over hers to apply pressure to the gunshot.

And he was about to fail again as blackness seeped into his periphery. *God, not now. Give me strength!*

Christian whimpered under the bed.

"Drop the weapon!" Emily's voice rang out.

CHAPTER 27

*E*mily pointed the gun at Lady Benton's back. She'd heard the shot and entered the bedchamber, no longer willing to cower in the closet.

Gunsmoke and the coppery smell of blood hung in the air. Lady Athol sat tied to a chair on the left, an expression of horror on her face. Jacob knelt on the bed to the right.

Where was Christian?

A crimson stain seeped down Jacob's sleeve from his shoulder, but he seemed too focused on stopping Lady Charlton's bleeding to notice.

Even so, the injured woman's breathing became labored, gurgling. She stared up at Jacob with a wide-eyed expression.

Muffled crying came from under the bed.

Christian.

His tearstained face peeked from underneath, but he seemed relatively safe.

Thank God.

"How lovely, the vicar's daughter." Lady Benton raised her hands and tried to turn.

"Stay where you are." Emily pressed the barrel tip against the woman's back. "Christian, go untie your Aunt Louisa."

"Em." Christian's face was red, and tears streamed down his cheeks.

"You can do it, Captain." Jacob looked over his shoulder, nodding at his son. "Your sister needs the *Pirate Slayer* to release the prisoners. Remember how I showed you by the stream."

Christian scooted out from under the bed and ran to Lady Athol's side. He started working on the knots in the rope.

"A vicar's daughter doesn't have what it takes to fire a weapon." Lady Benton scoffed—but didn't move.

"Oh? Your husband didn't mention who put that arrow in his shoulder?"

Lady Benton stiffened. A moment passed, and when she spoke again, her tone had softened. "How much for you to put the gun down and walk away?" She twisted to look at Emily over her shoulder. "I could do a lot for a budding artist like yourself. I have friends in the Royal Academy. Your paintings could go on exhibit." She harrumphed. "For that matter, I could have you installed as a board member within a week. Think of the fame."

Christian pulled out the last knot, and Lady Athol rubbed her wrist. Finished with his task, Christian scooted along the room's perimeter until he could safely reach Emily and wrapped his arms around her waist.

"I have the Father's love," Emily said, "and the love of my friends and family. What more fame could I want than that?"

Lady Charlton exhaled a long breath, and her head lolled to the side.

Jacob lifted her body so she lay on the bed properly. He brushed his hand down her face to close her eyes as if she slept and pulled the coverlet over her still form.

He picked up Sarah's weapon and rose, pointing it at Lady Benton.

"I'll take that."

Emily couldn't see most of Jacob with Lady Benton in the way, but assumed he confiscated her weapon. The flash of metal before he stowed it in his coat pocket confirmed her guess. Jacob side-stepped across the room, keeping Lady Benton in his sights, and scooped up his aunt's bindings.

"Point this at her while I tie her up." He passed the gun to his aunt.

Lady Athol did as asked, but her hands shook.

Emily held her pistol steady as Jacob wrenched Lady Benton's arms behind her back, tying them together with the rope.

The door banged against the wall, and Lord Sudbury burst inside, weapon raised, followed by the magistrate and constable. "We heard a gunshot."

"I'm glad you got my summons." Jacob shoved Lady Benton toward the doorway where the constable stood, but Jacob kept his hold on her.

Emily lowered her weapon, looped her arm around Christian's shoulders, and moved aside for them to pass. The steady calm she'd felt earlier dissipated, and her knees began to shake even though the immediate threat had passed.

"I'm with the Home Office. Lady Benton is to be detained for murder and for running a thieving guild of highway robbers."

Lord Sudbury's jaw dropped. "When did you start working for the Home Office?"

Jacob passed Lady Benton to the men. "We're going to need the coroner and some hartshorn." He patted the magistrate's and constable's shoulders to send them along. "And be quick about it."

The officials filed into the hall, flanking Lady Benton.

"Hartshorn?" Lord Sudbury flashed Jacob a quizzical look.

Lady Athol scurried out, taking her older nephew's arm. "I'll help you locate some."

"Jacob?" Emily barely got his name out before the trauma of what she'd beheld rushed in. They all could have died. Christian's mother lay dead. His young eyes had witnessed the whole incident. He'd probably have nightmares for the rest of his life. She choked back a sob, wanting to throw herself into Jacob's arms.

The front of his shirt was covered in Lady Charlton's blood, and his shoulder wound needed tending. He lifted his non-injured arm, and she stepped into his embrace, pulling Christian along with her.

"I thought..." The sob escaped her throat. "If you'd been killed..." She buried her face into his good shoulder.

His grip tightened around her. "God still has plans for me yet." He pressed a kiss to her forehead, and when she glanced up, he claimed her lips in a soft, endearing kiss. "For us."

Her heart leapt at his words. "I love you."

He flashed his eyebrows. "It's about time you admitted it." He swayed and leaned heavily against her side. "I love you too."

Did his words sound slurred?

Christian tugged hard on Jacob's jacket, and Jacob lowered to a crouched position at eye level with his son.

"I helped, didn't I?" Christian pointed his thumb over his shoulder. "I rescued Lady Athol."

"You are a brave boy." Jacob tussled his hair. "I couldn't be prouder of you, son." He blinked rapidly. "I must nap now, but when I wake, we'll take...the boats...out sailing."

Jacob slumped back against the wall, then tipped to the floor.

Emily pressed a hand over her mouth, biting back her scream. She dropped to his side. "Jacob?"

Lady Athol rapped on the doorframe. "We found the smelling salts. Robert is seeing the magistrate off."

Emily remembered Jacob making the strange request—a coroner and hartshorn. It was a miracle he'd stayed conscious as long as he had.

Christian accepted the bottle from Lady Athol and passed it to Emily. "Papa still needs naps? I stopped napping a year ago."

Emily uncapped the bottle and waved the smelling salts under Jacob's nose. "Wake up, my love."

EPILOGUE

A cry erupted from Emily's chamber at Brownstone Hall, and Jacob pounded on the door. He couldn't wait any longer.

His shirtfront was untucked, and his hair surely stuck out in all directions from his pulling on it. He needed to know if Emily was all right, and he needed to know now.

He beat the door with renewed fervor.

His mother-in-law opened the door. "Patience, Papa." She stepped aside to allow him to enter.

The midwife brushed by him, padding out of the room carrying an armload of soiled bedding.

"Congratulations," Mrs. Thompson said with a smile. "I'll give you two—I mean three—some time alone." She disappeared into the hallway and closed the door behind her.

Emily lay on the bed, their swaddled child tucked against her chest. Her hair was damp and stuck to her forehead, but never had anyone looked so beautiful. She waved him over. "Come and meet your daughter, Catherine."

He snuggled beside his wife on the bed, wrapping his arm about her shoulder. Moving the soft blanket aside, he peeked at the little pink face peering up at him. He brushed his index finger down the newborn's cheek, still dazed she was real and she'd finally arrived. "She's perfect."

"Phoebe will be ecstatic we've had a girl. She already has grand plans for our Catherine and her Molly to share a school-room, as we did." His wife yawned, not even bothering to cover her mouth. She seemed too tired to care.

He fingered the little tuft of dark hair on the baby's head. Perhaps she would have dark hair like her mama. "How old is Molly? She's giant compared to our Catherine."

"Six months. It won't take long for Catherine to catch up." Emily yawned once more. "She's already a good eater."

Emily'd had little rest. The pains of childbirth had come upon her as soon as they'd retired the night before, and now it was close to the evening meal. "You should sleep."

She shook her head and held little Catherine up to him. "After we introduce the baby to her brother and the rest of the family."

Jacob carefully extracted Catherine from his wife's arms, careful to hold her head. He'd never seen a baby so tiny. Not even his nephew, Nora and Robert's son, looked this small when he'd first met him. But Robert Junior had been several weeks old when Jacob first laid eyes on the lad, and Catherine wasn't even an hour past birth.

He tucked the white blanket around her and touched her hand. She curled her tiny palm around his index finger, and Jacob caught his breath.

He'd never had a chance to know Christian at this age, but God had blessed him with the opportunity to see Catherine grow in her mother's belly. He'd felt the first kicks, and now he held the precious infant in his arms.

He stood, and Catherine's face wrinkled as if she might fuss, but he rocked her as he'd seen Nora do with his nephew, and she settled.

He owed much to his brother and his wife for giving him Brownstone Hall as a wedding present. Robert and Nora claimed they already had too much to handle with their current holdings. They added how good Jacob had been for their aunt. Robert had arranged the plans with Aunt Louisa, who offered to stay at the dowager house. But Jacob and Emily would hear of no such thing. She was to remain living with them.

He lowered his head to his precious little girl. "Catherine. I'm your papa." His voice cracked, and he cleared his throat. "Your mama and I love you very much. I promise to always love you, to be here for you, and do my best to protect you from harm."

Catherine's tiny mouth stretched into a big yawn. She arched her back before settling and closing her eyes, still holding his finger.

He cautiously strode to their bedchamber entrance with such a precious package in his arms and swung the door wide.

Aunt Louisa, Mr. and Mrs. Thompson, and Christian rose from the chairs Maslow had brought into the hall for them to sit and wait. "May I introduce to you the precious and adorable Miss Catherine Ann Warren."

He held the baby out for them to admire before having them follow him back into the room where Emily could see them. Aunt Louise and Emily's parents—and even Maslow—gathered close for a peek, but Christian held back.

"A girl." He folded his arms, frowning. "I prayed for a brother."

Jacob chuckled and, with his free hand, aided Christian to climb onto the bed near Emily for a better look at his new sister.

The boy bent close. "Well." He sighed. "I guess God doesn't make mistakes."

"That's right." He smiled at his son. "His ways and timing are perfect."

Christian cranked his neck out over the baby. "You're right, Papa. It must not have been the right time for another boy like me." He patted the blanket. "You and Em are just going to have to try again."

Jacob couldn't resist winking at Emily, and a pink flush stained her cheeks. Amid stifled laughter and knowing grins from his relatives, Jacob placed a hand on his son's shoulder. "I will do my best to redeem myself."

Did you enjoy this book? We hope so!
Would you take a quick minute to leave a review where you purchased the book?
It doesn't have to be long. Just a sentence or two telling what you liked about the story!

Receive a FREE ebook and get updates when new Wild Heart books release: https://wildheartbooks.org/newsletter

AUTHOR'S NOTE

British legends and folklore speak of a notorious Wicked Lady as the first highwaywoman robber of the seventeenth century. Lady Katherine Ferrers was born in 1634 in Hertfordshire into a well-endowed family. Tragically, her father and brother died, and her mother remarried to Sir Simon Fanshawe before she, too, passed, leaving Katherine an orphan. Sir Simon's assets were cut during the British Civil War when King Charles I fought Parliament, and to recoup some of his lost money, Sir Simon married Katherine, age fourteen, to his nephew Thomas Fanshawe, age sixteen.

Katherine's marriage to Thomas was a failure. Thomas controlled and frivolously spent her inheritance, selling off much of her family's lands and property. Abandoning the marriage, Katherine moved to Markyate Cell, her father's former home, where legend has it that Katherine met and fell in love with a farmer named Ralph Chaplin, who moonlighted as a highwayman. He recruited her, and the pair rode out together, hunting and terrorizing travelers and absconding with jewels, wares, and coin. Little historical information is known about Ralph Chaplin's existence, and it's questioned whether he was shot during a raid or captured and then hung at Finchley Common.

Katherine supposedly continued her devious career without her lover until she picked a wagoner traveling alone near Normansland to raid. Unfortunately for Katherine, an armed man hid among the bales in the wagon and lethally wounded her. Rumor has it that the Wicked Lady rode back to Markyate Cell and died. Her bloodied men's clothing was found balled up outside a secret entrance.

While my intent was not to prove or disprove any rumors or legends of the infamous Wicked Lady, many of her stories stimulated my imagination. Katherine Ferrers's tale was fascinating to model *Redeeming a Rake's* own wicked ladies after. If you'd like to learn more about Lady Katherine Ferrers, please check out some of the sources listed on my website: https//:lorridudley.com/the-wicked-lady-resources/

FROM THE AUTHOR

Dear Readers,

I'm so grateful for you. Thank you for reading *Redeeming the Rake*. I write because I believe readers should be led on a heart journey. Romance should allow for an escape from everyday life. It should also lead us to a better understanding of the human condition and how God views us.

I believe readers, like the heroines and heroes of stories, are not static creatures and can discover different aspects of themselves through empathizing with characters' comical mishaps and dramatic misunderstandings. I believe romance novels can depict a fallible human heart that can be made whole again by a merciful creator and remind us of the hope for the same.

It is my prayer that you will know how deeply loved you are.

A big shout out goes to Wild Heart Books, Misty Beller, and team, who have blessed me with the joy of being able to write and put my stories into print. It's lovely to work with such wonderful people, from editors and admin to the design team and marketing. Special thanks to Robin Hook, Robin Patchen, and Denise Weimer, who helped fine-tune my writing and grammar in *Redeeming the Rake*. You are amazing, and I'm so grateful for you.

Lots of hugs and respect go out to my launch team, spreading the word about my books. Keep up the great work! I'm honored to have a great set of critique partners in Megan, Tammy, and Barbara, and I appreciate the time and careful eyes of my beta readers. You are the best! Lastly, I'm forever grateful to God for blessing me with such a great and supportive family.

God is good.

Blessings,

Lorri

ABOUT THE AUTHOR

Lorri Dudley has been a finalist in numerous writing contests and has a master's degree in Psychology. She lives in Ashland, Massachusetts with her husband and three teenage sons, where writing romance allows her an escape from her testosterone filled household.

Connect with Lorri at http://LorriDudley.com

WANT MORE?

If you love historical romance, check out the other Wild Heart books!

A Summer on Bellevue Avenue by Lorri Dudley

In the world of the elite, reputation is everything...

Wealthy heiress Amanda Mae Klein is set to marry the man she loves, Wesley Jansen—the only person she trusts to help ease her anxiety among the social climbers of high society. Then the daughter of a union boss falls down a flight of stairs at Wesley's oil company's office in the middle of the night...and the woman claims Wesley pushed her.

Seeking solace from the growing scandal, Amanda flees to the mansion-dotted seaside of Newport. Wesley follows and sets about disproving the rumors while winning back the trust of Amanda. But soon, Amanda finds not only her social status but her life at risk. As grievous events pit the two against each other, will their love find a way to survive?

❧

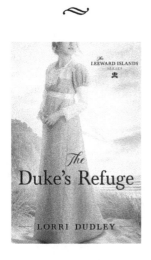

The Duke's Refuge by Lorri Dudley

When love comes in a tempest, who knew it would wear pink?

Georgia Lennox has traded in her boyish ways for pink gowns and a coy smile to capture the eye of the Earl of Claremont. However, on the day she's convinced the earl will propose, Georgia is shipped off to the Leeward Islands to care for her ailing father. But when she arrives on Nevis, the last thing she expects is to learn that her abrupt departure was not at her father's bidding but that of the infuriating, yet captivating, island schoolmaster. And now her plans may well be ship-wrecked.

Harrison Wells is haunted by the memories of his deceased wife and hunted by the women who aspire to be the next Duchess of Linton. Desiring anonymity, he finds sanctuary in the Leeward island of Nevis. He's willing to sacrifice his ducal title for a schoolmaster's life and the solace the island provides. That is, until unrest finds its way to Nevis in a storm of pink chiffon—Miss Georgia Lennox.

As Georgia and Harrison's aspirations break apart like a ship cast upon the rocks, a new love surfaces, but secrets and circumstances drag them into rough waters. Can they surrender their hearts to a love that defies their expectations?

∾

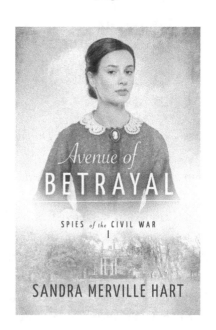

Avenue of Betrayal by Sandra Merville Hart

Betrayed by her brother and the man she loves...whom can she trust when tragedy strikes?

Soldiers are pouring into Washington City every day and have begun drilling in preparation for a battle with the Confederacy. Annie Swanson worries for her brother, whom she's just discovered is a Confederate officer in his new home state of North Carolina. Even as Annie battles feelings of betrayal toward the big brother she's always adored, her wealthy banker father swears her and her sister to secrecy about their brother's actions. How could he forsake their mother's abolitionist teachings?

Sergeant-Major John Finn camps within a mile of the Swansons' mansion where his West Point pal once lived. Sweet Annie captured his heart at Will's wedding last year and he looks forward to reestablishing their relationship—until he's asked to spy on her father.

To prove her father's loyalty to the Union, John agrees to spy on the Swanson family, though Annie must never know. Then the war strikes a blow that threatens to destroy them all—including the love that's grown between them against all odds.

Printed in the USA
CPSIA information can be obtained
at www.ICGtesting.com
CBHW070715230724
11999CB00016B/216